Mindful Things

Mya Duong

Arborville House

This is a work of fiction. Names, characters, places, and incidents either are the product of the author's imagination or are used fictitiously, and any resemblance to actual persons, living or dead, business establishments, events, or locales is entirely coincidental.

ISBN: 0999334603
ISBN 13: 9780999334607

FIRST EDITION

For anyone who has ever felt out of sorts, not realizing the strength buried deep inside.

Acknowledgments

WORK CANNOT BE done alone. Thank you to the following people for their support, encouragement, advice, expertise, and friendship: Jonathan Maberry, Indy Quillen, Laura Taylor, Diana Padgett, Taylor Hobbs, Jonathan Oliver, Angela Johnson, Carolyn Burch, Jennifer Ebner, Traci Steckel, and Richard Mellinger. I'm grateful to be able to express my fears and frustrations, and for giving me your time.

Contents

Preface

THE HEAT MOVED out of my body. My fingers and toes felt numb. I wasn't sure I could move them. I lay frozen on the damp ground, covered by a wool blanket that felt like tissue paper. The silence of my body felt deafening. Even my once robust heart failed to pump the warm blood through me.

The darkness became fearful. I couldn't escape. But the voices spoke of another light. A great, blue light wrapped in vapor lingered in the vastness. The voices called out again. They called my name and they pleaded with me. A man touched my face with feather lightness. I knew his touch, even as it faded.

"She's so cold," he whispered.

"Hurry, give this to her."

I understood what came next. I tried to reach out to him, one more time.

An energy force approached. My body suddenly stirred, and my mind flashed back.

Mother . . . Father . . .

CHAPTER 1

Lauren

I LIVED IN the metropolitan city of Chicago, the third largest city in the country. Actually, I was in the suburbs like most families. We used to move around every few years for Dad's work or Mom's advancements. Before Chicago, it was Atlanta, Georgia, and before that it was Billings, Montana. I've also lived in Boston, Park City, Utah, and Portland, Oregon. The hardest part of moving was making new friends—I was good at that—then abruptly leaving. My siblings adjusted well to the changes—they expected the brief stays with no sadness or attachments—and moved on.

I didn't care for Atlanta. Too hot and too stormy, and we lived far from any points of interest except the local mall. My parents drove me everywhere and supervised my trips, or I would solicit the help of my sister, Chelsea, and that felt restrictive. When you're a burgeoning teen, making new friends and forming a good impression became vital. My quest proved short-lived since we only stayed in Atlanta for a year.

Dad accepted a partnership at a downtown law firm in Chicago. They made him an attractive offer, so he took it without hesitation. In Atlanta, he worked all the time, which worried my mother. He seemed tired and anxious beyond the hectic lifestyle.

My older brother, Isaak, would be returning home this fall. Fresh out of Princeton at the mere age of twenty-four, he planned to join my father's firm before starting law school. "The Prince" was coming home. He fit the image perfectly: chestnut wavy hair, Ivy League education, avid tennis and golf player. Things came easy to him. It also didn't hurt that my father was already established.

My parents always stressed the importance of a good education. Reading and studying became second nature in the Reed household. We excelled in high school and started taking college prep courses during senior year. Demonstration by our parents and the genes passed down from them helped us to succeed. We were overachievers.

It didn't explain me. I was adopted; my biological parents were killed in a tragic car accident when I reached the inquisitive age of four. No history, no other family, and no survivors of the horrific crash except for me. At least, that's what I've been told. I just don't remember anything about it.

I once belonged to a Paul and Simone Lewis, the only child of the ill-fated couple. I have no memory of the Lewises. One day, I found myself at St. Bartholomew's Home for Children in Portland, Oregon amongst the other children, destitute and alone. They didn't call places like these orphanages anymore, even though it belonged to a church. The word "orphanage" described institutions in third world countries where hundreds of unwanted children waited to be adopted. At St. Bart's, only twenty parentless children lived. Adoptive parents preferred the babies over young children, leaving the rest of us to wait longer. Sister Grace told me that the Reeds—Oren and Helen—were excited to meet me. They had learned of my situation, read of my progress here at St. Bart's, and were looking for another child—not an infant—to add to their family. I remembered seeing my mother's honey-colored hair and warm hazel eyes, and the way her face relaxed when she saw me at St. Bart's for the first time. Dad squeezed her hand and said, "It's her."

"You must be Lauren," my new mother said in a sweet voice. "I think you would fit right in with our family. We have a son and a daughter that are *so* happy to have a sister."

Since then, I've never looked back, never doubted their love for me. They became the parents and family I know. I felt as if their blood and their genes flowed through me, that I was *their* biological daughter, not an outsider. When I turned sixteen, I became curious about my real parents. I mean, not knowing where I came from haunted me a little. I think almost any adopted child feels this way. Everyone asks themselves, *what were my parents like? Why did they give me up? Did they not love me?*

In my case, a car accident took my parents.

That's what the nuns told me. It's written in my documents.

My search on them came up empty. Nothing. Not one piece of information on a Paul and Simone Lewis as a couple and with a child. I aborted my plan and decided it was futile to search for people who gave me life but didn't exist in my world. I vowed to never go looking in the past, as it clearly meant, once was. The Reeds gave me a life. They provided for me and gave me everything and anything I ever wanted or needed—all the love any parents could give.

Today, I packed to move into my apartment: MY OWN PLACE. My parents let me stay in the dorms for one year, and then allowed me to get a place with a roommate for the following years. They asked me to move home since the university was close by, but I relished a little freedom and persuaded them to allow me the college experience. How many people can live close to home, go to Northwestern University, *and* have her best friend as her roommate?

Raegan Kilpatrick came into my life like a flare from a torch the year prior to high school. Her bubbly personality and quick wit—like her bright red hair, now a deeper scarlet—was so contagious, we became instant friends. She moved from sunny and warm Albuquerque, New Mexico to frigid Chicago where her father became manager of Pucelli's Meats and Deli, a popular market to get your delicatessens. Only in Chicago do the Irish and the Italians work closely together.

Raegan and I have been inseparable since then. We weathered the final, dreaded year of middle school only to endure the awkwardness of freshman year. Yes, *freshman year,* the first *real* year of your teenage life.

Forget thirteen, I was still a child. I couldn't even apply for a temporary license. Freshman year. It wasn't so bad after all.

Oh, the migraines are coming again.

The throbbing pulsations from my head felt heavier today. I reached for a cold compress and placed it on my head. They've been getting worse in the past year, more frequent and longer in duration with each episode. I wasn't stressed, and I tend not to over worry. The headaches began when I turned twelve, coming out of nowhere like someone constantly pounding on the front door. My mother thought they were brought on by hormonal changes, the kind you get when approaching womanhood. I've always believed the teenage transformation weren't the real reason. I've had CT scans, MRIs, and EEGs, but nothing showed up. Since we moved to Chicago, I always went to my neurologist, Dr. Uri Sendal. The last time I saw him was about six weeks ago.

"So, you're having those headaches again, aren't you? More frequently?" he asked then, after having my eyes follow his finger in an H motion before causing them to converge. He didn't sound surprised.

"Yeah, they come and go, but it seems more often. Sometimes, I don't have any warning." Dr. Sendal gently pressed my face. He then took out the penlight and did the same routine of shining the light back and forth in my eye.

"It doesn't have to be a specific stimulus that's causing the head pain. It could just be a random disruption in your brain's motor activity. Are the medications helping?"

"They did before, but I've stopped taking them. They don't seem to do anything for me any longer. It's like my body, especially my mind, rejected them. Sometimes it's not pain I feel but something taking up space that shouldn't be."

"Interesting," he'd flatly remarked. He sat down at the computer and began to type. He looked up at me again through his correction lenses. "What about the narcotic? Does it seem effective? You previously mentioned that you only take it when it becomes extremely painful. Does this happen often?"

"I rarely take them." I looked at him seriously. "Mom was visiting me at the dorm after winter break when I had my last major event. It felt like my brain had stretched out and started to . . . to crack . . . to hatch, but in a bigger way. The pain medicine helped at the time, but it made me feel as if my mind had shut down, not in a tired way, but had stopped moving."

Dr. Sendal let out a nervous laugh. "Stop moving. That *would* be a tragedy." His brows furrowed. He asked a few more questions like the ones he's always asked, then scribbled a note on his prescription pad. "This is a new one. It might help during an episode."

I've grown to rely on and trust Dr. Sendal. My parents admired him and speak warmly of him. He's also a family friend. He was one of the reasons we moved to Chicago. But, honestly, I don't know if he can help me.

"Say hello to your parents, and do tell them to visit when they can. It's a shame we don't see each other often." Dr. Sendal reminded me of Mr. Spock from *Star Trek*. It wasn't his appearance, but in his manners—intelligent, scientific, and unemotional. Practical.

In every new place we moved, my parents knew a few people. We originally planned to relocate to some small, unknown college town called Pocatello in Idaho. My father received an offer at one of the firms, and my mother was given academic privileges at Idaho State University, where she would have taught in the history department. Mom has this thing for the dead, meaning people who lived at another time that may or may not have made their mark on history. She felt strongly about connecting with people of another era. Sometimes, I think she was born in another time because she talked about how simple life was before cars, and how you took your time and enjoyed life.

I couldn't imagine a life without cars.

We never moved to Idaho after Atlanta, because Dad argued with one of the partners, Stefan Keegan. He never mentioned him again after that incident, except on one occasion when I overheard my parents whispering his name, describing something about a mark, and "letting the others know." My parents wouldn't talk about the argument, so I stopped asking. I really didn't care anymore. We changed courses, leading us to my favorite city.

After Dr. Sendal made the initial contact, Aaron and Leslie Brandt, and Julian and Nadja Fozi quickly arranged for our family to settle in Chicago. They helped us locate a great house, initiated contacts to law firms, and introduced us to people who would later become family friends.

The head pain ceased to become anything worth mentioning. It might worry Mom if I made an issue of it. In the past, she dismissed them as irritations that would go away, usually saying, "not to worry." I once believed she didn't care, because she quickly changed the subject to a happier topic every time I had an episode. Now, when she does notice the disturbances, a look of fear and sadness crosses her face as if she'd lost something. So, I tried not to mention the nuisances.

I'd packed most of my winter clothes: boots, seasonal jackets, colorful scarves, thermal underwear, and of course, my skates. Chicago has some fierce winters that took me a long time to get used to. I still cope with the long winters, but I found ways to enjoy the erratic weather.

Did I mention I'm a pretty good ice-skater?

I've packed one suitcase and started to pack the summer clothes. I finished my finals early, leaving half of May and all of summer with no courses to take. My excitement grows as I think about the leisurely summer ahead. My parents planned a weeklong family trip to Connecticut and a few weekend getaways; otherwise, the summer would be open to any possibilities. I picked out some fun clothes for nights out and for parties. I'd also found a few outdoorsy clothes, which reminded me of my two summers spent at camp following my freshman and sophomore years. My father wanted me to have a normal and healthy youth spent outside the city.

Summer camp wasn't the sit-by-the-campfire camp to sing songs. We hiked, swam, pitched tents, learned survival skills, and canoed until our eyes couldn't stay open. Raegan and I forged lifelong friends from the summers outside Duluth, Minnesota. I'm excited to see the gang— Alex Beechan, Justin Kim, Cameron Witte, Gavin Dushane, Elsie Scott, and Noelle Henske. We try to stay in contact as much as possible, despite living in three separate states. Alex, Justin, and Elsie live in Minnesota, and Cameron and Gavin live in Wisconsin.

We planned a house warming party this summer. I'm eager to have my camp friends, college friends, and high school classmates mingle in one place. At this age, going to parties and hanging out with friends is what we do best. I turned nineteen this May, and I considered it a milestone—successfully completing high school and surviving my first year of college.

Freshman year. Again, it wasn't that rough.

When I turned eighteen, I made some life goals I plan to keep. I wanted to travel to foreign places I read about, receive a college education, play for the Chicago Symphony Orchestra, fall in love, and get married before I'm thirty. I really didn't have a specific order; I just wanted this for myself—dreams and goals like any other person. My major? Undecided.

Next to my pale blue Henley shirt, my long hair grows more raven each year. I envied Raegan with her natural ringlets and spirals, which seemed to always give her a carefree look. I lathered on a generous amount of sunscreen, making sure to cover my neckline and any exposed skin. I burn easily and seldom tan, but I'm not one to bathe in the sun—a benefit of living in Chicago. Many people have said that I remind them of a ceramic doll. I've also heard Goth queen mentioned. I took it as a complement.

The eyes reflecting back at me are the same mesmerizing color as the ones I'd always known. When I was a child, my pediatrician sent me to the eye doctor to have them examined. She had never seen such bright, emerald green eyes, and she wondered if I had any vision or nerve damage. I saw perfectly. Most people with green eyes have an iridescent hue or an olive color to them. Mine appeared startling. I thought they were intriguing and intense when I needed to be serious, and dramatic when I became playful. My parents never thought twice about my eyes. They just told me I was special. I used to tell my parents that I was the prodigious offspring of the devil himself or reincarnated as an evil sorceress. They didn't find that humorous.

I grabbed my luggage, sitting next to my maple and spruce cello. I'd bring it next time since it didn't fit in the car. Bach and I couldn't be separated for too long. Raegan, on the other hand, has laid out ground rules for when I was allowed to play the cello. I remembered her saying, "That big thing!" when I played for her. My parents wanted all their children to be involved in extracurricular activities. I opted for the grand cello over the violin. Chelsea was the pianist in the family. When she came home, she played Mozart, Beethoven, or Tchaikovsky throughout the house. Isaak picked up playing the guitar. He felt it suited his style—relaxed and carefree. It didn't hurt that the girls came swooning.

I stopped at my parents' office to pick up the concert list I'd left on Mom's desk. The shelves were lined with history books from nearly every culture, and the novels and reference books were scattered within. My father had a small section for his journals and law books. The teakwood paneling on one of the walls provided some warmth and lightness in this serious den. A soft, leather sofa was placed next to one of the walls and two fabric-covered, floral designed armchairs sat alongside the wooden panel. I would come in here to play the cello when they're not using the room.

My mother left teaching to pursue one of her myriad interests. She taught American history through nineteen hundred. After that, she'd say, "It's up to the modern historians to correct history." She was also fluent in French, Dutch, and the so-called dead language of Latin. Who speaks Latin nowadays? For the past year, she managed her own independent bookstore with a handful of dedicated employees. The bookstore has been doing well. It keeps her busy with long hours, but somehow, she manages to keep a watchful eye over me. Something I'll have to work on. Although it may appear Mom is scatterbrained, she's one of the most disciplined and organized people I know.

"Lauren, we're leaving in five minutes," Mom called out from another room.

My thoughts returned to finding the list. I dug through her unusually disorganized desk and came across a folded up note. Should I? I couldn't find the concert list. I opened the note: R S. What was R S? It was Mom's handwriting. I closed up the note, feeling guilty, and placed it back where I found it. Then, I came across a photo that looked familiar. It was a mansion I had seen in New Haven. I wanted to explore the place, but for some reason, my parents discouraged us from seeing the estate. I put the photo away, too, yet my mind went in all different directions.

"This is so wrong on so many levels," I said out loud. I traced the cabinet for a few moments next to Mom's desk. It wasn't locked, so I opened the drawer. My fingers magically traced the files that were placed in alphabetical order until I stopped at the R's. I found a folder for R S. I took out the only thing left in the file. It was a photo of a decorated room, which looked like the inside of that New Haven mansion. Before I could examine it further, I heard approaching footsteps. I quickly shut the drawer.

"Lauren, what are you doing? Mom and I are waiting," Dad said from the doorway.

"Found it." I held up the concert list that had been tucked away between some papers on Mom's desk.

"Okay, then. Let's go. We have a long day," Dad said, looking convinced.

CHAPTER 2

Glimpse

THE DRIVE TO my new place was shadowed with sullen grays and patchy whites instead of clear blue skies. I turned up the stereo so I could follow along to the music Chelsea gave me for my birthday. One of my favorite songs on the disk, *Fallen Angel,* came on and I was soaring. Mom cringed as the lead singer bellowed the refrain.

"You know I'm very proud of you, and how you're adjusting to everything and enjoying this college life," Mom admitted while I drove past our attractive neighborhood. "I know leaving home is something every kid wants to do. Just know your dad and I are so happy you decided to stay close to home."

"It's no problem. Besides, who can skip out on tuition money and helping me buy this car?" I reminded her, referring to my Prius I got freshman year. Everyone seemed to be so eco-friendly these days; I thought I'd do the same.

I pressed the gas pedal but saw Dad closing in through the rearview mirror. This car seemed to lack the firepower to race. My previous Acura moved with power even if it had over a hundred thousand miles on it.

I wish I could speed.

"I'd miss you guys a lot, the friends I know, and Chelsea going to school in Chicago."

Chelsea had one more year left in her master's program at the University of Chicago. She studied English Literature. She hasn't decided to join Mom at the store as a buyer or try out freelance writing. Chelsea's intimidating intelligence and looks that belonged in a Botticelli painting, with her flaxen-blond hair and penetrating azure eyes, made her seem fearless. Yet, she never bragged. It didn't stop the guys from following her. Only Finn seemed to catch her attention and keep her interested. My parents liked him, and they allowed him to come over as often as he liked. He didn't realize what he'd gotten himself into. There was no turning back for him.

We neared my new apartment. When I turned a sharp corner, Mom firmly held onto the car's safety handle as I drove over an uneven section of the road.

"They need to repair the street," she commented.

The beige-colored Craftsman-style bungalow was located on a quiet avenue, three blocks away from a major intersection. We occupied the left side of the house, the larger of the two units. I loved the way the mature trees in the front lawn made me feel like I'd never left home. My father's black car pulled up the driveway, but I didn't see Raegan's metallic blue BMW. I turned back to Mom, leaving the car to idle. "Did you think I was upset that I stayed around here?" I asked.

"Well, no, sweetie, I didn't mean it that way," Mom answered. "You know how sometimes we're extra cautious when it comes to you."

"That's what I don't understand. You and Dad are always *so* much more watchful over me than you were with Isaak or Chelsea. What did I do?"

"It's not something you did or didn't do," she began. "It's just that this world can be a challenging place, and we want to make life easier for you."

"But you have!" I insisted. "I just don't understand all the unnecessary—"

"You're here!" shrieked Raegan. "Let me help you get your stuff."

I turned off the engine and got out of the car, never taking my eyes off of Mom. She ignored my careful glances. Dad stood in the driveway, holding my stuff. I hugged Raegan warmly.

"Hi, Raegan," my parents said in unison. The large, newly furnished house, surrounded by rows of tulips in the front and lilac bushes to one side, resembled a haven, waiting for us with open arms and welcoming us with its two grand, arched windows perched on the second floor. A reception area appeared before us.

"The porch looks sturdy and freshly painted," Dad said, admiring it. "I think Mr. Patel keeps a well-maintained house and is pretty choosy who he rents to. You're not going to find as nice of a place with this type of lawn for student housing."

Raegan and I rolled our eyes. Dad was so attuned to everything.

Mr. Patel and his son came by yesterday, mowing the grass and doing a final inspection on the adjacent apartment. They trimmed the shrubs around the house and raked the fallen leaves from the neighboring trees, revealing the shaven green grass. My parents, Chelsea, Finn, and I had moved the heavy stuff yesterday. I noticed the new neighbors hadn't moved in yet.

I loved the rich hardwood floors throughout this house. Raegan bought a gently used Italian rug from one of her father's customers. The deep blue color background with black and white trim caught my eye. Golden swirls, bright paisleys, and ornamental flowers adorned it. If I stared too long, following the curves and passages in the rug, it resembled an intricate labyrinth with hidden doors and secret hideaways. I felt lost, searching for a way out. At a different angle, the markings could be mistaken for a secret message only translated by someone who knew its meaning.

Focus, Lauren. My thoughts returned to unpacking and setting up the new place. I headed for the kitchen to the open boxes.

"Lauren, I've put away some of your things. You can do the rest. You should have enough storage space for your immediate things. If not, there's always the basement," Mom pointed out, coming down the long and narrow staircase. "I think I'll take a look outside and see what Mr. Patel has done to the yard." She grabbed a bottle of water and went out the back screen door.

The Patels had installed a large wooden deck, which was shared by each house. I envisioned parties and barbecues and friends coming over for football season. I hoped our new neighbors wouldn't be bothered by a few get-togethers. They would certainly be invited.

It didn't take us long to put everything together, even after the dishes were done. The house came with modern appliances that made everything run smoother. I looked around the transformed kitchen: White. Clean. Wood laminated flooring. Livable. "I think if we have some folded chairs and several tables on the deck—one of the guys can bring a grill—and we'll set up enough lawn chairs in the yard, that should do," I said to Raegan, getting more excited about the party.

"Yeah. We'll have music and dancing. They'll want to play some games, do something fun in the back. I hope we're allowed to have a gr—"

That's when I heard Mom scream.

We looked at Mom. I heard her try to catch her breath, because everything went silent.

"Helen, what's wrong?" Dad called out from the upstairs window. He ran downstairs when she didn't respond.

Raegan and I ran to her, nearly tripping on the patio stairs. She stared wide-eyed towards the edge of the yard, facing some sparsely covered bushes in the adjacent yard. The sunlight appeared significantly less in this corner with the long tree branches providing extra shade, but I could see the open parking spaces from the house positioned diagonal to ours. Mom stood there, taking in shallow breaths.

"Mom, . . . *Mom*, what is it?" I wasn't sure what to do. She looked ashen. Her gaze alarmed me, and I gently shook her to provoke a response. She remained glassy-eyed. The sky turned this unshakable steel. The clouds blended into the flickering sky before the crashing thunder took over. It startled me. I felt the sprinkles falling on my anxious face.

"Helen, are you all right? Speak to me!" Dad demanded. "*What is it? What* are you looking at?"

Mom still didn't respond. I looked at a puzzled Raegan; she only shook her head. I searched for my phone. Seconds later, Mom's color began to return. She visibly relaxed. Her dazed glare dissipated to a coherent expression, and her hazel eyes displayed clarity.

"Oh, I'm so sorry," she said nervously. "I didn't mean to frighten everyone. Her hand shook slightly as she pushed away her cropped, honey-colored hair.

"Are you sure, Mom? You looked like you were in a trance." I glanced out at the yard, unconvinced that yard rodents had caused my mother's distress. "Maybe you should see a doctor."

Mom laughed. "Oh, no . . . no. I don't need to a doctor. I'm *fine*, really." She placed a hand on her hip and leaned toward that side. She picked up the water bottle and poured the water onto the lush, green grass. Dad's suspicious intensity disappeared. If he felt any concern, he did a good job of concealing it.

"Well, let's go inside and finish up," he suggested.

The sky cleared and light permeated through the sullen clouds. We walked inside in silence. Raegan shrugged her shoulders. I trailed behind her and my parents, taking small steps at a time. I stopped when I heard a rustling sound behind the bushes. Turning to face the back yard, I noticed a slight movement from the corner bushes—an after-effect of some kind of movement. My eyes narrowed to any possible fluctuation in scenery. I didn't see anything except for the wind dancing with the landscape. I felt its oddly warm breeze flow through me. It felt good and inviting. Then as fast as it came and disappeared, a rush of cold air settled into my bones, leaving a hollow impression. I stood there for a few more moments, deliberating whether to check it out for myself, but decided against it. Inside, I found Mom sweeping the floor. She didn't falter. Dad looked at her for a few moments then went upstairs.

"I'll help you finish the kitchen," I said to Raegan. We worked in silence—swiftly and efficiently. Mom looked quite calm, as if nothing out of the ordinary happened. I studied her, but saw no cracks in her façade. I quietly walked up the carpeted stairs without anyone noticing. I heard Raegan telling Mom a story from the hospital that her mother works at. They both laughed.

"Dad, are you sure she's all right?" I whispered. "She looked so freaked-out."

"Something just caught her off guard," he muttered, not looking up from the computer he was fixing.

"Come on, Dad. You saw her face. You saw how sick she looked. How do you explain not responding when we were talking to her?" I pressed. He continued to work on the computer, ignoring me. I knew he was concerned whether he wanted to show it or not. I didn't understand why he wasn't making a bigger issue of the situation.

He clicked away. He hadn't budged from programming Raegan's computer. I stood there with my arms folded across my chest. "Lauren, don't worry so much about it. Mom is fine. She'll talk about it if she feels it's important. Now finish up what you're doing so we can leave."

"*Fine.*" I marched to my bedroom. I decided this afternoon's event wasn't worth mentioning anymore, but I would store it away when I could have a serious talk with Mom.

"Let's go out for dinner," Dad said from the hallway. I followed him out. "Raegan, why don't you go with Lauren, and we'll meet the two of you at Anthony's Supper House off of Forrest." Mom already picked up her purse and jacket.

"Let me get a few things. Meet you by your car," Raegan said. She ran upstairs.

The open front door allowed me to watch my parents through the screen. I looked up at the rescinding, lead sky. More silver clouds reappeared. Dad put his arm on Mom's shoulders. She whispered something in his ear, as if she didn't want anyone to overhear. She nodded a few times to something Dad said. He seemed unmoved. He appeared to be in agreement with her.

I wondered what they were talking about. Mom's episode? What weren't they telling me?

Suddenly, Dad looked up at the front door. Out of his view, I stood there motionless until the dark Lexus drove away.

Someone was tapping her foot. "What are you doing by the door?" Raegan asked.

I turned around. "Nothing. Let's go. I'm getting hungry."

I put the disk I wanted in the player, keeping the volume low. "Didn't it seem odd to you how startled she was—like she saw a ghost—and then, *poof*, she's fine again?" I asked Raegan as we drove away from the new place.

"She was just caught off guard. You know, your mom is so well put together. Maybe a squirrel surprised her. I don't think she's going to let something like that bother her for the rest of the day," she responded as she dug through her purse.

"I highly doubt it was some yard animal. Did you see her facial expression? And the gap in coherency? That's what bothers me. And I couldn't get an answer from Dad. It's like he wants me to drop it. It's just weird, Raegan." She didn't respond. I continued to drive in silence, listening to the mellow tempo coming from the car's speakers. Once again, the sky became dreary. Large, omniscient clouds formed. The day would soon end, and the shadows would grow longer and less defined. Nightfall crept up slowly, signaling the beginning of quiet passages between creature and man, whoever dared to walk the pavements in the dark hours. I shuddered as I thought I heard a faint cry of warning from the hedges we passed.

My parents were already at the restaurant ordering food. The aroma uplifted my spirits. Fresh garlic bread, tomato paste, and organic herbs scintillated my senses while my stomach growled its emptiness. Raegan and I collapsed into the angular booth. I felt as if I hadn't eaten in days, nourishment being withheld like some cruel test. I wasn't sure how much longer I would be stable without real food to eat. The tablecloth wasn't an option. As the minutes passed by, my mind slowly faded, entering into an unknown abyss. It searched for some recourse, something to hold on to. I would soon fade.

"Lauren, have you heard anything I've said?" Raegan asked.

I blinked in surprise. "What? Did you say something?"

"Oh, forget it."

"Lauren, honey, are you all right? The food's coming," Mom reassured me.

The slim, dark-haired waiter brought our drinks, mixed salads, appetizers, and warm salty bread. I was glad Raegan had an appetite so my family wouldn't be the only people *really* eating. I began to eat with such ferocity; I almost forgot I wasn't alone. Everything tasted so good. I couldn't get enough. I started to feel whole again. The experience felt breathtaking.

I'd nearly finished my side dish when Raegan glanced at my plate, comparing her half-eaten salad to my remaining green specs. My parents easily finished their salad, and the antipasti had only a few morsels left when the waiter came out, bringing the main courses: ravioli, lasagna, pasta carbonara, pasta primavera, and pasta with lobster wine sauce. The meal could easily feed two families.

"Will there be anything else I can get for you?" the waiter asked. He looked surprised.

"No, this should do for now," my father replied.

Raegan laughed. She was used to eating with us.

"Very well. *Buon appetito!*" he remarked and sped off to another table.

I wasn't embarrassed at all the food we'd ordered. We were at an Italian restaurant where it's common to indulge. It looked incredibly mouth-watering. I didn't know if I could eat slowly.

We gorged ourselves on the entrees placed before us. Creamy sauces and the right mix of herbs and spices warmed our palates. In a short amount of time, we devoured the entire meal. Raegan trailed behind as she finished her lasagna. My body thanked me for the satisfying meal.

Most people felt sleepy after a hearty meal. I felt alert and energized. My brain became ignited. Everything moved at rapid speed, allowing me to process the last few weeks' events and every action around me.

The waiter returned to the table. "Do you need a box for that?" he asked Raegan.

"Yes, please." She looked at the empty plates.

"Will you be having dessert?" he asked my father, no longer looking amazed.

"Four crème brûlées and some coffee," Mom answered.

"Oh, none for me," Raegan said.

"I didn't think so," the slight waiter responded.

"I'd better keep quiet," Raegan said.

Moments later, he returned with the desserts and coffee. He handed my father the check. "If there's anything I can get for you, just let me know. Otherwise, enjoy your dessert."

I told my parents I would meet them at home after I drove Raegan to her place. We wouldn't move into the new place until Raegan started her job, therefore, my parents insisted I stay with them. They didn't want me to be alone in the large house. Raegan's parents agreed with mine.

"Don't stay out late. I feel another shift in weather coming," my father cautioned.

I've driven in the rain before without any problems. I took a longer way home, because construction blocked several streets. I took a detour onto another road before reaching her familiar gated community of custom-built homes. We reached her place at nightfall, our surroundings cast in dense bleakness with only the streetlights providing modest illumination. Many of the homes didn't have the front door lights on as they normally did. We said our goodbyes, and I watched her step inside her Tudor style home.

Very few stars appeared tonight as we neared the summer solstice; unlike during the winter months when you can see so many twinkling stars shine across the sky. I was caught in a reverie of the night, staring at the twilight above, when I became startled by a bizarre screeching sound. I looked to my left, but only saw a man walking his dog. I turned around to find a jogger running in the opposite direction, moving away from my car. My senses peaked. I began to drive away. The shadows appeared to follow my car, moving with me at the same speed until I quickly accelerated. In the distance, I heard a woman's muted cries, which eclipsed my previous distraction. I looked around and glanced in the rear view mirror. No one lingered nearby.

My imagination? Perhaps.

CHAPTER 3

Contrasting Dreams

TAP, TAP, TAP, tap, tap.

After five days at my parents' place, I needed a change. Tomorrow, Raegan and I would be in our new place after she started her job at the pet store. The future vet got as much exposure by surrounding herself with the common domestic animals and the varied exotic creatures. For as long as I've known her, animals have been a constant, next to her own family. She promised not to bring too many pets to the new place.

Tap, tap, tap, tap, tap.

Oh, my pen just leaked.

I headed for my parents' office. A week ago my fingers came across the folded up note and that photo. For some reason, I wanted to see it again.

The room felt peaceful and relaxing. I grabbed another pen, but found myself seated at my mother's desk. The papers and letters were tucked away. Nothing out of order. I looked over at the file drawer. Should I? Shouldn't I? Even though I knew it was wrong, I reached for the handle. Locked. I let out a sigh of relief.

Laughing to myself, I headed for the family room. No wonder they called me daily, sometimes twice a day. That wouldn't change once I was on my own. At least when Prince Isaak returned, they would be preoccupied. Chelsea would also be available once her term ended.

For as long as I could remember, I felt my parents' worries and anxieties, especially when I wasn't home, which included high school and freshman year of college, or when I was with my friends. They did seemed more relaxed when I spent time with my camp friends. They developed an instant connection to that group, only calling a few times during my absence. Mom and Dad are loving and supportive parents. However, the knots in my stomach and the tiny voice inside my head told me they kept important secrets.

Ugh. The headaches returned. I rested my head on the family room sofa. The pain pushed through to the center of my forehead, growing larger as the seconds passed. I felt the heaviness sitting in the middle of my head, the tightness spreading to the periphery. I tilted my head forward, covering my eyes with my hand. I closed my eyes, but I didn't sleep. I began to drift, somewhere between here and the unknown there.

Please let me find that restful place inside of me.

It's the prairie again. It's daylight, and the sun is apparent, with the sky a soft, deep gray, adding a lovely shade to the perfect day. A cool breeze blows through the field, and I find myself standing there . . . waiting . . . watching. I close my eyes long enough to allow the fresh air to travel around me, blowing my long hair freely and moving between my fingertips. I pause for a moment before selecting my next course of action. I don't have a plan. I decide to walk through this field of weeds that resembles wheat barley, the fields I've seen so often driving on the country roads, with stalks reaching my knees, sometimes hips. It's quite peaceful in here, all alone inside my thoughts.

My headache subsides. A burst of wind buffets me, sending a slight chill to my inner core. I walk faster, with feelings of regret. It's time to leave. My safe domain is collapsing. I pick up my pace to a slow jog. My body remains stiff. I nervously look around. Where's a safe haven? Something or someone is coming. Getting closer. Every sense, every instinct inside of me shrills alarm.

I'm now running swiftly through this never-ending maze. Is there an opening or a way out? I feel lost; everything looks the same. I can't remember where I've been. I don't know where to go. I don't see any of my previous tracks. My awareness remains heightened; something is following me. It's closing in. It's chasing me deeper into this overgrown field. The light is fading—daylight suddenly turns into evening. I begin to stagger. I look down and see the dense weeds trapping me in its sinuous arms. I fall . . . I've fallen to my knees and panic creeps into the gaps I've left open.

Get up! Get up before they come! I yell at myself.

I slowly stood up, only to stumble again as I tried to catch my breath. Forcefully, I push myself up from the frosty ground. The previously serene, gray sky now appeared livid and stormy. It's yelling at me. I hurry. I sprint even faster. I must get out of here. The dense maze of weeds holds me back. I push out into the lightness. I need to warn the others.

There are others? How do I know this?

I reach a section of land where the stalks are only waist high. I see a woman running just ahead, her brunette hair flying in the wind. She's not dressed like me, but she's fleeing this harrowing meadow. I run faster, catching up to her. We move side by side, as if we are one person.

"Hurry!" I yell.

She doesn't notice; she just keeps running. There's terror on her face, and pain. She knows something is coming for us. She knows what's approaching. We scurry even faster, trying to avoid the pitfalls in the ground. She inadvertently maneuvers away from the meager course; I follow her into the thicker brush. "No, don't go there!" I shout. She ignores me.

There's only a fraction of sunlight above the overgrown field. She leads us into more dense plant life, making it harder to move around. She stops for a moment to catch her breath before trudging forward. We see a slight opening in the branches and continue aimlessly through the treacherous maze, still searching for an opening that will lead us out of here. We finally reach a clearing, which we cross with ease. Once again, we're running into the exposed field. So tired. Our speed slows, but we're no-where near safe passage. She becomes sluggish.

"Don't stop!" I plead with her. "I'll help you. Hold on to me. I have to get us out of here!" I reach for her, and grab for air, not even touching her shadow. She's moaning in pain. She lingers in each spot. "You're hurt..."

She's injured. She's coughing up small amounts of blood. Her breathing becomes more labored. She's gasping for air. She grabs at her chest, trying to slow her breathing.

She attempts to wipe away the sanguineous fluid, only to expel more of the same. She falls. I fall with her on to my knees. I attempt to lift her up. I can't carry her, because I can't feel her. I'm not really here. I'm watching what I've always watched, the same dark and perverse story.

They're closing in. I can't see them, but they're here. They're not here for me; they're here for her. "Runnn! Get out of here!" I scream at this fragile woman. I'm crying because I know what's going to happen. I can't save her. . . .

She screams.

I scream.

My eyes shot wide open in the realization that I was no longer there. I was still lying on the couch. Another daydream, resembling a nightmare, flashed before me, only I was awake. *It's not real. Everything's fine.* The thumping in my heart began moving to a quiet, even beat, taking my respirations to a calmer place. I take two full deep breaths. I gulp down the cool water on the end table. The pulsating hunger continues.

The day terror quickly moved to a far shelf of my memory locker. It's where my confused emotions live, no longer an immediate concern. I walked to the immaculate kitchen. Silence. I thought about my parents. They didn't need to know. I've never mentioned these visions to Dr. Sendal, either. They would all think I'm crazy. Mom has never mentioned this kind of experience. Her episode in the yard was brief, like a mini stroke. If I told her about my visions, she would grill me. I wanted answers, not more worrying.

I don't recall ever dreaming when I'm asleep. Not ever. I asked Raegan about this. She said everyone dreams. I can't remember one dream. I remembered asking my father if people dreamed. He said they did. "It's part of the sleep cycle." But he never elaborated on them. In fact, he became brief and uneasy when I brought up the subject of dreaming.

My hands trembled and my stomach rumbled. I grabbed a few oranges and some milk from the stainless steel fridge, and then reached for the granola from the cherry cupboards. Two hours since my filling breakfast, and I'm famished. This last vision had drained me more than the previous ones.

After eating, I raced for my cello. Mom would be home soon, and I needed to unwind. The tightened bow was already in my hand with the cello lying comfortably against my legs. My hand felt sticky from the rosin. The music started out quietly before the adagio flowed in, then turned into an allegro movement. My hands kept pace to the music and the moving tempo. Not a note missed. The vibrato, coming from my left hand, knew when to act every time the bow made contact with the strings. My long fingers stretched above an octave at the neck of the cello. The music played on its own, carrying us to another place. As I moved closer to the finale, my reverie shattered at the sound of the garage door opening and footsteps entering the living room.

"Hi, honey. I'm home early. I thought we could spend more time together before you move out tomorrow," Mom said, coming through the door. She looked at the cello. "I can hear you all the way from the garage. I'm glad you're keeping up with the lessons and not letting the cello catch dust. We'll go to the symphony again this summer."

"Of course." I continued to play quietly as she spoke.

"I'm hiring another sales person this week. It's getting busier at the store." She looked around the room. "What did you do today?"

"Nothing too exciting. Played the cello, made some progress on a piece." I looked in the direction of the family room where the images took place. It felt like I was never in that room. "Just thinking about my new place."

Mom frowned. I decided to talk about school and the upcoming trips this summer. I thought about telling her about today's visions, but decided if she felt her backyard episode was insignificant then my visions could stay hidden a while longer.

⊷⊨● ●⊨⊶

The next day, I arrived at my new place before noon to find a dark Volkswagen in the driveway. *The new neighbors must have moved in.* I decided to do the friendly thing, and introduce myself. I was always taught to be polite. Besides, a useful neighbor might be an advantage. I could hear Raegan reminding me to find out who lived next door. I knocked on the wooden front door, and waited patiently for someone to appear. Nobody answered. I rang the doorbell three times before a car passed by the house—a quiet hum only a small car would make—causing me to turn around to see the slow speed it went. A golden Crossfire drove away. *Nice.* It wasn't a car you would see everyday. A female with long, blond hair sat behind the wheel. I returned to the neighbor's door, still uninvited. Through the bay window and into the darkened home, I saw a few simple furniture pieces on the living room floor and a small kitchen table in the dining area. They probably don't want to be disturbed.

I went back to my place to change into some running clothes. The neighbor inquiry would have to wait. Honestly, I really didn't care who lived next door as long as we could get along because I really liked this house.

I ran down the long, interlining streets, in the opposite direction of the business district, making mental notes of distinctive landmarks, street signs, and alleys to avoid. Nothing unusual appeared. I found a spacious park with similar-looking shops lined neatly next to each other on the same street a few blocks from the busy commercial intersection. My run complete, I headed home, showered, and started flipping through the channels when something scratched against the door.

"Heyyy," Raegan said. "I brought Oscar here to see if he'd like to stay with us. I couldn't bear to be apart from him." The brown and white beagle pulled her into the house. He looked newly washed. "Harper is staying behind. She's too comfortable at home. That big cat is so spoiled." Raegan liked anything furry and friendly. She has Oscar,

Harper, two fish swimming in a bowl, and an active hamster waiting upstairs to be fed. "Is it okay with you if he stays?"

"Oscar can stay with us," I cooed. I let him come onto my lap. He stopped moving around and made himself comfortable, but his head pointed upward in the direction of the door.

Raegan tossed her bag into the living room, then went over to the kitchen to fill Oscar's bowl with food and water. He jumped out of my lap and in seconds, his face was deep into the bowl of water. I got up and heated the casserole and warm bread, and put the mixed salad in a separate bowl.

"So, I went over to the neighbor's place," I said.

"Did you find out who they were?" she asked. She stopped digging through her oversized bag.

"No. I knocked, but nobody answered the door."

"Are you sure you waited long enough?"

"Yes, I'm sure. I even rang the doorbell. There was a car in the driveway, but nobody came. It did look dark inside."

"That's strange. I came by earlier to drop off some stuff. I didn't see any cars. But there's one now." She looked outside the bay window, staring at the dark car. "And nobody answered?"

"Nope."

Raegan faced me again. Her eyes narrowed then widened, along with a smile on her face. "It doesn't matter. You have to find out who they are. I really wouldn't mind if there were two cute guys," she joked.

"Don't you already have Tim Perez and Davie Merton wrapped around your finger?" I teased.

"It doesn't hurt to keep the circle open," she said with a grin.

They weren't serious interests, just friends she spent time with while she waited for the one who still caught her attention. I got up to put away the leftover food. The refrigerator was well stocked, which looked more suited for two hungry college men instead of two active, young women.

"I bet they didn't want to answer the door," she said.

"Maybe. They might not be ready to see anyone. Or someone was sleeping," I responded.

"Who sleeps at this hour?" she harped. "I just think it's rude that nobody answered the door." She began putting the dishes away.

I sighed. "I'll try another time. I don't want to be pushy. Besides, does it really matter as long as they don't bother us?"

"Or do you mean, *we* don't bother them." She snickered. "You know, we could start making more noise and see if they do anything."

"Let's just wait and see."

I took Oscar outside to do his evening routine. It wasn't completely dark outside. We walked around the landscaped yard. He sniffed at the bushes and the trees. A sizable patch of newer grass covered an area that once appeared to be a thriving garden. In the left corner of the yard, two mature elm trees stood overpoweringly next to a raspberry bush, which overlapped the russet-colored fence that formed the back edge of the yard. Oscar ran from end to end, brushing himself up against the maple trees in the far right corner, and grazed at sporadic points along the wooden fence.

"Oscar, let's go inside," I called out.

I looked at the bushes again surrounding the elm trees, which divided this yard from the corner lot, remembering where my mother stood that day, staring into oblivion. If you looked at it more carefully, it was an intimate corner of a shady area with small gaps for light to penetrate during the daytime. In complete darkness, I could see why it would be difficult to differentiate the grassy spot from the scenery.

An unexpected gust of wind blew in as soon as we moved closer to the house, sending a chilling sensation through my spine. I shivered. A warmer spell followed. I stared at the colorful tulips along the back edges of the house, blowing from side to side, and the flowering rose bushes that became more entangled. I looked up to find a dim light reflecting from the far right corner window of the house. I saw someone move away. *That* someone's shadow remained visible. I walked closer to the house with the beautiful angelic flowers calling out to me, beckoning me to come closer. *"Lauren . . . Lauren."* Was it coming from the window or did my mind believe nature invited me? I reached out to the pastel rose bush, only to have a thorn pierce my finger. *"Ouch!"* The light above me turned off as I stood there, sucking the fresh blood from my wounded finger.

→═◎ ◎═←

The next day, I woke up later than Raegan; she'd already left for work. My part-time job didn't start until Wednesday, so I had extra time to explore the neighborhood. I took Oscar outside and gave him some fresh food and water. It was a good day to investigate the commercial district to see what kind of shops lined the busy streets. I got into my smoky gray hybrid and sped away.

A friend of mine suggested this up and coming boutique. I remembered seeing the red and white signboard that hung above the shop's entrance. The owner, a fashion connoisseur, supported local artists and showcased new men's and women's trendy clothes. I wasn't a person who always needed the latest style, but for some reason, I found myself drawn to the vibrant shop with all its colorful designs. The moment I opened the heavy, glass door, I felt complete. Did I lose something only to suddenly find it? Had I been thinking about a shirt I wanted to buy?

I rummaged through the tunics and printed jeans, taking my time and sizing up which outfit might look more flattering. I giggled like a child in a candy shop. I walked from one end of the store and circled to the opposite side before stopping at the invisible border between the men's clothing and the women's summer shirts. I was in my own world.

"I think this one belongs on your side," a tranquil voice stated, handing me the lavender shirt I accidentally placed on the men's side. I turned to warm gray eyes staring back at me. The edges of his lips curled upward. The brightness in the store seemed to enhance his custard and yellow ochre-colored hair.

"Oh, thanks," I responded. I reached for the blouse, my hand momentarily touching his. "My mistake." I couldn't help but look into those eyes that smiled back at me. My internal temperature rose ten degrees.

He wasn't anyone I'd seen before because I would have remembered his face. He stood before me with a familiar presence I couldn't place. There was something about him that eluded anonymity, yet triggered a dormant response in the recesses of my mind.

"Hey, are you okay?" He waved his hand back and forth in front of my face. "You look sort of lost." He grinned.

"What? Oh . . . I . . . I was thinking about trying on this shirt."

"I think it would look very nice on you, but I'm sure anything would," he said.

"Thanks." I blushed, still gazing into his inviting eyes. What was it about him? I've never seen him before and yet everything inside of me stirred wildly. I wasn't sure if I felt fear or curiosity. "Oh, I don't know. It's rather plain. Maybe something else might look better—something more colorful." I reached for the nearest blouse. "How about this floral one?" I joked.

"Flowers with jagged edges? Looks like it could cut you. It's too flimsy, don't you think?" He pointed to the racks of clothes. "Hmmm. Sometimes it's the simple things that stand out the most." He stood there, studying my frozen face.

Just breathe! I scolded myself. "Simple is good."

This time, he turned away. His soft, gray eyes conveyed reservation. His lips turned upward. "Like I said, you can make anything look good."

I narrowed my eyes. "That doesn't sound very original. More like something from a movie. You probably tell every girl that."

He looked confused. "No," he said flatly. Steel eyes looked directly at me. "Never." His smile disappeared, leaving tightly pressed lips. He continued to stare at my heated face, searching beyond my startled green eyes to some unknown place, perhaps looking for my hidden soul. I was shaking. His probing gaze persisted, but his eyes appeared more relaxed. "Never," he whispered, again.

Every nerve twitched in my body. Even my throat dried up. I pleaded with myself to find an escape, but my feet wouldn't move. "My roommate is waiting for me." Instead of waiting for his response, I spun around and darted into another section of the store, weaving through the crowded racks. I hid behind the long, spring dresses. *Coward.* I closed my eyes until I could regain my strength. I reached for my phone and texted Raegan:

Shopping. V Cute Guy Alert. TTYL. L

I sent the message, laughing at myself for feeling like such an idiot. I usually don't get this nervous when I talk to guys. He was an exception. Perhaps his good looks and the way his gray eyes pierced through me caught me by surprise. I glanced around. I didn't see him. I scanned the busy store. No traces of the mystery man. *Oh!* I purchased that lavender tunic and left.

Clothes shopping would never be the same. I couldn't shake that piercing gray gaze—familiar . . . gentle. What was it about him? My mind raced to find ways that I might run into him. I giggled. He might be a student or live nearby. What if I never saw him again?

Oh, Lauren. I can't believe you're obsessing over a guy you don't even know. I refocused again, pushing aside the silly schoolgirl fantasies. I put my belongings away and turned on my computer. I had emails from the Minnesota friends, several high school friends sent messages, and there was a note from my music instructor. Alex asked if Raegan and I got settled into the new place. A casual romance between Alex and Raegan began during our first summer in Duluth. They remained close friends despite going their separate ways, but I knew better. Justin and Elsie were still together. Elsie said they would visit Cameron and Gavin who studied at a college in Platteville. Noelle wrote about her family, school life at Loyola, and her summer job. She lived in the Chicago area. Mrs. Persson, my Evanston Township instructor, wanted to know how my lessons went with Professor Sobel, and if I'd applied for an internship with the Chicago Symphony Orchestra.

I stopped reading my email when Oscar started to bark. I could hear Raegan rushing through the house before she ran up the stairs. She was short of breath. I felt embarrassed.

"*Who* was the guy you met?" she demanded. I gave her a description of the mysterious man, and how I acted strangely at the boutique, not leaving out any details. "But you're always so calm around guys. I can't believe you were so nervous," she said, surprised, as she sat on my neatly made bed.

"I know," I agreed. "And I didn't even get his name. He was already gone before I had a chance to ask." I thought about the intense look in his eyes. "It was so strange. He was familiar somehow, yet, I couldn't understand why. I've never seen him before." I thought back to the way he seemed to analyze me. "Seriously, Raegan, he just stood there staring at me with those big gray eyes, like in a dream. If I even dream, he just stepped out of it."

"He must have been *dreamy* by the way you look." She imitated my facial expression.

"*Ew!* Get off my bed. You smell like animals," I joked. We both laughed. She left me to swim in my own thoughts.

Dreamy. He must have been a dream.

CHAPTER 4

Exchanges

I REFUSED TO waste my energy thinking about someone I'd only met briefly. It was silly, and I haven't seen him in a few days. Besides, I had the summer to think about—warm days, spending time at the lake with friends, and being on my own. Tomorrow was my first day at the school library, where I'd be working a few days a week.

Mom called this morning despite the fact that I had dinner with them yesterday evening. She reminded me that Isaak would be home on Friday, and we would have a family get together on Saturday. Isaak was moving home until he could find a place, even though I knew he'd be persuaded to stay longer. He'd be starting a new job at my father's firm.

He won't ever leave. He won't ever be able to escape.

I hopped into my car, thinking I'd do the usual coffee run. The quiet engine moved along newly paved roads. As I inhaled, I smelled the toxic fumes of melting tar magnified by the sun. I wasn't sure why it affected me so much. I soon turned into this isolated coffee shop that I noticed during my shopping trip the other day. Nothing could ruin this perfect morning!

The usual wrought iron tables and chairs were situated outside the café with the dark green pull-down awning tucked away, allowing the sun to shine freely. I entered the inviting cafe, inhaling the freshly brewed espresso and the rich blends of coffee beans being crushed. The lighting was subdued, a few lamps stationed at designated tables for reading and studying. I ordered my Columbia roast. Several strangers gave me friendly greetings and a few polite glances as I walked to the furthest table from the door. I looked down to see if I had any stains on my clothes.

A group of students gathered at the center of the coffeehouse had combined four tables. They were debating their schoolwork. A couple seated to the right of me was locked in a staring contest, in contrast to an arguing pair at the following table. Their voices became louder. I noticed mothers with their children along the windows, each parent coddling or instructing her young. The service line stretched out to the entrance. Even during the summer, midday was busy this close to campus. My head turned when a mug dropped to the floor, coming from the quarreling pair. It didn't break. I carefully glanced in their direction, only to find two unhappy people looking over each other's shoulder. A twinge of sadness came over me. I turned away and decided to ignore the rest of the customers coming in and out of the main entrance. My book waited for me. In seconds, I became engrossed in the novel. The cafe ceased to exist in my undisturbed realm.

"Do you mind if I sit with you? It's crowded in here today," a familiar voice asked.

I looked up to see those amused gray eyes, this time accompanied by a wry smile. "Uh . . . sure. It's free," I muttered, my face flushing.

"*The War of the Worlds*, that's a pretty intense book. You must be a pretty serious person," he probed.

"I like my science fiction. H.G. Wells was so ahead of his time. Nothing like a grand invasion to shake up the planet," I answered, unable to say anything else. I stared at him. "And no, I'm not always a serious person. It depends."

"On what?" he inquired.

"On whether the person is funny or not. I mean, if you can laugh at yourself and joke with people around you." I closed my book. "It would be so dull taking yourself seriously all the time."

"You have a point. I've been known to take myself too seriously. What do you suggest?"

I shook my head, confused. "You want me to tell you how to be less serious. You're joking, right?"

"No, I'm serious," he said with a straight face. Then, he chuckled. "There I go again, siding with heaviness."

I held back a smirk.

"Okay, if I got up on stage and did a comedy skit, would you find that really appealing?" he asked. His gray eyes looked at me warmly. Then, the patience disappeared and turned into annoyance. Now his transparent eyes began to laugh at me, and his arched mouth added to the ridicule. He frowned, then squinted. I saw the irritation on his face. Did he really say, "Are you slow or something? Don't you get it?"

"Well, I wouldn't find *you* funny." I turned away from his incredibly handsome face and reopened my book to a random page. My face burned. I reached inside my purse for my keys.

"Hey, I wasn't making fun of you. I was just trying to be funny. I guess that didn't work."

"Oh." I turned to face the stranger again. "I knew that."

We looked at the warring couple because the young girl just yelled an expletive at the guy sitting across from her. She then threw money in his face before rushing off. He looked distraught. He quickly picked up the bills, leaving the coins on the floor. He followed after her, calling out her name. The loving couple next to them now fed each other tiny bites of chocolate cake, their eyes continued to play adoringly at each other. She looked amused. The beautiful stranger watched them. He produced an amused smile, then turned my way. I turned ruby red.

He's just a guy! Granted, a very good-looking and charming guy. Pull yourself together!

"Is that book any good? You seem to still be on the same page."

Oh! I looked away again, struggling for recovery.

"You can tell me what you think, but I've already read it. I didn't particularly like the book. Too depressing," he said. "The world was being destroyed, and we were struggling to survive the battle of advanced machinery."

"I've read it before, when I was in high school. I had a sudden urge to read it again. I found him ingenious," I responded, now more in control.

"Mr. Wells was ahead of his time with modern machines and alien invasions. Who could have known greater forces would jeopardize the human race?" he commented.

"It would be frightening waking up one morning to find half the city destroyed and running to safety. But that's all fiction." I found myself twirling my tightly made ponytail and quickly stopped.

"If that ever happened, some form of invasion, what would you do?"

"Well, it's not going to happen because I don't believe in it, at least not in Martians. I suppose war and destruction can happen, and that's a tragedy. I guess I would have to fight—or run—if it *truly* were an alien invasion."

I studied the stranger's serious face. He moved his eyes down to the open page I had in front of me. When he glanced back up, he was looking over my shoulder with distant eyes. "If only the human race could win. . . . " he said.

What did he mean by that?

I wasn't sure, but I wanted to know. He was interesting to talk to; the conversation felt genuine. I took more sips of my now tepid drink. He nearly finished his while I was talking. The afternoon sun emphasized his natural yellow highlights. He had a subtle cowlick that was controlled, allowing a mature look instead of a young boy image. His slightly styled and layered waves neatly covered his head and were trimmed over his ears with a few tight waves forming at the nape of his hairline. It was a classic look, so effortless in its natural form. I quickly lowered my eyes and began to outline the rim of my cup.

"You didn't tell me your name," he stated.

"Lauren. Lauren Reed," I murmured.

"Lauren," he whispered. "They gave you a lovely name."

"What?"

"It's a nice name," he said.

"It's the name I remember, the one they called me at the orphanage," I said. "I was adopted. My birth parents' name was Lewis. The Reeds have been my parents since I was four."

"I see," he said. "That must have been very difficult for you to lose your parents."

"I suppose so, but I don't remember anything about my birth parents. It's hard to miss people you never really knew. I only remember living at an orphanage, and the Reeds coming there to adopt me. I was four years old. They've been great—the best." I sipped my increasingly bitter coffee. "They were killed in a car accident."

"A car accident? Did the Reeds tell you that?" He looked surprised.

"No, that's what the nuns told me. It's also in the documents."

"Did they tell you anything else about your parents?"

I hesitated.

"You don't have to answer. I didn't mean to pry." He looked regretful. "Your family is not my business."

I pushed the coffee cup away and started on the water. "That's all I know about the Lewises. I'm sure they were good people. At least, I hope so. Like I said, I have no memory of them."

"Nothing . . . nothing at all?" he questioned further.

"Nothing."

"Did they mention any other family?"

I felt comfortable talking to him about my family and my former parents. I'm not sure why it felt so easy to confide in him. "Just me. No other family that I'm aware of. I must be an only child. I tried to do a search on a Paul and Simone Lewis, but nothing came up."

"No other family," he repeated with melancholy. He looked away, somewhere in the distance. His previously shiny gray eyes turned desolate.

"Just me," I mimicked. "I'm pretty happy with the life I have. I think if it ever came up again—the need to search for my biological parents—I'd talk to my parents and my brother and sister, too. We're a close-knit family."

"Ah, yes, your siblings. You have *other* family members," he chided.

I wasn't sure what he meant by that. Maybe he was an only child. "As I got older, I assumed the real story behind my adoption wasn't from a car accident. I thought they abandoned me, just left me. I really did believe it was a cover up for the truth."

All the students left the center tables, abandoning two dedicated classmates to unravel the encrypted notes lying in front of them; a long, extensive mystery, no doubt.

"I can't imagine they would. I'm sure your parents cared about you a great deal," he spoke softly. "Why do you think they abandoned you?"

"Because I didn't find any answers about my past. No trails connecting me to them."

"I'm sure your parents didn't leave you. The story would be too hard to fabricate," he said reassuringly. "Anyone leaving you must feel ashamed." He looked down at his empty cup.

"I don't believe they left me on purpose," I insisted. "It doesn't matter anyway. I have everything I want."

A brief silence entered the table. Even the afternoon rush had settled into a comfortable speaking level. "Well, I have to go." He got up quickly.

I started to stand. "When will I see you—"

"Maybe we'll run into each other again."

I hope so.

"I have to get something to eat," he mumbled.

"I do, too," I said hastily.

I waited for him to invite me along, but he didn't say anything else. My moment of excitement turned sour. Defeated, I resolved to let him go. He got up, grabbed his empty cup and his keys. Several athletic looking guys from another table turned their heads at us. He frowned.

"My name is Quinn," he said before walking out the door.

⇢⊨◉ ◉⊨⇠

I decided to keep this interlude to myself. I wasn't ready to share Quinn with anyone. I needed to find out more about him even if I never saw him again, a thought that became disturbing.

Who was he?

Today was my first day of work, only four hours of orientation and training. I dressed in a cream colored shirt, wore a contemporary plaid skirt I found in a magazine, and grabbed my tan mules. My hair was already up in a tight, modern do. I grabbed a pair of fake tortoise glasses and left.

The beaming sun filtered through the driver's side window and the fresh air streamed through the open window on the passenger side. I took in a heavenly breath. Not a cloud glided across the cornflower blue sky today. Every creature stirred around me, awakened by the May spring after a long and hard winter.

When I got to the library, it was busier than I expected for a Friday prior to summer sessions. I reacquainted myself with a few students I met on my interview before putting my belongings away, and followed my trainer, some Spanish major named Ethan. He gave me a peculiar look. I laughed under my breath.

"The vending machine is over there." He pointed to the distant hallway after readjusting his retro glasses. "The employee lounge is to the right, the bathrooms are past the lounge, and you must know your way around campus by now because you're a . . ."

"I'll be a sophomore, and yes, I can make my way around," I said confidently.

"I'll show you how we check out books and locate microfiche, and how the library is divided. You can take a break whenever you want as long as it's not too busy, unless you see one of the professors looking for something. Help them out unless you want to hear it from administration." He walked me through the library, drinking his caffeinated soda. "We basically use the Dewey Decimal system to catalog the reading materials."

I followed him for the next hour, carting the returned books back onto the shelves, scanning student IDs, and putting up some posters the university allowed to be posted. He left me alone to sort through my pile of English literature books before sitting down at the main desk with his magazines and another can of soda. I moved across to the media room where I found the music collection. Barbara Mandrell and Elvis Presley disks were placed in the same pile as the Nine Inch Nails CDs. I cringed.

"Hey, Lauren. How's your first day going?" asked Linda Nguyen, the friend who'd told me about this job.

"Not too bad. It sounds simple enough and the hours work well with my lessons. The supervisor is giving me plenty of flexibility for the summer," I told her. We moved out of the media room to a large cart of books along the science row.

"Great! It'll be fun having you here, someone to talk to. It's pretty laid back," she began. "Hey, remember when I mentioned volunteering at one of the downtown soup kitchens? We plan to meet next week and help out at mealtime. Do you still want to do it?"

"Sure, it sounds like fun. We could do something afterwards."

I'm one of those people who gets involved in clubs and organizational roles. Class president my junior year in high school, student council member, involved in the school orchestra, played sports, and active on many student committees while maintaining my honor student status. My parents were driven and my siblings were talented; therefore, I should be the same. They never forced me to succeed, only encouraged me to do well. I didn't want to let anybody down. I needed to be perfect. Anything less was not acceptable.

"I should let you get back to work since it's your first day," she said.

Ethan brought another cart of books. I divided up the numbers according to the numeric order along the shelves and compared those with the correct numbers attached to the spine of each book. My own efficient way to separate the numbers for the higher shelves and for the lower levels became effortless. I grabbed a nearby footstool in order to reach the upper rows.

"I could hand you a few so you wouldn't have to climb down each time to grab more books," the magical voice said to me.

I felt myself losing my balance when Quinn spoke, and I imagined a scene where the girl in the library fell off a stool only to be caught by some handsome young man. The thought seemed appealing, and I became tempted. I really felt that I would faint.

"I can manage," I said stiffly, now facing eye level. I took off the fake glasses.

"Your eyes are unusually green."

"A defect since birth. An unexplained aberration."

Quinn didn't laugh. He kept looking into my eyes. I couldn't move; I was held fast. He continued to stare without flinching. He seemed so familiar, but from where? His silence mesmerized me. I expected some electrical impulses to trigger my memory, allowing me to recognize the person standing before me. Creases formed between his reflective eyes, and his frustrated face turned doubtful when he returned to the present setting. He shook his head several times, as if responding to a question he'd asked himself. He gave me a crooked smile then turned away to reach for more books. We finished the work in silence. On occasion our hands touched during the passing of select novels. I tried not to linger too long like some silly schoolgirl caught up in her first crush.

"I think that's everything. I'll see what else I have to do," I said, not wanting to leave this spot.

He walked with me down the long, quiet row until he found a table. I headed for the media room again. I asked another student to switch tasks in order to work closer to Quinn. As I slowly walked back to his table while trying to control my eagerness, two friendly girls approached him and sat at his table. *Our table.* They chatted away about how hard they've been studying this past year, and how they planned to get a head start for the fall semester so they could take accelerated courses next term.

You look like you need it.

One of the girls laughed and threw her lush, blond hair near his face while the other female inched closer, batting her long, fluttery lashes. She whispered something in his ear. She attempted to get cozy with him. I needed to do something. The sisters of Medusa circled their prey before the final descent—the ultimate kill—and the human would turn to stone. I nearly choked on my breathing, unsure if he would perish or just annoyed at the intruding females. The wavy, dark-haired sister hissed at me when she noticed I was still there.

"Don't you have work to do?"

"I'm doing it. I didn't realize I was such a distraction," I said sweetly.

Her face turned sour. "Well, get to it instead of just staring at us." She flashed a condescending smile.

The blond sister laughed. "Who cares? Forget about it."

I remained steadfast. Quiet and unshaken, Quinn appeared unmoved by their luring ways. He closed his eyes as if meditating. A sardonic smile rose from his perfect lips, and he opened his beautiful slate eyes, turning my way. "Lauren, are you ready to help me find my book for class."

The dark-haired sister scowled. She looked at me with icy blue eyes. The golden-haired one began her search for other victims.

"It's this way." I pointed in a direction far from the crowded table.

Neither girl looked at me as they made sugary attempts to see him again at a party or around campus. I fumed inside, and then shook it off. My heart crumbled. Quinn politely exited the table and followed me down the corridor.

I'm just as pretty as they are, I thought.

We stopped at the technology rows. I began the chore of dividing the numbers in calculating speed, while trying not to be distracted by the attentive observer who leaned against the metal shelf. I glanced over my shoulder for a moment. He flipped through the pages of his mundane book. I moved further away, loitering at a nearby row, and fumbled to straighten several hardcover texts. I felt his concentrated stare as I stood there pushing each book into place. A sly smile formed on his handsome face. Heat flooded my cheeks.

I moved closer to him. His smile remained amused, and his eyes stirred. I pushed away pieces of my floating hair. He gracefully walked to the other side of the towering shelf. Large volumes and thin books separated us like a lopsided wall in a cell, but somehow the gaps between each row allowed light to pass through. They were dividers that couldn't keep us apart. He gazed upon my warm face again, stealing minute glances in between intervals of fictitious reading.

My defenseless heart beat louder and louder, flowing at a rate too fast for the organ to hold. I wasn't sure how much longer I could withstand the pressure inside before a chamber would erupt.

"Oh, Lauren. There you are," Ethan interrupted. "Why don't you take your break? They'll think I'm working you like a slave."

My reverie shattered. I felt an artery completely sever, allowing fluid to pour out of my body.

Moments later, I regained consciousness. "Um, sure, why not?" I looked over my shoulder; Quinn had disappeared. I looked down both aisles and saw no trace of him. I let out a heavy sigh. I picked up the dated book he dropped on the floor. I flipped open the book and found a folded note.

Meet me tomorrow at 11:00 at this park.   *Q*

He wrote directions to the park. I had passed it during my run on Monday. I smiled in anticipation. Hope was restored.

CHAPTER 5

The Moonlight

I GOT READY to meet Quinn at the park. After trying on numerous out-fits that screamed, "You're trying too hard!", I opted for a pair of comfortable jeans and the lavender shirt I bought. I powdered my face and applied a neutral lipstick, giving myself a sun-kissed look.

My phone rang. Mom, of course.

"Hi, Mom, I'm on my way out," I muttered into the phone.

"It won't take long. I know I've asked you this before, but have you noticed anything unusual in your neighborhood, or anyone . . . strange?" She sounded more curious than worried.

"No, I haven't seen anything strange. Did you hear something in the news?" I asked.

"No, nothing like that. It's just . . . well, you're on your own, and I guess I'm just being a mom and worrying," she admitted. "Are you meeting new people?"

I wasn't ready to tell her about Quinn. She'd been leery of a few boyfriends in the past. "No, Mom. Just hanging out with the people you already know."

"All right then, I'll see you tomorrow. Love you."

"Love you, too."

I hung up the phone and got into my car. I drove faster than normal because I didn't want to be late for my date. I giggled to myself. Maybe we would extend the date and go somewhere else after the park. When I pulled into a parking spot, he was already waiting for me. He found a picnic table near the center of the park with some shade. The clear sky and the warm sun shone down on us. It was perfect. Quinn wore dark jeans and a fitted, pale green shirt, revealing defined muscles and a healthy physique. I tried not to gaze for too long.

"I brought us some burgers and fries." He reached into the bag and set the food on the table.

"Great, I'm hungry, too. I wasn't sure if we would go out to eat." I was relieved. Nothing could go wrong today. I started for the mammoth burger.

"One of the best in town, I was told," Quinn remarked.

I took a sip of my water. "It's very good."

Quinn took a bite of his, then stopped eating. He picked at his fries and took small sips of soda. Then, he stared in the horizon. "I just want to make things clear," he began. "The other day at the coffee shop, I wasn't sure if you thought I was being rude because I didn't ask you to come with me. I needed some time alone to think after seeing you," he admitted.

To think about what?

My curiosity and contentment stood on level ground. The joy I felt of just being next to him overpowered my hunger. I couldn't let that happen. I took another bite of the greasy burger.

"You see, you remind me so much of someone I still care about," he whispered.

I stopped chewing on the food. *Still* and *care*, all in the same sentence—present tense. The words paralyzed me. I almost choked on a piece of burger. I grabbed my drink to wash it down my throat. I felt ill. Even worse, it felt like someone just kicked me in the stomach.

Can't breathe.

The shock and injury to my system jarred me. My heart sank to the deepest low with my mind sifting through all his possible meanings. A broken heart, his long lost girlfriend, someone he's waiting for—a wife? I tried to look composed and supportive even when the knife penetrated the first line of defenses. I knew if I looked down, I would see blood seeping through my clothes. I reached for my stomach. Quinn could probably tell that I wasn't well. My eyes felt heavy. What was I thinking? What was I expecting? All this time, the deep stares into my eyes weren't meant for me. He was still in love with the one he had lost.

I thought I was special.

"Oh. Is this *someone* here?" I asked apprehensively.

"I think she's long gone."

Did she leave him?

"So, you came to Chicago to see her?"

"No. When we last spoke in New Haven, she left suddenly. She had to leave." Quinn gave me a probing look.

"And you're still looking for her?" I asked.

"Yes and no," he said.

The blade moved further inside, nearly touching a vital organ. The internal bleeding began. The breach would set off a collapse of the entire foundation, leaving everything in ruin. I would fall. I didn't know how to stop the destruction.

"That's why I'm here. I searched for two years before I gave up. I stopped searching . . . when I met you."

The pain medicine was delivered and the numbness took over. The experts continued to work on the leak, patching the hole to prevent further loss. It would be a temporary fix. The sun would shine again even if storm clouds lingered. I felt hopeful. But could I replace the loss he felt? How do I compete with the memory of his past?

"I can't make any promises, but I'd like to see how things pan out." He looked optimistic. "Unless you're already involved with someone."

"No, no one special at the moment." I looked at my lap.

"I'm sure you've had relationships. Maybe you were in love?" He cringed.

"I've had boyfriends, but not anyone special. Some were short-lived. No . . . never in love," I admitted.

"I think it's wise not to rush your feelings." He looked relieved. "We could get to know each other, and you would *think* you were falling for me. But once you got to know me, you'd soon realize I'm not Prince Charming."

I turned away from him.

We ate the rest of our lunch in silence. Small threads of thin, white clouds moved into the pale blue sky. The air became cooler. It didn't bother me. I was with Quinn. Even though I had numerous questions, I didn't want to ruin the rest of the day. I debated if I should ask about his past or wait until he told me. The knot in my stomach grew. It was as if Quinn could read my thoughts. He jumped to his feet, grabbed my hand and pulled me up. He threw away the bags.

"Let's go for a walk."

His hand felt soft and warm, holding mine in a protective manner as we walked through the bustling park. We received approving glances from random strangers. I looked up to see a slight smile. Small creases formed around his eyes underneath the baseball cap he wore.

"I'm surprised you didn't ask me where I came from," he blurted out.

"I was waiting for you to bring it up, but since you are, why don't you tell me more about yourself?" I invited, my curiosity growing.

"I moved to Chicago from California. I started out in Fresno, made my way to Sacramento, and ended up in Santa Cruz," he began.

"That's when you were looking for . . . her," I interrupted, swallowing hard.

"Something like that. I did some searching, and Chicago became a possibility," Quinn continued. "So I tried my luck. I've been here for eight months."

"I love Chicago." I reached for my sunglasses and put them on. "Where did you live before California?"

"I'm originally from Connecticut—New Haven." Quinn stared at me with one of his probing looks again. I wasn't imagining his intensity. What was he trying to tell me? I hid behind my dark glasses.

We continued down the streets, my hand still in his. Our animated conversation dominated every move. Every life form bloomed and anything that moved, moved all around us. A new day marked a new beginning, and I was part of it. We became the children in the playground of life.

Minutes turned into hours. I felt increasingly tired—not tired of being with him—but drifting into another state of mind. He noticed my gradual fading and steered us back to the park. He walked me to my car.

"I can't believe we were gone that long. I'm not even tired." I leaned against the car.

"I don't know about that."

"Hey, you didn't tell me about your life in Connecticut."

"Another time," he murmured. "You need rest."

I was weary, but I wasn't ready for the day to come to a close.

"I have an idea," he said, smiling mischievously. "I think a real evening out is in order," he suggested.

"What did you have in mind?" I inched closer.

"Let's go into the city tonight—for music at the symphony," he said.

"I love classical music! How did you know?" My enthusiasm soared. I began to wonder if he was real.

"Just a feeling."

I felt elated. He already had tickets.

"I'll pick you up at your place," Quinn said.

Raegan would be at her parents' house tonight. I smiled mischievously. I stood by my car with the door partially opened. I wasn't sure if he was going to kiss me; I just hoped. As if on cue, he brushed away locks of my hair that fell on my face. His tender hand stopped at my burning face, now inches from his. His smooth lips curved upward. He framed my face in his careful hands. I closed my eyes . . . waiting.

Instead, he planted an enduring kiss on my forehead.

My shoulders slumped. I felt the sting of disappointment, but I quickly recovered. There would be more opportunities!

I raced home to get ready for my evening. By the time I set my alarm for a nap and put my head on the pillow, I fell into a deep sleep.

--→►◉ ◉◄•--

I shot upright to the sound of the buzzer. I made sure to take extra time to get ready like I had just spent it at an exclusive spa, slipping into my maroon-colored satin dress that I saved for special occasions, and applying just the right amount of make-up. My hair was up in a twist, so the sparkling blue jewelry that Mom gave me stood out. I stepped into my heels and felt extra tall. The doorbell rang. The person in front of me resembled a man who had just stepped out of *GQ*, dressed in a jacket and tie and hair styled in a *Gatsby* fashion.

"Lauren—*wow*—you look great." He beamed.

I glowed. "And you, as well."

He stood at the door for a moment. "Here, these are for you." He handed me a colorful array of wildflowers—forget-me-nots.

"Wildflowers. How did you know I like these?" I asked, pointing to the little blue, yellow, and violet flowers.

"You mentioned them in our conversation," he reminded me.

I put the flowers in a vase and closed the door behind me where they would be kept safe, just like the delicate flowers they were. Quinn opened the passenger door to the black Audi for me.

"I like your car."

"Thanks, it's not mine. I'm borrowing it. Mine is in the—shop," he said.

We spoke casually during the drive downtown. The evening sky had not reached the city; it was still early with the days growing longer as summer approached. The concert was at eight.

The immense foyer was filled with elegantly dressed people sipping wine and chatting within their small groups. New money mixed with old money. I felt insignificant next to these finely dressed admirers of the arts. I kept my chin up.

"You're outshining them," Quinn murmured.

Chandeliers and brilliant lighting lined the grand hallway, adding a touch of refined style to the lavish room. We waited patiently before taking our seats.

"You really do look wonderful tonight," he whispered into my ear. "This suits you." He motioned to the room around us.

"This is just me dressing up. I'm normally not this made up," I admitted. "I love the music—it's a part of me. I feel it when I play my cello. It gives me life."

"Then you won't be disappointed with the evening."

"No, not with you here."

He took my hand as we walked together into the great hall. We found our seats in the lower balcony, high enough to watch the whole orchestra but not too far so that we couldn't see the details in the instruments and the expressions on the musicians' faces. The lights dimmed. The conductor opened his arms with a commanding motion to dictate to the orchestra what his intentions would be. Tonight would be a tribute to Mozart, one of the greatest composers. I soaked in the rich sounds of each stringed instrument and studied how the cellists performed against the violins and the violas, as they played off one another. The stringed instruments resonated in harmony with the accompanying brass ensemble. With each passing page, the music grew louder and louder with more fervor until it reached a crashing frenzy, only to be brought down by the whim of the conductor's baton.

Early in the performance, Quinn took my hand into his warm and secure hold, and I noticed him stealing glances as I surrendered to the music. I looked his way, feeling pensive. At times, the orchestra mesmerized him. I didn't think he noticed me peering at him until he began to smirk, and the small creases formed around his pewter eyes. Again, I looked at Quinn to see his handsome and serene face, but this time I noticed something different. There was a man several rows above us staring in our direction. He had greasy, dark hair and angry eyes and what appeared to be defined lines embedded in his face. It seemed the stranger was trying to figure out who we were. He continued to glare at us, especially at me, before turning away to watch the orchestra with dead eyes. I felt goose bumps cover my skin.

We neared intermission. I wanted to take a closer look, and confront him if needed. The stranger would then realize he made a mistake, a case of mistaken identity.

When the lights came on, I nudged Quinn. "There's a man staring at us." I nodded in the direction of the stranger.

Quinn turned around. "What man?" He scanned the empty seats behind us.

The stranger was gone. I scanned the balcony, side doors, and lower floor. He was nowhere to be found in the mass of dark suits, and there were too many people moving around the great hall to notice a single person, albeit an odd one.

"Lauren, is everything all right?" Quinn asked. "You seem a little upset."

"I thought that man was watching us, but I didn't recognize him. He didn't look familiar." I shook my head.

"There's no one there, but if you said you saw someone, we'll stay alert." His face filled with tension. He brushed a side of my cheek. I flushed. "Let's wait outside," he suggested.

I followed his lead. I felt out of control, not my normal. He led us through the buzzing crowd, weaving between tight spaces and group photos. The air in the hallway cleared my daze, but kept my heavenly mood. A cheerful man offered to take a photo of us. I reached in my purse and handed him my camera. We posed with arms wrapped around each other, smiling into the flashing camera. It was natural and unforced. I couldn't ask for more. I would always remember this evening.

Quinn and I found a spot away from the dense crowd. "Feeling better?" he asked.

"Much."

We stayed put, still too mesmerized by tonight's performance to care about what the other concert members were doing. I looked up at the piercing stars visible through the glass ceiling. I wondered if there were angels sitting on the tips of each star looking down on us, smiling favorably at us. This felt right. We were right. I'd forgotten about the mysterious man.

"I'll be right back."

I walked to the ladies room on the far side of the hall. Surprisingly, it was empty. I took out my compact to powder my shiny face. The reflection staring back at me glowed with happiness. I reached for my lip gloss and applied it, when suddenly, I dropped the gloss into the sink. That stranger approached me in the ladies' room.

"What are you doing in here?" I demanded, taking a step back. He grabbed my arm. "Ouch!"

"Don't scream and don't say anything to Quinn, unless you want more trouble."

My heart was racing and I was shaking. How did he know Quinn? I suddenly froze.

"Now, listen carefully and no one will get hurt. Just a friendly reminder that Raefield is coming for you. You've known this all along. Do not resist, and do what's expected of you. Everybody wins."

Me? What was he talking about? Who was he talking about? "Let me go!" I tugged at his arm. The strange man finally released me. I couldn't believe this. I stared at him, studying the lines on his face. "You've got the wrong person. I don't know who Raefield is. And how do you know Quinn?"

The stranger narrowed his eyes. "Don't lie to me. You can't escape from this."

"I'm not! I don't know what you're talking about! I don't know who you are! You seriously have the wrong person!" I looked around the bathroom for some kind of weapon I could use. I saw nothing. I didn't even have perfume to spray in his smug face.

The stranger's eyes widened. He stared at me for a few seconds before giving me a pursed-lip smile. He took a step back, then left. My mouth hung partially opened. I was still shaking. I drew in a deep breath.

Everything will be all right. You're safe. Nobody got hurt. This was a horrible mistake.

Was it really a mistake? I couldn't make sense of what had just happened. I didn't know him and I certainly didn't know Raefield. My heart raced, and I tightened my lips. The air moved slower. I looked at my drained face.

Pull it together, Lauren.

Someone else came into the bathroom. I took a step back again. I looked up at a woman coming towards me. "Are you, Lauren?"

"Yes," I said, hesitating.

"There's a Quinn outside. He seems really concerned."

I took a deep breath out. "Oh . . . thank you." I walked past the woman. I opened the door to find Quinn standing on the other side.

"Are you okay? I wasn't sure if you left."

"I . . . wasn't feeling so well. But, I'm better now." I wanted to tell him everything that had happened, but I remembered what the man had said to me. I didn't want to put Quinn in danger.

"Do you want to leave?" Quinn asked.

"No, let's just enjoy the rest of the concert."

We walked back to our seats; the concert had resumed. I looked over my shoulder, and saw that the stranger's seat was empty. I shuddered, and then hardened my thoughts. Whoever he was, he had left. I wouldn't allow this man to ruin my perfect evening. This clearly was a huge mistake. It was the only explanation for what just happened. Yet, he knew Quinn's name. Was Quinn in trouble? Maybe he knew Raefield.

I looked over at him. He appeared calm.

The rest of the concert was a harmonious success, which included silent exchanges between us. The audience gave the maestro and the performers a standing ovation.

We walked out of the theater into the busy Chicago streets, the bright lights and speeding cars moving all around us. Everyone seemed pleased with the performance.

"Should we go for a walk? The night is so clear." He glanced up at the sky.

The fresh air felt good. My mind was clearing. I wanted to ask Quinn if he knew the stranger, but he hadn't seen the man. Perhaps the stranger forgot to take his meds. Or the full moon somehow made him crazy. Whatever the reason, I pushed the bathroom incident away.

Yet my thoughts kept returning to the stranger knowing our names.

We strolled hand in hand down the well-lit streets, turning onto a less obvious road. A dimpled moon beamed down on us, its luminous reflection guiding us on the darkened road. Stars twinkled above us in the night sky. Too magical to explain.

"Now you can tell me more about yourself," I urged.

"There's not much to tell. Like I said, I moved from Connecticut to California and ended up here. Besides, you might change your mind once you get to know me."

All I could see was a perfect person. "What about your family? Are they still out east?"

"They are, and my younger sister lives with them."

"You're still in contact?"

"No, I don't talk to them much. I haven't spoken to them in a while." Quinn looked down at the ground, then across the street. He walked more slowly. He still wouldn't look at me, but he reached for my hand. I remained silent. He must have sensed my curiosity because his pace picked up.

"My family is great—loving and caring. We're close, and they're very supportive. I tried to look out for them; they know I've done my best. They know I've tried to look after *everyone* I care about." He glanced at me.

I wanted to reach out to him. I wanted *him* to embrace *me* this time. "Look out for them—are they sick?"

"No, not ill . . . just worried." He appeared distant.

I didn't want to pry, but I needed to know. "What are they worried about?"

Quinn laughed. "You ask a lot of questions."

"Only when I'm interested," I said.

His manner changed again. He moved closer.

"My sister, Sophie, she's very devoted. She was really upset when I decided to leave, but she understood," he reflected.

"She sounds wonderful. You should visit them."

"I can't . . . not now. I don't think I will ever see them again," he said, wavering. "When I decided to leave, they knew I might never come back."

"I don't understand."

"It's hard to explain." He seemed to be thinking back to some distant memory. His expression turned thoughtful.

How can I be so stupid? I suddenly realized he must be regretful, that his decisions had been poorly made, and being here wasn't what he planned or expected. He was probably thinking about *her.* It made sense now. *I* was the one having all the elated feelings and the romantic notions. Not him. *How can I be so dense?* I wanted to run.

I closed off my weakness. "Then you must be sorry you left and sorry you're here. You probably *wish* you hadn't. You probably wish you were still back there," I said, childishly.

Quinn refocused. He looked puzzled. Then he was quiet, the moonlight concealing his enraged face. *"Sorry?* No, I'm *not* sorry that I came here. And I'm not *sorry* that I'm here with you," he snapped.

He grabbed me by the waist, pulling me away from the nearby streetlamp and holding me close. We were out of sight, shadows that could barely be seen by the naked eye. He leaned closer. First, it was a gentle kiss, his soft mouth on my waiting lips. Everything stopped moving; I was held. Urgency followed. The energy in my body rushed forward, pushing to the center of the commotion while trying desperately to save the life that was nearly cut off. My body screamed for air, pulling me closer to the source it believed gave me life. I never felt Quinn pull away. Not once.

I had completely surrendered.

I thought I heard the giant moon laughing down on us, revealing us out of the darkness. I became moonstruck. Even the stars had joined in on the production. A wicked laugh suddenly woke me from my eternal bliss.

"Wow," he finally gasped.

"Wow," I mimicked, catching my breath. "I guess you're not sorry."

We walked back to the car, a pearly full moon trailing after us. I looked up again. A cinereous stain began to cover the edges of the once unblemished jewel.

-⇥•◌ ◌•⇤-

I couldn't sleep after an exciting day and evening. I wished I could dream so that my dreams were filled with Quinn. They would be of us talking and laughing, everything bursting with life with no strangers waiting and no haunting figures lurking in the darkness.

Sleep still hadn't reached me when thirst took over. The house was pretty quiet without Oscar, but I could hear the hamster in its cage and the fish in its bowl. I meandered into the darkness to the lifeless kitchen. A reflection in the backyard from the far corner lot caught my attention. I grabbed my glass of water and stepped outside into the brisk evening air. The same right corner window was lit tonight, but I saw no outlines around the windowpane. I hadn't noticed any cars in the driveway when I'd arrived at home. I lingered in the moonlight, smiling as I moved aimlessly around the dewy yard, still in my reverie of this evening. The corner light suddenly dimmed. I sharpened my eyes to catch any image standing at the window. Everything remained still. Any other person would have been on alert, but I felt surprisingly calm.

CHAPTER 6

Family

I ARRIVED AT my parents' house in the early afternoon to help my mother prepare for the evening. I haven't seen Isaak since spring break. He was only here for a short time to settle the details at the firm. It was going to be nice having my big brother around again.

Quinn and I had plans tomorrow, a movie in the afternoon followed by dinner. More dates. I thought about him constantly. I wanted to spend more time with him. I needed to see him. Normally, I would gradually get to know a new guy, waiting a few weeks before I spent a significant amount of time with that person. With Quinn, it was different. The time we spent wasn't enough. I needed more. My usual collectiveness was being challenged, but I didn't care. We had to work out. It felt right.

I wasn't ready to tell my family. All the concerns and all the questions they would ask seemed too much until I knew them myself. I wanted Quinn to get to know my family, and I wanted them to get to know him. Even Raegan didn't know. I planned to tell her soon, maybe tomorrow. I needed her in my corner. I needed her thoughts and support. She'd met every guy that I had dated.

"Hey, kiddo, are you going to fold those clothes or just keep holding onto them?" Isaak asked, standing at the doorway.

I hadn't realized I was folding and flattening out the edges on the same shirt. "Isaak! I looked for you when I got home, but Mom said you went out," I cried. "I'm so glad you're home!" I ran over to him and gave him a big hug.

"Whoa . . . easy. I'm right here. Hey, I haven't been gone that long." He looked puzzled. "You're never this excited to see me."

"I know, it's just . . . I don't know, I'm suddenly feeling overwhelmed, like I haven't seen you in ages. I've missed you so much!"

"I've missed you, too," he said cautiously. "You're going to be seeing more of me unless Dad turns me into a workaholic," he joked.

"I won't let him. We're going to make excuses for you so that you can't work all the time." I hugged him again, more tightly this time.

Isaak almost lost his balance. He let go of me and put his hand on my forehead. "Is everything all right? Well, you're not burning up. Maybe we'd better get you something to drink."

We went downstairs. I already felt flushed. He poured me a glass of water, and I gulped that down in seconds. He poured another glass and I drank that as quickly, too.

"Hey, slow down. I wouldn't want you to drown." He looked baffled. "You're drinking water as if you haven't had any in days."

"Any what?" Dad asked, coming into the kitchen.

"Lauren's inhaling the water."

"Are you ill?" He reached over and touched my face.

I felt fine except for the extra emotions. I hugged my father for the longest time, afraid I might lose him.

"And doing *that*," Isaak pointed.

I didn't move. I still held onto my father. I finally let go when he pushed me away. "Sorry, Dad. I'm not sure what's gotten into me. Maybe I'm just tired."

"No worries." He patted my back. "Any father would love to have his daughter care so much." He and Isaak exchanged a perplexing look.

"C'mon. I'll let you beat me in Ping-Pong." He grabbed my hand and we headed for the lower level.

We remodeled the basement years ago, turning it into a second family room. We installed a flat screen television with an extensive video game system. Isaak had the largest collection of games I've ever seen next to some of the guys from my high school. Even Chelsea enjoyed an occasional video game. Dad had purchased a Ping-Pong table, because Isaak had begged him. He and my father played tennis as well. There was also a workroom, which allowed Isaak and Dad to build anything wooden.

We played several matches of Ping-Pong. Imagine, a little plastic ball being the most important object to a player. How could something small and insignificant have a central role to winning? After playing table tennis, he challenged me to a fierce round of video games. One in particular, where the people on earth defended themselves against alien invaders, reminded me of the conversation Quinn and I had had about *The War of the Worlds*.

"Lauren, can you help me with dinner?" Mom called from the top of the stairs. I left Isaak to defend the world and headed for the gourmet kitchen. Its tranquil and down-to-earth feeling was uplifting. Mom kissed me on the cheek and examined my face with scrutiny. "Dad said you weren't feeling well."

"It's nothing. Probably too much excitement this week—moving and all—but I'm fine," I assured her. I moved to the other side of the island kitchen and started cutting the fresh vegetables. She watched me through narrowed eyes before she returned to frosting a chocolate cake.

"Tomorrow shouldn't be busy. I thought we could do something in the afternoon," she suggested.

"Oh, I can't. I already have plans. Soon, okay?" I grinned, my eyes fixed on the island.

I continued to slice the colorful vegetables then poured a light Italian dressing over the mixture before steaming. The baked potatoes were already in the oven, and the tenderized and marinated steaks waited to be broiled. A car horn sounded. Chelsea and Finn had arrived. They sauntered through the front door, Chelsea leading the way and Finn close behind.

"Lauren, are you settled in your new place? I want to swing by and see it now that I've finished my exams. We could have lunch." She tossed her golden mane over her shoulders.

"That would be great." I looked over to see a poised Finn standing beside his trophy girlfriend. I imagined them having perfect children some day. "Hey, Finn, glad you made it."

"I wouldn't miss your mom's cooking," he complimented.

"How thoughtful of you," Mom answered. "Dinner will be ready in thirty minutes. Your father is in the study and Isaak is downstairs playing his silly games." She waved her hand in a dismissive fashion.

They headed for the library. I searched for the nicer dinnerware. I wasn't looking for the fine china, but this was Isaak's first family dinner since coming home. I decided to make it special. The potatoes baked to a golden brown in the oven. I mixed a mushroom wine sauce to sauté over the steaks. Mom found a vintage red wine she liked for special family occasions.

"Let's eat," Isaak said, inhaling the aromas coming from the kitchen.

We gathered around the rectangular oak table, Mom and Dad seated at opposite ends. I sat next to Isaak and Mom. Dad and Isaak were in a heated conversation about a merger of some company.

"—But the law states if you merge with a company, and that current company offers a certain benefit package, than the newly merged entities should have equal representation," Isaak stated.

"Not necessarily true. If the original contract of the existing company outlined the compensation for only those employees, and until the second company is fully merged with the primary corporation and a new, binding agreement is made, then and only then will both groups share the same profit," Dad corrected.

"Unless there was a clause stating any new employees would be subject to receive the profits gained within that time frame if they were hired during—"

"Gentlemen, please save your discussion for another time." Mom smiled a lovely smile of appreciation.

Isaak and Chelsea have the same smile as Mom—friendly, polite, lips curving at a similar angle, and full. My smile looked similar, a well-crafted imitation of the same expression after years of watching her smile.

Chelsea and Finn conducted their own quiet conversation, eyes locked on each other and hardly moving an inch to break up the silence. It was sickening. I went back to cutting my tender steak into bite-sized pieces, but I suddenly lost control. I dropped my fork and knife. They thudded on the table before falling to the ground. Mom looked shocked. A quiet eruption suddenly surfaced in my head. I didn't know where it came from. I felt dizzy and shaky. My eyes seemed to have tripled in size.

Whoa, something's wrong.

A general ache reverberated throughout my head, the pressure building up internally. Next, a terrible sensation of localized pain, a gouging and splitting feeling at the front and the uppermost portion of my poor head. It was the most intense sensation that I've ever felt. I didn't know if a break along the fissure lines of my skull had occurred—if that was possible—but the pain intensified even more. Reflecting from the butter knife left on the table appeared an imbedded blue-green vein, not normally seen under the skin, which rose from my right temple in an erratic contortion.

I couldn't take it any longer.

"*Ahhh!*"

Mom looked horrified. She ran to my side to see if I'd choked on my food. My airway remained open. All conversation ceased, all eyes locked on me.

I couldn't speak; I just stared wildly with my mouth partially open. They spoke. Their mouths moved to form words, but no sound came from their lips. I saw fear and anxiety on their faces—the *horror*. My family, standing in front of me, moved in slow motion as I watched them fuss over me. The visual information processed in my head, yet another part of me transported to what I believed was inside my head, if that was possible. A bright green, intensifying object surfaced from nowhere, blinding me within.

When the excruciating pain reached maximum intensity, my head shook inside. Without warning, a split came from the solid green object. It emitted bright green and white laser lights. Extensive cracks occurred along the jewel. I screamed in pain. I couldn't tell if any sound came out of me, because everything became muffled. I saw double, and those images threw me off balance. I reached to steady myself, trying to grab at anything in sight. Two Finns stood before me—one with red hair, the other with blonde. Combined, he formed one person, a strawberry blond. This *thing* clearly played with my mind. My mother moved from triple form to single form. I couldn't stop the repetitive shifting. Their alarmed faces overlapped each other like macramé. I wanted to reassure them, but I couldn't find my voice.

"She looks like some swamp creature, and her eyes are glowing green. Hey, Chelsea, remember that movie we saw?" Finn asked. I watched my sister smack his arm in slow motion. My parents glared at him.

"*Lauren . . . Lauren*, say something!" Mom yelled.

I could hear again. My breathing slowly came back in rapid pants. I felt my heart and lungs communicate with each other, dictating to my body what was normal and what was overworked. My mind told me I was still alive. The cracks began to seal and the breaks vanished into a solid, crystalline form. The light began to dim inside my head and the pressure subsided. I was no longer inside my mind. The blank stare broke, and I returned to reality.

"I think I'm going to vomit!" I said.

I rushed to the nearest bathroom. The relief came instantaneously. The poison, and its accompanying treachery, departed my system.

As I became myself again, everything around me appeared the same. I looked at my washed up self in the mirror. The contorted vein sank deeper inside my head with only its shadow remaining. I took in a few deep breaths, then splashed cool water on my face. It felt refreshing. I emerged from the bathroom to an apprehensive family.

"Lauren, you look *terrible*," Finn scoffed again.

Chelsea hit him harder this time.

"Ouch!"

Mom rushed to my side again, this time holding my face firmly between her hands and checking for injuries. "Are you hurt?" She inspected my head and neck for signs of trauma. "You gave us quite a scare. What happened?"

"I . . . I don't know what happened." I felt dazed, my pride dented. "I'm fine—really, aside from feeling extremely drained. I'm okay. Did I have a seizure?"

"I'm not sure, sweetheart. It looked that way." Dad came to my other side. His fearful expression disappeared.

"Do you remember what happened? We were trying to say something to you, but you didn't respond. I thought you went into shock. Lauren, we were so scared." Mom put a hand over her mouth. She shook her head.

"You really had us worried," Dad said.

"I didn't mean to scare anyone. Everything's fine. See?" I moved around the room, displaying no injuries with my balance intact.

"Well, Lauren, that was quite a performance. You really can put on a show," Isaak remarked.

Finn laughed, and Chelsea rolled her eyes.

"I think I'll go lie down. Guess I'm not one hundred percent. I don't think I can eat anymore." I didn't want to talk. I couldn't tell them what I'd seen.

"Lauren, do you think it's a good idea?" Chelsea asked. She glared at Finn, putting her index finger to the center of her lips.

"I think I'll feel better once I get some rest." I looked at my parents. They didn't pressure me into staying. Their calmness after my ordeal puzzled me.

"Lauren, I'm curious," Dad said. "Did you see something?"

"What do you mean?"

"During your seizure, do you remember any of it?"

"Just some lights."

"I'm going to let Dr. Sendal know what happened. Maybe you should pay him a visit," Mom said.

"No, I don't need to see him. Really, everything's fine. If this happens again, then I'll go see him." My parents didn't look totally convinced, but they didn't push back, either. "You can check in on me as many times as you like."

I went to my room, and slept until eight the next morning.

⟶⟿ ⟻⟵

When I awoke, my mother was in the kitchen drinking her morning coffee. She was dressed in a camel-colored suit with a designer scarf wrapped around her neck. "How are you feeling?"

"Great, like I've slept for two days." I was famished. I began making breakfast—ham, eggs, toast, fruit, and juice.

"Do you want me to stay home?"

"No. I feel fine, like nothing ever happened. If anything, I feel more energized. I have plans, anyways."

"Okay, we did check on you a few times last night, and you looked quite peaceful." She seemed convinced.

I wasn't sure what was happening to me. All of these changes and visions meant something. Was I losing my mind? No, there must be a reason. What reason? One day, soon, I would talk to my parents about my experience last night regarding the signs and visions. The truth would surface somehow and the truth was the only thing I could hold on to.

Maybe I should visit Dr. Sendal.

⤐ ⊜⤙

I got back to my place before one in the afternoon, knowing Raegan was home today. Her BMW was the only car parked in the driveway. I hadn't seen the neighbor's car in a few days, but I thought he or she could have been here yesterday while I was gone.

"Hey, I'm back," I said, coming through the front door with my cello and bag. Oscar came running. "I've missed you, little fella."

"I'm in the kitchen," she called out. I set the instrument down and walked over to Raegan. She was making lunch. "I'll fix you a sandwich, because I know you'll want one eventually."

I smiled at her. "How was it at your parents?"

"Fine, the usual," she said. "How was yours?"

"Uneventful." I thought about the seizure-like episode at dinner, the flashing lights. I needed to figure this out on my own before telling her.

"What's new, then?"

I hesitated. I didn't know where to begin. "Remember when I saw that guy at the clothing store?" I started. "Well, I ran into him a few times, and we've been talking, more like we've been spending time together."

She stopped making the sandwiches. "I. Can't. Believe. You. I can't believe you've kept this to yourself and you *didn't* tell me. I tell *you* everything."

"I know. I'm sorry. I just didn't know if it would go anywhere." I sat down at the kitchen table. "I ran into him twice since the store incident. Once at this coffee shop I found, and the next time on my first day of work."

"At work—really? How exciting."

"He's so nice . . . and caring, and . . . Oh Raegan, I'm really falling for him. I think about him all the time," I said, beaming. "But there's this part of him that's so mysterious and sad."

Raegan's eyes went wide. She nodded her head a few times, mumbling in between bites of her chicken salad sandwich, "I totally know what you mean."

I told her everything he'd told me about himself. I told her about the concert, the kiss—I even told her about the strange man.

"Seriously, I'm not imagining anything. It was so bizarre. But Quinn was really concerned."

"How freaky." She looked sympathetic. She paused for a moment, and then started to giggle. "So, was he a *really* good kisser?"

"Excellent." I flushed again. We laughed, and Oscar couldn't stop barking.

"When do I get to meet him?" she asked.

"Today. As a matter-of-fact, he's coming over and we're going to the movies—a comedy. Do you want to come?"

"He's coming here? Today? No, I can't go with you." She laughed nervously. "How do I look?"

"You look fine. I'm worried about me." I touched my hair, making sure it wasn't out of place. "He'll be here soon. I'd better get ready." I finished the sandwich, gulped down some water, and dashed upstairs to freshen up.

Quinn arrived at two. On time. Again. I heard Raegan answer the door. "Hi. Is Lauren here?"

"She is. Come in. You must be Quinn."

"And you must be Raegan. She talks about you a lot."

"And she's mentioned you," she said. "Oh, Lauren. Quinn is here."

"Do you want to come with us?"

"Oh, no. I have things to do," she answered. "Another time."

"Hi." I came down the stairs. I always thought that was sweet when the girl came down the stairs to the waiting boy.

"Shall we go?" he murmured.

Raegan mouthed the words "he's so hot" as we left.

"I thought we could walk since it's not that far."

We started down the sidewalk in silence. I could go anywhere with him. Even in silence, nothing felt awkward. He reached for my hand as we walked through the neighborhood to another stunning day. He felt familiar.

"When I was living in Connecticut, we used to walk down similar streets like this one except for all the cars and the street signs." He reached up to grab a maple leaf from a dangling tree branch.

"Your street didn't have a lot of cars?"

"Not at all." He became very quiet.

He must have lived in a rural area that didn't have many cars. Maybe he was embarrassed.

"I'm not concerned that you didn't live anywhere fancy. You shouldn't be ashamed that you didn't have a lot of resources."

"Actually, we were more fortunate than most people. My family owned a hotel and a restaurant, The Maxwell Inn, hence the last name. We practically lived there."

"Maxwell," I repeated, clinging to the name tightly around my lips. "Tell me more," I urged.

"My parents, sister, and I worked at the family inn. My father had a dedicated staff, and business was booming. We frequently had people from the East Coast stay at the hotel, and sometimes from the outlying states. Europeans who traveled to America or other foreigners who sojourned here stayed with us. We even had dignitaries and movie stars visit. New Haven was close to the sea, and the port was a bustling establishment for the fishery industry.

"The lobby had a large crystal chandelier with an impressive lounge for the travelers who needed to relax after their long and arduous journey. It was a vast room—bright and airy and tastefully designed by an English designer with the assistance of my mother, who had an eye for detail. The bellhops waited attentively on the side to escort the guests to their rooms. The French doors opened up to the spacious property, connecting the bay to the hotel."

It sounded like a magical place. "I've been to New Haven many times. My family often takes trips to Connecticut—Bridgeport and some coastal towns along the way—and of course New Haven. But I don't remember seeing a Maxwell Inn or a restaurant with that name." I scanned the recesses of my brain to all the quaint and charming attractions along the coast. Nothing came up.

He hesitated. "It's not there anymore. The name Maxwell is associated with other trades under the title Maxwell Incorporated. It's a conglomerate now that's made up of a few community banks, some restaurants, and one or two shopping centers. My family worked there until my father passed away, and my mother sold the shares to my father's brother and a few business partners to keep the hotel running." His face turned serious. "Apparently, my uncle, his children, and a few associates feuded over money and the hotel was lost. The bank that tried to salvage the hotel was in my mother's family, and because she was the sole heir, she changed the parent company to Maxwell. The incorporated came later and the rest is history."

I felt the loss he must have felt. It sounded like he hadn't spoken to them in a very long time, longer than he'd portrayed in earlier conversations, yet here he was, still a young man. These events must have happened when he was quite young.

"I wasn't there to continue the family hotel, and it appeared from what I've read that my sister and her family, who controlled half the hotel, tried to carry on the family business until it was ruined by my uncle. They managed to find other sources of income and lived a comfortable life. She—" He abruptly stopped himself. We had stopped walking, too. Quinn became silent, looking down at the cement ground.

His sister? She was younger than he was; yet he spoke as if the timeline was condensed and had a large chunk missing. Him! "You lost me somewhere. It sounded like it's been more than just a few years since you've seen them." I shook my head. "Oh, never mind. It's not important." My empathy returned. That's why he couldn't see them anymore and make amends. They were gone. He was an orphan, just like me!

"Well, your home is here now," I said.

He cleared his throat. "Speaking of home." We moved closer to a looming tree; he turned to face me this time. "I've been meaning to tell you this, but I didn't want you to be alarmed. I wasn't sure if I should have mentioned something sooner."

I waited for his response.

"I already knew where you lived before the night at the symphony." Did he see me go into my place? Did he live nearby?

"Because I live next door."

Instead of being surprised and alarmed, I was overjoyed. Quinn had been there all along. *He* was the mysterious person next door. Maybe it was my adrenaline that spilled over, and maybe it was that nagging feeling I've had that was just confirmed. I grabbed him, and we slipped behind the oak tree. We began kissing, more than a friendly kiss. We searched for the comfortable places we'd found the last time, but we weren't lost. Our heated mouths connected and explored. He ran his feverish kisses along my aching neck and back to my waiting lips. Normally, this type of display would have bothered me, but I didn't care if anyone saw us. The movie would wait.

CHAPTER 7

Strange And Strangers

I COULDN'T WAIT to tell Raegan. She would have never guessed who lived next door. The lights in her room were off; I would wait until tomorrow. Quinn went back to his place—next to mine. I wondered if he was still awake. Maybe he was lying on his pillow thinking. Were his thoughts about me? I wondered if he thought about us. I'm certain he wasn't thinking about me. He probably took everything in stride and let a natural course take over, not rushing anything and not expecting too much.

Gosh, I was tired.

I decided to do the same when sleep weighed heavily over me.

The next morning I woke up to the sound of doors slamming and heavy objects moving around, coming from the other side. I quickly freshened up and went downstairs, only to find Raegan lurking around the bay window between the curtains.

"What's going on?"

"There's someone moving in next door, and he's very good-looking," she reported.

I casually glanced out the window, noticing a dark-haired person and what appeared to be his parents carrying boxes. He removed items from a black Audi, a car that looked like the one Quinn used when we went to the concert.

"He is nice looking." *Although not like my Quinn,* I thought.

"I'll have to make myself neighborly soon," she remarked.

I straightened the magazines on the coffee table and picked up Oscar's toys from the floor. Raegan didn't notice. "I have some interesting news," I began. She still didn't turn around. "It turns out that Quinn is the mysterious person who moved in next door, the one with the Volkswagen."

"*What?*" Raegan completely turned around. "No way! How did you find out?"

"He finally told me."

"Can this be a coincidence or what? This is fate. It has to be. How else can you explain this?" she said with excitement.

"I don't know. I still can't believe he's living next door—this close. Honestly, Raegan, when he told me, I almost died." I thought about the oak tree. "I think about him *all* the time, and the more time I spend with him, the more I'm falling for him. Maybe it is fate." We both made a dreamy expression.

"Well, some of us have to get to work." She grabbed her keys and purse. "See what you can find out." She winked at me as she walked out the door.

I chuckled. I raced to my cello for my needed practice. I had to meet with Prof. Sobel for my Monday lesson and wanted to be extra prepared. After two hours of practice, my hunger reached a critical level. I couldn't think anymore. I walked to the empty kitchen and put together a deluxe brunch in record time. Quinn still hadn't stopped over. After my morning routine, I headed for the neighbors. Large boxes and furniture pieces were scattered on the front porch. The adjacent front door was wide open.

"Hi, neighbor," I mumbled.

"Oh, hi," a voice responded. "Were we too loud?"

"Oh, no. Just taking a break." I scanned the clutter. "I see you have a lot of work ahead of you."

"I should be able to get this mess out of the way by later today." He looked at all his stuff. "I'm Garrett, Garrett La Rouche. I just moved in."

"I noticed. I'm Lauren. I thought I'd stop by to say hi and to see if you needed any help. Raegan and I live next door," I said, pointing to the other entrance.

"That's right. You're *the* Lauren. Quinn did mention."

I blushed. This was good. Quinn mentioned me. I decided not to ask about him. Let Garrett do the talking. "Are you a student here? Raegan and I go to Northwestern."

"Yeah, I'll be a sophomore, unlike Quinn who'll be a senior. He's not carrying as many credits this quarter as me. He'll be working at the bank. You know, that's where he's at right now," he informed me.

"Oh." I felt my body cave in. Of course, he worked. Most people did. I wondered if it was a bank that belonged to his family.

"He likes to stay busy. He always has plans he's working on."

"Like what?"

"Work . . . establishing himself with the company . . . looking out for the people in his life."

I was floating on air.

"Did he mention how we met?" Garrett asked.

"A little bit."

"We met in Santa Cruz. It was August, still very warm. I was on vacation with my parents, doing a little surfing. For some odd reason, they wanted to go there, a trip before school started. Anyways, we were at the beach one day and I see Quinn. He looked pretty down, kind of worn out. He just seemed lost. We started talking, and we realized we had a few things in common. He mentioned he was looking for someone . . . and let's just say I helped him come this way." Garrett looked justified. "He stayed in Santa Cruz long enough to take care of a few things, then moved to Chicago in September. He's been staying at my parents' place until now. I guess it turned out to be a good deal." He gave me a big smile. "He's a good person, someone you'd want on your side."

I'd have Garret to thank some day. "I've got to get to practice. I'll let you get back to unpacking." I returned that smile and waved goodbye.

I went back to my place. My phone buzzed with three messages: One from Linda telling me she'd pick me up on Tuesday if I needed a ride to the soup kitchen, one from Noelle asking for a ride to the fashion show on Saturday, and one from Sherry who was giving us the tickets for the runway show this Saturday. I had no messages from Quinn. I left for my lesson.

Sherry Gibson, a towering six-foot tall model, went to my high school. She'd put college on hold when the Ford Modeling Agency signed her as one of their models. She knew the ins and outs of the modeling world—Paris, Milan, London—she'd been to all those places. She had first-hand information on when the designers would showcase in Chicago. Sherry was also the one who suggested the clothing store where I first met Quinn.

The summer heat felt uncomfortable as I reached Prof. Sobel's informal studio located near campus on a quiet cul-de-sac. "Professor Sobel, it's me, Lauren."

The older, stout man entered the lesson room where I patiently sat. "Well, Lauren, it's good to see you. Have you been practicing?" he asked in a bubbly manner.

"I have. I'll go over the music I've been working on." I began doing some warm up exercises before I started on the composition. The bow on my right hand moved quickly along with the movement of chords from my left hand through the beginning of the piece. I didn't slow down when I approached the refrain. My energy still soared.

"*No, no, no!* That's not right," he lectured. "You're playing so stiff, like a robot. No smoothness or definition in your style." He shook his head several times. "This isn't a race. *Flow* with the music, move your fingers like this and the bow in a more relaxed way, not this choppiness, this rapid progression into nowhere that you're doing." He grabbed my instrument, demonstrating the correct way to play the song.

I didn't know what was wrong. I thought I had been playing well, but obviously other matters consumed my mind.

"I don't want to take the metronome out. I know you can read the music well," he announced. "*Feel* how the notes would sound, how they would make sense. *Hear* the chords." He moved his hands and swayed his body in a rhythmic fashion. "And *please*, slow down."

I thought back to the symphony and how it flowed in a harmonious way. I suddenly felt lost in a trance with my eyes closed. I began to engage my instrument with as much enthusiasm as I could muster. The piece began to make sense; it played on its own. The music took over. Each note spoke to the next note in some orderly fashion.

"Yes, yes! That's right. *Feel* the music. Play like you mean it," he asserted enthusiastically.

The rest of the lesson went much smoother. I thanked the professor for his invaluable instruction and left the cozy studio. I headed for the grocery store to pick up some basic items and grab the ingredients needed to make the chicken burritos that Raegan liked. The store was crowded as usual with too many carts lying in the narrow aisles. I found the olives and salsa. As I was leaving the condiment aisle, a middle-aged man dropped what appeared to be a grocery list.

"Sir . . . sir, you dropped this," I said, following after the man. I gave him his list.

"Oh, I must not have been paying attention. Thank you. That's very kind of you," he replied.

"No problem." I started to turn away, but the stranger grabbed my arm, pulling me back. At first I thought he wanted to thank me again. He looked at me sharply. I saw the urgency in his face.

"Lauren, be careful. Some of *those* people are around . . . and they come to do harm," he warned. "You must not let them get to you."

"*What?* Hey, how do you know my name? What people?" I insisted, pulling my arm away. He didn't reply, only gave me a sympathetic look.

"You can't trust everyone. Sometimes it's hard to tell who's looking out for you and who's not."

This man scared me. I felt confused. I looked around the store to see if anyone had followed us, but I only noticed busy shoppers.

"Just be careful," he whispered. "Some of them are here. And they'll try to find you anyway they can." He squeezed my limp hand. "I'll pray for your safety." He quickly sped away.

"Wha . . . what people? Hey, wait a minute! Who are you?" He kept walking. "Come back here!" I called out. Other shoppers looked at me. I stood there dumbfounded. I had never seen this man in my life, and I couldn't figure out how he knew my name. *Why would anyone be looking for me?* "Strange," I muttered under my breath, shaking my head. I purchased my items and left.

My mind cleared during the ride home. *It's just a fluke.* Yet, as I thought about it further, the crazy man at the concert crossed my mind. *Could there be a connection? Maybe they knew each other, and it was somehow related to Quinn, and not me.* I replayed what the stranger in the grocery store had said about not knowing who's really looking out for you. I dismissed that thought. This was all coincidental. Besides, Chicago did have its share of colorful people. My focus turned to the possible circumstances waiting at home. When I got home, I didn't see any cars in the driveway.

I checked my phone again. No messages. I went to the kitchen to make dinner. No cars pulled into the driveway, and no sound came from next door. I sighed.

When Raegan came home, we decided to eat in front of the television. I turned the channel to this reality show about two college students stuck at their parents' house and following their parents' rules. She looked over at me a few times, but didn't say anything. Why was I so worried? We'd spoken yesterday. Quinn consuming my every thought needed to stop. I only made it through half the show when I got up from the sofa.

"I think I'll take Oscar outside," I finally said.

"Okay, I'll throw the dishes in the dishwasher and clean up while you do that."

I led the dog to the spacious backyard. I teased Oscar with a toy so that he would start barking. Nothing stirred inside Quinn's house. I saw a dim light in one window, knowing it was Garrett's, but I didn't see any lights on from the room that belonged to Quinn. Disappointed, I returned inside with the satisfied dog following behind.

"I think I'll go to bed early tonight. I have to work tomorrow." I sauntered unremarkably to my room.

I lay awake in my bed, unable to find a comfortable position. I felt myself tossing and turning throughout the night until a dull sleep slowly crept in.

-->|=◎ ◎=|<--

The next morning, I awoke feeling groggy and achy. My dark hair was all matted. The person in the mirror looked like a wretched witch without the wicked. I didn't feel like a fairy princess waking up to a magical day after meeting her prince, a fantasy falsely placed into every girl's head. I ignored that person and got ready for the day, a strong, black coffee in hand.

Ethan waved to me from the main desk. He carried a soda in one hand and fumbled through a small stack of magazines with his other hand. The return pile overflowed onto the floor. I picked up the ones off of the floor and threw it into another bin. I headed for the media room; it was a good distraction. I couldn't sit around thinking. Subconsciously, I checked the table where Quinn sat, only to find a student sleeping with drool hanging from his mouth. I noticed a cozy couple tucked away in a secluded aisle, laughing and kissing. *Ugh.* I turned away from the scene, working swiftly and mechanically, not letting myself surrender to the tiny pangs that ate away at my insides.

"If you work any faster, there wouldn't be anything left for the other students to do," the magical voice said.

I turned to face a smiling Quinn, my excitement barely contained. "Oh, hi. I didn't realize you were standing here."

He wrinkled his face. "You weren't home so I thought I'd stop by to see if you were here. I've been really busy with work."

The biting sensation stopped; I was healed. We walked through the wide rows while I continued to put away the rest of the library books. Then we headed for a corner table.

"You should stop by my place after you're done with work," he suggested, stroking my hands.

"I have this volunteer thing at one of the soup kitchens, but I'll come over afterwards," I said.

He only stayed briefly today, observing me on occasion while I continued my effortless job. The aching glances were still apparent even though I tried to stay poised and indifferent. Unfortunately today, he actually read some paperwork he'd brought. When he needed to leave, I watched him walk down the long, angled corridor. Pieces of me trailed behind.

"Ethan, do you mind if I leave early? I don't have much to do, and there's enough people looking pretty bored."

"Fine with me," he said, not looking up from his magazine.

The cumulus clouds had multiplied since my arrival at work. I would have found some beauty in the painted horizon if it weren't for the grim undertones. I ignored the dismal sky and drove to meet Linda. The lines at Winton Hall had already formed across the room to the entryway. The former hall was a small convention center, but had deteriorated from the lack of use and the decline in the neighborhood. When the shops began to close and the transient population moved in, the once attractive neighborhood at the edge of the city assumed an older image. The former charm disappeared.

I found Linda standing at the designated table with four other volunteers serving the hungry masses. "Lauren, over here," she called out.

I poured hot soup into bowls. The cooks laid out the ready-made food—some from local donations—onto the long tables for us to hand out to the hungry people. Three busy serving tables separated the great hall into an organized system.

"I hope we have enough food. I saw some of the cooks carrying in more supplies from the delivery trucks. The refrigerators were stocked this morning before the shelter opened," she informed me. "I heard that some of the local restaurants were delivering extra meals."

"It looks like they have this really organized." I continued to place the turkey and the stuffing on the plates, alternating with the chicken and rice. "Linda, about this evening, I need to get home after we finish. Okay?"

"Oh, sure, no problem. Some of the others were talking about going out, so I might join them." Linda frowned.

We worked diligently for the next hour. More people came through the double doors, and the workers quickly wiped up the vacated tables from the previous customers.

"My dear," a silver-haired woman said to me, reaching for my hand. She led me aside. "You do such good work helping us out." I smiled. She looked so frail and hungry. The woman kept staring at me with her wild, glaucoma like eyes. She then touched my startled face with her long, boney hand. "Lauren, you're so young. I don't know if you can handle this." I stiffened. She caressed my surprised face again, her fine fingertips tracing my stiff jaw line. "So much pressure placed on such a young and innocent girl. Oh, what they want, they will try to get . . . at no cost," she rasped.

"I—I don't know what you're talking about." I shuddered at her touch, removing her cool hand from my frozen face. "Who *are* you?" I demanded.

"Just a messenger. A feeble old woman in this random bowl of marbles."

I think you're losing yours! I took a step away from her.

"Don't be afraid. I'm not going to hurt you."

I hesitated. I wasn't afraid of this woman. I wanted her to leave me alone. "How do you know me?" I insisted.

"I know a lot about you," she replied.

I just stared at the old woman. I didn't know what else to say. Linda was watching us the whole time.

"Your mother was so proud of you. She loved you so very much. She wanted to protect you—yes, she did. She did everything she could to protect you from them," she narrated.

"*My mother? How* do you know my mother?" I hissed.

"She was so lovely, just like you. And look how you turned out, all tall and beautiful, helping poor people like us," she carried on. "She's here with you . . . right here." The elder woman pointed to my palpitating heart.

"*What* about my mother?" I demanded in a low voice. "*Tell* me." Tears blurred my vision.

"Keep her there, close by."

"Please, tell me about my mother," I begged.

The ancient woman turned and walked in an unhurried manner down the aisle between the dining tables; leaving me with the fundamental questions I knew I would someday ask. I stood motionless, allowing the leftover fluid to run down my weary face. I didn't have the energy to go after the woman. I felt defeated.

Linda looked confused. "What was *that* all about?" She motioned to some of the other volunteers to take our place.

"I really don't know. I've never seen her in my entire life."

"Here, let's take a break. The lines are slowing down." She led me to the open seats where the other volunteers sat. "I'll get us some food."

She took off for the serving table, leaving me to dwell on what had just happened. The pangs of hurt and frustration ate away at me. *Nip, nip.* I wasn't sure if I could ignore her words. Who was that woman? How did she know my mother and me? A coincidence? Twice in one day, and now my mother—my *birth* mother—was involved.

The safety net had been cut.

No! I won't let this happen.

I turned off my emotions. I gathered myself together, firmly holding back the sadness and confusion I felt.

Linda returned, carrying the hot meal with the help of one of the other volunteers. "Feeling better?" she asked.

"I'll be all right." I gave her a brief smile. "Let's not talk about it."

I turned around to search for the woman, but I saw no trace of her in the crowded room. I ate in silence while Linda talked cheerfully to the other students. She looked at me from time to time, less worried than before. I needed to see Quinn and tell him what had happened tonight. Then, I thought about the man at the symphony and the stranger at the grocery store. After encountering this woman, I couldn't deny the connections between these three people any longer. They knew me, and possibly, they knew each other. Why couldn't I remember them?

We left Winton Hall in the evening hours. The sky was dark with a harried-looking undertone still prevailing as the crescent moon guided me into the night. It was the shining staff I sought. I drove swiftly down the winding roads and through the quiet, well lit neighborhoods until I reached the familiar street. My haven. Both front porch lights and the street lamps were on. I felt safe. Raegan was talking on the phone to Alex. I motioned to her that I was going next door. Quinn might be able to make sense of today. I stood there until he answered my knock, his gentle eyes inviting. I stepped inside as he held open the door.

"How was the soup kitchen?" he asked.

"Fine . . . the usual . . . just busy," I replied.

The apartment looked different with all the furniture in place. It had a masculine touch and simple designs with no frilly décor. We slumped onto the comfortable sofa, and he turned on the TV to a quiet speaking level. My willpower caved in. I couldn't hold back the tears any longer. They began to stream down my pale face.

"What's wrong?" he gently asked, wiping the tears away.

I buried myself into his broad shoulders while he held me in his protective arms, and I allowed myself to pour all my frustration over his clean, white shirt. He listened attentively as I told him about the grocery store incident and the older woman at the soup kitchen.

"—And I was so shocked, I couldn't say anything," I cried in between gulps.

"You didn't know any of those people?" he questioned. "Yet they knew you. From what you've said, it sounded like they were warning you," he repeated.

"I've never seen or spoken to them in my life. And I rarely mention my birth parents, especially to strangers." My sobs were quiet now. "And they knew my name."

"Has this ever happened before?" he asked, his tone more urgent.

"No . . . never. Just today."

"Are you *sure?* Think back."

"I . . . yes, I'm sure. Only the people that are close to me—you being the most recent—know that I'm adopted *and* the circumstances around it."

He remained quiet. He tenderly held me in his arms, in the same way one holds someone who was lost and only recently found. It felt firm and distant at the same time. A part of me sensed he'd kept something important from me. What wasn't he telling me? What couldn't he tell me?

He planted several tender kisses to the side of my face, stroking my unruly hair. I continued to calm down, lying comfortably on the sofa with him wrapped around me—a security blanket. I felt more relaxed. I fell into a restful place. Then I shook abruptly when the haziness of sleep encroached my mind again. He remained still.

"Do you want to stay here or go back to your place?" he murmured.

"Stay here with you."

I followed him to his room, nearly asleep from the exhausting and emotional evening. He quietly put me in bed without stirring my now peaceful condition. As I drifted, I felt completely at ease with Quinn at my side, keeping my fears away. I jerked several times, waking to find him holding me more tightly and kissing the back of my head until I fell back to sleep. Quinn stayed with me, never left my side.

->==() ()==<-

I spent nearly every waking hour that week with Quinn, whether he stayed at my place or I stayed at his. The encounter with the two strangers disappeared from my mind. I became wrapped up in my life with him. Everything went smoothly. I wanted to tell my parents about him, but decided to wait until Sunday.

Today was the fashion show on Michigan Avenue, the pinnacle event of the fashion world brought to downtown Chicago—a sneak peak of the upcoming styles this fall. Sherry was one of the models chosen to represent the designer's clothing line. Raegan, Noelle, and I wanted to cheer her on. Raegan sped through the busy and congested streets of Chicago, trying to avoid the hostile drivers and the lost motorists. Surprisingly, we found a parking spot within walking distance of the show. Girls with high heels should not have to walk far. I dressed in a fashionable spring dress, with a thin belt to accentuate my waist, and carried a designer purse. This was my first runway show, and although I didn't plan to purchase any clothes, it was enough to see all the beautiful people on the catwalk. The designer made his appearance in New York and Miami, stopping in Chicago for the weekend before heading to Los Angeles.

Sherry put our names on the guest list. We sat next to the reporters and the photographers. Everyone was buzzing. I decided to find Sherry before the show opened. She was having her make-up done. The make-up artist and hairstylist simultaneously worked on her, giving her a very dramatic look. Her tiger-eyes were emphasized with rich, deep hues and her powder puff lips were glossed in a neutral color. Some light rouge was applied to her flawless, cocoa skin before the hairstylist covered her face to spray the finishing layer on her hair.

"Lauren, over here," Sherry called out.

"You look great. I can't even recognize you," I said. "We're all here, and I wanted to wish you good luck."

"Thank you. I'm a little nervous because this dress is so short and my heels are extremely high. Nothing I can't handle," she laughed. "Isn't this exciting? There are so many people from the press here today."

"It's pretty crowded out there. The media is out in front, but I've seen a few reporters walking through the place. They kept the lights pretty low," I reported. "I think it'll be a success."

"Of course it will! The designer is *such* a genius. Look at me." She made a striking pose in front of the mirror for us to see. Her entourage applauded. I looked around the room, only seeing perfectly thin girls, probably sixteen to twenty-five years of age. They must only eat carrots.

"Margaret, don't you think she could be in pictures?" Sherry pulled me next to her, in front of the blazing mirror.

"She does have some natural beauty. Hmmm . . . I see some red spots," the make-up artist said to me in her Russian accent. She flashed a bright white, rotating lamp in my face, examining my skin closely. "It's not bad. It could be better."

I pulled away. "I'll meet you later."

The lights dimmed further, and all the photographers were positioned in the media section, ready with their flashing cameras when the first girl strutted out onto the runway. The techno dance music echoed in the background. Praise and applause came from the anticipating crowd. The fashion show previewed the designer's fall and winter collection: bright whites, neutral hues, and deep reds were splattered all over the Amazon models.

Raegan and I became engrossed in the show, our eyes catching every detail of each outfit splashed onto the open floor. We were in awe of the beauty. Sherry walked out in front of us for the second time, now wearing an evening ensemble of black and white chiffon. Even Noelle couldn't keep her eyes off the clothes. She made editorial comments with each passing design. We were taken to the land of make-believe, where fashion plates were the norm and expensive, designer clothing became mandatory. The super models set the bar, at least five foot ten and glamorous.

Someone tapped me on the shoulder. "Lauren, don't look over there, but there's a woman staring at you," Noelle whispered, moving her eyes across the podium.

"What?" My attention was still diverted.

I slowly looked to where Noelle mentioned, finding an exotic and breathtaking woman staring at me. I didn't recognize her. Our eyes kept meeting at the gaps between each model walking across the stage. She gave me a smile, and her deep eyes, though not narrowed, had an unfriendly, piercing look to them—demon like. I quickly looked away.

"Do you know her?" Noelle asked.

"No, I have no idea who she is."

"Then why is she staring at you?" she insisted.

"I have no idea," I whispered. I sank back into my chair. Everything felt tighter. I wanted to hide in between the seats, to escape the shadows closing in. Yet, I couldn't deny this any longer. Was she one of them, too?

Concentrating became difficult for the rest of the show, but I somehow managed to clap when Sherry walked onto the runway again, prancing on stage in another designer dress. Noelle noticed my uneasiness, but didn't say anything. The wealthy looking woman still glared at me, tightening her finely arched brows even after the applause started and when the designer came out to take his bow. Noelle grabbed my hand, squeezing it lightly. I hid behind several people until the lights fully came on and the crowd began to rise.

"Lauren, did you do something to that lady? She's looking at you like she wants your blood," Raegan asked, leaning over to me.

"That's not funny, Raegan. Lauren doesn't even know that woman. We're not sure why she looks so mad," Noelle said. "Let's go find Sherry so we can go to the after party."

The mysterious woman finally looked away. She reached inside her elegant purse, pulling out a pair of tinted glasses. With her eyes now covered, she walked toward the exit. We waited until everybody got up before we followed the woman. I needed a closer look. Maybe she really wasn't looking at me in that awful way. I haven't done anything to deserve her vehemence.

Sherry came by us. "Hey girls! How did you like the—"

"Just a minute. We have to follow this woman," Noelle whispered.

Sherry looked confused, but followed Noelle's adamant lead to the door. We trailed behind the elegant woman, hiding in the darker corners, and stopping long enough to space a distance between her and us. The stranger reached into her purse for her phone before exiting through the door. She stepped into an exquisite Bentley, a car I could never afford in my lifetime.

"Wow."

"Shhh. She'll hear you, Lauren. Come closer," Noelle hissed.

"That's some car," Raegan whistled.

"I'll say. Very expensive. I've seen a few of the top paying models in something like that. It's usually the company they keep that can afford something that nice," Sherry said.

I watched the chauffeur close the passenger door, making his way to the driver's seat. The front windows had been rolled down. He wore a black cap and some dark sunglasses, but there was something strangely familiar about the way he appeared and the angle of his face. When he got into the driver's seat, he took off his chauffeur's hat, ruffled his dark, unkempt hair, and removed his sunglasses. There, in the side mirror, I saw the reflection of his defined face, a face I would never forget.

"*Huh!*" I shrieked. I hid behind the double doors. He rolled up the windows so that the tinted black glass concealed the inside of the car. They drove away as I stood there with my mouth wide open.

"What is it?" Noelle demanded.

"I know that man. I saw him last week when I was at the symphony." My throat tightened and my stomach churned. We all remained silent, and I couldn't move my lips to get another word out.

CHAPTER 8

Revelation

MY MIND FELT busy as much as my head felt full. I looked around at the elaborate after party, and thought to myself, I didn't belong here. But, it was Sherry's day, and I knew the others wanted to go to the party. Who wouldn't? I put on my polite face in order to survive a strained social event of nodding on cue and smiling at random jokes, sipping whatever cool beverage came my way as if I knew the latest trend.

"Are you one of the models?" a handsome, well-dressed man asked.

"No, I'm a friend of one of the models," I replied, lifeless.

"Oh. You look like you can use a drink. Something I can help you with?"

"No. I'm fine."

"This isn't a place for pretty young girls to stand alone. Why don't we sit over here and you can tell me what's troubling you." The man leaned closer. He wore cologne that was strong and masculine. "Or, if you like, my Ferrari is just outside. We can see how fast it goes."

"I have to go."

"Suit yourself." He walked away, moving toward a group of young, giggling girls.

"Lauren, where have you been? C'mon, let's mingle. There's a lot of interesting people here," Raegan said, grabbing my arm. "Let's go find Sherry."

I looked at all the happy people. "I'm ready to go home."

"*What?* We just got here."

"I know. I'm sorry."

Raegan's face turned red. She stared at me for a few moments with wide, green eyes. Her mouth opened up to say something, but then she closed it. She spun around and headed for Noelle and Sherry, who were talking to a group of attentive young men. Raegan whispered something into Noelle's ear. Noelle turned to me with a blank stare on her face, then said her goodbyes to Sherry. I could see Sherry's disappointment, but she managed to wave at me with a big smile as the other girls walked towards me. I lowered my head.

"I think it turned out well for Sherry," Noelle said as we walked to the car.

"I'm really sorry, you guys. I just couldn't handle it anymore."

Noelle nodded. Raegan remained silent.

As we got closer to Noelle's place, the mammoth trees with its lily pad sized leaves felt familiar and inviting. I found comfort knowing she lived in a secure place. Noelle finally broke the ice and said, "Don't worry too much about this. Sherry said she'd try to find out who was on the guest list. We'll find out who they are. I'm sure it's just some mix up."

We hugged Noelle, and I got into the passenger seat next to Raegan. A coincidence. I hoped this was just a coincidence, but after the grocery store run in, the soup kitchen event, and then seeing him twice and having both people vehemently stare at me, I knew better. I just didn't know why.

Raegan was suddenly upbeat and bubbly. "So, Alex, Justin, and Elsie might visit next weekend to go to this concert in Chicago. They know the lead singer, and they said the band is pretty good—rock, I think. They're coming on Friday and staying until Sunday. Gavin and Cameron haven't decided if they're coming. I told them they could crash at our place or maybe Noelle's, even at my parents' for a night would be fine. I don't think your parents would mind. This way, they don't have to get a hotel," she said.

"It would be fun to see them," I said flatly. I wanted to be supportive because I knew how she felt about Alex.

It would be great to see the gang again and catch up. They could meet Quinn since he was a part of my life now. He should know my friends. I knew they would really like him and think he was good for me. I felt much better as we reached the serene house. Quinn's black car was parked in front of the tan bungalow, and my improved mood just rose a few degrees. I hurried inside to change my clothes. He must have heard me coming home because he opened the heavy, maple door before I could even knock.

"You're back. I've missed you," he said softly.

I was at the top of the mountain. "I wasn't gone that long for you to miss me, but since you do, that's even better," I cooed.

Garrett was doing laundry in the basement, so we decided to steal the couch before he got back. I craved the alone time, even lying around in front of their large television set. I needed the reassurance. Instead of holding me closely, Quinn tickled me unmercifully until I fell out of the leather sofa.

"What are you lovebirds up to?" Garrett teased.

Quinn flushed. "We're just sitting here waiting for you."

"Sure, sure. In that case, you don't mind if I make myself comfortable and watch the basketball game, do you?" He plopped his tall and muscular physique in between us and placed a playful arm around my hunched shoulders. I pretended to be disgusted. Garrett played with the remote, switching channels and surfing for the game he recorded. He lifted his muscular legs onto Quinn's lap and laid his large head on mine. "Ah. That's more like it. Now I'm really set."

"Garrett, your head is getting heavy," I moaned. I tried to move his heavy body off of my lap. He pressed extra weight on it.

"Easy man. She's not as strong and heavy as you are," Quinn cautioned. "Lauren doesn't have the strength like you do."

"Give her time and she might. You'd be amazed at what she could do." Garrett winked at a scowling Quinn. "If you two want, the armchair is pretty comfortable."

We both got up at the same time, leaving a very happy Garrett with his television. "We'll be upstairs if you need us," Quinn said.

I followed Quinn, clinging to the back of his cotton navy shirt. The hallway was simple and ordinary, only one picture hung on the lifeless wall—the Northwestern Wildcats football team. Garrett's decorating, I assumed. We entered Quinn's room, stepping over a creaky floorboard at the entryway. The wooden floor and oak baseboard were similar to mine. Aside from his bed and dresser, he had a preprinted picture of a bridge and what looked like the shoreline of New Haven on his cream-colored walls. Something was missing.

"You don't have any photos of your family."

"I didn't bring any with me. I didn't have time," he muttered.

"You must have left so fast. You probably forgot."

He remained indifferent. He looked over at the shoreline picture, then back at me. Quinn reclined further into his firm bed, a wry smile forming from his lips. I curled up next to him.

"Ah, this is much better than the couch. You look more relaxed without Garrett's head on your lap," he mused.

"It was getting a little bit heavy. I always feel better when I'm here with you. You seem to have a way of making things right."

"Not always." Quinn removed his arm around me and rested his head on his intertwined his fingers. He looked up at the bland ceiling, staring somewhere else in some distant memory. "I've been known to make my share of mistakes . . . mistakes I don't ever want to repeat."

His eyes looked reflective. He faced me again. "But that's different now. I'm here with you and that's what matters."

He reached over to touch my face, our warm lips meeting. He needed me, and I needed him. He never came on too strong, only with the same intensity that I showed him: two souls becoming one. We were somehow separated and living in different worlds, carrying this unknown void neither one of us could explain. But somehow, we were joined together by chance, the undeniable realization that we'd deliberately crossed paths. It was too remarkable to explain.

"Wow," he muffled, reaching for air.

"Wow," I said, trying to slow my breathing.

"Do you always kiss like that?"

"Only with you," I said, smiling.

He frowned. I could see the pictures forming inside his head. I was amused. At this juncture, I couldn't see myself with anyone else. I wouldn't be with anyone else.

"Everything pales next to you." I reached over to wrap my arms around his neck. "No chance."

"Then we should do that more often." He drew me into his arms, and I rested my head against his chest. "Speaking of racy events . . . How was the fashion show?"

"Oh, that." I winced.

"What does that mean?" His eyes narrowed, and the softness disappeared.

I let out a breath. "Remember when we went to the symphony?"

"Yes."

"And I mentioned that man staring at me."

"Go on." His face tightened.

"Before I get to the fashion show, I forgot to mention something else."

Quinn's expression remained tight. "What happened at the symphony?"

I cleared my throat. "When I went to the bathroom, that man followed me there."

"What?" Quinn looked shocked. "Lauren, why didn't you say anything? Did he hurt you?"

"I . . . I didn't want to make a big deal about it. I didn't want you to jump to conclusions. He didn't hurt me. I thought he was some crazy man, who confused me for someone else." I described the man. I told Quinn about what the stranger said about Raefield coming. I told him I didn't know who he was or who Raefield was. That was the truth. "It was just a bad mistake."

Quinn shook his head. "He was warning you?"

"Yeah, something like that."

Quinn closed his eyes like he was trying to ward off a pounding headache. He then opened those steel eyes. "Please tell me if this happens again. Okay? Something could have happened to you."

"Okay. Nothing bad happened. It was just a freak coincidence."

Quinn frowned. "It's not a coincidence."

"What do you mean?"

"First, tell me what happened at the fashion show."

I sighed. "Well, I noticed this glamorous woman staring at me. She had dark, wavy hair, and she was finely dressed," I began. "She didn't seem unfriendly at the beginning. It was kind of strange how she smiled at me. It seemed polite at first, but then I realized she looked spiteful instead of friendly. She stared at me until the end of the show. I didn't know what to do. The girls even noticed. Honestly, I had no idea why. I've never seen her in my life," I assured him.

Quinn clenched his jaw so tightly, I thought he might crack a tooth. Still, he remained a rock.

"We followed her after the show. She never said anything to me. She got into this amazing Bentley, and we waited until the driver got into the car." My voice wavered. "And when he turned to look into the side mirror—probably to see if they were being followed—I saw that face."

"His face," Quinn said. He turned onto his back.

"It was the man from the symphony. I *know* it was."

Quinn stared at the ceiling. The walls could have fallen over, and he still would've stared at the bland ceiling. I worried more about him than myself.

"It really is them," he finally said.

"Who are you talking about?"

"I don't know how they managed to find you."

"Quinn, *what* are you talking about?"

He faced me again. He looked wary. "People that I know. People your parents know.

I was puzzled.

"How much have your parents told you about your past?"

"Everything I've told you before. I never mentioned the encounters to them." I tried to remember if they'd ever mentioned anyone similar to the people I'd described to Quinn. No one came to mind. "What do they have to do with my parents?" I sat straight up in bed, really staring at him this time. "And why would you know those people?"

He remained quiet.

I glared at him. *"What aren't you telling me?"*

He looked at me again, troubled. "Where do I begin without sounding . . . judgmental?"

"Let's start with the mysterious pair."

"Yes . . . them. But first, tell me. Did your parents honestly tell you how you came to live with them?

"I *told* you before. My parents were killed in a car accident. The Reeds adopted me. There's not much to tell except for the memory of a four-year-old, and after that I've always been with my family. What are you getting at?"

"Do you remember if they mentioned any significant people?" He sat up beside me, his face displaying his concern.

"Like who?"

"Lauren, I don't mean to upset you, but it's important we know exactly what your parents have told you." He hesitated. "Have your parents ever spoken to you about your birth parents?"

I felt the sting in my eyes. It was like a gentle slap in the face, just enough to warrant a protective shield. I drew back from him. The mention of the strangers responsible for giving me life opened the floodgates of conflicted emotions. I didn't understand why I felt this way. I'd spoken about my adoption before without feeling the heartache.

"What do my *parents* and my *past* have to do with those people?" I asked.

"Perhaps it's time you ask them."

⟶⊨⊙ ⊙⊨⟵

Irritation stirred inside of me. My mind raced in so many different directions; I couldn't decide which thought was more important. What weren't my parents telling me about my birth parents, and why does Quinn know something about those people? I didn't understand the connection.

"You're home early tonight. How is—?" Raegan started to say.

"I'll talk to you later." I climbed the narrow staircase to my cozy room and closed the door behind me. I was losing control. The protective layers came apart. My mind wandered into the memory banks and into the hidden, locked chambers that I rarely sought. I felt leery, afraid of what I might find.

Stop it! I can't go there.

Opening the locked drawer next to my desk, I sifted through the copies of my birth record. I needed a focal point. My phone buzzed with new messages.

"Lauren, I'm sorry if I upset you. I'll understand if you're mad at me. I'm here if you need me. I just can't go into details."

"Hi, sweetie. Your father and I had to go out of town at the last minute. The Fozis are with us. Isaak is home if you need anything, and Aaron and Leslie Brandt are just a phone call away. We'll be back from Connecticut in a few days. Love you!"

What were my parents doing in Connecticut, and with the Fozis? Why did Quinn want me to talk to them about my past? I'd have to wait until the middle of the week to make sense of this new connection. I needed to talk to Isaak. He would tell me. He couldn't deny me the truth.

"Hello, Lauren?"

"Isaak, I got a message from Mom and Dad, said they were out of town. Why did they go to Connecticut?" Music blared in the background.

"Some last minute business trip. They'll be back in a few days."

"I need to talk to you."

"What? I can't hear you," he shouted. "Listen. I'm out with friends and it's loud here. I'll call you later, okay?"

I went back to sorting through my personal files. I didn't find anything unusual, just the standard certificates and a few old photos of the place I'd once lived. A picture of me with my new family, posing with the other children and the nuns stood out. It was the last day of my life at the center. So young. The photo didn't give me any clues, not even a hint of what I was looking for. I closed the drawer to my past. My mind felt tired, and my bed reached out to me.

I slept restlessly, waking up a few times. I gave up in the middle of the night. The brilliant moon magnified the night—much brighter than usual—leaving an impressive spotlight in the middle of my room. At first, I thought I was dreaming. The pale blue curtains were opened, the window left ajar, allowing the night sky in along with the icy breeze. I was drawn to that peculiar moon. I stood there mesmerized, alone with my private thoughts, touching the thick glass of the window for reassurance. And in the image reflecting from the glass, I saw a glaucous mask form on my weary face. Emerald eyes stared back at me, but this time I didn't recognize the face that mirrored my expression. I stood placid, unsure why I felt drawn to the haunting light like a stranger forced onto the stage created by this transient night.

"Lauren, don't be afraid," the voice said.

"Who's there?" I broke out of my psychotic daze.

The ethereal wind blew into my room, waking me further from my recent place. I took a few steps back, and looked around, only to find my familiar bedroom. The room darkened again, cast in the same blackness I remembered when I'd fallen asleep. I looked up to the sky with focused eyes. It was quite still. The quarter moon appeared less impressive than moments ago. Now, it seemed quiet sitting in the muted sky. Everything would change. I wasn't going to be the same Lauren that I had always been. Somehow, I always knew. It was a wretched feeling, no longer hidden by the fortress I'd created to keep the growing details from surfacing. The walls became permeable. My life would now take me down a path I was meant to travel.

⇥⊙ ⊙⊷

Three painfully long days passed without seeing Quinn. I wanted to be close to him, but spending time apart seemed liked what we needed. My work and my lessons continued. I didn't want to spend time with my friends, and I wasn't in the mood to go into the city. Quinn phoned a few times. I messaged I would be in contact soon. I wasn't angry with him. I needed to think, but he continued to appear in my every thought.

I couldn't stand the silence any longer. I marched over to his place with an agenda in mind. "Truce?" I asked when he answered the door.

"Truce. There was no battle on my part." He reached out to me, bringing me into his familiar arms. He continued to hold me close, in a tight embrace as if I were slipping away.

"Some air?" I moved back a few inches. "What's the matter?"

"I'm not letting you escape, I guess."

"You don't have to worry about that. I don't plan to."

He led me into the roomy kitchen where he was making dinner. "Why don't you have dinner here and we can talk," he suggested. He continued to mix the fresh vegetables with the sautéed meat already cooking in the enormous pan. "I'm sure you have an appetite."

I was ready to eat whatever he served. I reached for the stoneware. He placed a large amount of steamed rice and covered it with the vegetable medley. It smelled delicious even before I took my first bite. "So, are you going to tell me how you know those people?" I asked between mouthfuls of the hot stir-fry.

Quinn took a sip of water. "I've met them a few times. If they are who I think they are, then the driver and the person at the concert was Nicholas Argenti. The wealthy-looking female you described sounds like Mercedes Kar. They work closely together, but they work for another man—Raefield Sinclair. We call him Raef." He stopped to pour more water and drank it down right away. "She can be ruthless, and she often gets her way, but don't underestimate Nicholas. He's no angel. He doesn't have a reputation for being kindhearted. In any case, I've had to deal with him on a few occasions. I usually try to avoid them."

We'd barely eaten half the meal when my willingness to know more superseded my appetite. I pushed aside my dish.

"Unfortunately, your parents know more about them than I do," Quinn said.

"Which leads me to wonder how *you* know my parents," I interrupted. I searched for any facial changes in him, but his face remained unreadable.

"We've met before . . . on a few occasions . . . a long time ago," he reflected. This time his expression wandered. "They're good people—your parents—they've seen a lot. And they would be the people who can best give you the answers you're looking for. Just keep in mind that they really do care about you. We all do." He looked at me meaningfully. "Even if I haven't always been the greatest of people." He quickly got up from the table, and walked to the kitchen sink.

He'd mentioned this before—his imperfections—and how he didn't believe he was a wonderful person. I didn't see the flaws he thought he had. I didn't understand how he could think so poorly of himself. He was good and caring. He had a quiet strength one could rely on. Quinn stood out far from ordinary. He was everything I had been looking for. In the short period of time I'd known him, he has come to mean more to me than anybody I've previously known. Yet, an extensive history was still missing from his limited explanation. I thought about coaxing the truth out of him.

Quinn walked back to the table. "Try not to charm your way into having me tell you more until you talk to your parents," he said, sighing.

"Am I charming?"

"Without even trying."

We talked for the rest of the evening about his time in California. He mentioned it was hard for him to adjust in the beginning to living on the other side of the country and to learn the modern era, but he was a quick study and adapted well to our current technology. More mystery. *The modern era?*

"I met some people who I could relate to. I stayed with a family that owned a vineyard, worked part-time in the wine producing business, and commuted for my studies. When I moved to Sacramento, I was following a lead, but it turned out to be a dead end." He showed no expression. "Again, I met some people who had similarities to me, but they were wanderers. I felt uneasy associating with them. I wasn't sure they understood their purpose or place in this world. They were always . . . searching. I didn't feel like I was in danger, but I didn't want to take my chances." He shifted from his chair a few times before going to the fridge for more water. "After that, you already know I moved to Santa Cruz where I met Garrett and his parents. He probably told you that I wasn't the happiest person at the time. We put our heads together and devised a plan for me to move out to Chicago. It was a gift that I had met him knowing it would lead me here."

He looked at me adoringly. I was elated. He stole a kiss from me. It wasn't a forbidden kiss from two lovers who were banned from seeing one another. It was an invisible bond stronger than welded steel that was pulled together by a powerful, magnetic force—a negative and a positive pole naturally seeking each other. We were those people. I pulled away from my natural selection.

"The people who were like you, would they happen to have special talents beyond this world? Powers that the average person wouldn't have or couldn't explain?"

Quinn's face lit up. He didn't take another breath. His bright, pewter irises became radiant. "And what do you suspect?" he questioned.

"That some people, including yourself, have certain talents given to you . . . maybe at birth and perhaps learned over time."

He looked at me, and a wry smile formed from his lips. "And if it were true, would that bother you?"

"Not in the least bit. I find it appealing." I moved closer to him. "I just have to wonder when my talents will surface."

Quinn only raised his eyebrows. I had Pandora's box in my possession, but I hadn't decided if I should open the box. Maybe I could take a quick peak, knowing a small look would never be sufficient. Once the lid was open, I would want to dig further. The secrets would naturally unfold. It would be too tempting to avoid. Quinn, on the other hand, was the guardian of the box—the trusted keeper. He wasn't going to rush in and reveal everything he knew nor would he allow anyone to gain its possession. He would wait for the right time. He was the person who kept the lid closed to avoid premature chaos. I thought of my parents.

"How long have you known?" he asked.

"It wasn't concrete for many years, just a nagging feeling I couldn't explain. I always felt different, but I knew there were forces that guided me or warned me."

"Warned you?"

"Alerted me when something wasn't right, as in trouble was coming. I tried to ignore the signs, push them as far away as possible. I thought it was my imagination, that I was hearing voices. I *believed* I was going crazy even though I knew I was very alert. My senses seemed to go beyond the natural instinct." I reached for my glass of water. My eyes never widened during this animated tale. Quinn and I walked over to the sofa.

"Yes," he whispered.

"Is it possible that I'm the only one who can hear certain voices? Certain warnings?"

"It's possible, but I would have to see if I can hear or feel what you hear the next time a sign occurred."

"When I have a really bad headache, I sometimes have visions, not always pleasant ones. I knew I wasn't dreaming."

"No dreams. We don't dream."

"During my last major episode at my parents' house, I found myself literally looking inside my head, if that makes any sense. I could see my mind at the same time I was thinking and seeing everything in front of me."

"Really?"

"My family looked scared. They watched me stand there like a zombie, not responding to their pleas. But during that time, I became focused on the shiny emerald inside of my head."

"A gem," Quinn said.

"It held me there. It was so brilliant, so alluring . . . and mysterious. I never felt any danger. I reached for it. Then it began to unfold."

"And?" he asked impatiently.

"And that's it. I came to," I said.

"Lauren, I think you and I both know you saw more than you're telling me. I may have a higher level of awareness, but I can't read minds," he lectured.

I flinched. "I can't either. So when you're ready to tell me what you know, I'll be more than happy to share *my* experiences." I had two tens and an ace in my hand, waiting for the final call.

"Sometimes, we do things to protect the people we care about and to keep them out of harm's way." He had the king and the ace, or he was a professional bluffer.

I wasn't going to fold just yet. "In my visions, I see this woman. She's sick." I took a deep breath. "Someone is after her; they're dangerous. I know her, don't I?"

"Yes," he said, drawing in a breath.

Thunder shook the house. Quinn's glass rattled on the wooden kitchen table before coming to a standstill. I didn't expect rain because the sky had flaunted shades of blue all day. But it came down in heavy, slow drops, imitating hail, then transformed into a quiet, rushing flow. With rain, a melancholic air surfaced from the gloomy skies and muddied the greenery. I felt a peaceful surge flow through me, the kind you experience when other fears aren't as grave as you expected. The rain also washed away old memories, bringing new life and hope to the surface.

Lightning flashed in the sky, causing the lights in the house to go out. I waited for thunder to follow as it usually does in a rainstorm. No sound came forward except for the creaking sound of our feet as we climbed the stairs. I withdrew my hand. I didn't care who had the winning cards or how much was in the money pot. Quinn would tell me everything I needed to know when the time was right. I knew some of the answers already. Most importantly, she wasn't in pain. My previous thoughts became magnified by my higher level of awareness and perhaps from the rock inside my head.

"Will I see her again?"

"I really don't know."

The lights flicked on. The hallway lit up again and the street lamps flickered outside his window. The rain quieted to a light sprinkle. It felt soothing. I watched his peaceful face make an effort for sleep. His masculine brows relaxed above his eyes and his long lashes and closed lids sheltered his thoughts.

"You should try to get some sleep. Let your mind rest after today's discovery," Quinn suggested, his eyes still closed.

"I just want to know. The people who killed my parents, are they after me? They must want me dead, too." I kept my fears hidden deep inside. My reasoning remained within reach.

"I don't think they want you dead, but I do believe they're after you, most likely to own you or to control you or to see what you might be able to do." This time he looked at me with those intense gray eyes, a hint of fluid surrounding his irises.

"And my parents tried to stop them. They had been protecting me, still protecting me in some way. Did the Reeds know my real parents?"

"You should ask your mother." He turned away.

It wasn't his place to tell me. I needed answers.

Mother.

CHAPTER 9

Connections

I QUIETLY STOLE away from Quinn's place early in the morning. He looked peaceful in a deep, tranquil sleep. I thought back to last night. I touched my face with the back of my hand the way he did. The sensation sent pulsations through me. Quinn had pushed my hair away from my face before tenderly kissing me as he has done many times. His hand found my waist and his fingers traced the hills and valleys of my body. I wrapped my arms around my stomach.

I pushed the pleasant thoughts to the back of my mind. The conversation we'd shared last night surfaced again. Even though I could talk to him about anything, and he understood me and knew my weaknesses, I couldn't help thinking about her. When would I get to know her? I couldn't blame him for not telling me about his connections to my family. One look at his warm face, and he owned my trust. He didn't know what I'd seen, despite the possible distortion of the truth. Next came my parents. Could I really blame my loving and protective parents for withholding vital information from me? I wanted to believe their reasoning was sound.

The wheels of my transformed mind seized my thoughts and the information coming into it in organized compartments. It pulsated with each nerve integrating itself around the gem like a transmitter for information to flow. I felt energized.

Before work, I looked up Nicholas, Mercedes, and Raefield on the computer. The only name that matched Nicholas was a person in Corsica, an island off the coast of France. The photo didn't match the person I'd seen. I found articles regarding a wealthy socialite who showed up at parties in New York, Chicago, and Philadelphia. In the limited photos that were posted, I only saw a profile or a fuzzy image of what looked like Mercedes. She wore a hat, or she looked away. Another article stated that she owned homes in New York and Chicago. I cringed. I came across another reporting of a Mercedes Kar, who attended social events in New York, Boston, Chicago, . . . and Connecticut—*New Haven*, Connecticut.

Oh, Quinn . . . and my parents.

My mind raced, my fears replaced by anger. A slow rage surfaced. It wanted to push out. I became startled by this newfound emotion.

Calm down.

Were they in danger? Would something happen to them . . . to me? No, I wouldn't let it. Mercedes needed to be confronted. Her every move should be known in order to safeguard the people around me. I thought back to Quinn describing her as ruthless. My hand made a tight fist. And finally, there was Raefield. What was his role in all of this? I searched for Raefield—Raef. Nothing. Another dead-end. I went back many years. *Nada.* I didn't even know what he looked like.

This became too much. My hunger escalated. I went downstairs to an empty kitchen and fixed myself a large breakfast. The food distinction hit me again. I should have known why we needed so much. After I finished my breakfast, I called Mom.

"Hello?"

"Hi, Mom. It's me."

"Oh, Lauren, I've been trying to call you. Raegan said you were out with friends, but that you were fine. I'm sorry we left so suddenly. I missed seeing you on Sunday. We can have dinner another time."

"Sure. It's okay. I got your messages. I didn't have time to get back to you." I hesitated. "You'll have to tell me about Connecticut."

She paused. "Oh, it was nothing. Everything's fine. Just some things your father and I had to take care of," she said quickly. "It was nice being in Connecticut again, but I'm glad we're home."

Just like Quinn, they had this unusual attachment to Connecticut. It was a nice vacation, but Chicago was for me.

"I'm coming over tonight. We can spend some time together."

"That would be great. I'll make something special. Listen, honey, I have to go. We'll talk soon."

Goodbye, Mother.

My bed called to me. I needed a nap if I was going to make it through work—four easy hours. I couldn't begin to understand what went through their minds.

What was I thinking about?

Everything suddenly grew dark.

--)═◉ ◉═(--

My alarm clock shook me from a heavy sleep. I jumped out of bed, grabbed the cold coffee from the carafe, and poured it into my favorite mug. Yuck! It tasted bitter. The sediments sank to the bottom of the pot. I threw it out. I didn't need the artificial stimulant; I had my own.

A loud motor roared outside. Mr. Patel was mowing the grass. He waved to me when I left the house. This would be a good time to ask him if I could paint my room. He turned the engine off when he saw me coming.

"Well, Lauren, are you settled in? Everything okay?" Mr. Patel asked with a smile.

"Fine. We really like the place. You've done a great job of fixing it up."

"And the new neighbors—they're not any trouble, are they?"

I smiled. "No trouble at all. They've been great." I couldn't dream of a better situation.

"The only reason why I ask is . . . well, Garrett and his family seemed very nice and responsible. I wasn't sure about Quinn, because his references were vague. I didn't find much in his rental history, but Garrett said he always lived with family members and that he was living at the La Rouches'. He seemed nice enough."

"Oh, Quinn has been a perfect neighbor. He's *very* responsible."

"Good. I wouldn't want to upset your parents, especially your father."

"My father?"

"I don't know if I should say anything to you, but he wanted to make sure this was a safe and pleasant neighborhood before you moved in. He was very thorough," Mr. Patel explained, chuckling to himself. "He's a little protective of you."

"I know." I tried not to roll my eyes. I could only imagine all the questions and inquiries he made before letting me rent this place.

"Can you blame him? I'm a parent, too. I know these things. Besides, your father is very respectable. A good family man."

"Thanks for letting me know, Mr. Patel. I have to go to work." I began walking to my car.

"Oh, Lauren, I almost forgot," he said.

I turned around.

"The other day . . . let me think . . . oh, yes, it was Saturday. You girls weren't home. Neither was Quinn or Garrett. Anyway, I was fixing your neighbors' kitchen window when I noticed someone walking around the house." He looked puzzled, then slightly bashful. "A very attractive woman, who was dressed for a party, was looking for you."

"Me?" My jaw tightened.

"She said she was a relative of yours and wanted to know if you needed a ride to some fashion show. I think she said it was downtown." He pretended to shift the gears on the riding lawnmower, like he was driving it. "The car she came in was one of a kind."

Mercedes. Looking for me. I clenched my hands.

"But, I remembered your parents expressing their wishes that no strangers were allowed. Whatever that meant. So, I told the lady you didn't live here. She left with some driver waiting in the car. I figured if she was family, then she would contact you."

I smiled warmly at Mr. Patel. "You did the right thing. I don't know her."

He started the lawnmower again and drove away. I climbed into my car and sped away.

Ruthless.

⋆⟶▣ ▣◀⋆

Work seemed to be a good escape with the library as my hideaway. I wasn't running; I was retreating. I let out a nervous laugh. They weren't making a social visit, that's for sure. My thoughts drifted to defensive boundaries. Motion sensors and guard dogs appeared. I would have to tell Quinn. We needed to keep track of them. I suddenly found myself looking over my shoulders.

The library noise became louder. For a Wednesday, people actually used the library since the summer sessions had begun. I picked up the assignment roster and checked it. Project day. The tack boards needed to be redesigned for the summer school classes and for campus events. Digging through the craft boxes, I began to lay out some colorful patterns and precut trim on the open table.

"Hey, Lauren, you're here."

"What's up, Ethan?"

"I want you to cover the last hour at the desk. I have to leave early. Linda, Brianna, Simon, and Aaron will be coming in at two when Tasha, Devon, and Suki leave."

"Sure, no problem." I went back to sifting through the boxes. Ethan still hadn't moved. "Is there something else?"

"Yeah, I almost forgot," he began. "Yesterday, some girl was looking for you."

"Oh? Was it Raegan?"

"Your roommate? No, it wasn't her. She didn't give me her name. I think she was a college student, maybe a graduate student. She had mid-length blond hair."

I didn't know who would be looking for me at work. I picked out some oversized letters and some construction paper in purple and white.

Ethan adjusted his glasses. "I was going to tell her that you'd be here tomorrow, but then she started asking a lot of questions."

"About me?"

"Yeah, it was kind of strange. She said, 'Did she work a lot?' and 'What is she like?' It didn't sound like someone you knew that well."

"Did she say anything else?" I pushed the construction paper away.

"Something about meeting up with you and your new boyfriend."

The alarms went off inside my head. What stranger knew Quinn and I? And where I worked? It wasn't Mercedes or Nicholas.

"So, I told her you didn't work here. I hope I didn't cause you any problems." He studied me cautiously.

"Oh, no. I would've done the same thing. It's probably an old friend I haven't seen in a long time." I laughed nervously. "No harm done."

Ethan went back to manning the desk. I filtered through anything and everything within the last three weeks and the months prior to today. Empty. I couldn't think of a person who fit his description. I decided to work on the project even though my thoughts lingered. During the last hour, I relieved Ethan. The library was nearly empty by mid afternoon.

"Hey, Lauren. Glad you're working today. I wanted to ask you about Saturday," Linda said. "I heard the fashion show was exciting . . . and a little bizarre."

"Just a little bit, but it was nothing."

"Did you find out who the woman was?" she asked.

"Yes, but not through Sherry. Someone else." I didn't want to bring up the volunteer day, either. It was odd enough having several unknown people approach me. Now this.

"I'm sure it was all a mistake. Maybe she couldn't see who you were."

"Right."

"I'll stop by later. You've got some customers." Linda motioned to two students waiting to check out some books and another person standing in line. I perked up.

"I'll see you later, Linda."

She walked by Quinn, pausing briefly, and looked back at me, her dark eyes amused. I quickly took care of the two students. Quinn leaned against the oval desk.

"Have you been here long?" I asked.

"No, only a few minutes." He acted aloof. He began playing with the stapler.

"I didn't want to wake you up this morning. You looked so comfortable."

"I wouldn't have minded. I expected you'd be gone this morning, but I didn't realize how . . . " He paused.

"What?"

"How much it bothered me that you were gone, like you had left me." He didn't make eye contact.

I laughed softly. My fears disappeared. "You don't have to worry about that. It'll never happen."

He looked relieved. "I'd search for you, even if you didn't want me to." His stark eyes spoke to me. "No matter what."

"Something else is bothering you."

Quinn paused, doing that looking-through-my-eyes kind of stare. "I'm just wondering if your changes are magnifying your emotions? If this is all real?"

I stared at him. "I'm pretty sure I know how I feel. Have I been labile?"

"You're dealing with a lot of energy and newfound emotions, and that's bound to throw you off."

"I guess I can see what you mean." I reached for his hand. "No, I'm quite certain how I feel."

Quinn gave me a half smile. His questioning look disappeared.

"Quinn, I have something to tell you."

"What?"

"Before I came to work, I ran into Mr. Patel. He said that some woman came over to our house, looking for me on the day of the fashion show. The woman sounded like Mercedes."

Quinn stiffened.

"She told him that she was a relative of mine, which I didn't believe."

"No, she's not," he said sternly.

"But, he also told her that I didn't live there. My overprotective parents insisted I remain anonymous."

"They're very wise."

"Do you think they've been following us? I've never noticed anyone unusual around here, but Chicago is a big city."

"It's possible. It would explain Nicholas showing up at the concert."

I shuddered. I needed to be more vigilant.

"Lauren, I don't want you to get too worried, like you have to live in some cocoon. We already know they're looking for us, especially you. We just have to anticipate their next move. Most importantly, we have to find out what they really want. If I know those two, all this glitz, money, and modern culture might keep them occupied for a while. Greed can be very alluring."

I didn't want them to control my life. I had a great life, good health and opportunities, and the best family and friends anyone could ask for.

"There's something else." I hesitated. "Ethan, the assistant manager, said some girl was looking for me yesterday. He didn't know her name. He thought she was a student. The odd thing was, she kept asking a lot of questions about me."

"What kind of questions?"

"If I worked a lot, what I was like, and meeting up with you and me. The only people that know about us are Raegan, Garrett, and today Linda suspects something is going on between us. Do you have any ideas?"

"I can't think of anyone."

"Ethan was suspicious, so he told her that I didn't work—"

"Lauren, I have to take care of a few things. Come over later."

"I'm eating at my parents' house tonight. What's this all about?" I asked as he sprinted for the door. Where had he gone in such as rush?

Moments later, Linda approached the main desk. "Okay, who's the guy? And don't tell me he's just a friend."

I blushed. "Someone special."

"Are you guys together? He's really good-looking, but I'm sure he's smart, too." She looked at me quizzically. "Can't say I've ever seen him around campus."

"Yes, we're together. He's a student. He transferred here from California in September. He'll be a senior this fall."

"You guys look good together." She paused. "All the other boys will be disappointed."

"*Whatever,*" I remarked. We both laughed.

⇢►═◉ ◉═◄⇠

I stepped out of my car. For a few moments, I just stared at my former home. It was still home, a safe place where we could all meet and be a family. So, why did I feel like my family could fall apart? With a trembling hand, I turned the key and slowly opened the door.

"Mom, I'm home."

"In the kitchen, honey," she called.

"Everything smells so good. What are we having besides the roast? I can smell baked fruit."

"Steamed spinach with almonds, roasted tomatoes, potatoes au gratin, and for dessert, blueberry tart. They're in season."

I grabbed some plates and silverware and headed for the dining room to set the table. Dad and Isaak weren't home yet. I could start with Mom. Persuading her might be easier than I expected, after all, I was her baby. I walked over to the stove to arrange the tomatoes in the frying pan; she worked on the roast.

"Mom, you know I would come to you if I had any concerns, right?"

"Absolutely."

"And you would tell me things if I asked you, right? Important things?"

Mom stood at the island. "Sure, Lauren. What do you want to tell me?"

"Mom, I met someone. He's very nice. I think you'll like him."

"Oh?" She looked at me with narrowed eyes.

"He's a transfer student. He's from California. I'd like you to meet him soon, maybe next week."

Mom looked away. She turned her attention to the spinach. "What's his name?"

"Quinn . . . Quinn Maxwell," I said proudly.

She looked at me again, this time without expression. She searched my face. Then, she returned to checking on the roast and the potatoes. I waited for a laundry list of questions.

"I think once we finish the potatoes, the roast should be done. The fruit, cheese, and wine are set out. Oh, and only brown the tomatoes slightly before placing them in the oven. I'll put the spinach—"

"*Mom,* is that all you have to say? I'm surprised you're not grilling me with questions."

She looked at me this time. Her face softened. "Lauren, I know we're overprotective, but we trust you. We've raised you well. You've made a lot of responsible decisions." Her face began to tighten. "You *will* tell us if there's any reason for concern, won't you?"

Her reaction surprised me. "Of course, of course. And I want you to meet him."

"Whenever you like."

"Good. Then it won't be a total surprise to see him . . . *again.* He told me you've met before."

She stopped what she was doing. Her eyes remained focused on the table. "What did he tell you?"

"Only that he knows you and Dad, and that he says you're good people."

"Anything else?" She looked at me with cautious eyes.

"He wouldn't elaborate on *why* he knows you, but he did mention that you and Dad are the best people to tell me about . . . my birth parents." My emotions remained intact. I gathered all my courage to speak freely. *"Mother,* is there something you'd like to tell me?"

She dropped a plate in the sink, making a hard clanging sound. It didn't break. She looked straight ahead, her eyes widened. Then, she turned her face away. I noticed her eyes glistening, but it was a shadowy light. Mom still wouldn't look at me.

"Mom, are you okay?" I asked softly.

She straightened her cropped hair. She took a few deep breaths in and focused on the food in front of her. "We'll put the spinach in last. Let's put the tomatoes in the stove."

"Mom, I *think* I deserve an explanation."

She sighed. "All right. I knew this day was coming. We feared you would push us on this." Mom appeared sad. "Your father will be home soon. Let's talk about it then." Her eyes pleaded with me.

"If you think that's best," I whispered.

We finished preparing the dinner in silence. I didn't want to unleash the mayhem. The silence between us felt like walking on a landmine. I wasn't sure what to expect. Was I about to open Pandora's box and release the chaos? Or would it be less dramatic? If I didn't find out about my past, I would never be satisfied. I would always wonder. . . .

I sided with less chaos.

"Helen . . . Lauren, we're home." Dad and Isaak appeared through the walkway by the garage.

"Mom, dinner smells good. I'm ready to eat. Hey, Lauren. They told me you were coming. What's the occasion?"

"I just wanted to visit. I wanted to spend some time with my family."

Mom didn't look at me. She swiftly set the food on the table. "Wash your hands."

We sat down. Isaak and Dad began talking about work. Mom ate slowly. Dad looked at her a few times. His eyes stayed with her after he noticed she barely touched her food. His face appeared solemn. I waited until everybody had had enough to eat before I released the chaos.

"Mom, is everything okay?" Isaak asked.

"Everything's fine. I'm just tired. How's your dinner?"

"Great, as always." Isaak reached for a second serving of food. "Lauren, I'm surprised you're not completely done with your meal. Microwave cooking *must* leave you hungry."

"Funny. I do know how to cook," I retorted. "Mom, everything's delicious." I suddenly felt guilty.

Mom looked up at us. "I wanted to make tonight's dinner special for Lauren. We always love it when she visits us." She looked directly at me. "You mean the world to us."

"You didn't have to go to all this trouble." I felt worse.

"It's never any trouble to see you, sweetheart," Dad responded. He looked at Mom again and then back to me. "We'd do anything for you."

"You're so spoiled," Isaak teased.

Mom set her partially eaten meal aside. Dad and Isaak were almost done with their second plateful. Mom rose from her seat and began to cut the dessert. "I think tonight is a tribute to Lauren, our precious daughter, and your wonderful sister."

"Okay, okay." Isaak rolled his eyes.

"I think Lauren would like to say a few things. Perhaps we can all go into the family room where it's more comfortable." Mom handed us the dessert. We walked into the other room like orderly children forming a straight line. Dad remained quiet. He trailed behind Mom.

"So, what do you want to tell us, Lauren? I'm curious now," Isaak questioned.

"Well, Mom and I were talking . . . about me."

"Naturally. What else?" Isaak's jovial nature disappeared.

"Isaak, give her time," Dad cautioned.

I stood in front of my family with a ready-made speech. "First, I'd like to say what a wonderful and supportive family I have. You're the greatest. I wouldn't be where I am today without you. I *really* mean it. I love you guys." I held back the tears. "Chelsea isn't here with us, but she already knows how I feel." I paused again. "But, I've been thinking about who I really am. Some interesting and important facts have come to my attention, and I think it's time I learn the truth. I *deserve* to know the truth."

Dad looked somber. Mom was fighting back the tears. Isaak leaned back into the sofa.

"The good news is that I've met a wonderful person. His name is Quinn Maxwell."

Isaak quickly turned to Dad, his royal blue eyes widening.

"Yes, Mom and Dad know him. I'm not sure how, but he thought it was best that I start with Mom and Dad." I turned to them. "He'll tell me what he knows after I speak to you. He's important to me, and I want you to get to know him—again. I'm assuming Isaak doesn't know him yet."

"Of course," Dad whispered.

"So, I'd like to direct this to Mom and Dad. What do you know about my birth parents?" I didn't flinch.

Dad turned pale. Mom just stared at the floor. Isaak stayed quiet, but he kept looking at our parents.

"I know this is difficult, but I have a right to know."

Dad looked at Mom. She looked up this time, nodding her head several times.

"Your birth parents . . . they weren't killed in a car accident," Dad began.

"I didn't think so." I stopped pacing as Dad began to speak again.

"Their names weren't Paul and Simone Lewis. There was a note affixed to your jacket when you were found, stating you were Lauren

Lewis, the daughter of Paul and Simone Lewis. The note was placed for good reason. I'm sure the car accident story came about to protect your identity. A reliable source told us that you were brought to the center from a local hospital that said your parents were killed in an automobile accident. Naturally, the center made their inquiries and nobody responded or fit the description," Dad said. "Your parents' names *had* to be changed."

"But we knew your parents weren't killed in a car accident," Mom quietly said. "After an extensive search, we found out where you were and headed for Oregon to get you. Do believe me when I say you *are* family, that you have been our daughter."

I soaked everything in. Nothing they said made me waver. The debate inside my head continued on. "So tell me . . . who's Phillip?"

My mother looked stunned. It reminded me of the time we found her in my yard completely dazed. But this time she had found her voice. *"How* do you know about Phillip?"

I cleared my throat. "Now it's my turn to confess. Remember when I had that episode in the dining room, the day of Isaak's homecoming dinner?"

"Yes," they said in unison.

"I saw something." My parents sat upright in their seats. "I saw something green and shiny that looked like a large emerald. I'm not sure *what* it was or *why* I saw it, or why it's even in my head. I guess that would explain the headaches even though they never saw anything on the scans." I decided to sit down; the emotions began to stir. "And somewhere between the pain and the bright lights, a figure showed up."

My mother began to weep quietly. My father reached for her. "Oren, it's okay. She has to know."

"He came to me. He reached out to me, and I reached out to him. I felt safe." My tears came down. "I asked him who he was and he told me." Everyone was silent. "Is he my father?"

"Yes," my mother said, sobbing.

I took a few moments to get my thoughts organized. "I don't fully understand what's going on."

"Helen, do you want me to tell her?" Dad asked.

Mom gathered herself together, her shoulders positioned upright. "No, I should be the one to tell her." She looked at me with careful eyes. "Phillip, your biological father, . . . is my brother . . . my twin brother."

I slumped back into the chair. My mouth hung open. I wanted to say something, but nothing came out. I was crying and screaming and elated at the same time. The recent news and my tangled emotions rushed to my head and back out. I was a De Boers. I was daughter to Phillip De Boers and niece to the former Helen De Boers.

"Lauren, say something to us. We're very sorry we didn't tell you. We've wanted to tell you so many times. I've struggled many times, asking myself when we should tell you. You have every right to know. You should know about your parents. We understand if you're upset with us. We were afraid we'd lose you. We love you very much. But most importantly, and know this to be the absolute truth, we hid your identity only to protect you," my father spoke quickly.

Isaak reached for my true aunt and uncle. I was in a state of flux.

"And my mother? Who was she?"

"Her name was Faye. She was a caring, beautiful, and loving mother. She wanted us to take care of you. She wanted to make sure you would go on."

Why have I heard those names before? My tears poured down my face. My sweet, caring mother had been taken from me. The parents that I didn't know had pushed me out into this life to give me another chance, a *fighting* chance. I had to be strong. I had to do it for them.

The hidden identity, the strangers, and my birth parents were all part of a world that was tied to me. I was at the center of the web, with the net getting larger and more entangled by each person connected to the other person. But who was I really? The slight resemblances to my mother and my siblings weren't my imagination. We were family. The blood that ran through my veins was linked to theirs. Somewhere, deep inside my buried thoughts, I believed it was possible.

"And this would make us all witches?" I asked them.

"In the flesh as real as life," Mom responded. She didn't look surprised at my revelation.

The box stayed open. My birth parents had tried to protect me. The Reeds, my other parents, have been protecting me. Even Quinn played a role. His motives were still a mystery to me above anything else. I vowed to find out his involvement. I ran over to my family and hugged them warmly. They were still my family, now more than ever. We held each other for quite some time as Mom and I dried our tears.

"I'm glad this is out in the open now," Isaak said.

"Well, not everything," I responded.

"What do you mean?" Dad asked.

"There are some people I'd like to ask you about." I looked down at the wooden floor, and guilt churned inside my stomach. "Do the names Mercedes and Nicholas sound familiar?"

"Did Quinn tell you about them?" Mom asked.

"No. Quinn and I saw him at a concert. He didn't say anything to me; he just stared at me. At intermission, he approached me. He was warning me, but I didn't know what he was talking about."

"*What?*" Mom asked, alarmed.

"He didn't hurt me. I think he realized I didn't know who he was."

Mom and Dad looked at each other like they just exchanged a silent conversation. Mom turned to me. "What else happened, Lauren?" she questioned.

"When I went to the fashion show with my friends, I ran into Mercedes. She only stared at me unpleasantly, and left. I saw both of them. I didn't know them at the time. When I told Quinn what had happened, he identified them." I decided not to worry my parents further by telling them about the visit to my apartment.

"I was afraid this might happen," Mom said. "Have they made further contact or threatened you?"

"No, that's it. Quinn wasn't sure what they wanted with me, but that we should anticipate their next move."

"I think he's right. We've been following Mercedes ever since we found out where she was. She's only made herself more public in the past year. We knew she hadn't approached you until now. And Nicholas . . . he's harder to track, but you can always expect him to be close by Mercedes," Dad informed me.

"Quinn mentioned someone else, someone they work for." I dreaded the next piece of bad news, but I had to know. "Who's Raefield?"

My family looked at each other. I knew Raefield was a major player. He was *the one* I needed to be worried about.

"Raefield is someone who carries a great amount of appeal, someone who's drawn to great power. He's quite convincing, and can appear trusting. That's when he knows he can win you over. You just want to believe in him, and then he turns on you. We thought he might be in Connecticut. Julian and Nadja Fozi went with us because they came across some old journals from a former witch. There was a depiction of Raefield in detail," Mom said. "But it was a false alarm. He wasn't there."

Yes, the sudden trip out east. My parents went to confront him. They've sacrificed so much for me.

"Did he betray my parents? Is that how they died?"

Mom covered her mouth with her hand, nodding to the questions I was afraid to ask.

Everything felt tight. Pressure building. And my legs felt wobbly. "Should I be worried about Raefield? Do you think he'll come after—"

"Ahhhh!"

"Lauren!" It was the last thing I heard my mother say.

CHAPTER 10

Voices

"DR. REYES, DR. Munroe, what do you think is happening now?"

"I'm not sure. Her drug tests are negative. All her lab values and her vital signs are normal. Heart, liver, and kidneys are working just fine. She hasn't responded to any painful stimuli, just flaccid. Not even reacting to light." A man's hand picked up my arm and let it drop. "I don't know why she can't wake up."

"Dr. Jankowski, her recent head scans and neurological tests have found nothing. She's breathing somehow, even if her respirations are only ten. Her pulse is strong. Everything is . . . so normal. She's a mystery," a female said.

What are you talking about? Of course, it's normal. I'm lying here in this bed while you guys are treating me like a guinea pig.

How did I get here?

"We could run a few more tests, but I don't think we'll find anything new," the female said.

I'm pretty comfortable right now. I don't need any more tests.

"Let's wait, Dr. Reyes, until we talk to her parents again," Dr. Jankowski responded.

They were mumbling to themselves. I couldn't see anything.

"She's been like this since before eight last night," said Dr. Munroe, the man who lifted up my arm.

Was I dreaming? Impossible. I don't dream, unless I do now. Wait until I tell Raegan. It smells so clean and sanitized in here. Lemon bleach. And there was a lot of noise coming from outside this room—bells, whistles, and people shuffling around. I wondered what was going on. I searched my memory banks. I've seen this before, on one of those hospital shows where the patient wakes up and realizes she was in a hospital.

Oh, no! I'm in the intensive care unit.

"She does look comfortable," Dr. Reyes said. They flipped through some paperwork. "It's too bad how this happened. She's so young."

What do you mean?

"I know. It's hard to believe she was enjoying a quiet evening with her family when she lost consciousness. She's been like this ever since," Dr. Munroe said.

The dinner.

"I hope she can wake up," he commented.

I do, too.

"Remember the twenty-five year old girl they brought in recently who was biking without a helmet?" Dr. Reyes asked.

"Yeah, that was sad."

It wasn't me. I can't be. Ohhh, wake up, Lauren! I tried thrashing around in bed. I couldn't move.

"Let's bring them in," said Dr. Munroe.

I heard them leave and moments later returned with more people.

Mom, Dad, is that you?

"Mr. Reed, Mrs. Reed, we have every indication that your daughter is comfortable, that she's not in any distress. We're not sure what's really going on. We've looked at all the possible biological reasons as well as any traumatic possibilities that could cause her to be in this sleep-like state. We'll keep you informed if we notice any changes."

"We understand, Dr. Jankowski, that you're doing everything you can for her. Her doctor, Dr. Sendal, will be here momentarily," my father said. "He's well-aware of her kind of condition. It won't be necessary to do further testing." He paused for a moment. "I realize it's been four-teen hours since she's eaten, but do you think she can have some form of nutrition beyond the fluid running through her veins?"

Tell them, Dad. I'm really hungry. This water stuff isn't holding me.

I tried moving my arms and legs again. Nothing. Not even a rustling of the sheets. I wiggled my nose internally. The oxygen itched. I didn't need it. I tasted salt and sugar and something bitter, like liquid vitamins.

"If she doesn't wake up soon, we can feed her through her nose. There's always a stomach tube for long-term care if things don't progress. But let's not go there just yet," Dr. Jankowski told my parents.

Get me out of here! I won't do it.

"And just to let you know, we have the finest neurosurgeon and neurologist following her case. They're very hopeful."

My head is fine, thank you. Please don't disturb the rock.

"We appreciate everything you've done for her," my mother said. "We just want her back."

I heard footsteps walking away and the sliding glass door close. Someone sat on my bed. *Mom, is that you?* Her hand touched mine.

"Oh, Lauren. I wish you could say something. I don't know if you can hear me."

I can! I can!

"I have no idea what happened. That gem must have done something. But don't worry, they're taking good care of you here, and we're trying everything we can to wake you up. Dr. Sendal is on his way." She held my hand even harder. "We'll have Raegan visit later when everything settles." She took a deep breath, keeping silent for longer than I expected. "Poor Quinn. He called you last night when you didn't return home. We told him you were here. He knows what happened. He's been at your side ever since. I can see that he really does care about you."

Quinn!

"He stepped out for a moment. We've all been taking turns staying with you."

I'm so happy you finally spoke to him. Tell him to come back. I tried telling her, even though she couldn't hear me. *I must look awful.*

"Lauren, I have to tell you something. Please don't be angry with me." She took another deep breath, pausing again for a longer time. "I wasn't going to call Quinn. I wanted to wait. I should have told you this sooner, but that day at your apartment when I had my spell, I wasn't ill. I . . . saw Quinn on the other side. I was startled and surprised to see him. It was . . . unexpected. So there, I've known him before. I'll leave it up to him to tell you the rest. My real concern is that if he came into your life now, did the other two follow him to you or have they just been waiting? *Please* forgive me. We're just trying to look out for you."

Oh, Mother. I wish I would've known. I'm not angry with you.

"My mind was racing that day. I wasn't sure what to expect from him or them."

No, Quinn wouldn't lead them to me. He had no idea.

"I was afraid you'd leave if you knew."

Leave?

"Helen, they want to examine her. And there's someone else waiting to see her," Dad interrupted.

Quinn?

"It's Annalise, her nurse. I won't be long. I just need to get some numbers and see how she's doing."

"Of course. Don't let us be in your way," Mom said.

"It's no problem. She needs the support right now. Is there anything you can think of that she might need?"

"No, she seems comfortable."

Annalise punched some buttons on a monitor. "Her vital signs are still normal." She placed the cold stethoscope on my heart. "Do you want to sit somewhere? There's a chair next to her," she said.

"Okay, as long as I'm not in your way."

Quinn, over here!

"That's strange. Her heart rate just increased to a hundred and twenty . . . now one thirty. Steven, what's she reading out there?"

"One thirty-two."

I heard my mother walk over. "Lauren, if you can hear us, try to relax. The nurse is working with you."

I'm trying. I wish I could talk!

"Lauren, I'm right here. I'm sitting next to you. We just want you to come back to us," Quinn said.

His voice. I would never forget it.

"One hundred and forty. And the pressure is high, too. I'll let Dr. Jankowski know. We'll give her some medication to slow it down." Annalise started to walk away, then said, "That's strange, it went up when you came over."

"Should I move?" Quinn asked.

No! Please stay.

"It shouldn't make a difference, but if this gets worse, I may have to ask everyone to step out."

No! I'm calm. Working on it. Please don't leave.

Quinn touched my arm, and then squeezed my hand.

"Annalise, it's coming down. I'd like him to stay with her if that's okay with you. I think it may actually benefit her."

Thank you, Mom.

"All right," Annalise said.

"Quinn, I'll be outside with her father. Dr. Sendal will be here soon. Chelsea and Isaak will be coming back."

My parents and the nurse left the room.

"Finally, we're alone." Quinn sat on my bed. "You really scared us. I barely slept last night and I haven't even shaved." He moved my hair away from my face. "I look much worse than you. You actually look quite peaceful in this bed, but I can't wait until you get out of here. They said you were fine." He stroked my face.

I need to get out of here.

"But we can't wake you up. Lauren, if you can hear us, was that a sign?"

I think so!

He reached for my hand. It was real . . . warm. It was his. He moved my hand up to his face so that I could feel the facial hair that grew overnight.

"I wish you would wake up. I'm a mess without you." He squeezed my hands even tighter.

I do, too. I could feel tears forming, but they weren't falling down my face.

"I can't lose you again. I *won't*. It would kill me."

Lose me again?

"It took me so long to find you. I almost gave up. I didn't know this was going to happen. I didn't mean for it to happen. It was the only way to save you."

Find me? Save me? What happened? I don't understand. You were looking for me? When? I attempted to shake myself free from this bed, but I remained a prisoner in this body. I wanted to scream.

"I know it was painful to hear about your family, but you needed to hear the truth. I don't know what's going on inside. The gem is changing you. How much? I don't know. They weren't sure what it could do. It holds a great deal of power, and only you may know what happens next. Lauren, it was the *only* way to get you out of there, even if it meant never seeing you again."

Someone placed this rock in my head for important reasons, but it put my life in jeopardy. It's changing me and I caused it to change. The past and the present crossed through the same dimension. I was the point of intersection.

"Lauren, I need to tell you this so you will always know how I feel. It's what I've told you time and again. I love you. I've *always* loved you. Will *always* love you. Only you."

I was crying inside. *I love you, too. I felt it, too.* My heart was moving out of my chest.

"From the time you and your family came into the hotel, I knew. We would be together. You knew, too."

The hotel?

The nurse interrupted us. "Excuse me. We're going to ask that you step aside. Dr. Jankowski, the heart rate is climbing into the one sixties, and sustaining. What do you want me to give her?"

No, I can control it. Wait.

"Let's give her a loading dose of Amio and put her on the anti-arrhythmic to slow it down. What's her BP doing?"

"Still high, see?" Annalise said.

"Let's do another twelve lead and get me her previous EKG." Dr. Jankowski checked my neck and listened to my heart. "What's this? It's going down."

"She's holding in the eighties. Look, her blood pressure is stable, too." Annalise said.

"Okay, let's just start a low dose drip so she's not bouncing all over the place."

"I don't think that will be necessary."

"And who are you?" asked Dr. Jankowski.

"Sorry, I couldn't be here sooner. I'm Dr. Sendal, her family doctor."

Dr. Sendal, you're here! Please, help me!

"We still need to keep her stable. She's not in the clear, yet."

"I couldn't agree with you more. But, I've worked with her for many years. She doesn't respond to medications like the way most people do. I think it could worsen her condition."

"Well, I'm her doctor while she's in the ICU. I know what's best for her."

"I understand you're just doing your job. Please, I want to help her, too. She's a unique individual with special needs. You can see for yourself by the images that came out fine, and all her blood work is normal. Your fellows are doing a fine job of working diligently with everything they know. You're not going to find a case like hers in any textbook." He moved closer to the head of my bed. "Let's just say her body constantly repairs itself quickly and adjusts to the insults thrown her way. See, you have the recordings of her vital signs. They're unremarkable. The temporary elevations were just a blip. Let me work with her."

Dr. Jankowski chuckled. "Dr. Sendal, that's quite a picture you've painted for us. Sure, she's a mystery and anything can happen at this point. We just can't leave her untreated."

"Dr. Jankowski, you've been extremely helpful in the care of our daughter. We're grateful for your expertise, but we'd like Dr. Sendal to take a look at her as well. We want her home again."

"All right, but my team is ready if she doesn't improve. You *do* have privileges here, don't you?"

"Of course. You can check the list."

I heard several footsteps leave the room.

"Quinn, it's good to see you again. It's been so long. We have so many things to catch up on."

Dr. Sendal knows Quinn? A spiral thread has been connected to a radial thread. The sticky outer layer continued to grow. But was the anchor point strong enough to hold us all?

"Of course, another time. Right now Lauren is my only concern. Can you help her?"

"I'll do what I can."

"Uri, is this typical?" my mother said.

"I've only experienced this twice, and on the second occasion that person was never seen again. He had a red garnet embedded in his head. It . . . it took a hold of him."

"What did I miss?" Isaak said, rushing into my room.

"Her doctors are letting Dr. Sendal look at her," Chelsea replied.

Chelsea, when did you sneak in? Isaak, you made it.

"Quinn, you should sit next to her. She seems to be receptive to you. Lauren, I'm going to examine you. Everyone is here. Let's find out what's going on," Dr. Sendal said.

Just wake me up. I took a few deep internal breaths as I waited for Dr. Sendal to work his magic. I needed to escape.

He carefully examined me—my eyes, my head, and my reflexes—like all the other doctors did.

"Lauren, I'm going to put something in your mouth. Quinn, you should take her hand."

I felt the drops slide down my throat.

"That's it, just relax. Let the medicine do its job. Oren, Helen, it may be too soon for the gem to come out. I'm not sure what it could do to her if we force it out. She's not ready for the exchange. I'm going to suppress the changeover."

Changeover? What have I become?

Quinn squeezed my hand tighter. I felt the worry in his grip.

"When do you think the rock could come out?" Quinn asked.

"Soon. It's only begun, but I haven't noticed all the transitional signs."

"Signs? What do you mean?" Chelsea asked.

"Helen, has she been approached?" Dr. Sendal asked.

"Yes, Phillip came to her. I don't know if Faye has been in contact," my mother whispered.

"She vaguely mentioned seeing images, and I think more than once during an episode. It sounds like Faye." Quinn became quiet. "But I think they were distorted."

"Good. It's as I expected. What else?"

I felt the contractions in my arm move outward. I felt the impulses going through the nerves and muscles of my arm. My mind suddenly communicated with my arm without me forcing a movement.

"She's squeezing my hand!" Quinn exclaimed.

I heard many footsteps coming closer. My family surrounded me, probably watching my next move. They would watch over me—be my eyes—because something was approaching. . . .

The light came again. It was so bright. I knew pain would come next.

"Lauren . . . Lauren, can you hear us? We're all here," Mom said.

"Lauren, please answer us," Dad pleaded.

Just focus, Lauren. It won't hurt you. Let it pass.

"Her grip is getting tighter. Lauren, hold on. Let it come to you." Quinn kissed me on the forehead. "It won't hurt you."

I was blinded again, inside my head, from the bright green and white lights shooting out from the emerald. I waited for the pain, but it never came, only the memory of it surfaced. This time, I knew what to expect. I welcomed the encroachment.

"Lauren, you have to be strong. We can't be there to help you. We're always with you."

"Daddy, don't leave me. I don't know what to do."

"Trust yourself. You will find a way. Your friends and family will help you."

"But . . . how?"

"It will come to you."

"Lauren, they're coming. Be careful. There are others. We don't know who they are. We love you . . . always."

"Mother! Stay with me."

"Helen, hold onto her other side," Dr. Sendal directed.

"Let them teach you. They're your family. Learn from them. And be happy."

"No, . . . Mother, I want to stay with you."

"You can't. You must live this life. You must survive. Promise me that you will go on."

"Mother!"

My eyes shot wide open. The bright exam lights shined in my wet eyes. The heat rushed to my face. I felt my heart and lungs work harder until my body forced them to slow down. I looked around the room, still dazed. I really was in the hospital.

"What's going on?" demanded Annalise. She looked around the room. "She's awake. Steven, get me Jankowski."

"Lauren, I'm right here," Quinn said, taking my hand.

I could see everything and everyone. The hospital bed, the lighting, and the equipment in the room looked real. I remained motionless, afraid to move, fearing the worst. What if I can't move? I wiggled my toes. My thoughts were here, but my visions were still fresh, waiting at the edge of my mind between here and there. The salty tears tasted real.

"Everything's going to be fine. We're here with you," Mom consoled. "You left us for a while, but you're back." She wiped my face with a warm cloth.

"Can we sit her up?" Isaak asked.

"Slowly," Dr. Sendal said.

"Lauren, I'm your nurse, Annalise. How do you feel?"

"Um . . . fine, I think. Hungry." I wasn't there anymore. The figures in my head became blurry; their shadows lingered within the soft tissues of my mind. Even their voices became indistinguishable. It grew hazy again.

Now they were gone.

I thought back to their esoteric words. This was my life now. I have to be here, for them and for me. I moved my hands and feet some more, then reached to my left.

Quinn.

"Her numbers look good. Lauren, do you want to sit up higher?" the nurse asked.

"Yes."

My head was raised, but I didn't feel dizzy. In fact, I felt great. My stomach began to growl. My family started laughing.

"I think that's a good sign," Dad said.

"Well, Lauren, welcome back. You gave your family quite a scare. How do you feel?"

It was Jankowski. I recognized his decisive voice. The other two physicians looked perplexed—Reyes and Munroe. They had no idea. And standing not too far away was Dr. Sendal, who became seemingly quiet.

"I feel great. When can I leave?"

"Not just yet. Let's take a look at you and see if there are any changes. We can get you something to eat. If everything checks out, you can move around with some help." He turned to my parents. "I'm going to talk with Drs. Huang and Kellner."

"Finally, some food," I said.

"Dr. Sendal, what happened in here?" Dr. Jankowski questioned.

He was expressionless. "I examined her, she didn't respond. We were all talking, and then she woke up."

Dr. Jankowski frowned. "That's it?"

"She woke up on her own," Dr. Sendal replied.

"See, I'm healed."

Dr. Jankowski still didn't look convinced, but without evidence, he didn't have reason to argue. The other doctors came over and assessed the revived me. They were thorough and looked amazed. Then the trio left.

"Lauren, you mind telling us what that was all about?" Isaak inquired.

"Your guess is as good as mine. I think you would know more considering you watched me go down and out. I was gone for awhile, wasn't I?"

"You were asleep for about thirteen hours," Dad commented.

"Seriously, what was it like being in another dimension?" Isaak asked.

"Different . . . and strange. Exciting . . . sad." I looked at my parents.

"I think you're doing great. I'm sure we can take you home soon," my father said.

I turned to Quinn. His face was filled with concern and relief. I gave him a reassuring look.

"I think she's turned around," Dr. Sendal said. "You're in good hands. Lauren, I'll see you in a week, sooner if you need me. Helen, Oren, we'll be in touch." He turned to Quinn. "Come see me when you can." Quinn nodded.

My eyes narrowed. I was the only one looking at him. He didn't return my questionable stare. He quietly followed Dr. Sendal out, walking through the sliding glass door.

"Lauren, I know you have questions, but our concern is that you continue to improve so that you can come home. We don't want you to have any major upsets while you're here. We're curious if you had another encounter. I suspect the rock was acting up, maybe even before dinner," Mom said.

I nodded my head.

"Mom's right, Lauren. Take it easy. You've been through a lot. We'll figure things out when you get home," Chelsea added. She reached for the remote and flipped through the channels. She stopped at a comedy, but I wasn't in the mood for laughs.

"Since you're better, I think I'll head back to the office and see what needs to be done. Dad, I'll let them know you're still here." My father nodded. "Call me if things change." He kissed me on the cheek. "Take care of yourself. Don't let the thing work you up."

I reached for his hand. "I'll be fine. Thanks for being here." I watched my brother leave. I felt anxious seeing him go. I wasn't worried about him—he always took care of himself—but something didn't feel completely right. My mouth opened to form the words I wanted to say, but only my mind responded. *Don't go.*

"Here you go, young lady. I'll set this in front of you. You must be hungry." She opened up the cover to the main course—turkey with gravy, mixed vegetables and stuffing. "You're very lucky. Not many people in here get to eat."

"Thank you. That will be all," Dad hastily said.

Chelsea and Mom found a channel they could both agree on—a book review on a talk show. Dad sat in the chair that was previously occupied by Quinn. He was still gone. *You bet he has a lot of explaining to do if I have to drag it out of him.* My mind ruminated as I shoveled food in my mouth. Could I be that devious?

"Maybe you should slow down," Chelsea said.

"I'm fine. My body is craving it. It's not like I was Sleeping Beauty and asleep for a long time." We both laughed.

Speaking of princes, why wasn't he back yet?

"Mom, when I get out of here, I'm going to have Quinn take me home."

"Oh?"

"Mr. Patel told me you knew Quinn lived next door. You seemed okay with it."

"We wanted to see what he would do," Mom replied.

Quinn came through the partially opened glass door. I searched his face. I didn't see anything revealing, just his usual calm and warm face.

"Sorry I was gone for so long. We started talking, and I lost track of the time."

No one looked up except for me. "Okay. I just missed having you here." He sat down on the edge of my bed. From the corner of my eye, I thought I noticed my father smile.

"I'm glad you're all here," Dr. Jankowski said, coming through the door. "I see your appetite hasn't diminished. Good. I've talked it over with the other physicians, and Dr. Sendal, as well. We don't normally discharge people from the intensive care, but they feel you're fine to go home after we see how you do walking around. I'd like you to follow up with your doctor, and if there are any questions, just call my office." He waved to my family and me. "Take care, Lauren. I'm truly amazed."

"Thanks, Dr. J." Home. That's where I wanted to be.

"If you don't mind, I'd like to take her for that walk." Quinn helped me to the edge of my bed.

Annalise came into the room. "Lauren, do you feel dizzy?"

"No, I feel great."

"Everything looks good." Annalise swiftly took out the line in my arm and the tubing that drained clear, yellow fluid into a bag. "Okay, you're free to move around."

"Let's go." Quinn grabbed my robe, and we left the sterile room.

We passed the nerve center of the intensive care unit. Busy, noisy, and serious. Several of the staff members stared at me in awe and amazement. I was glad to be the one who could walk away from here. I thought about running, but quickly changed my mind. The long hallway was well lit and serpentine in shape—a passageway to the main hub. I wasn't sure what lurked behind each door. It held my curiosity for only a few seconds.

"I don't think we should go too far." We stopped at a corridor in front of a set of elevators where two adjoining hallways reached out. I became drawn to it. An internal pull pushed me to one of the hallways.

"Are you tired?" he asked.

"No. I'm glad to be out of that bed. It was getting uncomfortable."

"Let me know when you get tired so we can go back. Unless you need me to carry you?"

My face lit up. *"That* would be a nice idea. Let's just stand here for awhile." I gazed to my right, feeling satisfied and utterly complete with the memory still fresh in my mind of the words he meticulously confessed to me when he thought I was asleep.

"What are you thinking about?"

"Something you had said." My face felt warm. I wanted to revel in the moment for as long as I could, but my mind was puzzled. What hotel was he talking about? I never went to his family's hotel. I must have heard him incorrectly.

Then something caught my attention.

"Lauren . . . Lauren. What are you looking at?"

"Did you see that?"

"See what?" He looked to where my eyes were fixed, but it was gone.

My eyes widened. I turned back to him. "It was a woman. I saw her at the soup kitchen. We have to find her."

"Lauren, are you sure? I don't see anyone." He looked down the narrow hallway again and then looked at me skeptically. "We can't go running down the hallway. I don't want you working yourself up."

"But it was her," I scowled. "She's following me. What does she want with me?" My mind raced again. "Maybe she wants to tell me something."

"We don't know that for sure."

"You *do* believe me, don't you?"

"I want to. I just don't know if the rock is playing with your mind or if you really did see a woman." He became solemn. "Let's go back. You've had a long day. I don't want them to find more reasons to keep you here."

"But . . . it was her," I pleaded quietly.

He didn't respond.

"Fine."

We slowly walked back to my room. I looked over my shoulder, only to find an empty hallway. On the ceiling where we just passed, the forth panel of florescent lighting was partially out where the bend in the corridor began. The lighting wasn't even. A shapeless shadow seemed to linger for a moment before growing smaller until it disappeared. Goose bumps formed on my skin as I stood there locked in my mind, trying to make sense of everything. I felt Quinn's hand tug at my arm.

Those eyes.

"There you are," Annalise said cheerfully. "I have your discharge papers. You must be excited to go home."

I nodded hastily. She read through the instructions quickly.

"Take care of yourself and call your doctor. I'll have one of the assistants take you out."

"That won't be necessary. If you can bring us a wheelchair, we'll take her out," Dad said. "I'll go get the car."

I quickly got dressed into normal clothes. "Let's go," I urged.

Quinn pushed me out of the intensive care unit, Mom and Chelsea following closely behind.

"Lauren, Quinn, you should eat at our place before you two go back to the apartment. Honey, are you sure you don't want to stay with us tonight?"

"No, I'll be fine. Quinn and Raegan will both be there. Really, nothing's going to happen."

We passed the same hallway where I saw the frail woman. It appeared less secluded and frightening. *I'm sure it was my imagination.* Dad waited in front of the hospital. I turned around to scan the crowded lobby. The stranger was nowhere in sight.

I'm being ridiculous.

"Lauren, I'll see you at your parents' place." Quinn took off for the parking lot.

I watched him leave. A smile formed on my lips, knowing he would spend time at my parents' place. If it weren't for my staring, I wouldn't have noticed a figure standing off to the side, behind a corner edge of the hospital. She put an index finger up to her lips.

"Chelsea, do you see her?" I froze.

"See who?"

"A woman standing there," I whispered.

She turned to that site. "Lauren, I don't see anybody. We'd better get you home."

I looked again at the corner edge where she'd stood. Nobody was there. I replayed the image in my head. Maybe my mind just played tricks on me. It had to stop. They would send me to the other floor if this charade continued. My mother looked at me, puzzled. I couldn't face her. I quietly got into the car.

As the Lexus slowly moved away, I turned around to face the towering hospital, a center for sick people. It wasn't for me. I wanted to get as far away from it as possible, yet it brought me closer to them. Now, nothing appeared unusual. I could see clearly.

"Stay with me." I thought I heard those words drifting in the air.

Chapter 11

Pieces of Me

"You're the best! Are you sure?"

"Yes, I'm sure. A week is enough time to recover. Tell them to come. The concert will be fun. Besides, I want them to meet Quinn."

"I can't wait to tell them! Woo-hoo!" Raegan ran off to her room.

I felt excited, too. My friends would be here at last. I longed for their companionship. They understood me without me having to explain anything to them. It was a natural bond. Even Quinn thought it would be a welcome change. My parents graciously offered their place to any of my friends for the night, longer if they needed. The guys would bring tents, giving Elsie exclusive rights to the house. We would see my family at lunch on Saturday.

I picked up the broom to clean the house. I don't know why I started for my bedroom when I was already standing on the first floor. A natural pull tugged at me, which needed confronting. As I stood in my room and stared at the locked drawers, I wondered, what am I looking for? My adoption papers were the only things hidden away. I turned the key and searched inside the lackluster compartment. The same papers placed in this drawer were still here. I flipped through the documents and the files until I hit an object that didn't feel like the back slat of the drawer. I worked my hands all the back in the compartment. A box. I quickly withdrew the metal object. It was stunning. The delicate, shimmery silver and gold chest had been placed in the same drawer with my past. I ran my fingers along the edges of the box. The deep-set grooves that covered the entire precious chest resembled an intricate maze. It reminded me of Raegan's rug. I attempted to open the case, but it wouldn't open. A tiny lock sealed the chest shut, standing in my way of discovery. *Where was the key?* I searched the drawer again. No key. I tried using a bobby pin, a paperclip, and a letter opener. Still locked.

Just think. Instinctively, I placed my right thumb along the edges of the eyelet. The mysterious box opened. *How did I know?* Hidden within the velvet lining was a delicate bracelet of white gold. The polished band was shaped by thin, intertwining waves fastened to each other and intersecting each other to form the bracelet that connected to a centerpiece. I carefully lifted the bracelet from its case. A deep blue and purple stone was affixed to the center of the bangle. It reminded me of natural spinel. I carefully placed the bracelet around my narrow wrist—a perfect fit. The gem began to glow brilliantly in purple hues. My lids felt heavy from the light shining in my eyes. Yet, I felt mesmerized. I couldn't pull away. There was a faded, beige-colored piece of paper folded over at the base of the chest. Quickly and gently, I opened up the note.

My Daughter,
This is yours. Keep it safe, and with you at all times. Remember its use. When you are ready, use it wisely.

Your Mother

Faye.
Oh, mother. What does this mean? I wish you were here.
My bracelet—but how? I didn't remember ever wearing it. And what was its purpose? I searched my memories, but found no recollection. I rotated my wrist—left, right, left, right. The precious gem remained unaffected. Making a tight fist, I tried willing the stone to do something

wonderful. Anything. It didn't respond to my commands. *Oh, why doesn't it just tell me what it can do?* I returned to housework. I folded some clothes from the laundry basket and picked up the clothes off of my bed, hanging them neatly in the closet.

What? What just happened?

Everything became dark for a millisecond, then an opaque hue covered my eyes. I could still see everything, but something wasn't quite right. I grasped at the air. *Where am I?* I looked at the full-length mirror. I was . . . invisible. A ghost. I touched my newfound trinket, dangling around my right wrist. *Oh, mother, is this what you meant?* I walked back and forth across the floor in silence, holding in my growing panic. My hands remained in front of me, my clothes the same, and the bracelet, . . . it glowed. I looked at my bed. I hopped onto it without making a dent in the mattress.

Impressive.

The door.

I couldn't decide if I should open it or try to walk through it.

You can do it, Lauren.

Climbing off of the bed and still amazed that I didn't leave a mark, I closed my eyes to the solid bedroom door. *One, two, three . . . oh, this is kind of scary!* I slowly opened my eyes. *I did it! I didn't feel anything.* I stood in the hallway. I had crossed over! Everything looked the same, just slightly darker.

I hope I can reappear.

I looked at the door again, thinking I would try to leave my eyes open this time. I was indecisive. I told myself not to be afraid. *Okay, here I go. Just breathe.* My foot moved forward. The wooden door passed through me without causing me any pain as I kept my astonished eyes open. I was inside the bedroom again. I had passed through it without leaving a trace.

Unbelievable.

Footsteps sounded on the stairs. *Raegan.*

"Hey, Lauren, I just got off the phone with Alex." She knocked on the door several times before letting herself in. "Lauren? Lauren, where are you?" She stood in my room looking everywhere. "Lauren, are you in the bathroom?" The room was silent. "That's strange, I thought she was here," she mumbled to herself and left.

Wow.

"Lauren!" The dog was barking now.

I didn't know how to get back to my normal form. I started pacing again. *Think . . . think! What was I doing when I made myself disappear?* I moved to the closet again where I put away my clothes and where the bracelet's magic unfolded. Repeating the same actions as before, I sifted through my clothes, but soon realized my fingers went right through the garments. I slumped onto my bed. *What am I going to do?* Panic and despair invaded my normally rational mind. I wanted my physical life back.

"Please bring me back," I chanted. I rubbed my hand over my forehead. *Think, Lauren.* The idea floated through my head since the moment Raegan began to look for me, now rushed forward to a reality without me directing. I took in a deep breath. Then suddenly, a moment of blackness reached out and left. I was here again in full form.

"Whew. That was close." I looked at myself in the mirror. It was the physical me. My relief felt overwhelming. I reached for my phone, and texted the only person I knew who could help me:

Quinn, I have to see you. Now. I'm coming over.

I quickly gathered my stuff, including the mysterious box. My answers waited on the other side.

"Hey, where have you been? I've been calling your name. Didn't you hear me?" Raegan demanded.

"I've been here. I must have been listening to music." I looked for my shoes.

"What? Impossible. I've looked *everywhere* for you. Isn't that right, Oscar?"

"I have to see Quinn. I'll talk to you later." I rushed out the front door.

I knocked and stood there for a moment before he opened the door.

"Hi. Everything okay?" he asked, looking somewhat confused.

"I'll explain. It's nothing bad. Can I come in?"

"Would I ever say no?"

I walked into an empty house. Garrett was gone. Quinn had paperwork spread across the coffee table. "What do you have to tell me?" He reached for my hand, leading me to the familiar sofa. Before we could sit down, he stopped to stare at my new piece of jewelry. He looked troubled. "Where did you get that bracelet?"

"That's what I came to tell you. I found it in a drawer, the same *locked* drawer with my adoption papers. I don't know who put it there. I was somehow drawn to my room when I was standing downstairs. I couldn't do anything else until I found out what I was supposed to look for. Can you explain this? Here, it came in this unique box." I gave him my interesting little trunk. "And there's a note inside from my mother."

He examined it closely, turning the box at different angles and holding the box up to light. He shook his head. "I don't know what the box means. The markings could be symbols or signs. It could be some secret message. Or not." He carefully opened up the letter and read what turned my emotions. He looked at me thoughtfully. "It was clever of Faye to put this note alongside the bracelet. Do you think Helen put it there for you to accidently find?"

It was strange of him to differentiate my two mothers by their first names. By doing so, their importance sealed my existence and offered me guidance to unravel my confounding life.

"I don't know if Mom put it there. That would be the logical answer, but I don't know why she didn't tell me," I replied. "I guess she wanted me to find out on my own."

"That bracelet you're wearing can be quite useful, but not as powerful as the rock inside your head. If used correctly, the bracelet allows you to become invisible." He looked at me critically. "Lauren, did you make yourself vanish?"

"It was an accident. It just happened." I quickly turned away.

Quinn's lips tightened. He brought me closer to him. "Please don't do that again unless I'm there with you." He let go of me so that we faced each other. "It's not a toy. It has some serious consequences. I know you didn't mean to. You were curious, and you didn't know what it could do. It has an extraordinary draw to its owner." He studied my face carefully. "Kind of how you are to me."

My mouth hung open.

"It belongs to you, Lauren. A gift from your family," he whispered.

"How is that possible?"

"Believe me. It was designed for you and given to you by your parents."

"How do you know this? Quinn, tell me what's going on."

"Shhh, I don't want you to get upset."

"By not telling me what you know, you're upsetting me." I stood there with my arms crossed.

"Lauren . . . please, I promise. I *will* tell you everything when the time is right. I have my reasons. I'm thinking about you. I'm doing this for you."

"I don't see how you're doing this for me, by not telling me the truth. Don't you think I deserve to know the truth?" I gave him a stern look. "I would understand. I *know* I would. And maybe I can make sense of all this, and it would be behind us." I tried to convince the person I cared about the most to tell me about my past. It was like standing outside of my life, watching it move along and waiting to see what would happen next.

"I don't know if *it* will never be a part of us." He tried to hide his worry. I knew he was thinking about Mercedes and Nicholas and others, as well as my newfound power. "And remember, you have that rock inside your head which seems to erupt at any given moment. Any extra stress on you could set it off. I would never forgive myself if it caused you any harm or put you to sleep so that we couldn't wake you up." His eyes never left mine. "You have to trust me. I *will* tell you. Everything. And if it makes you feel any better, I think you're already finding out some of the answers you're looking for on your own. A natural course seems to be flowing." He gave me a wry smile.

"Are you talking about the hospital?"

"What about the hospital?" He looked hesitant, but asked, "Lauren, is there something you'd like to tell me?"

"When I was in the hospital, I heard things." I settled onto the sofa. "I wasn't completely asleep. At some point, I woke up when the doctors were talking about my condition. That's when I realized I'd been taken to the hospital after that fateful family dinner when I found out who my parents were," I confessed. I watched his face soften. His pewter eyes lit up, but with a cautious glow.

"Then you heard everything."

"Yes," I whispered.

Quinn walked over to the TV console and began to rummage through a drawer, as if desperately searching for something important.

"Quinn?" I reached for his warm hand.

"It's true. I love you. I've loved you since the day I first met you. I always will." Quinn moved into the lonely kitchen. Again, he dug through some random drawer.

I couldn't speak or move. Internally, I was soaring. I shook at my weakened limbs in order to reach out to him and to tell him what I thought. I dashed to the place where my heart drifted.

"I feel the same way, too. Quinn, I love you."

"Lauren . . . I . . . it's hard to explain."

"What? Have you changed your mind?"

"No, that part is clear." He looked at me decisively.

"Then there's nothing more to say." I closed the kitchen drawer. "At the hospital . . . What did you mean by 'the only way to get me out'? It sounded like you were referring to the rock in my head and the hotel. Quinn, have I been there? I know I wasn't imagining the conversation." Pandora's box flew wide open. I waited, watching as he deliberated, then walked back to the living room. I followed behind him.

He sat down in the sofa. "Yes, you were at the hotel. That's where we met. But you can't seem to remember. The rock in your head has somehow managed to block your memory."

"When was I at your family's hotel?"

"Many times. A long time ago, although it feels like yesterday."

"I can't believe I don't remember the trips with my family and the hotel . . . and meeting you. I *should* remember meeting you. How could I forget?" I delved through my memory banks again but nothing emerged. "Tell me about our first meeting. I want to know everything," I pleaded.

"You came in with your family. It was a pleasant September afternoon. You had just arrived from Bridgeport."

"Then you've met Chelsea and Isaak," I interrupted.

"You had that autumn glow. You were happy and excited to be in New Haven, and a little scared. Your father had important work ahead of him."

"Dad brought work with him?" I thought back to our last trip to Connecticut. I don't remember my father bringing any work. I don't remember being there in September. It was mid June. We were in Connecticut for two weeks. We flew into Bridgeport, stayed there for a few days, and visited the harbor. We stopped at coastal cities like Milford along the way before reaching New Haven. It wasn't a long road trip. I remembered Isaak and my father playing tennis at the hotel we stayed at in New Haven. I recalled going sailing with my family, all of the restaurants, walking around the city, and listening to music—classical and vocals—on several evenings out with my family. But, I can't remember being at the Maxwell Inn or anything he's mentioned. And disturbingly, I couldn't remember meeting Quinn or his family.

"Like I said, it's caused you to forget. Someday, when it comes back, you'll remember everything."

I didn't want my lack of memory to ruin his account of me. I would have to be patient. "Quinn?"

"What is it?"

"Have we been together since then?"

"Yes."

My life started to come full circle. I was still myself except for a large part of me was missing, which included Quinn and my time at the hotel. Who was I? My phone buzzed for the second time. "It's Raegan. She says our friends will be here at five."

"Then you'd better get ready. That's plenty for today. I'll see you later." He came over and kissed me long and hard, long enough so that I would know everything would work itself out, and strong enough to remind me that I was his. He finally let go. "That's definitely enough for today."

"Uh . . . okay. I'll stop by later." I tried to catch my breath.

Yes, I trusted him. I had to. I needed to leave all my trust with him. He carried my heart.

CHAPTER 12

One Kind of Family

"THEY'RE HERE! ALEX, Justin, and Elsie are here. I don't see Gavin and Cameron. I'm sure they're coming." Raegan adjusted her clothes again. "How do I look?"

"Like sunshine over the clouds. Relax. Just be yourself." I gave her a quick hug.

She opened the door before they could even knock.

"Hey, what service. We made it, thanks to my expertise driving," Alex declared.

We embraced each other like it was ages since we last spoke. It felt like family.

"That's because of your speeding. We're early. I hope you guys don't mind," retorted Elsie.

"Of course not. Come in. Our place is your place." I helped them carry in their bags and brought Elsie's belongings upstairs.

"Cameron and Gavin are twenty minutes behind us. They took a different route, of course, since they were coming from Platteville. We went through Eau Claire and Madison slowly." Justin turned to Alex. "The cops were out. Genius here remembered some of their hiding places. Rockford is terrible to go through."

"I got you here safely and ahead of schedule. What more can you ask?" Alex and Raegan left for the kitchen. They found a tight corner to stand in. She was playing with his dark brown, wavy hair. I understood their attraction to each other.

154

Alex and Justin had tried to get the others to move to Minnesota, unsuccessfully. Cameron and Gavin chose to stay in the small town of Platteville, near the southwestern border of Wisconsin. Their parents wanted them close by—somewhere safe and away from a major city.

"Hey, Alex. Let's put the camping stuff out back. We'll put it up when the others get here," Justin called out.

"Yeah, let's wait for the *girls* to get here just in case they need some help."

"You're too much, *Lexi*," Elsie chimed in.

"Keep it up, Elsie, and you'll be hitching a ride home. Maybe I'll let you sit on top of the car."

"Funny." She scowled at him.

"Okay, you two. Let's have a fun weekend," Justin responded.

The guys went outside to retrieve the camping gear from Alex's Acadia. Oscar followed their every move, but he didn't growl at them. Raegan slipped through the door as well.

"So, tell me, Lauren. Who's this new guy?" Elsie asked. "Raegan says he lives next door. I can't believe it."

"Quinn. He's great. Everything I ever wanted. He'll meet us later. He's more the serious type, which is fine with me. I think you'll like him. His roommate is pretty nice, too—Garrett. They're going to the concert with us," I said, feeling a lot of pride.

"You have a good eye when it comes to men. Me? I haven't dated anyone serious except for Justin," she said, reflecting back. She reached into her purse and pulled out a brush, brushing the ends of her straight, straw-colored hair. "Okay, during the six months we were apart I had another boyfriend, but that didn't mean anything. Justin and I will probably get married after college."

"You two are right for each other. I can tell."

"Tell what?" Justin asked, walking into the living room.

"About people. She's got a good sense about people," Elsie replied.

"Well, sure she does. She's like us," Justin responded.

"What?" I asked him.

"Oops. I guess that was premature." He shrugged his shoulders. "Haven't your parents told you? Sorry, Lauren, I didn't mean to spring it on you like that. I thought you'd figure it out by now."

"She's been a little busy with the new man and being hospitalized. Oh, Lauren. We were going to tell you, but your parents made us promise not to say anything until they had a chance to talk to you," Elsie explained. "Don't be mad at them."

"*My parents?* What did my parents say to you?" Again, their involvement in my past had reached my friends. My friends had known about me before I did. This was dizzying.

"Didn't you notice how your parents seemed to relax more when we were around you, like at camp and when we visited?" Justin asked.

"Yes, I picked up on that."

"Your parents knew we were like them. They trusted us to let them know if anything was going on. And they knew we could defend ourselves if it ever came to it," he explained to me.

"I had my suspicions, but I couldn't quite figure out why. I guess the gem in my head was blocking my true intuition even if it was trying to protect me," I said. "You see. It's also blocking my memory. There's another part of me that I don't know about."

"*You* have a gem? I've only heard of a few people who were given the source, but they were people of the past. They all had it embedded in their head," Justin stated. "Does it hurt?"

"Sometimes, but I've always been able to keep it under control except recently."

"Wow, I can't believe it. You're one of them," Justin said, marveling.

"How many of us are there . . . I mean with similar abilities?"

"You, me, Justin, Alex, Cameron, and Gavin. Noelle and Raegan aren't like us. We're thinking of telling Noelle because she's been in our group for so long, and we can trust her. I don't think it'll be hard to convince Raegan. Alex can cover that one," Elsie said.

"And my family." My friends nodded their heads. *And Quinn and Garrett.*

The back door opened as Oscar ran in, followed by Raegan and Alex. "Hey guys. What are you up to? We're playing Frisbee outside," Raegan said.

"I wonder where Cam and Gavin are. I'm getting hungry. Raegan says you made a buffet," Alex said.

"We stopped two times for food. You're still hungry?" Elsie commented.

"I'm a growing boy."

"He needs the energy," I said. I studied Alex.

He returned my steady look. "Lauren understands these things. *We* need the energy to keep going."

"Well, Lauren, at least there's more people here this weekend who can out eat you," Raegan joked. We all laughed.

Someone beeped his horn loudly. I looked through the living room window and saw the familiar Ford Sport Trac. Gavin and Cameron. "They're here," I said. I could see the wire-rimmed glasses that Gavin wore and Cameron's dark blond hair, now lighter in the sunlight. I headed for the kitchen. The others stood by the front door to greet the newcomers.

"We made it, no thanks to Cameron. We got pulled over." Gavin handed Cameron his glasses. "You should try these on. I only wear them when I get tired. They may help you."

"No way, man. I can see clearly. I just got distracted. I was getting hungry." Cameron set his duffle bag and sleeping bag on the floor. "Thanks for letting us crash here."

I waved to them from the kitchen. "I'm getting the food ready."

I quickly heated the meatballs, chicken wings, and fried chicken. Mom made some lasagna, which I placed in the oven earlier along with a loaf of bread. Raegan placed the green salad, fruit salad, chips, potato salad, and pasta medley out on the table next to the two kinds of desserts and the drinks. We had a feast.

"Help yourself. I'm going to take some food next door."

"Would that be Quinn?" Alex inquired with a wink.

"Alex!" Raegan said sternly.

"What?" He looked at her mischievously then turned to me. "I mean that's nice of you, Lauren, to think of your neighbors."

"I won't be long." I left the house to deliver the food. I wasn't standing outside for long before he opened the door with a surprised look on his face. "I brought you something to eat, and for Garrett, too."

"You didn't have to worry about us; you've got your friends to entertain. But, I'm not one to turn away anything from you." He escorted me through the door. "Can you stay for a few minutes?"

"I can stay as long as you want me to." I felt myself falling into a pleasant trap.

"You should spend some time with them. I don't think they'll like me too much if I monopolize all of your time when I'm supposed to be making a good impression." He took my hand, leading me into the kitchen.

"Quinn, about all this food. I assume it's what keeps us going, and thinking, and sharp."

"Uh huh. All people need food for energy. We just use it more rapidly without the sluggish outcome. It's the gasoline in our engine, and it's what keeps our powers alive."

"Speaking of abilities, you'll be happy to learn my friends are all like us."

"I know. When there's so many of them, and they're this close, all the energy they emit is overwhelming."

"Really? I can't tell. That must be why I never picked up on it all those years. I only had a feeling something was different, but then again, I always felt that *I* was different."

"That would explain how you never knew about your friends. You couldn't feel the energy. The rock that's protecting you has its weaknesses. We'll have to ask Dr. Sendal about it."

"I'm not glowing like you are?"

"No, not in that sense." Quinn chuckled. "It must be some sort of defense mechanism to keep you hidden, so you don't fall into the wrong hands."

"And keeping me from using dark magic?"

"That's misconstrued. It's only when someone abuses his power does magic appear evil. The darkness is the unknown."

"Then how do we prevent someone from gaining too much power and abusing it?"

"If one person were to gain a great deal of power and take hold of it, then it affects us all. We would become stronger. And if that person controlled and abused the power for his own purposes, he could be met with an antagonistic rival of equal strength."

"A way to balance out power."

"Exactly. The very fabric of our existence is survival, not survival of the fittest. That's why they may try to spread out their influences rather than have a supreme ruler."

"What other powers do we have? Spells, potions . . . magic wands?"

"Only if you want to carry a stick. Everything we do that is unique is very mind centered. There isn't an official book of tricks— at least not among our kind—maybe in another faction of witchcraft. Everything is illusionary, and matter and material can be bent. That would be something to create creatures from thin air and have the ability to constantly do magic spells." I could see the excitement in his shining gray eyes. "We can wield a greater sense of reality from what is currently there and put it into motion. For example, if your room is dirty, you can change it with your mind by miraculously making it clean in seconds. You can't suddenly make a cat appear in your room, but altering someone's mind is possible. It takes a greater power."

"Someone like Raefield."

"Exactly."

"So the weather could be altered?"

"Storms can happen. But abrupt changes in weather could be created from our kind."

I knew I wasn't imagining all the dramatic shifts in weather. They were real. And the bizarre hallucinations had all been signs. My subconscious had been alerting me. But who or what controlled it? I shuddered just thinking about who might be around the corner. "And vanishing. Do we carry the same tools?"

"No, each of us has a different method to disguise ourselves. You have the bracelet. I wear a very old watch. See?" He took out a gold watch for me to examine. It was unlike anything I'd ever seen. It didn't possess the numbering and handles of a regular wristwatch. I couldn't tell the time. I could only see the ratchet wheel, the metal wheels, the winder, and what looked to be the hard stones that a wheel's rotation axle might rest upon. It lay inside the watch.

"That's amazing. It moves so effortlessly like a watch, but I can't tell the time."

"You're not supposed to."

"And Dr. Sendal, can he create potions?"

"He's dabbled in a few tonics. He's been a physician for many years, and he's spent a great deal of time creating medicines and healing treatments for our kind."

"Then we do get injured. But I don't remember having injuries or scars." I checked my arms and legs.

"We heal very quickly." Quinn reached into a kitchen drawer and took out a sharp knife. He turned his left hand over, palm facing upward, and quickly slashed his hand. He didn't flinch. A river of red formed across his hand.

"Quinn! What are you doing?" I reached for a towel.

"Just watch."

I stared at the long incision, forcing myself not to put pressure on the wound. It was closing on its own. "You're healing."

"We can heal. But I wouldn't want to try a stab wound just to see how fast I'd recover." He looked at me seriously this time. "Remember, as long as the mind is sharp, we remain strong. If the mind weakens, we're vulnerable."

I hung on his every word. Survival versus demise. I would never let them get to me. "Quinn, how do we gain more power?"

"That's for another time." He planted a tender kiss on my forehead. It wasn't goodbye. "You'd better get back to your friends before they send out a search party."

"Will you come over?"

"Not today. Garrett and I are going out tonight. You should be with your friends. We'll join you tomorrow when you visit your parents. I promise."

I left his place for mine. My invisible self was still there. The physical me mechanically walked back to my door.

"There you are. We finished eating, but I saved plenty for you. You need to keep up your strength," Raegan said.

"I ate before they came over. I'll eat again later."

"Let's put up the tent," ordered Alex. All the men and Elsie left through the back screen door.

"Hey, Lauren. Can I talk to you?" Raegan asked.

"What is it?"

"I was talking to Alex and the rest of the gang. They . . . they told me about you . . . and them."

"Oh? What about?"

"You know . . . your talents. All of you," she whispered. Raegan hesitated, unsure what to say next. Then, she asked, "Is it true?"

"I don't know what you're talking about."

"Come on, Lauren. *You* have powers."

I hesitated for a moment. "What do you mean by powers?"

Raegan rolled her eyes. Then, her olive eyes softened to an innocent green. "I promise not to say anything."

"What would you be saying?" I asked, suddenly needing not to jeopardize more people.

"*Lauren!* You can't keep it a secret!" she hissed. "They already told me what they could do. They said you were just like them. *Special.* I'm going to find out sooner or later." She continued to stare at me.

I shrugged. "It's nothing."

"Nothing? It's not *nothing*, it's *something*. You should have told me. I'm your best friend."

I looked at her this time. "I didn't actually know myself until recently. Besides, I didn't know how you would react. Aren't you a little scared dealing with people involved in . . . sorcery?"

"I'm not afraid. It's not like you're involved in dark magic. Are you?"

"That's not my intention."

She thought about it for a moment. "Well, it is a little bizarre—and very cool at the same time. I've always known you were kind of . . . different." Raegan let out a nervous laugh. "That would explain all the food and the need for sleep. Oh, Lauren, I don't care." She hugged me tightly.

Raegan was like a sister to me. And she was right, she would eventually find out, even if it were before I could practice all the things I was capable of doing.

"Lauren, aren't witches supposed to be green-faced with missing teeth, big noses, and snarly hair?"

"Only on Halloween." We both laughed. I knew she would safeguard my secrets. "Let's join the others."

We watched our friends from the patio. They placed the stakes in and put up the enormous blue tent. Gavin and Justin pulled at the guy lines, making the four lines taut. Elsie and Cameron checked the elastic strainers around the tent, each pulling it tightly so that the rainfly would be stretched evenly and securely over the tent. Alex inspected the zipper under the canopy at the entryway.

"It looks secure. A rainstorm won't get in," he said. "This tent can fit up to six people comfortably." He looked at Raegan with a sly smile. Her face turned brighter red than her hair.

"C'mon, let's go get the air mattresses and sleeping bags," Gavin said.

As we walked towards the kitchen, a burst of cold water splattered at all of us. We were soaked.

Justin.

"Yup! I think the tent is waterproof." He laughed hysterically.

"You are so dead!" cried Elsie.

They ran towards Justin, Gavin pinning him to the ground. "I think you need to cool off." Alex hosed him completely from head to toe.

"It's c-c—cold! Okay, okay. I surrender!"

"Just so you don't feel left out," Alex said, laughing.

I ran into the house, keeping the muddy spots from falling onto the clean, wooden floor. I grabbed a handful of towels and headed for the backyard. But when I returned, the soaked group were nearly dry.

"Guess you don't need these."

"My hair is still a little wet," Justin said, reaching for a towel.

"I'm impressed. Can't wait to see what else you guys can do," Raegan said, still marveling from their little trick. "Think that's enough for today." She turned off the hose.

They gathered the rest of the camping gear and set up the inside of the tent. We then headed for the living room. "I think we should stay around here tonight. We have a busy day tomorrow," I suggested.

"I agree. Let's lay low and sleep well tonight," Elsie added. "We're used to sleeping a lot." She gave Raegan a knowing smile.

"We'll take the upstairs and get ready while you guys do what you normally do," Raegan said, smirking at Alex. "The bathroom is around the corner."

"We'll be sleeping by the time you ladies get done," Alex retorted.

"Funny," Elsie replied.

I quickly got ready, grabbing a pair of shorts from my dresser and a clean linen shirt from the closet. It was still warm out tonight. I slipped on my sandals. "I'll be downstairs," I said to Raegan and Elsie from the hallway. I heard muffled voices from the hallway.

"School is easy at Platteville. I'm thinking about graduating early or taking a year off," Gavin said.

"That's because you study too much. You should take it easy and not spend so much time in the books," Cameron said.

"It's easy work. I just get bored," Gavin said.

"Guys, whatever you decide to do, we should try to stick together. Something's going on. I can feel it," Justin said.

"Justin is right. I've noticed some odd changes. Can't figure it out, though. The word around is that we may be having some visitors," Alex added.

"Yeah, but we can't risk being too close," Cameron stated. "Remember that group in the Nevada desert? There were twenty of them, and they got raided. Only ten survived."

"I don't know. It might not matter anymore. The problem was they never divided up, and they stayed in an unpopulated—"

"Hey, guys. We're almost done. Any place you want to go tonight?"

"Whatever you want, Lauren," Alex replied quickly.

Something was going to happen. Even my friends noticed. It wasn't just me that had those feelings. They were warning signs. I wondered if Quinn and Garrett felt the same way, too.

"Okay, let's go," Elsie said.

"Raegan, take Alex, Justin, and Elsie in your car and I'll drive the rest. We'll meet at Dawes Park. There's an outdoor concert tonight. It'll be something low key. The blankets are in my car."

"Save you a spot," Raegan said. They got into her car and sped away.

It was a short drive to the park. I didn't want to get into a discussion about what I'd heard until I had a chance to talk to the rest of them. It was too important. I knew we had to make some decisions.

I parked near Raegan's car. I could see her mane from a distance. They found a secluded spot to the left of the musicians on a grassy terrain under a weeping willow. We headed in that direction. I was glad to see the music enthusiasts out tonight.

A cool breeze from Lake Michigan filtered through the park, a refreshing change from the humid air circulating back at home. Just imagine, thousands of years ago, a massive glacier forged its way onto this front, forming a great lake so vast you couldn't see the other side of the shore. It was an ocean of fresh water. And along the jagged waters, the minty scent from the pines trees glistened in the air, as did the heavy, brandy wine flavor of the oak trees swirled around us. We passed a noxious, strong odor from some invasive flowering bushes before coming across the sugary scent of the crab apple trees. I noticed the feminine musk of lilacs and inhaled the evening perfumes of jasmine. It was a perfect night along the shore.

"What took you so long?" Alex asked.

"I was being careful." I surveyed the park. I couldn't allow myself to be careless for one intoxicating night. The soothing, jazz music reverberated throughout the park.

"We already checked things out. We wouldn't be sitting here if we noticed anything suspicious," Gavin informed me.

"How can you tell?" Raegan inquired.

"It's like your senses has been quadrupled, as if someone directly tells you what isn't right," Elsie informed me.

"That's way too cool. I wish I could do that." Raegan leaned back and chuckled. "Obviously, you don't melt from water. Justin proved that. And Lauren here, she sometimes takes two showers a day."

"I like to be clean."

"And I haven't gotten sick from anything she's made. No funny soups in a kettle."

We all started to laugh.

"We can show you what isn't so funny," Cameron suggested.

"Alex, show her your arm," Elsie said.

Alex lifted up his left sleeve to reveal his tan arm, but it wasn't his biceps she was looking at.

Raegan grimaced. "What happened?"

"It was a couple of years ago. I was in West Virginia helping a friend out. Apparently, I ran into our kind, but they were renegades. They believed in a new order, away from the ancient world and apart from civilized society. They believed they were elitist—following their own set of rules. They insisted I join their cause. Naturally, I resisted." He rubbed the burn marks on his arm. Each wavy line was precisely the same in length and shape, and still crimson. "They're fire marks. They call it the four staffs of unity—strength, power, obedience, and command. I call it torture."

"When he didn't return, we got concerned. We tracked him down into the deep forest of a mountainside. He escaped, but he was weakened. They knew how to bring him down," explained Elsie.

"The countryside was beautiful . . . until you took a closer look." Alex traced the lines again. "It doesn't hurt anymore. It's just a reminder. . . . "

"I can't believe they did this to you," Raegan moaned. She leaned closer to him.

"They were crazed. Their minds weren't clear. Something more powerful had gotten to them like a disease eating away at the body. I'd never seen anything like it," Alex admitted.

"We didn't stick around to find out more. They knew we were one of them, and it wouldn't be long before they would come after us," Justin added. "Once we left, they never followed us. I'm not sure if they believed it was unsafe to separate from the group or if they were afraid to live in the real world."

"If this had been the sixteen hundreds, they would have been hanged for witchcraft," Gavin informed us.

"They had a ruling wizard. He tried unsuccessfully to take more control away from the others," Alex added.

"Can anyone make those marks?" Raegan asked curiously.

"The fire marks? It takes a powerful mind to cause that kind of damage since we usually repel injury," Alex said. "I've never seen anyone do such a thing. I've only heard of a few ancients who could burn the flesh." Alex looked at me questioningly. "Being like us . . . we grow up fast. Betcha Lauren already knows that."

I didn't know how to respond to his comments. I knew I wasn't ready to leave the safety of my current way of life. I also knew I might not have a choice.

The rest of the evening continued on a lighter note. There was no talk of evil spirits and forsaken witchcraft. We were young adults. Our lives remained ahead of us, filled with hopes and dreams. We lived in the present, a world in which magic lived and flowed among us. And if the vampires and werewolves, and the ghost and goblins, roamed the land, then they lived parallel to our existence.

--->=0 0=<---

Noelle arrived ahead of us. Garrett's Audi was already in my parents' driveway. I didn't worry about Quinn not getting along with my family. They'd become quite friendly and comfortable with him after my stay in the hospital. Even my parents paid extra attention to him.

"Mom, we're here." I stood in the kitchen, my friends forming a disheveled line behind me.

"Everyone, come in. I'm glad you could all make it," Mom said.

"I'll reintroduce everyone. This is Gavin, Cameron, Elsie, Justin, Alex, and, of course, Raegan." I turned to my family. "This is my mother, my dad, my sister, Chelsea, her boyfriend, Finn, and my brother, Isaak. And this is Noelle, Quinn, and his roommate, Garrett."

"It's so nice to see those I haven't seen in awhile and those who are newer to us. All the food is set up. Please, help yourselves," Mom said to everyone. No one hesitated. We circled the table in the dining room and surrounded the kitchen island. The scrumptious feast that my mother prepared was too delicious to ignore.

"You should try the crab cakes and cucumber sauce," Noelle said to Elsie. "I don't think I'll make it to dessert."

"We won't have any problems," she replied.

My father and Isaak made their rounds to each of the guests. Mom and Raegan talked about her family's trip to New Mexico this summer. I stood between the kitchen and the dining room, watching everyone mingle. Chelsea and Finn were having an animated conversation with Quinn, Garrett, and Cameron in the kitchen. Quinn laughed at Finn's jokes. His striking face appeared playful and relaxed. He noticed my quiet observation and smiled at me. I could look at him forever.

Elsie, Gavin, and Noelle stood at the opposite side of the kitchen, discussing the concert tomorrow and who should drive. Alex suddenly moved closer to me.

"Raegan said you were out for some time at the hospital before you woke up. I wonder what caused it."

"It was nothing," I mumbled, barely listening to him.

"Lauren, what do know about Quinn?" Alex asked.

"Huh? What do you mean?"

"You haven't known this guy for long. How well do you *really* know him?"

A sharp sting poked at my sides. "Enough to know that I care about him and that he cares a great deal about me."

"Yeah, yeah. They all say that. I don't know. I'm not sure that I can trust this guy." He shook his head.

"*I* trust him. My family likes him. Our friends seem to get along with him. Alex, what are you trying to tell me?"

"There's something about *your* Quinn that I don't like. He's got a story."

Quinn suddenly stopped listening to the people around him and looked at Alex and me. He frowned. Alex stared back at him, disapprovingly.

"Look, I don't have all the facts, but I will. You're Raegan's best friend, and you're one of us. We look out for each other."

"But . . . Alex . . . *please*, he's one of us."

"Are you *sure?* I don't know. I'm having my doubts. If he turns out to be one of them, then this could mean the survival of us versus them. They've been known to infiltrate."

"Lauren, is everything okay?" Quinn put his arm around me.

"Lauren and I were just talking about friendship. We understand these things, *don't* we, Lauren?"

"I don't know, Alex. She doesn't seem to be having such a good time."

"Alex, is there a problem?" Isaak approached us from nowhere.

"I was having a friendly conversation with Lauren when Quinn rudely interrupted us," Alex said.

Quinn's eyes narrowed at Alex.

Raegan walked over to us. "Lauren, are you monopolizing Alex? He's so outgoing; he can't help himself. Alex, Lauren's mom wants you to help her carry some boxes from the garage to the house."

"Of course, Mrs. Reed. Anything you need." He walked to the dining room where my mother waited.

The kitchen conversations turned quiet. The others glanced over at us.

"He's upset you, hasn't he?" Quinn moved his hand along the back of my shoulders. "I don't know what that was all about, but if he's bothering you, I could easily take care of it."

"Quinn, it's fine. Alex is my friend. It's just a misunderstanding."

Quinn frowned. I couldn't look into his eyes, so I turned away. Isaak disappeared from our small group. He stood next to my father, whispering something to him. Chelsea and Elsie looked at us again.

"Lauren, help me put this food away and we'll pack some things for you and your friends. Noelle, can you take everyone to the family room where it's more comfortable?" Chelsea directed. I was now alone with my sister. "I noticed Alex and Quinn weren't too friendly with each other the entire afternoon."

"Alex doesn't seem to trust Quinn. He doesn't know him. He hasn't given him a chance."

She didn't respond. We continued to pack up the food and place the leftovers in the refrigerator. I felt confused. In a way, Alex was right. I really didn't know Quinn that well even though he said we've known each other longer than I could remember. He had an unfinished story to tell and a mysterious past that he never fully explained. I shook my head. Could I trust him?

I moved all the doubts to the back of my mind and focused on the present and the important people around me. Putting on a cheerful face, I smiled like the happy hostess everyone expected. The rest of the afternoon went smoothly with Alex and Quinn at opposite sides of the house. My friends and family never tried to bring them together.

"Lauren, let me know if you need anything," Mom said, looking at Alex and Quinn.

After the goodbyes, we left the house in four cars. Quinn and I were silent the entire trip home. I dropped off the food and we headed for Lincoln Park to meet my friends.

"Lauren, I know he's your friend, but I'm not sure he's such a good influence on you. He's got you upset and that bothers me."

"He was just being concerned, the way you are."

"Are you going to tell me what it was all about?"

"It's nothing at all, just Alex getting worked up. He does that sometimes. It keeps him on his feet."

Quinn didn't say anything else, but I knew he wasn't going to forget it. I buried Alex's accusations to the back of my mind. It was my weekend to spend with Quinn and my friends. I would show Alex. I would prove to him that Quinn was like us.

"Hey, Quinn. I'm glad you came out with us," Elsie said cheerfully.

"I hear you and Garrett spend time on the waters," Cameron said.

"We try when we can," Quinn replied.

"Good, because we're taking a spin around the lake. We're getting two boats and they're letting us take the wheel," Cameron said.

"Listen, Quinn. No hard feelings, okay? I was just giving Lauren a pep talk," Alex said apologetically.

"Don't worry about it," Quinn mumbled.

I kept my eyes on Alex, but he didn't look at me. He quickly walked over to where Raegan and Gavin stood. He acted playful—talking and laughing and being Alex.

The instructors waited for us by the dock. Initially, I headed for the first boat, but it was full. I strolled to the second one where Alex, Raegan, and Gavin played musical seats. Quinn grabbed my hand and we climbed into the boat.

"We'll go this way, around the lake, where there are fewer people. I'll give you a quick tour, and then let each of you try it out. She's a fast one," the captain said.

Quinn and I found two comfortable seats in the back. Raegan and Alex vied for a place at the head of the boat. Once we settled in, the captain eased us away from shore. He guided the boat around a bend through some murky sludge and choppy waters before heading out to deeper parts. The heavy blades ripped through the tangled weeds in the shallow waters until we finally moved effortlessly to calmer places. The resilient motor roared. We passed the first set of foam buoys. We went far enough in order to make the transition. Gavin took the wheel from the instructor.

"Don't worry, Raegan. I won't go as fast as you drive," Gavin said.

Raegan gripped the handrail.

Gavin maneuvered carefully and at a moderate speed. He avoided the heavy currents from some motorists who passed us not too far ahead. Then he sped effortlessly along the designated route—a simple path moving at a straight angle. His short and tightly curled dark hair glistened in the sunlight from the water drops flying in the air, and behind the aviator glasses, his amused eyes partially concealed his enthusiasm. The droplets now covered us like an afternoon spring rain. But we didn't care. We were having fun. Gavin made a final wide turn. The instructor praised him for his skillful driving and considerate awareness.

"See? I told you I could drive." He slowed the boat closer to the starting point to pass the wheel to me.

I had only driven a motorboat a few times, much less powerful than this Yamaha Output. I took the helm, anyway. At first, I crossed to the right before making a wide loop to avoid any sharp turns close to shore. Then I glided across the shimmery lake at a steady pace, proving I could flow with the current. It felt easy.

An unexpected burst of wind blew onto the waters we traveled along as the waves pushed harder on the lake. I coasted onward despite the sudden warning. I felt fearless. We reached my friends in the other motor craft across the waters. The MasterCraft they drove moved as fast as ours until we glided at the same speed. Then they decided to make a sharp left turn. I could hear the screaming and laughter coming from their boat. The captain instructed me to slow down and directed me to turn back.

"Not too bad, young lady," the captain said. "Who's next?"

"I think I'll pass. I don't want to be too reckless," Raegan said. "Quinn?"

"I'm good."

"In that case, I'll take her out," Alex said. He grabbed the wheel of the boat.

Quinn and I took the seats at the head of the boat. My life jacket remained securely on. I knew Alex was proficient in speed boating. He's spent many summers on the Minnesota lakes, navigating through treacherous waters. I waited for more. Alex passed less powerful boats and a few luxury cabin cruisers until he raced smoothly across the waters. The sun reached eye level, leaving sparkles of light blindingly across the lake. My shades were no match for the powerful sun. Alex continued to move us deeper into the lake, avoiding sudden turns and any loops. I looked over at Quinn. He just looked ahead. I closed my eyes for a moment, letting the cool air fly around me.

It became longer than a few minutes. The waters began to take a different form—midnight blue and charcoal gray with the lapping waves moving heavy and high. I turned to find a barely-visible shoreline disappearing. Even the sky turned a dirty white haze. Yet, Alex didn't slow down. He was steady and confident. We motored along as if we headed to some planned destination.

"Maybe you should turn this around!" the instructor shouted.

Alex forged ahead. He was on autopilot. We came across the first set of bright red, conical buoys. It was a guide for cargo ships to know when they neared land. Even though we went exceedingly far, I felt alive and free. I wanted to go further to the unknown. My dark mane blew wildly in the wind. I wasn't sure why I did what I did next. I think I became caught up in the thrill of the ride. Quinn stood up for some reason, possibly in response to my sudden movement. He looked at me strangely. I leaned over the ledge, nearly tipping over the metal rail. I inhaled the lake's fresh breeze. Quinn's hand reached out to me, but I only smiled at his worried face.

"Hey, be careful, miss! He's driving pretty fast!" I heard the instructor call out.

"Alex! What are you doing?" Gavin bellowed. *"You're going too far! Turn the boat around!"*

"Just wait! You'll see." Alex sped even faster.

The light broke through. Quinn grabbed me before I lost my balance, but I wasn't falling. I was in complete balance. Raegan shouted my name, wondering what I was doing. I didn't respond. I was soaring. Raegan called out to me again, this time shrieking in laughter and fear.

"Alex, where are we going?" she asked.

"You'll see!"

"Turn this boat—," the instructor yelled right before turning completely silent.

The eruption unleashed, but I was still in control. I didn't feel the pain. I looked at the frozen man: he was statuesque and very lifelike. I looked at Quinn and smiled. He held onto me, his eyes wide and stark.

"*I knew it!*" shouted Alex. "*Here we go!*"

"What's going on?" screamed Raegan. She held tightly onto Alex.

I couldn't stop it. It came out of me. The energy was too great for me to hold on to. But I didn't want to. I let it escape freely.

"*Lauren, your eyes are glowing!*" Raegan yelled. Gavin's mouth hung wide open. Alex looked justified. Quinn let go of me but stood nearby. He looked scared.

Gavin held onto his seat. "Are we really—?"

"*Yes, we're flying!*" Alex roared.

The speedboat took on another capacity. Instead of gliding through the waters, it floated in the air at the same speed as if it were in water. I gave it wings, and it felt good to have that control.

"*Woo-hoo!*" Alex bellowed. "*Look at us go!*"

"*Lauren, you rock!*" Raegan yelled in excitement.

It was effortless. I couldn't feel the work I put forth, only the energy flowing out of me. The boat merely followed my internal command. As we continued to climb, the city's skyline shrunk in the distance, and I knew we reached a level unheard of for people traveling outside of planes. We moved smoothly and freely in the misty white sky as the moisture rose and settled on my skin. The lake moved so far away. I was still amazed.

We continued to fly across the lake until the sky turned deep blue again. I was still glowing. I thought about the heavens cushioning us in a blanket of white. I didn't want to think about falling. That would not happen today, or ever, if I could help it. In this high altitude, my friends and I were protected from the normal struggles of oxygen loss by the carefree way everyone acted. Even Raegan was immune. She came up to me, cautiously.

"Lauren, how do you feel? I'm afraid to . . . touch you. You look the same except your eyes are so green . . . and they're still glowing."

"Like nothing at all. It's a breeze." The energy still circumvented inside of me. I felt its electrical surge move through my veins and organs and flow out of my skin.

"This is amazing. I've only heard of people doing this. I've not actually seen it," Gavin said, no longer frightened. "Wait 'til I tell the others."

Alex remained quiet at the wheel. His observant eyes remained focused.

"Lauren, let's turn around and go home," Quinn said with caution.

I ordered the boat to turn around and travel back to land. It did as instructed, moving smoothly and at a steady pace. Again, it felt effortless to command. We flew southbound at the same speed we had departed. The eerie clouds we passed dispersed this time so that the blue sky came through. I allowed the boat to slowly descend like a plane ready to hit the tarmac.

The boat glided downward with ease until it gently touched the crystal blue lake. I let go of the control and allowed the propeller to take over. Alex was ready at the wheel. I smiled at Quinn victoriously. Quinn motioned to the instructor and turned back at me.

". . . *I said, let's turn this boat around!* Huh? Oh, I guess we're moving that way," the instructor said, looking puzzled.

"Did you say something? We're almost to shore. I didn't want to go too far," Alex said. He drove us in the direction of the late afternoon sun. The instructor remained silent. He sat quietly in his chair, looking out at the waters and shaking his head. Gavin and Raegan quietly laughed in the back of the boat.

"How do you feel?" Quinn asked.

"Good, but somewhat tired, like my energy suddenly went into hibernation. Hungry, too."

"That's what I expected. You used a good amount of energy up there. You're probably using your reserves to avoid being depleted."

"That was fun. We should do that again."

Quinn frowned. "Let's save the showing off for another time."

My other friends waved and shouted to us from land. Alex steered the boat until he stopped along the side of the wooden dock, against the padded cushions. We quickly tied the ropes to the dock and left the instructor standing behind us.

"*Where* have you guys been?" Elsie asked.

"We took another route. Lauren took us sight seeing," Gavin scoffed. Instead of looking surprised, they appeared interested. Gavin and Raegan followed the first group to the car. I lagged behind with Quinn and Alex trailing me.

"The next time you want to make a point, do it on your own time. *Not* at Lauren's expense," Quinn lectured.

"Relax, *Quinn*. She was fine. I wanted to see what she could do with that rock in her head. And it gave me a chance to see how *you* would react," Alex said.

"What's that supposed to mean?" Quinn snapped.

"For starters, the stunt you pulled in the boat with the instructor. Very clever. I would have done the same thing if greater powers had descended upon me. What else can you do?"

Quinn remained silent, but I knew he was fuming. *Oh Alex, why can't you see Quinn is one of us?*

"No answer, huh? Can you see why I have my doubts? I'm not sure what you might do next. Maybe you're hiding something. Maybe you're working for them. We have to be careful nowadays." He stopped his ranting for a moment. "I'll give you credit for helping her out, and for not letting her fall into the lake. But, you knew we were watching you."

"Don't *ever* think I would hurt Lauren," Quinn said sternly. "If you have a problem with me, I'll be glad to settle it for you. Don't *ever* expose Lauren like that again. Got it?"

"Whoa . . . take it easy. We don't want to make a scene," Alex said.

"How do I know you're not one of them?" Quinn asked this time.

"You don't. You just can tell. Besides, I've been with them for years. If I wanted to harm them, I would have done something by now or be destroyed by the group," Alex said. He dashed to where the others were walking. He put his arm around Raegan's shoulder.

I slowed down in order for Quinn to catch up to me. He looked saddened. "I'm sorry you had to hear it. Alex is wrong, you know. I'm not one of them. I would never hurt you in that way."

"I know. He doesn't know you. He has no idea how caring you are. And don't be sorry. I needed to hear what he was thinking. He can be so reckless sometimes and push people to the edge. He just needs convincing. And at the same time figure out the next step." I lowered my face so Quinn wouldn't see my thoughts.

"You feel it, too?" Quinn asked.

"Without a doubt." We walked silently to the car, hand-in-hand. The smoky gray clouds and bleak sky moved in. Despite my growing fears and the possible danger we faced, this was where I wanted to be. Here, with my friends and with him.

CHAPTER 13

Bonds That Tie

THE DRIVE DOWNTOWN was surprisingly smooth with traffic flowing at a steady pace for a Saturday evening. Gavin took Raegan's car and Alex drove his. Garrett followed Alex's deep red SUV.

"I could bump him if you want me to," Garrett said.

"Don't waste your time. It'll cause more damage to your car," Quinn said. "He's not worth it. I have bigger issues to deal with."

"Lauren, we're just having fun. We don't mean any harm to your friends. Alex is a little uptight, but I can see why he's uneasy. We had a long talk. He'll try to settle down when it comes to Quinn," Garrett said.

"Lauren, don't worry about me. I can take care of myself. Alex doesn't scare me. I'm more concerned if he gets you worked up," Quinn said from the back seat.

"Anyway, he showed me his fire marks. That's pretty wicked stuff." Garrett quickly glanced at Quinn then turned right back to the wheel. "I've seen it once out west, on a man who had a similar mark, but it wasn't as defined as Alex's."

"He's had it rougher than the rest of them. He gets worked up and is vigilant about his surroundings, but it doesn't mean that the rest of my friends aren't as sharp. Alex likes to live carefree. He doesn't want another sect ruling him," I explained.

"Don't we all? Our freedom means everything to us. We live among everyday people without drawing attention to our kind. Those who wish to live apart and away from wizards, do so in seclusion or as secular," Quinn said. "The ones who bring harm and chaos are the people that could destroy our existence. They want power and control. They want to send mankind back to the repressive days of the ancients."

"Lauren, we're like everyone else, but we've been given special powers for some unknown reason. Why? I'm not sure if it's for some higher purpose or because certain people are meant to have greater abilities. My parents aren't like me, but they've accepted who I am," Garrett added. "It was passed on to me."

I knew they were right. I just had more at stake, and an identity still undiscovered. Plus, a precious stone that people would kill for.

Cursed gem!

We reached the Revival Theater where Alex and Justin's friend, Connor Justice, and his band, Justice's Revenge, were headlining. Being friends with the lead singer got us free tickets into the venue. Adam Tran, along with the female vocalist, Sydney Knox, and the rest of the band had performed this past spring on a worldwide tour and now made Chicago their home. They'd just recorded their second album, *Under Pursuit*, in which my current favorite song, "Fallen Angel", had made its debut.

"Let's go inside before it gets too crowded. I don't want to have to stand in line with everyone else," Alex commented.

"You wouldn't want to come off as being a commoner, would you?" Justin remarked.

"Unless you want to stay out here, be my guest. I suspect there'll be quite an interesting mix of people in no time." He turned around and said to us, "Quinn, Garrett, you're going to like the show. Connor is a great performer."

"Lauren, how do I look? Do you think Raegan's top looks good on me?" Noelle asked.

"You look great. The guys will be after you." She wore Raegan's Chanel top, a pair of dark denim jeans, and metallic black heels. Noelle's rich, brunette hair and blunt bangs shaped her sweet face and brownie–colored eyes. Tonight, with the extra makeup on, she'd transformed herself into a vixen.

"What are we, decorations?" Cameron glowered.

"That's not what she meant. You guys are great . . . like brothers," Noelle quickly said.

"Brothers. How typical," Cameron mumbled.

"I'm Alex Beechan, and this is Justin Kim. We're friends of the band. They're all with us."

"Let me see . . . right. Okay, let's tag everyone and you can go this way." The bouncer showed us to the door.

"Alex, Justin, glad you made it. It's going to be big. We played at Baker's Hall last week. Like the place, but it's too crowded," Connor said. "These must be your friends. We're having a party after the show. Stick around."

"Relax, he's not one of us," Quinn whispered in my ear. Connor had tattoos on both arms and wings of a dove along the side of his right neck.

The hall filled up fast. The lights were already dimmed but not completely turned off. Everything from punk rock to gothic to metal to prep boys and even glamour girls walked through the door. We found our seats in center front, but would move to the pit shortly.

"This is so exciting. I *love* their songs. Lauren and I have all the lyrics memorized," Raegan informed everyone. She took out her cellphone and began taking photos of the hall. Gavin took out his new camera.

The laser lights and atmospherics came across the stage after the main venue lights were turned off. The drummer, bassist, Adam, and Sydney came on stage to the roar of the crowd. A fog wall formed on stage. Sydney set herself up at the keyboards: her platinum blonde, pixie hair glowed in the lights. The drummer began pounding away, setting the tempo of the song as the crowd roared to the music. There was no opening act tonight.

Connor came on stage as the CO2 jets spouted at various points. The crowd went wild, chanting his name. His dark hair was styled with enough glue to paste a wall, and the theatrical make-up he wore and the tight, dark pants and white T-shirt made the girls scream. He bellowed out the first song along with Sydney in a rhapsodic harmony. I felt captivated. I sang to the lyrics and swayed my arm like the rest of the crowd. Quinn stood behind me, his arms wrapped around my waist. He was really enjoying the show.

Alex and Justin walked toward the stage. I noticed the crowd willingly move away. They wore gold bands on their right third finger. I held onto my bracelet. Elsie wore a pendant necklace of an intertwining circle within a circle. Both Gavin and Cameron sported silver bands tonight. I knew Quinn wore his watch.

The concert played on with Connor stopping after every other song to address the crowd. They performed songs from their current release and included a few hits from their debut album. The fans screamed and shouted for more. The array of lights and pyrotechnics mesmerized. In the fog that rose, Connor looked death-like but held onto his emotions as he belted out the murky lyrics. A spotlight flashed on Adam's solo performance. His blue-streaked hair complimented his deep cerulean lips. Then *Fallen Angel* came on. I was bewitched by the slow, haunting melody.

> *. . . I followed you into the wondrous place*
> *Here alone you hide your face*
> *Staring at the glassy pond*
> *Shadows of broken dreams*
> *Can the midnight clearing be more than just a scheme?*

If in my eyes you are the light
Of angels span above great height
Now fallen from the highest nest
Only to search in the deepest night
For the time to mourn gone is rest
Woman child your day has been put to test
You run no more
The old leave as new time lives
Is innocence once was how she gives
Now I've fallen, fallen like the angel
Guardian to the night of shadows
Fallen, and run this way, to the age of days before such times
Fallen, and run so fast, along the edge trapped here to stay. . . .

Then something disrupted my mood. My supernatural friends diverted their attention, too, from the hypnotic performers to the shadows approaching us in the mist. Their relaxed demeanor faded. Their eyes became fixed and focused, and their bodies held a defensive posture. Something moved towards us even if I couldn't feel the energy emitted. I felt defenseless.

"Well, what do we have here? A gathering of great minds. Hello, *Quinn*, so good to see you again," scoffed Mercedes. She approached us as every head from the audience turned to face us. "You remember Nicholas." The quiet, scar-faced man nodded once with cold, dark set eyes looking away from us.

Alex glared at Quinn. His fists formed tight balls, ready to strike. My other friends were less dramatic, but the seriousness on their faces told me they weren't amused. Even a cheerful Raegan found silence to be appropriate. Quinn's face remained stern as he looked at the new guests on the floor.

"And who do we have here? Could this be our *precious* Lauren?"

"Don't even *think* of touching her," Quinn growled. Garrett stood close by, waiting. I wasn't sure what he was capable of doing.

"Touchy, touchy. Relax, fearless one. I wouldn't *dream* of hurting Raef's prized possession." She came over and weaved her gaunt claws into my hair. "She is a pretty one."

"Don't touch me."

She took a step back, her clever smile regaling. "Lovely Lauren. You and I are going to be good friends. In time, you'll have no choice but to depend on me." She suddenly stopped herself. She crossed in front of me, moving from side to side. She began to scowl. *"What* is this? It can't be. *Nicholas,* what do you make of her?"

The somber man edged closer. "She's different. I can't feel a pull." His eyes narrowed and turned back to a vexed Mercedes. "Are you sure we have the right person? She's not like us."

"Of *course*, I'm sure. She's the same person," Mercedes snapped. She looked at me furiously. *"What* have you done to yourself?"

"Nothing. I've done nothing wrong."

"See? She's not the same person. She's no use to Raefield any longer." Quinn and Garrett moved closer to each side of me.

Mercedes kept a sharp eye on me as she sneered with contempt. "Oh, I'm sure we can find out what's really going on," she hissed. With a sudden wave of her hand, the hall came to a standstill except for us. "There. She's still one of us." A clanking noise rose from a distant corner on the stage, and a curtain slowly moved in the direction of the sound.

"Boys, let's be amicable about this. We are . . . family in a sense."

"You're no relative of mine," Alex grumbled.

"Silence! I could easily destroy you with a draw of my hand," Mercedes said. She gave Alex a hard look. I gripped Quinn's hand.

"I highly doubt that. Should we test it out?" he retorted.

"That's enough! Mercedes, what do you want?" Quinn demanded.

"Quinn, I knew you could be reasonable. This is merely a peaceful mission. We just want a closer look at our darling." Mercedes inched closer to me. Quinn and Garrett remained at my side, neither one flinching. Alex continued to glare at Mercedes and Nicholas.

Mercedes put her cool hands to my face, lifting it up at an angle. I kept still. "She is quite stunning. I can see why she's held you for so long." My friends looked at Quinn, puzzled. Garrett was the only one not surprised.

"What do you want with Lauren?" Elsie cautiously asked.

"To keep a close eye on her. You never know who else might be drawn to her. Don't worry. We don't plan to harm her. She's too valuable to us."

"How do we know you won't change your mind?" Quinn insisted.

Nicholas broke his silence. "You have our word. Raefield wants her alive at all cost." The strangely quiet and austere man smiled wryly. "Think of it this way, we could be protecting you from some vagabond group who would like nothing more than to rip the gem right out of your head. Even Raefield would be tempted."

I gasped. I felt the arteries in my neck tighten.

Mercedes started to laugh. "Nicholas, you can be so honest sometimes. Let's not scare the witch right out of her. You know the gem may be useless without its host." She turned to me. "No need to fret, dear Lauren. You are expected to remain alive as requested by Raefield."

Even in the dim light, I saw Quinn's face turn red and the veins pop out of his arms. His viselike grip eased. Before he could bellow something, Mercedes put her hand in the air to stop what he might have hurled at them.

"Let's not start a pointless conflict. When you look at the bigger picture, we really have similar ideals and interests. It would be a shame to set such a dividing line between us when, in reality, if these regular humans ever knew what we possessed, you know what they would do," Mercedes said.

"We've heard enough. I want you out of here before this turns into a meaningful conflict," Quinn said through clenched teeth.

There were only silent exchanges and angry looks between my friends. I hesitated to say anything else, lest start an unofficial war.

Mercedes grew furious. "You mean these *normal* people you find so important who would turn on you given the chance? They're nothing compared to us! We would benefit from a few less." With that, Nicolas and Mercedes drew a sharp blade into two defenseless, frozen strangers.

"Noooo!" I started to charge at them for what they'd just done, but I felt an arm yank me back. I scowled at Quinn. Even my friends looked angry, terrified, or in shock.

"Let go of me, Quinn!" I pulled him so hard, he nearly collapsed into me. My strength surprised me.

Mercedes let out a deafening laugh so high and grating, we found it unbearable. She waved her hand in the air and the venue came back to life. The awakened audience looked confused or some just continued to dance like nothing had even happened. In seconds, the pair left the hall. I just stared at where the two had stood.

Then, a girl screamed. And another person alerted everyone of the bodies found on the floor.

The audience panicked. People shouted about dead people on the floor and yelled for help. Those at the center section of the hall ran toward the exits as the band stopped playing. Fear and chaos dominated, confusion sweeping through the hall. I wanted to scream. I couldn't believe this was happening because of me. My world was falling apart. Now, my friends were forced to be a part of this tangled, paranormal life I hadn't chosen.

⇥▅◯ ◯▅⇤

An hour later, the police cleared everyone out and the crime scene technicians removed the two bodies. Raegan and Noelle held onto each other tightly. Two other girls cried about the friends they'd just lost. I couldn't say anything. I didn't feel anything but anger. Quinn stood nearby, observing my unbreakable hold. I couldn't take my eyes off the scene. A summer breeze blew in, which eased the coldness I felt.

Alex became restless. He paced the pavement, pointing his finger at Quinn. "*This* is all of your doing. Ever since you came into Lauren's life, it's been nothing but mystery and strange events. Now there's two dead people and those crazy witches are after her."

"Just hold on, Alex. You don't have all the facts. Quinn didn't bring them here. They've been looking for her for quite some time," Garrett said.

"*What?* How can you explain the coincidence?" Alex fumed.

My thoughts finally broke away from the flashing red and white lights. "It's my fault. They wouldn't have been here if it wasn't for me. This tragedy happened because they needed to show their will, directed at me. They killed two innocent people. I can't begin to tell you how sorry and angry I am."

Elsie looked sympathetic. "No, Lauren, it's not your fault." She put her arm around my shoulder. "Nobody knew they would come and do this. But now we know what they'd do just to make a point."

"But why surface now? Why suddenly make an appearance after all this time? Unless it was because they knew *he* was around." Alex looked scornfully at Quinn again.

"Alex. My parents have been tracking them for the past year. I think they've been here longer than that, and definitely longer than Quinn has been in Chicago," I said.

Quinn let out an audible sigh. "Lauren, Alex is right. They've kept away from you until I came into your life again." He looked away. I shook my head. I didn't want to see him hurting.

"Quinn, man, don't be so hard on yourself. You said they've had leads on her longer than you have, that they were able to set out looking for her before you had the chance." Garrett glanced at the others for support.

"They don't want to harm me. It's the gem they want. They have strict orders from Raefield not to touch me. Maybe they wanted to make sure no one else would get to me, or take me away." I shot a serious look at Quinn. The idea sounded good right now.

My friends looked puzzled. Yet, they didn't ask any questions even though I'm sure they had many.

"Let me get this straight. From what Mercedes said back at the hall and from what you're telling us now, you and Lauren have known each other longer than the month we were told?" Alex bluntly asked.

"Yes. But the stone in Lauren's head has made her forget. I know it's hard to understand, but I need your cooperation in letting me deal with this on my own terms. You understand the eruptions in her head can happen when her mind is overly challenged. Until she can fully control the impulses in her brain, she's not completely safe from her own self."

They looked at each other then back at Quinn. "Sure, Quinn, we got you," Gavin said.

"Yeah, no problem," Cameron said. The girls all nodded in unison. Only Alex remained silent. He nodded mechanically as he stood away from the group.

"I've been getting better at controlling what I want and how to wield the power I have. Remember the boat excursion?" I glanced over at Alex. Again, he said nothing. His expression only grew darker.

Raegan suddenly spoke up and said, "Hey, that's great that you've known each other longer. Just wish I could remember Lauren telling me about you. Her memory must be blocked." She stopped herself before going any further. "I think we're going in the right direction. She'll remember everything soon."

"Yes, I only hope she can. But if that doesn't come, the new memories will be just as wonderful." His gray eyes appeared supportive. I could be hopeful again.

-→═◉ ◎═◄-

Back at the house, our mood became less somber. My friends kept a normal tone as they told stories from the enormous tent. I checked my phone for messages. Mom called to ask how my weekend was going with my friends, and I also got a message from Sherry.

"Hey, Lauren. Sorry it took me so long to get back to you. I'm at another fashion party as you can tell. About that woman . . . her name is Mercedes Kar. She's quite wealthy and attends a lot of fashion premieres. She's been seen around some important people but has stayed out of the media except for the past six months. Hope this helps! Bye, darling, and can't wait to see you again. Say 'hi' to everyone."

That confirmed what I already knew. What is Mercedes really up to? I thought anonymity would serve her better. Then, I thought back to what Quinn said about the high life appealing to them—the money, the power, and what wealth can bring. My analysis broke. Alex suddenly approached me from out of the darkness.

"Hey, Lauren. I just want to apologize for giving Quinn such a hard time. Whatever is going on, I'll try to keep an open mind. You can understand where I'm coming from. He doesn't give us much to go on, but I'm sure he has his reasons. Just . . . be careful, that's all," Alex said sincerely. He stood against the wall next to the kitchen door facing me on the patio. He pointed his flashlight downward. "And, Lauren, we'll understand when the time is right that you may have to leave. We'll be here if you need us." He went back to join the others in the tent.

I didn't know what to think. Was I going somewhere, or would I have to leave in order to save myself and those around me? The thought passed me briefly in a surprising acceptance of what might occur, followed by a wave of sorrow in leaving my home, the place I knew so well. When the time was right, I would know what to do.

Or would I?

I looked up at Quinn's bedroom to see the light still on. Was he as concerned about the future as I was? Something kept him awake. I went back inside. I couldn't do anything else tonight except to stay here with the people I cared about. That was enough for now.

⋙ ⋘

Sunday morning arrived like a completely different day. It felt as if last night might never have happened. My friends and I were in a festive mood. The only sadness that lingered today was the fact that they would be going back home. It hit Raegan the hardest. This weekend had brought her and Alex closer than they'd been since our summers in Duluth. We ate out for brunch, Quinn and Garrett joining us. The atmosphere felt less strained.

"We'll be back after the Fourth when you have your party. We'll try not to bring the entire campus," Alex joked. I suspected Raegan would be visiting them at least once before their return to Chicago.

Noelle said her goodbyes and left us right after lunch to go to work. I could see Raegan holding back her tears. They locked in an embrace, standing away from the rest of us.

"Quinn, if you ever want to go north, just let us know," Gavin offered.

"Or, if you decide to come to Minneapolis with Lauren, we have extra room," Elsie added. "But don't take too long to decide. We may be making some changes in the near future." She gave Justin a wary look.

"What changes?" I asked.

"We've been talking about moving. Only recently was the issue pushed." Justin looked at me cautiously.

It started to happen. The plans and the constructed ideas were in motion, perhaps taking seed long before this weekend. This time they were serious.

"I think Chicago would be a great idea," I told them. "It would keep us closer."

"Yeah, I think now more than ever we should stick together," Justin answered. He looked back at Elsie with certainty. "Everything happens for a reason. It'll work itself out." She didn't look convinced.

"We better get back. Gavin and I haven't decided what we're going to do. We agree with Justin. This time sticking together is a better idea than living in different cities—strength in numbers—but we may head as far north as Clam Lake before coming to Chicago. There's an old friend we'd like to see. We'll let you know." Cameron started to laugh. "Too bad there isn't a car that would take us cross country without fueling up. You never know when you need to run." He headed for the black truck.

"It may not happen until after Halloween. We'll let the others get settled first . . . keep it from being too obvious," Gavin said. He got into the passenger side. The dark truck headed in the direction of the ninety-four freeway.

"Okay, I'm ready. Let's go," Raegan said, urging us along. She watched as Alex's SUV headed for the freeway.

"Don't be too upset. We'll see them again, sooner than you think." She looked at me curiously, now with a sparkle of hope behind her olive eyes.

Quinn drove us out of the parking lot of the restaurant and in the opposite direction our friends had taken. This time it was Raegan who stared out the window. She didn't look distraught, as I had been the day of the fashion show. Then again, she didn't have two strangers following her. No, Raegan was simply quiet, almost too quiet.

"I think we should see Dr. Sendal. We need to get a better understanding of what we're dealing with, and what he can do to help us," Quinn said.

"I agree."

"I'll call him and let him know we're coming over this afternoon."

CHAPTER 14

Treats and Tricks

DR. SENDAL'S IMMACULATE condominium was filled with heavy furniture pieces, paintings—replicas of past masters and modern works of art—shelves of books along the deep-colored walls, and figurines scattered throughout the house. His place conveyed that a worldly person lived here.

"Excuse the mess. I haven't had time to clean, and my cleaning lady is on vacation," Dr. Sendal apologized. I didn't notice a mess. Everything looked neat and organized with an antique flare. "Can I get you anything to eat or drink? I just fixed myself some hot tea."

"Don't go out of your way. We just ate," Quinn said.

"No trouble at all. I made a full pot." He walked through the swinging, mahogany door into the kitchen. I looked around his living room for the one piece of artwork you couldn't buy at the store: family photos.

It was strange. I knew Dr. Sendal was a widower. He spoke of his wife briefly when he dined at my parents' place, and I remember my mother telling me that she passed away due to scarlet fever, an old scourge. On one end table, I found photos of him and his colleagues at a conference and with some friends on a tropical vacation. I walked over to the marble mantelpiece where vases and candlesticks and more photos lined the shelf. There were scenery pictures of Lake Michigan, Chicago, Paris, and a city that looked vaguely familiar. New Haven.

"Lauren, what is it?" Quinn asked, standing up from the coffee colored leather sofa.

"Take a look at this."

Quinn came over and looked at the photos. "It looks like New Haven. Must be fairly recent." He examined the photo like an antique specialist. I think he memorized every detail of the harbor city. Quinn still didn't look at me, as he returned to the sofa.

The swinging door opened again with Dr. Sendal carrying a tray of tea and coffee and a few sweet treats neatly lined on a porcelain plate. "Here we are, an afternoon snack." He poured the hot beverage into each cup. Dr. Sendal finally asked, "What's on your mind?"

"I'm sure you know why we're here." The seriousness returned to Quinn's face.

"Of course, I do. But does it need to be so . . . grave?" Dr. Sendal steeped the tea from the tea ball in the porcelain teapot. "When I was young," he said, chuckling. "A long time ago. I took myself very seriously. I thought I was fighting time, that my life meant nothing unless I did something . . . *was* someone. So I always rushed, and I worked hard, but I never enjoyed the life a young man should have. My parents even said I had the mind of an adult. They were right. Everything seemed so urgent to me . . . until I met Sarah, my bride. She changed me. She taught me how to enjoy this life—*live* this life—even if it could end tomorrow. And if despair stood around the corner, waiting in the darkest places to consume the life in me, I should wait and be patient until my perspective changed. It usually did. What I believed to be lost or troublesome or even dangerous had a way of settling into place." He met my gaze. "What can I do to help?"

I'd never seen this side of Dr. Sendal. I knew a serious and educated person with a pleasant demeanor who came over to my parents' place on occasion. It was refreshing to see a personal side of him. In his fifties, he appeared closer to his forties. Only a few strands of gray hair covered his head.

"Dr. Sendal, there's several things we want to talk to you about," Quinn began. "What can you tell us about the rock in Lauren's head? You said it was too soon to remove it. I'm wondering if it should be removed at all. Could it be catastrophic for Lauren?" Quinn gave me a rueful look.

"You bring up a valid point. As I had said in the hospital, it's too soon to remove the gem. Honestly, I don't know what would happen to Lauren if we prematurely extracted the rock from her head." He turned to me apprehensively. "In my limited experience, I've only successfully removed a stone once before its time, and that person miraculously returned to his previous state. I've witnessed another rock being removed from another person."

"What happened to that person?" I asked.

"It wasn't a good outcome."

I felt a chill run down my spine.

Dr. Sendal turned to us again and said, "If you're concerned about the possible harm the stone could do while it's in your possession, I think it would benefit you to look at it in a different light. Aside from causing her to forget, think of the advantages it has." Dr. Sendal refilled his empty teacup.

"You probably noticed she isn't as recognizable to us as she should be—an added bonus when some undesirable person is looking for her. And the additional power she has puts her ahead of most of us." Dr. Sendal grinned. "I'm sure you've tested out some of your newfound abilities. What have you discovered?"

"That I can make myself disappear, which I found out was basic to all of us. I can walk through doors while invisible, and I can move objects around me."

"Yes, yes."

"Move *many* people around me and float in the sky."

"You were able to fly?" Dr. Sendal asked excitedly.

"Yes, carrying a boat full of people—fly across Lake Michigan above the clouds without much effort."

"Amazing. I can only whisk myself through several rooms and reappear in another."

"Move across several rooms? I haven't tried that one." I looked at a studious Quinn.

"You haven't shown her that trick yet? Basically, we can move from place to place without being seen. It's similar to being invisible, but we can't go very far before reappearing. Otherwise, we'd get to places much faster. You, on the other hand, might be able to cover more ground."

"Another way to sneak up on people." I was slightly amused. I wanted more. "Dr. Sendal, besides having a stone imbedded in my head, how does someone gain more power?"

Dr. Sendal raised his eyebrow. "By killing one of our own."

I didn't look at Quinn. I remembered Alex mentioning Quinn had extraordinary powers. I also knew that Alex possessed more skills than my other friends. His time in West Virginia had been difficult. Survive or be killed by the deranged pack.

But who could have Quinn fought? And why?

"Lauren, try to make yourself reappear outside like this," Dr. Sendal instructed. He brought his arms to the core of his body in a defensive position with his hands forming a fist. His eyes were closed. In a few seconds, his body spun so fast that, in several blinks of the eye, he vanished from sight.

"Look over here." Quinn led me to the living room window of the condo.

We looked down at the ground from four stories up where normally a birch tree stood, only now Dr. Sendal was leaning against the white tree. He looked up at us. I moved away from the window. "And I can do that?"

"Lauren, I'm sure you can do better," Dr. Sendal said, standing behind me. "For now, try to focus on the same tree. Get a feel for it."

I did what he said. I focused on the sole birch tree across the street. It wasn't hard to concentrate. I felt the energy surge in my mind, singling out the tree and back to me. Like a powerful force of nature, I felt myself spin incredibly fast with every particle of me moving as one until I became nothing but the passing breeze in the living room where Quinn and Dr. Sendal stood. In a rapid moment, I reappeared outside, standing next to the edge of the same tree Dr. Sendal had stood near.

I did it! I transformed myself from one place to another. My growing powers felt sensational, and I wanted to learn every magical trick possible. Finally, coming into my own in this supernatural world. I felt like an undisputed witch!

In the same way as I came to the tree, I would return. I focused on Dr. Sendal's place. He and Quinn watched me from the window. A heartbeat later, I disappeared. "Looking for me?" I asked, walking through the swinging kitchen door.

"Excellent! You moved well. That was very fluid." Dr. Sendal clapped his hands in approval. "The movement from one point to another is so fast, no one can really see the spin before you become like dust. The inertia. Your molecules just float in the air momentarily before reaching its destination."

"Show me something else."

"You don't want to take a break?" Dr. Sendal asked.

"No, I feel good. I don't feel hungry at all. In fact, I feel energized."

"Me, too," Quinn responded. He looked over at Dr. Sendal. "What did we just have?"

"A special drink. I call it the vitality tea. Do you like it?"

"A special drink?" I asked.

"Yes, it's something I came up with. It's a mixture of special herbs. I was surprised to be able to find the ingredients so easily. The drink gives you lasting energy. It keeps your strength going without leaving you hungry. It's especially useful in times of famine."

"That's amazing, Uri. How long does it last?" Quinn asked.

"It varies with each individual. I would say what we consumed today should last us another six to eight hours. With Lauren, I'm not sure."

I gained a whole afternoon and the beginning of the evening without eating—the *need* to eat. I was amazed. Raegan would be shocked. My grocery bills could be cut in half. I chuckled to myself.

"Let's try something else. Quinn, why don't you show her your trick?"

"I'm not sure it's such a good idea."

"She'll find out sooner or later."

"Yes, Quinn, why don't you *tell me* about your trick," I insisted. I was ready.

Quinn hesitated. He didn't make eye contact right away. When his pewter eyes gazed upon me, a quiet alarm and worry overshadowed his gray eyes. He reached for me, touching my warm face until heat emanated from my skin. I was falling.

Dr. Sendal cleared his throat.

"Right," Quinn said. He walked closer to Dr. Sendal, touching his head with both hands. He concentrated, but he didn't look strained. Neither did Dr. Sendal at first. Then it happened. It wasn't physical pain that came from the wise man. It was another kind of pain, something we all have felt.

"Okay, that's enough," Dr. Sendal said, moving away from Quinn's grasp. "I was trying to block it, but you were persistent. Have you been working on this?"

"I haven't used it since the time I was in California, when I was in Sacramento."

"It's quite strong. Stronger than the time we had tried it out. I . . . I was fighting." Dr. Sendal regained his composure. "In any case, you were able to dig deeper."

"You've tested this out before? Guess I'm not surprised. Obviously, you two have a history." I looked directly at Quinn. "What exactly did you do?"

"I was able to go inside his mind, pull out his fears and his grief, and bring them to the surface. At that level, I can magnify his most intimate concerns and turn them into a nightmare, giving him a strong sense of emotional pain." He looked apologetic. "It's very easy on regular people. They have no boundaries. With us, it takes a little work. We have some ability to fight it off, but most of us eventually succumb to the pain."

I felt uneasy. Even I seldom allowed my fears to surface. I couldn't. I casually glanced over at Dr. Sendal. He didn't look distressed.

"Lauren, please understand that I don't do this for some twisted pleasure. I would never hurt anyone intentionally." His eyes pleaded with me.

"I know. It's something you have. In some way, it's there to protect you from others." I thought about Alex. I'm sure he could do the same thing.

"Lauren, if you don't mind, and I'd only ask this of him to see what he can do. Let's test it out on you. He'll stop if he goes too far," the doctor suggested.

"I don't think we should. Rock or no rock, I couldn't inflict that type of pain on her. She's been through enough," Quinn asserted.

"No, it's okay. I want to try this out."

"Lauren, I can't. We can try something else."

"Quinn . . . *please*. I need to know. Do it for me. I have to find out if I'm strong enough."

"No, Lauren. Ask me something else. This hurts me too much to do this to you."

"*Oh, pleasssssse*. Do it for me."

"I said, *no*."

"*Humph!*"

"Lauren, don't."

I didn't say anything to him. I just turned away.

He let out a heavy sigh. "I hate it when you do that."

"Do what?"

"That! The adorable face."

"I don't know what you mean."

Dr. Sendal quietly laughed at us.

"I promise, I'll pull away if it's too much."

Quinn shook his head. He came closer to me and placed his hands around my head. "Try to relax. You're not going to feel anything at first, but when I'm able to break through the barriers, try to fight it."

I felt eager and somewhat nervous. However, I did what he asked, taking in a few deep breaths. I felt completely calm in his hands. I looked up at Quinn and only saw his piercing gray eyes staring at me. They were warm and intense. They were the eyes I knew.

He began concentrating. I didn't fight him.

Nothing.

Quinn focused on my head again. He wrapped his hands tighter around my head and his concentration intensified. Again, nothing happened. I remained still and unshaken. Quinn redirected his strength on my thoughts. Still, I felt nothing.

He let go with a relieved sigh. "I can't break through."

"Try harder," Dr. Sendal ordered.

I could feel the energy circumventing around Quinn. I knew then what I could do to him at this moment. It became enticing. But I held back and allowed him free reign. He searched and pulled and gnawed at the steel case I left so easily unguarded.

"It's too much. It won't leave her," Quinn said, trying to catch his breath.

"That's wonderful!" Dr. Sendal cheered. "The gem is very strong. Lauren, you have another advantage."

I smiled. "If Quinn can't break through, that means I should be able to hold up against anyone—including Raefield."

"Let's not get ahead of ourselves," Dr. Sendal cautioned. "But technically, yes, you can hold your own."

"And you're not going to have that chance against him," Quinn remarked.

Dr. Sendal contemplated. "Lauren, I want you to try this on Quinn. He has a strong mind, stronger than mine. Try it out. Let's see what you can do to him." He took a few steps in the room and turned back to me. "But I want you to practice control when you break through. If my theories are correct, you should be able to penetrate and cause quite a disturbance."

"I can handle it," Quinn said confidently.

"Don't be too sure. What she brings up can cause some pain for you both."

My mind picked through the possible reasons he could have been upset regarding the people in his life. That included me. I thought back to the first few conversations we'd had. "I promise I won't go too far." Quinn was silent. I reached up to touch his beautiful face and placed my hands around his head. He stood very still.

"Now concentrate, Lauren. Try to draw out his pain. Bring it to the surface as if he was telling you."

I did what Dr. Sendal instructed. I focused on the depths of Quinn's mind to the places where his fears stood. It was fairly effortless moving around the complex organ. The energy felt electrifying yet subtle, surging through me to the person intended. Quinn stiffened. His walls quickly came up, but my strength pushed through the barriers like knocking over toy blocks.

Quinn tightened again—a second line of defense rose. This time, he released an internal force. The energy coming from him felt intoxicating, swimming along my vanity. I almost forgot the primary reason for my intrusion. Then something stalled me. His will collided against mine. My concentration intensified as I pushed onward. I felt overwhelmed by my own strength and my ability to command someone as advanced as Quinn, but I managed to stay focused.

The doors suddenly opened.

I was inside. I was in the control center. My mind swiftly began to search his. I weaved through the soft spots, deep into the frontal portion of his mind, through the minute channels, and through the microscopic impulses that spoke to one another. There were a few obstacles in my way, invisible steel walls which barricaded the outside world from entering the intricate and now exposed mind. However high the hurdle, I overtook it. I entered his memory banks, sitting above the mighty brain stem.

He fought me.

My will proved stronger.

He attempted to put up more blockades. But I was already inside, drawing out the deep-seeded emotions he kept buried. He tried futilely to pull away, but it was too late. I had him in my grasp, and I wasn't letting go. The answers sat inside.

"Lauren, maybe you should pull away," Dr. Sendal cautioned.

I ignored the doctor. I ignored Quinn's internal pleas that eventually gave into defeat. He knew I was stronger. He knew I would find out.

"Lauren, he's struggling."

Someone was running. He was running to *her* . . . to the person he loved. He was anguished. He was enraged. He was angry with himself for not being there, for not seeing the danger she was in. But it was too late. They had gotten to her. She was captured and she was weakened, weakened to the point that she was so frail, only a faint pulse was left. He was upset. He desperately held onto her, trying to give her life while she lay lifeless in his arms. And there was blood on his hands—someone else's blood. He quickly wiped it away before taking an object that was given to him.

The sky turned charcoal, a means to an end, an end at the lighted path turned dark. Everything that was predicted played out. Only the image of hope survived—barely. She was gasping. His pain became unbearable. He carried his grief along with hers, a burden so heavy it shook him. But he knew he had to endure . . . carry on for her. And there were others standing by, waiting anxiously, grieving in their own way. There were others coming. They were closing in, dangerously close. He was afraid, but he was more afraid of not being able to save her. He spoke to her tenderly yet in vain. He was hurrying; they were hurrying. The others were leaving. They had to leave. It was the only way. In her weakened state, she reached out to him, calling his name for the last time. His tears fell on her. It was the tears of anguish and sorrow, his love for her. He wiped them away so that her face could be seen through his gray eyes one last time.

It was me.

"Huh!" I abruptly let go of him. All the energy used to control him quickly ricocheted back at me in a force that caused both of us to fall backwards. I was speechless. I held onto my throat, gasping for air.

"Quinn . . . Lauren, are you hurt?" Dr. Sendal rushed to us, guiding us onto the sofa.

Quinn leaned forward, his head bowed, his hands covering his face. No words came from him except for the heaviness of his chest. I was too stunned to say a word.

My voice finally surfaced in broken pieces. "It can't be. I . . . I wasn't there. It . . . wasn't me."

Dr. Sendal stepped away from us. He vanished into the kitchen and returned in mere seconds, carrying some cold water with him. "Here, drink this."

I looked at it skeptically.

"It's just water."

The fluid tasted good on my palate, hydrating my shaken up body. Quinn still hadn't moved. He was like a bomb waiting to go off. I wanted to reach for him, but decided not to disturb his needed space. I turned to Dr. Sendal. "What I saw . . . could it be true?"

"What did you see?"

"I saw him running to someone. That person was me. He held me while I lay dying in his arms." I shook my head in disbelief. "But that can't be right. I'm here."

Dr. Sendal looked regretful. He moved back into the burgundy chaise lounge already deep in thought.

The silence became too long. "I saw three other people, but I couldn't see their faces. I was focused on Quinn's emotions. They were trying to help. They knew danger was coming and they were leaving."

Quinn looked up this time. His face was stricken with grief. "Lauren, I'm so sorry," he finally whispered.

"*No,* that can't be right. I just twisted things. You said that I could take your darkest emotions and turn them around, make them into your worst fears." I got up from the couch, shaking my head. This was too confusing. It wasn't right. It didn't happen. I nearly fell over the coffee table as I took a few steps back.

Quinn grabbed me before I could fall. "I wish it were true, that it didn't happen. I would trade *anything* to have it not take place."

I regained my balance. "But it doesn't make any sense. I'm *here.* I'm alive and well. When did it happen, and *why* can't I remember?"

The room teetered between reality and the outer limits. I was its balance point, trying desperately to gain control of both sides. But I was losing that ability, and soon I would be knocked off to fall into the unknown.

Dr. Sendal gently said, "Lauren, the rock. Everything you know about your past has been forgotten. Give yourself time to take this in. It *will* make some sense once you understand."

"Lauren . . . *please.* I wanted to tell you for so long, but I couldn't hurt you again," Quinn pleaded.

"Hurt me again? *How . . . how?"* I could feel the hysterics creeping up.

"I would have died if anything happened to you. I would have gladly given my life to save yours. *You* are my life." He looked down in shame. I could only stand there and try to make sense of what they'd told me. It was as if they spoke about a different person in another time. Tears streaked my face. Quinn looked defeated. "They tricked me. They tricked us all. I couldn't get to you before they got to you."

"Tricked us? Who . . . *Raefield?"* My tears felt like a storm. "He was trying to kill me? Like what he did to my parents?"

"No, I don't think so. You happened to find out. You knew something was wrong and you went to try to save your parents, but it was too late." Quinn hesitated, his sympathetic eyes bore into me.

"No, no, no! Tell me this isn't true!" I sobbed in his arms.

"I wish I could. I wish I could make this all go away, and make your days be filled with only joy and not sorrow." He held me tighter as I wilted in his arms.

I gulped and tried to find the words. "Why? Why my parents? Why me?"

Quinn put me down in the chair. "They found out what Raefield was up to, and they tried to confront him. I was told it was an accident; they weren't supposed to die. And you weren't meant to be there after it happened. You had been weakened." Quinn paused briefly. "You knew something was wrong. You went after them even though you weren't yourself. You were going to attack them, as anybody would have in reaction to what had happened. It was one of Raefield's followers. He came after you despite Raefield's orders to leave you alone. He was jealous of you because Raefield prized you—singled you out—believing you to be special." He stopped to wipe the tears from my face, just like in the vision. "Believe me. I didn't want to cause you this much pain."

My parents. My poor, selfless parents confronted the man who planned something they couldn't live with and lost their lives. I became an orphan on the same day I nearly died. Where was the justice? Where was the balance in this magical world that only left us with broken lives and broken hearts? And now, I'm being followed for the powerful gem I possessed.

I hate this rock!

"The others found you before anything else could happen. They were able to buy us time to save you, to get you out," Quinn continued.

"No. I don't want to be a part of this!" My head spun. Something started to move rapidly through me. I felt a tremendous magnetic pull reaching out its powers, unleashing. . . .

"Lauren, quickly, take this and drink plenty of the fluid," Dr. Sendal ordered hastily.

I drank the medicine that sat in rainbow swirls on top of the familiar beverage. It didn't take me long to finish the tea. I took another cupful of the herbal remedy. It was calming. Dr. Sendal poured a third cup, and I quickly finished that as well. I felt the energy surge inside of me until I started to fade. Soon, my weeping turned into a quiet whimper until I had fallen completely into something strong, holding me as far away from today as possible.

"I'd better take her home."

The last thing I remember seeing was Dr. Sendal giving Quinn something in a pouch.

Chapter 15

Quinn

I WOKE UP to the evening sky. A quiet brilliance stood before me with the moon shining in my face, as I lie comfortably warm from the summer night with every detail coming back to me. Closing my eyes, I pushed the agony and the response I felt away so that it would only be a passing memory. It wasn't a world of today, but a mystical world—beguiling in origin—with its own set of laws. In this supernatural world where horrible things happened to good people, to people that I loved, existed for some unknown reason. Where were the spells that heal and the bright and starry magic where dreams came true? It wasn't floating around in this universe. It wasn't here with me.

Someone quietly knocked on my door. "Come in," I said in a hoarse voice.

"You're finally awake. I didn't want to disturb you," Mom said, coming into my room. "We wanted you to sleep."

"What time is it?"

"It's Monday night, about nine-thirty. You slept a whole day. I called your work to tell them you weren't feeling well."

"Thanks, Mom. I really wasn't."

She sat next to me on my bed, deep in thought before forming the words she wanted to say. "You've had quite a journey, more than you asked for and more than anyone ever expected. You've been amazingly strong about this whole thing, more understanding than I gave you credit for. I'm just sorry this had to happen to you." She looked at me with distressed eyes.

"Mom, I'm so tired of people being sorry about everything. It was out of anyone's control. Yes, it was a horrible thing, but it's over. We can't change the past, and we can't bring them back. We have to focus on what's happening now. *I* have to move forward. They would want me to." I moved the covers closer to me like an added security measure. "Time to be a big girl. I have to deal with today. I have to do what's in my power to turn this around. Besides, I'm not the only one who has lost someone."

Mom looked sympathetic this time. "You're right. We've both lost important people we can never replace. They would want us to have the best life possible, to go on." She placed a tender hand on my warm cheek that only a mother could elicit. "Oh Lauren, you've always been so strong. I just hope we haven't pushed you over the edge."

"I'll let you know when that happens." We both chuckled.

"Just know that you're not alone. We're here, and we'll do everything in our power to make things right. Together," Mom reassured me.

"That includes Quinn and my friends?"

"Yes, all of them."

"I take it he's told you everything, from the time my friends arrived, to the concert, and from Dr. Sendal's place."

"Yes, every trick—everything—in full detail."

"Good. We need to all be on the same page and share what we know. I have to start making plans."

"Shhh. You need to take it easy for a while. Doctor's orders."

"Oh . . . fine. You're right. I'm still feeling a bit weak, but tomorrow I should be steady on my feet."

Mom kissed me on the cheek before getting up. I watched her head for the door. "And Mom, thanks for everything."

"Lauren, you don't need to thank me. That's what family is for."

Family. It meant everything. "Mom, one last thing."

"What is it?"

"The box. Did you put it in my room?"

"Yes, it was given to you by your parents when you were young. Only you can release its gift. Keep it safe, and always keep it close by." She hesitated by the door. The moonlight casted just enough light so that I could see her loving face, now cast with concern. "Lauren, you were very lucky that nothing happened to you when you tried on the bracelet. I had hoped Quinn would have been there with you for guidance. Heaven knows what could have happened if you weren't careful."

"Everything's fine, Mom. Nothing bad happened." I felt a sudden twinge of guilt. "I'll remember that next time. Quinn already voiced his opinions."

She sighed with relief. "I just want you to be aware that you're not dealing with any simple toy."

"Got it." It was my turn to turn the tables. "And you're going to tell me when they gave this to me because my memories are only of you and Dad since I was four."

Even in the semi-darkened room, I could see the strain she hid. "Yes, that would make it difficult to have two sets of memories. I'm going to leave that to Quinn. He feels it's his place."

Quinn.

"Mom, can you let Quinn in? I'm dying to see him."

"Of course. He's eager to see you. Be gentle with him, okay? He still feels a great deal of guilt."

I nodded thoughtfully.

"Lauren, he really is a good person. He cares a great deal for you . . . more than you know."

Again, the gaps that needed to be filled in would have to be rendered soon as the object of my inquiries will undoubtedly be entering my room. I wanted and needed the answers. I'd been patient long enough. The door closed. Seconds later another soft rap sounded on my door. "It's open."

Quinn slowly entered the room, as if approaching a fragile person, afraid he would break me, physically and emotionally. I extended my hand to him. He looked hesitant. "I wasn't sure if you were up for company, but your mom said you wanted to see me."

"Quinn, I always want to see you. You're stuck with me. You don't have much choice. If you go, I go. When you run, I run. We're tied like that."

A wry smile formed on his lips. "You may want to let go of me first before everything blows up."

"We'll both jump before it gets too bad."

He lingered by the door for a few more seconds before planting himself squarely on my bed. Quinn drew my hands into his warmer ones, tightly closing mine into a fist. "Lauren, I'm just so sorry— "

"Stop it. I'm tired of everyone being sorry. I'm not a child."

"I know you're not. I didn't mean it that way. It's just . . . your life could have been different, less painful if we . . . no, if *I* had done things differently."

Frown lines began to form on his beautiful face. It pained me to watch his bright eyes fade. I knew he wanted to tell me something important. I only wanted to say what I felt might alleviate his remorse.

"They tricked everyone. You couldn't have known. I felt it when I went inside. I understood the confusion, the deception. I *saw* your pain. And when you found out, it was too late," I said gingerly. "Let's put it behind us and focus on the present. My parents would have wanted me to."

"Yes, they loved you dearly."

Dearly. If only I could remember them.

"We have a lot of work ahead of us. I'll need to start soon, get everyone's thoughts and ideas. Figure out what to do next."

"Whoa. Slow down, love." He stroked my hair as if I were an unruly child needing a touch of discipline. I looked at him with wide-eyed innocence. "The world isn't coming to an end. Tonight, you rest. You have tomorrow to scheme all you want. You can't afford to have another close episode."

"Will it continue . . . my lack of control?"

"It's hardly a lack of your control. You're dealing with some heavy surprises about yourself. It's a lot to take in. I'd say you're handling it fairly well, almost internalizing each new episode that would be burdensome for most people."

"I know what you mean. It doesn't feel as heavy as I thought it would. It's like a mist floating around in my mind, just enough that I would remember, but barely a constant thought. Is that me, or is it the rock?"

"A little bit of both, I think. Your mind is stronger, but I'm not planning on testing it to its limits."

"But I need to work on it. I can tell when it starts to let go. I can feel when I'm able to control those thoughts and emotions, put them safely away so that the gem isn't disturbed, so that *I* won't be disturbed. And when I'm able to do that, I can use the gifts given to me. Quinn, please, I know I can. Teach me. Help me to learn what I'm able to do. Help me to control those emotions and turn it around so that I'll know my own powers." I stared at him. "Don't be afraid to tell me about the past. I need to know."

He studied me momentarily before he chuckled. "Look at you. Without even trying, you could extract the secret formula of the next big product. The poor sucker would have no choice but to hand it over to you, willingly of course, in order to have piece of mind. You haven't lost your touch."

"I don't know what you're talking about."

"Your power to persuade. I was trying very hard not to give in. You almost had me, but you weren't trying that hard. Dangerous. So casual in your attempt, and it was luring enough. I'm not sure what might have happened if you really tried."

"I guess I'm going to have to test it out. Hmmm, it must be the gem. I never thought of myself as that convincing."

"I don't know. Maybe it's a little bit of both. You probably didn't know what you were capable of. Yes, quite dangerous you can be." Quinn stroked my face, following the jaw line to my lips. His fingers moved across them teasingly. I tried not to tremble. Only he could elicit the heat coming from my face, which began to travel onto his hand. He smiled in amusement.

I swallowed hard, trying to regain my control. My voice became husky. "In that case, I'll try harder."

He quickly pulled away. "Let's leave it as it is. I see treachery down the road."

"It doesn't have to be," I cooed, the sweetness returning to my voice.

"Goodnight, Lauren. You're too hard to resist, but I have to be strong . . . for your sake and mine. We don't want the neighborhood awakened by a lightning storm." Quinn gently kissed me, lingering on my lips, and then too quickly he left.

Wait, please stay, I tried to utter the desperate words that didn't come out. The room seemed to have turned two shades darker.

Alone, I would be tonight, by myself, now cold in my room.

Sleep quickly descended upon me.

⋙ ⋘

My lesson with Prof. Sobel went smoothly and effortlessly. I thundered through the morning with his praises. I felt like myself again . . . stronger. I was alert, full of energy, and stamina. And my mind settled easily. It was light and quick, absorbing everything I wanted to learn. I needed more knowledge. I wanted to push my mind further to the places unknown. It moved in me like a separate entity, yet working in concert with my body.

"Good morning, everyone!"

"Afternoon, Lauren," Ethan grumbled, reaching for his caffeinated soda.

"Hey," Aaron and Devon mumbled.

"Hi, Lauren. You're bright and cheery today. What's with all the extra energy?" Linda asked.

"I'm feeling extra energetic, like I've slept for twelve hours. Actually, I have, a whole day in fact." I laughed to myself. "It's been a great day. I feel like I can conquer the world."

Linda raised an eyebrow. "Are you all right? Heard you were sick yesterday. Maybe you should take it easy."

"I'm fine, couldn't be better. Wow, I feel great. It's going to be an amazing day. A new day," I rambled.

"Err, Lauren. What's going on?" Linda asked.

"What do you mean?"

"Why are you acting so funny, like you're on something?" Linda narrowed her eyes. "*Lauren*, what did you take?"

"What? I didn't take anything."

"Then why are you acting so—*whoosh?*"

"I'm energized. It's a natural high."

"Well, can you come down a few notches? Not that I mind the enthusiasm, but can a mellow Lauren please come out?" she joked.

I laughed. "Fine, I'll just be dull and serious and work in my little corner." We both chuckled.

She was right. It came out. My energy exceeded my normal self. Even with this newfound positive attitude, I still allowed my exuberance to escape my control. But was it really harmful? Was it actually from the gem or due to my extra long sleep? I searched my mind, passing from last night to the afternoon at Dr. Sendal's.

What had been in that tea?

I came to a complete halt. My mind stirred, but I managed to rein in the outward energetic emotion. Control.

"Lauren, not to break your trance, but you've got company." I followed Linda's gaze. Quinn.

"You'll cover for me, won't you?"

"Uh huh. What else am I going to do on a slow day?"

I made a beeline to Quinn in the history section. More irony. I would have laughed if he'd managed to find the neurosciences section on his first attempt.

"It's nice of you to show up at my work. Miss me already?" I hugged him.

"You know I can't stay away." He smiled warmly. "How're you feeling today?"

"Better than ever."

"Oh?"

"In fact, I seem to be bursting with more energy and vitality than usual. It seems that since this morning, my brain has been hungry for anything and everything it can absorb. I just got it under control so that it's not pouring out of me for everyone to see. Care to explain?"

He studied me carefully before saying a word. "I'm really not sure. I expected something like this to happen from the extra tea you drank, although I'm surprised it's lasted this long. How's your appetite been?"

"I haven't been that hungry, and I've obviously been able to maintain my strength. What's in the herbal remedy?"

"His special blend. Whatever it is, it works and it keeps us going. Do you remember anything else that Dr. Sendal did?"

"Dr. Sendal did something else? Wait . . . yes, I remember. He gave me something to stop the eruption. It was like in the hospital. I remember him telling me then, and I remember him saying it to me before I drank his remedy. That's how I was able to sleep for so long and not dwindle from the lack of food. But this after-effect, could it still be from the tea?"

"I have my doubts. You obviously aren't having an episode, so most likely it's from the tea *and* progression of the gem."

"The rock is evolving?"

"In theory, it's like another brain, working and learning just like your own. Even though it's tied to you, it can have a mind of its own, as we've seen. It might extend away from you—figuratively, of course—to seek something important to you, perhaps a thought from your subconscious even before you've had the chance to really think about it. Kind of mind boggling, don't you agree?"

"Yes, overload without the overkill."

"Remember, it's also a powerful entity that contains some of your hidden talents."

I was a two-headed monster. I frowned.

"And you're not some deformed person. You're more special than you know."

I felt better. I knew he could explain what was going on with me. Really, I wasn't overly concerned, just curious.

"Lauren," Quinn said in a soft tone. "How did you sleep after I left you?"

"I wanted you to stay. And I tried reaching out to you before you left, but found myself fading. Next thing I knew, I was alone in the dark, falling into a deep sleep. Somewhere, I remembered your kiss. Did you . . . do that?"

Quinn looked satisfied. "I wanted you to surrender to the night. You were getting too excited, and I thought too much information would push you over the edge."

"I think by now I've already scaled a few walls. Any other surprises would be commonplace." I searched Quinn's face for hidden truths. I came up blank. "Can I expect more heavenly nights or is the kiss of death next in your bag of tricks?"

Quinn frowned. "Lauren, how can you even think I would do any-thing to harm you, let alone destroy your life? Haven't I made myself clear by now? Have you any idea . . . any idea at all what that would do to me? *Do* you?"

A few students from a nearby table looked up at us. I ignored them. "I . . . I didn't mean to say that. I was just joking." I suddenly couldn't see my own humor. His facial expression said it all. Death was not a subject he could joke about.

We stood there in the longest silence, my heart ready to thunder out of my chest for the pain I'd caused him. Quinn's face finally relaxed. "I'm sorry. I didn't mean to be so hard on you. I know you didn't mean it. It's just . . . I can't lose you again."

There it was. Lose me again. The same reference that Quinn made regarding my relationship with him spelled out for me dur-ing my coma-like state in the hospital. That lost segment of my life seemed to hold an essential part of me, and what happened between Quinn and I. But I was determined to keep my head above water. I knew Quinn was close to telling me everything. He has to, there's no other option.

"No, I don't plan to be away from you. That much should be clear."

"Let's not talk about this anymore. They aren't my favorite memo-ries," Quinn said.

"Agreed. So, I'll meet you at your place tonight?"

"With open arms."

I watched him slip out of the building without distracting anyone. His image lingered. Even though we hadn't known each other for long, I couldn't imagine a life without him. He'd become a permanent fixture in my daily life, engraved in my every thought. He felt my pain as I felt his. We'd formed a single unit composed of two parts without losing our own identity. And time never played a role in how comfortable I felt around him. We were people who'd loved each other for an eternity. I knew that truth in my heart of hearts.

"Earth to Lauren, please come in," Linda said.

"Oh, I was just thinking about Quinn."

"Obviously. Anything good?" she joked.

"Let's act like we're busy before Ethan finds us real work to do."

The rest of the day dragged. I didn't mind. Quinn remained in my thoughts. *What couldn't you tell me?*

I drove home through the familiar route with enough lasting energy. The light snack at work still kept me alert. I decided to go on a run. By the time evening approached, Raegan arrived.

"Lauren, guess what?" Raegan yelled.

"You're going to Minnesota."

"That's not fair. Did you read my mind?"

"No, I don't have that talent. I just knew. It's pretty obvious."

"Oh." She deliberated for a brief moment then said, "You should come with me."

"I can't."

"Bring Quinn with you. They've invited him, too, and you guys can leave whenever you like. It'll be fun."

"Sounds great, but I think we'd like to spend some time around here before the Fourth and before the party."

"The party. I can't wait. I've told everybody it's on the weekend after the Fourth. Do you think I should get a totally new look? Something more trendy?" Raegan played with her hair, forming a different do each time she looked into the bedroom mirror.

"I think you look fine."

"Maybe I should cut it off. Alex thinks it would be way cool if I tried a very short look."

"He would. He'd probably help you shave it off if you let him. But I think you'd regret it."

"Guess you're right. He'd want me to try the rebel look for a few days then he'd get bored. I'll just straighten it. Men, they're *so* picky." She started to laugh and returned to fussing with her red mane.

That was my cue to get up and leave. Before I made it through her door, Raegan turned to me with a more serious look. "Lauren, is something going to happen? I mean, are you in some kind of trouble?"

"No, why do you say that?" I felt a twinge of guilt.

"It's just—and please don't say anything to Alex—he said to try to stick together and look out for each other. He wanted to know if anything unusual was going on. I wasn't sure what he meant by that."

I let out a light chuckle. "Everything's fine. I can take care of myself. Besides, don't we always look out for each other? That Alex. He always wants to know what his friends are doing."

"Okay. I'm being paranoid. He had me worried about you." She gave me a tight hug, like I was going to leave her without saying good-bye. "You'd tell me if something was going on, wouldn't you?"

"Of course I would. Try not to worry."

Raegan looked convinced. I went to my room, thinking about what Alex had really said to her. Aside from having Raegan keep an eye on things, he might be expecting Mercedes and Nicholas to visit. I thought back to the odd conversation we'd had that night on the deck when he apologized for being so rude to Quinn. I remembered him mentioning he would understand if I had to leave.

Alex, what do you know?

I quickly put on a fitted, pale blue shirt and some denim shorts. I grabbed an overnight bag with the things I needed. In seconds, I crossed over to his side of the house. Garrett answered the door with his friendly smile and amused brown eyes.

"Lauren, nice to see you again. Have you come down from the ecstasy or should we call for a sedative?"

I wondered if Quinn kept any secrets from Garrett. "Oh, no. I'm pretty mellow by now. My run used it up."

Garrett let me inside where Quinn sat at the edge of the sofa with a Scrabble game in front of him.

"Looks fierce. Who's winning?" I asked.

"Quinn so far. He knows a lot of ancient words."

"What?" I asked.

Quinn ignored Garrett's comments.

"I mean, he's older than I am so he has that advantage of knowing more words than I do. But I should be able to overpower him once he starts to fade."

Quinn looked up from the game, his eyes amused. "I've already had my fill. I should be good for the rest of the night."

"We'll see who takes the reins. Unless, of course, I forfeit. Then, we'll never know who's smarter," Garrett gloated.

"Can't handle defeat, can you?" Quinn teased.

"Letting you win is hardly a defeat. I'm feeling the need to be charitable."

Quinn and I both rolled our eyes.

"I'd love to stay and rub it in your face, but there are ladies waiting for my attention. Lauren, it was nice seeing you again. Stay as long as you'd like, and try not to have an episode tonight. Poor Quinn has enough guilt on his hands." Garrett gave Quinn an over-sized wink and then grabbed his keys, chuckling as he made his way out the door.

Quinn shook his head, then allowed a laconic smile. "Just ignore him. He gets rather mouthy when he's being competitive."

"I'm not offended. I thought he was rather funny. Why be so serious all the time?"

"Do you think I'm too serious?"

"No, but I have the feeling you worry too much about hurting me and allow some mistaken guilt to take over."

"You're probably right. I've beaten myself up for so long, feeling remorseful for not being there for you and for letting you down. It won't happen again."

The confusion started up again. *Wait, just wait, be patient.* Even though his face didn't show his concerns, I knew he was hurting again.

"I've always been in good hands, with family and friends whom I love and who, hopefully, love me back. Life has always been good to me. Only you were missing from that memory."

Quinn began to relax. But somehow, I couldn't break away from that slight feeling of desperation. A sudden void engulfed me. It was the same hollow emptiness that invaded me from time to time, an un-explained force to shadow my days. Was it the void of Quinn all those years against my quivering heart? It made perfect sense! I had accepted the incompleteness as life's natural course.

Quinn became mindful again, his own discomfort dissipating. "When I searched for you those two years, not knowing if you were alive or dead, and not knowing how you lived, it tore at me. I wal-lowed in my own conviction. My sanity slipped. I tried to live my life, survive on my own in ways I'd never imagined by learning the world around me. Holding onto hope of finding you was the only thing that kept me afloat." Quinn's deep gray eyes met mine. He searched through me again for that lost soul. "I almost didn't ap-proach you. I battled with the idea even before we met at the clothing store. Disrupting your life might be a mistake, but my own needs outweighed your undisturbed life. I finally decided to give into my wishes and see for myself if you were happy. Honestly, I thought I could just see you once, see if you remembered anything, just look at you one time, and I could leave you alone and in peace. When we met again at the coffee shop, finding out that you were alive and well, and seeing that you've had a happy life lifted some of that weight. But it wasn't enough to excuse me for my actions."

I opened my mouth to interrupt, but he placed a finger against my lips.

"When you left me . . . when you had to leave so quickly, part of me left with you. The person that remained seemed dead to the world."

My heart reached out to him, to wrap its coiling red mist around his broken world and to shield his pain. The words that would normally follow an emotional gesture failed me. I seethed in my own ineptness.

"It's important that you understand what had to be done, needed to be done. It was the only way."

"You keep talking about losing me and saving me and doing something unbearable, but it needed to be done. This is all so cryptic. Quinn, tell me . . . everything . . . from the beginning. *Please.*"

Quinn released a heavy sigh. "You're right. It's time you know about the past."

Finally. The truth.

"Lauren, think back to when you searched inside my mind. What did you see?"

"Quinn . . . why? I've already told you what I saw. I twisted your pain around. It wasn't real."

"You weren't fabricating anything. What you saw was real. You read my pain as I had seen and felt it. You didn't even have the chance to pull it out and twist my suffering to your advantage, a talent we have when dealing with a potential enemy."

"I had let go."

I remembered the pain he'd felt that afternoon as I looked inside his mind. It was surreal. It felt real, but I pushed it away, believing it to be some convoluted image I'd made up. I didn't want to picture it again. Yet how would I ever know if I didn't allow my curiosity to see the horror that had reached into the depths of my mind? Gradually, the images penetrated my brain and took form. I really was the girl in his arms. When? Why?

"Try to remember the scene. What did it look like? What did you notice through me?" Quinn instructed me.

I dug deeper into my mind to picture what he had seen. There was a forest, thick and vast. Quinn moved very quickly, running faster than the average human, and using his talents to cover more ground. Horses ran wild and in a stampede. Some were saddled and trained, grazing in the field or near their owners. I remembered seeing dirt roads, long and winding unpaved roads. Was this countryside undisturbed? Quinn reappeared in a city, more like a village with cobblestone streets and charming old-world buildings lined up next to each other—turn of the century picturesque.

Through his mind, I saw flashes of an old Victorian mansion: dark, gothic, nearly resembling a medieval castle. More horses waited along the circular driveway, and a grand carriage with its own fastened steed stood in front of the arched entryway. A carriage! Quinn instinctively ran elsewhere, to the edge of a forest as he followed his anguish.

Light passed into darkness. The fear of something momentous escalated. Another carriage stood in the distance, waiting patiently for its passengers. There, between the shadows of day and the dusk of evening, a group of unusually dressed people hovered anxiously around an ailing girl.

Me.

I lay on the cool ground, covered by a wool blanket and the hem of my long, burgundy skirt showing. A memory flashed through Quinn's mind of happier times exchanged during a wintery Christmas. Quinn reached down to hold me in his arms while he fought the rage that flowed through his body. Through Quinn's eyes, I was barely alive, only a thready pulse remained, and I was quite delirious. He cursed in horror from the blood he suddenly noticed on his hands. Removing the blanket that covered me, he saw the fresh blood on my white blouse. He quickly examined where the blood came from while reaching for the bandages to cover the wound. I reached out to him and called his name in my struggle for air. He was distraught.

"She's so cold," Quinn told the stranger.

"Hurry, give this to her."

The stranger gave Quinn the hard object. It was a shiny, emerald green stone, a gem I knew all too well. Quinn looked up in despair at the stranger, searching for hope in the face of the person who was no stranger.

Dr. Sendal.

"*Dr. Sendal?* What was he doing there? And my parents, the Reeds?" I stared wide-eyed at Quinn. They were all there. And they were dressed in clothes from another era.

"You saw all of them. You know it's true. Lauren, you were lying in my arms. We were trying to save you."

The truth. I felt it deep within my being, even if I didn't remember being there. My parents and Dr. Sendal stood around me.

"The horses, the roads, the mansion, and the carriages . . . even the clothes we wore. It was another time."

"A long time ago," Quinn responded.

"Quinn, when did this happen?"

"Nineteen hundred."

"As in the turn of the century, *nineteen hundred?*"

"That would be the one."

"You mean to tell me that you, and I, and my parents and even Dr. Sendal, have been around since nineteen hundred? I don't get it. How is that possible?" I shook my head. "Wait, on second thought, anything's possible at this point. Why haven't we aged?"

"We do get older. We just happened to cross through time."

"As in time travel?"

"Exactly. I know it's hard to believe. When I first learned of it, I thought it was some ancient tale meant to scare children and adults. It's impossible, but when you look at the abilities we've been given for some unknown reason, transporting ourselves to another dimension isn't so hard to grasp. Once you see it for yourself, you never doubt it again."

Time travel. In my wildest imagination, I would have never guessed the possibility of time travel. Sure, scientists still debated the idea of traveling through time, a theory of particles passing through some bend in space that man has yet to discover. And through books and television, it was made possible because our imagination to dream of the most wishful dreams meant that we could cross through time. In this reality, we'd achieved it.

"How do we go through time? Everything that I've read or seen talks about a portal."

"It's not a door you open or some metal chamber you climb into. It's almost spirit like in its approach. It can't be dictated, and it can't be controlled. There's no rhyme or reason to when it occurs. You just sense when it's approaching."

Quinn became distant. His thoughts seem to travel to another time and place, as mine moved in that direction as well. We had both been a part of that life. I could believe in time travel. It wasn't so hard to fathom after knowing what I could do and after seeing what I'd seen. Believing in ghosts now seemed trivial.

"It's a heavy mist unlike anything you've ever seen, more like a dense fog, thicker than the marine layer that covers Chicago and blankets the lake on an overcast day. This great force seems to descend from the sky. When it comes down and covers the ground, it opens a door to another time. What makes this fog so unique is that beyond the white of the mist is the blue outer layer."

"A blue vapor, having enough power to take us to another place. I'm having a hard time believing something so fine can do so much. What's in the mist?"

Quinn chuckled. The heaviness he carried around seemed to disappear just like the clouds. "A greater force beyond you and me. Something powerful enough to send us through time."

"Than it must have something to do with our innate abilities. Who or what gave us these gifts, and what created the fog?"

"Who created anything? God? The Big Bang theory? It's a mystery. It's been passed from generation to generation like folklore of people who possessed special powers. In the randomness of existence, talents were thrown in the mix and a super species, if you need to call us something, was created. As to the mist, it's a complete unknown how it works."

"So this great force could come down at any time, and we would be able to cross over to the past and even the future. Do you know what this means? I could see my parents again."

"Whoa, it's not that easy. Do you remember how old you were when the Reeds adopted you?"

Something clicked in my mind. "I was four."

"You and the Reeds left at the same time. My guess is that somewhere during your travels, you became separated from them. Lauren, the portal doesn't always keep you at the same age. I believe there are layers within the portal that we slip into and come out a different age."

"Like being born again," I muttered to myself. "My parents still wouldn't be here, because I was somewhere else. That would make sense. I was four when the Reeds found me at the orphanage. They were still adults but younger than the time when we left the field at the edge of the forest." I turned to Quinn. "Are you the same age as you were when you left?"

"I think I'm somewhere in my late twenties. Remember, I lived in the present time for two years before I moved to Chicago," he reflected. "I was fortunate enough to get here when you had reached adulthood. In theory, we're both a lot older if you count years, but, in fact, our age gets recycled and we're new again because of the lapse in time."

"Exactly when were you born?"

"Eighteen seventy-four. You followed afterwards, arriving to the world we once knew in eighteen seventy-eight. You were born in Bridgeport, Connecticut."

Connecticut. If not for my family's yearly trips to the northeast, I would never have formed a connection. My preexisting life had been based in a place I didn't remember. Chicago became the only home I knew.

"It was by pure luck that your family decided to move to New Haven." His smile was contagious.

"Then I'm an old woman." My head continued to wrap around the idea of living in a time before cell phones, computers, and even cars. We even predated World War I. I wondered if I had gone to school or to dances, and if I cooked and sewed all-day and only went out with a chaperon like a proper young lady. Did I tend a garden and roam the countryside on a fearless steed?

Quinn seemed to recognize my newfound discovery. "I hardly call nineteen old. You're just beginning," he said. "Your father had been appointed mayor of the city six months before your arrival. You had been staying at the Reeds' place until your move to New Haven. Your house was nearly complete, and fortunately for me, your family decided to stay at the hotel for that remaining time. I thanked my father for his wisdom in arranging your family's stay."

Your father had important work ahead of him. The Maxwell Inn. Yes, it made perfect sense. My family and I had moved to New Haven from

Bridgeport. I had stayed at the Maxwell Inn where Quinn's family had been prominent citizens of the community.

"Tell me more about your family's hotel, and your life in Connecticut. What was it like?"

"It was the best experience anyone could ask for. You could say that my parents were grooming me for this career. We lived in a section of the east wing. It was pointless for us to reside in a separate house when we spent so much time at the hotel. There were two restaurants—a small, intimate cafe and a more formal dining area. We also had a theater with an informal lounge for entertainment in the north wing next to the restaurant. Of course, there was a smoking room in the hotel for the gentlemen of those days to discuss life in the changing new world, the growing economy, and politics. It wasn't socially proper for women to spend time in the hall, but only to be announced if they came searching for their significant other. Besides, who would want to spend time in a smoky room killing your lungs?" Quinn added in jest. His glassy eyes reflected the love he had for the hotel.

"The grand lobby was always bustling with people. I can still see the weary travelers and the extravagant luggage that were sent by carriage or train to be delivered to the prospective rooms. People came in riding clothes, in simple dress, and in fashions of the time, especially the evening wear. The formal attire in those days took forever to put on. I prefer today's leisure style to the many pieces."

I saw the lobby with the crystal chandelier and French doors opening up to the property through his eyes. "It sounds like a grand place."

"It was a sight. A wooden hotel—light and airy—built for modern times. Running water, indoor plumbing, and a mix of gas lighting and electricity made staying at the hotel quite memorable. We even had central heating." Quinn looked at me knowingly. "You have to remember that those worldly conveniences we take for granted were a luxury to most people.

"During the Civil War, New Haven positioned itself well in supplying the region and outlying areas with industrial goods and supplies—carriages, rubber goods, weapons, and household luxuries. Its location proved vital to the city's prosperity. Population growth spurred during this time. After the war, people wanted to move forward, prosper and embrace life in building today's society. We were already involved in the industrialized age, so when the hotel was completed in 1890, it was designed with as much sophistication and modern amenities as possible. The hotel is also where you entered my life."

I felt his excitement. Through his memories, my imagination took me to the Maxwell Inn where we had met so long ago in another life.

"It was 1898. You were twenty when we met. Your face glowed with the autumn sun. You stayed close to your family, quietly observing everything and everyone around you. I made my way to introduce myself to you. Your eyes softened as they are right now. And your smile spoke like your eyes, warm and free of the defenses you had put up. I knew my life was going to change at that moment."

"And mine has changed since you've entered my life. Quinn, I can't bring back those memories, but I know that I don't want to lose you. I'm sorry you had to leave your family and the place you loved to find me. I feel terrible. You've had to sacrifice so much, only to find out that I can't remember who I am. And this thing in my head might explode at any given moment. I don't deserve your love."

"What are you saying . . . that it was all a mistake? Lauren, I love my family very much, and I wish the hotel had continued on with my mother and my sister. But it's enough knowing they had a good life. You're my family, too. That's what matters."

"You're mine as well. I just feel that your life could have been better, living in Connecticut, continuing the family business, and having a family of your own, away from memories of me. You even lost two years searching across the country in a place and time you weren't prepared to live in. I can never give you any of that time back."

Quinn looked at me puzzled. "You think that I've lost a great deal? My life couldn't be without you in it. We made that promise to each other. I couldn't have it any other way. It was because of me that you went to confront Raefield on your own. I was too caught up in my own world, thinking I needed to expand the business instead of listening to the warning signs. They were good. They knew how to get to me. They knew how to separate us, make us weaker before attacking."

"Quinn, stop it. It wasn't your fault. You didn't know what was going to happen. I wasn't even supposed to be there. I went on my own."

"It's no excuse. I should have listened to my instincts. I wasn't there to help you. I wasn't there to get you out. You took the fall. You nearly died. I haven't forgiven myself for that, but I'm trying to make it right again. I promise to work hard so that you can believe in me." His eyes pleaded with mine. "I don't need to hold onto the old memories. I just want the ones with you. So, if you can forgive me, then let's make another promise to stay together."

"You don't have to ask. It's already done. I can't be without you."

CHAPTER 16

A Haven

QUINN AND I hit the highlights in downtown Chicago on a beautiful June day. We sampled every delight along the Grant Park neighborhood in one of Chicago's many lakefront festivals—the Taste of Chicago. I wouldn't go hungry. If I could store away the abundance of food I consumed, the energy need could be spread out for days. A wishful thought.

We reached our fill, and it would last for hours. I felt strong and renewed. Even my fears and worries seemed to be a lifetime ago. The eruptions and wild visions hadn't returned, and Mercedes and Nicholas somehow disappeared from the face of the earth.

Between our schedules, Quinn and I continued to spend every moment together, which only made us closer. Our thoughts even moved parallel to one another. And after learning about my past and the connection we shared, I understood what had been missing for so long.

My days with Quinn, however, left little time to spend with Raegan after our friends returned to Minnesota. I knew she was happy. Her face glowed every time she talked on the phone. They would return to Chicago for the house party just two weeks away. The whole neighborhood might even show up.

"Quinn, when you left the old New Haven, where did you go?" I asked as we entered the Shedd Aquarium. I was glad to leave the over-crowded park for a more serene place.

"I actually stumbled right into modern day New Haven. It was my plan to go there first, since this was where we had lived. But when I arrived, it wasn't the same. I had hoped some remnants of our life would still be there. I thought you might have returned. I was sorely disappointed." We slipped into silence, walking hand in hand where colorful fish glided by in over-sized tanks.

"I first went to the hotel. I didn't know what to expect. You could only imagine my frustration when I couldn't find the hotel or any Maxwell Inn. I had hoped it survived into the new century. It's now a waterfront district. At least the land went to good use. After recovering from my disillusion, I went to your parents' house. By this time, I knew to expect many changes. Again, I had hoped you'd be there." Quinn shrugged. "Wishful thinking on my part."

I watched the large fish circle the massive aquarium. Their lives seemed simple and carefree. I envied them.

A beluga whale approached the thick aquarium glass. He opened his mouth, making whistling and clicking sounds that echoed from the opening at the top of the pool. He looked fearless. I touched the glass where he pressed his blunt nose. He didn't swim away.

"Your house, a Queen Anne Victorian, is still standing with a replica of the same fence enclosing the property. The city kept the home and remodeled the place under the historical society's guidance. Helen and Oren should take you there."

"I've been to the home. My parents have taken me there several times, perhaps to see if I could remember anything from my previous life, and maybe for my mother's sake so that she could hold onto some memory of her brother." We moved on to the next exhibits. I enjoyed the peaceful darkness the aquarium offered. It gave me a chance to search through the past.

Nothing.

"It's funny," I said. "The museum curator said that no photos were salvaged from a fire in 1900, which started in the master bedroom, supposedly killing the owners of the house—my parents. There was no mention of a child belonging to Mayor De Boers and his wife. An old clipping displayed at the house only speculated about how the fire started and why they didn't try to escape. But it was cut short by an editorial that the mystery had been solved. A cigar left at bedside had started the fire. The unfortunate couple were sleeping, most likely inhaling the fumes, and unable to escape the toxic surrounding." I stopped to look at Quinn. "We both know that isn't true. Whoever put those bodies there did it for a reason. They didn't have sophisticated technology in those days to identify charred remains. What's even stranger is that the curator said when the renovations were started, there was minimal damage to the master bedroom. According to the society's notes, the original woodwork still covered a great portion of the bedroom."

"I read the same thing and did my own investigation. What I found was rather interesting. When the city took over the property in 1903, they left all the original furniture and knickknacks around the house, but they couldn't find any photos of your family. I looked everywhere, too—the bedrooms, the living room, the parlor, and your father's study. Lauren, there were photos of you and your parents throughout the house, not only in the master suite. Someone took them. Why?"

I shrugged, not knowing the answer.

"The house had six bedrooms," he went on. "What had once been your room was meticulously altered to resemble a guest bedroom. Your personal items disappeared, as if to make it appear you never existed. I'm not sure why, though. Perhaps to protect your identity? I assumed Raef was behind the entire cover-up, but I suspect someone else had ulterior motives."

For some reason, I had been eliminated from existence. No history of me, no evidence that I've lived. Only a limited biography of my parents' life and a brief summary of my father's interrupted term was given. Why?

"For the record, your father didn't smoke. Anyone who knew him could vouch for that. They may have thought it was suspicious, but probably dismissed the idea, thinking he might've enjoyed a cigar on occasion. If they suspected foul play, they kept their mouths shut or their concerns were ignored."

After listening to Quinn's disturbing account, I realized some important details were missing. "Quinn, who owned the home after the fire and my parents' supposed death?"

"I think it was a private investment firm. For whatever reason, they had a stake in the property. They held onto the place until it was sold to the city three years later for historical preservation purposes."

I glanced at the large glass front of an exhibit. The sea turtles and the lionfish and the moray eel all lived in harmony. They swam in the same waters, breathed the same oxygen, and ate from the same pool. They took what they needed to survive, but not more than what was naturally programmed in their genetic makeup. We went far beyond those boundaries.

Quinn looked at the same creatures I observed. "After I left your place, I had to make my way around the city with what I had, which was nothing. I didn't want to stand out from everyone, but I also needed to get by. I found a local bank and was able to get money for food, clothes, and a place to stay."

I could only imagine what he'd done to borrow money from a bank.

"The library was my key to what I had been looking for. At first, I had to confront the minor challenges of moving quickly from one century to another. The change in technology was overwhelming. The automobile really advanced from the late 1800s. The computer and the smart phone were extraordinary." We continued the tour down the maze-like tunnels, passing playful young children and their parents. "I'm lucky to be a fast learner. I found some records of my family in the archives. As I mentioned before, my sister and her husband controlled half of the hotel, but with the poor management of my uncle and his associates, the hotel nearly went bankrupt. The bank, already holding a heavy lien on the hotel, assumed the title of the hotel and repaid its creditors. But, before the transaction could take place, a raging fire burned down a good portion of the magnificent hotel. I suspected arson, but it was never proven. They decided not to rebuild. The insurance company paid out the money. The bank took most of it to pay off the debts, and the rest went to my sister and my uncle. They managed to stay in New Haven and live a productive life."

"What about Raefield and his people, and Mercedes and Nicholas? Weren't your family afraid of them?"

"During that time, they had their concerns, but the hotel and their life was in New Haven. Raefield and his people never bothered my family. They actually felt safer knowing more people of their kind lived in the same community. There was talk of a movement to eliminate people who walked in the shadows of demons. It was said that all people who practiced the evil ways of witchcraft should be destroyed."

I shuddered at the thought of past persecution.

"After I left, I can't say if Raefield ever bothered my family or if they had feared him, but they carried on."

My heart ached for him and his family. I hid my guilty feelings. We needed to move forward. We had to connect the past into the present in order to protect the unknown future.

"Don't be alarmed, but I was curious to see if Raefield was still around. I wasn't going to knock on his door for an afternoon chat."

"You didn't! Quinn, you could have gotten yourself killed. What were you thinking?"

"I was just curious if he'd managed to survive. I wasn't going to expose myself. I knew if he found me, he might find you. I wanted to see if being in New Haven was dangerous for me."

"And?" My grip on his arm tightened.

"The old mansion was still there but no signs of Raefield or his people. Not even Mercedes and Nicholas. I didn't feel the energy pull when I got near the estate. I assumed it was safe. It, too, had been preserved by the historical society. I looked around the old place, searching for clues and hidden messages that could have been left behind. I didn't find anything worth remembering."

I sighed. The thought of Quinn going to the home of Raefield, the person who killed my parents and whose men nearly sent me to my death consumed me. And still I wasn't safe. I couldn't be free. I was hunted. I would have to conquer or be destroyed.

Control. I needed control. My strength needed to win over my emotions. *Gently now, come down carefully. That's it.*

"Lauren, are you all right?" Quinn studied my face carefully. "For a second, I thought those emerald eyes of yours were awakening. Should we stop?"

"No, I want to hear more." I didn't move. I found the necessary inner balance.

"I did more searching. I roamed the city for two days. It wasn't home anymore. My life . . . you, it no longer existed. I felt the emptiness. New Haven changed so much. Modern life took over, and with the prosperity of a convenient life also gave rise to poverty and crime. The warmth and vitality I remembered was no longer there," Quinn recalled, his mood somber.

I wrapped my arms around his shoulders. "You're home now with me, here in Chicago. We can start again. You can tell me everything about yourself and me . . . about us."

Quinn smiled. "I'd agree to that. This is home now."

My heart sang out. "What happened next, after you went to Raefield's mansion?"

"My stay in New Haven was done. After about four days, I gathered everything I needed and headed for Bridgeport. It was a long shot, but I still needed to exhaust all possibilities."

We moved further into the oceanarium. The rooms and the hidden alcoves came alive with the most exotic and varied sea creatures on display.

"I doubted you'd go there. The Reeds would've thought it unsafe to take you to Bridgeport. But I tried to keep some of my hope alive. I racked my brain to remember where the Reeds had lived. I'd only been to their home once with you and your parents, so it was hard to locate since the geography had changed so much. It was destroyed years ago when the city was developing. At that point, I felt rather defeated. Honestly, Lauren, I didn't know where to go. There wasn't anyone to turn to. I wasn't even sure how old you might be or if you even survived."

I'd had my parents and Chelsea and Isaak to lean on. My family. I'd had good friends and a place I knew as home. Quinn had been forced to start over—alone. He'd left a good life where his family and the people he knew had created a place he called home—*for me.*

Undeserving.

I closed my eyes. No, I couldn't criticize his decision to come here. He'd made it clear that his life was with me and my life was with him. Perhaps he would have been in greater danger had he stayed. I wouldn't devalue his decision. I would, to the best of my abilities, do anything to make him happy.

"During my search in New Haven, I came across several Helen and Oren Reeds. I wasn't sure if your parents had kept their names or used an alias. I called two of them, one in Oklahoma and the other in New York. Neither of the Reeds fit the description. I only had two other options on the list."

I might have been discouraged if I'd been in Quinn's place.

"I left Connecticut and drove to Philadelphia to see for myself the other possibility. I found a Dr. and Mrs. Reed with the same names, and to my surprise, they had a fourteen-year-old daughter. I made an appointment to see the practitioner, and you can guess how I felt when he showed up. He didn't look anything like your uncle—shorter, darker hair with glasses. The photo of himself with his family said it all. His daughter was blond and her face was nothing like yours." Quinn's lips curled up.

"After I left Philadelphia, I went to Fresno. There was an antique dealer with your mother's name and a teacher with your father's name. What did I have to lose? I needed to keep trying."

We entered Neptune's Temple—elegant portico that housed the aquarium's glass dome, built to compete with visions of Paris. I felt like we had stepped into a Greek temple, ominous and sacred, yet safe enough to house the wonders of the ocean within its protective glass walls. We stood inside the nerve center that branched out throughout the aquarium. I felt the turmoil begin.

"Flying was a godsend. I was in complete awe at how far we had advanced in the successful transport of passenger carriers," Quinn said, looking amazed.

I never thought about the importance of flying.

"Of course, I could move very quickly on my own, but to travel across the country without stopping, that was a feat."

"And you obviously stayed in California, despite the dead end. That must have been discouraging." I was wishful. It was bordering on torment. He had longed for me. I knew he had suffered. How terrible for him to have suffered. I knew he was alone, wondering where I could be.

Selfish, selfish, selfish!

How could I want to inflict pain upon his already guilt-ridden conscience? He searched for me. He had come for me. Wasn't that enough?

What was I becoming?

I quickly killed that misguided notion. It was horrible to think that way, my self-centered needs above his well-being.

"How much did Garrett tell you?" Quinn asked.

"About what?"

"I know Garrett spoke to you about the time I was in California. What did he say exactly?"

"He didn't tell me much. He said that he met you at a beach in Santa Cruz when he was on vacation with his parents. Do you surf?"

"Don't change the subject. I want to know what he said to you."

"It's nothing, really. He said that you two started talking and realized you had things in common. You were looking for someone . . . a girl, I assume." *Me,* a small voice in my head answered. My genuine concern and welfare for the man who had crossed through time for me returned. I wanted to return that favor, console him any way I could.

A mischievous grin formed across my lips.

Quinn looked at me puzzled. "Lauren, are you sure you're okay?"

"I'm fine."

"We knew we were similar. That's the beauty of knowing when one of our own is around. I told him why I was here, that I was looking for a girl. I didn't mention that I had traveled from the past. I wanted to wait until I could trust him. He's been my savior. He said that he would help. It was a miracle that he lived in Chicago." Quinn's face beamed.

"Why did you stay in California so long? I'm surprised that you didn't find my parents in Chicago."

"Thinking back, I'm surprised myself that I couldn't trace them to Chicago. Your father is a lawyer and your mother manages a bookstore. They would've been exposed. Yet, any personal information that could compromise their identity seemed to be hidden or removed from public knowledge. You can't find them in any form of media."

I nodded my head. "If you searched for the bookstore, the owner is listed as Chelsea Marie, and my father goes by Landon, his middle name, as the namesake printed on the firm."

"Something to keep people guessing," Quinn remarked.

"Just like me."

"But they don't have a gem. I mean, Chicago is a large city, and you could easily get lost or hide in a city this large."

"Or they knew how to disguise themselves."

"That's it!" Quinn said out loud.

"They wore a disguise?"

Quinn chuckled. "No, they could cover up their identity. I've heard of this before, people who could shut off that energy flow so that they couldn't be traced, so that an enemy within couldn't feel their presence."

"My parents can do that? Amazing."

"I wonder if they can alter their appearance when faced with a person they can't trust. They could hide from—" He abruptly stopped talking and narrowed his eyes on a spot across the darkened room.

"*Quinn*, what is it?" I hissed.

Before I could say anything further, Quinn grabbed me by my wrist and we darted out of the foyer. We didn't reach the outer rim. We came to a standstill by the towering pillars. The whites of those eyes came towards us. They were eyes I knew and eyes that I feared.

"Quinn . . . Lauren, where are you going in such a rush? We're always meeting like this in such dark places," Nicholas said with a touch of sarcasm.

"It's late. We're just getting something to eat," Quinn said in a steady voice.

"I think that can wait. I have a few words for you both."

My feet pointed straight ahead and my leg muscles tightened. I scanned the environment. *Conquer or be conquered.*

It started again. Something stirred inside of me. *No, not yet. Take control. Be the owner.* The veins in my neck pulsated. The nutrient-dense blood pushed its way upstream to fill the cavity. So much blood and air was being forced into my head. I felt dizzy. And my own animated heart beat out of control.

Quinn gently touched my face to ease that rage. I let go of the tight grip I had on him.

"Lauren, you will *learn* to control that power of yours and put it to good use. When the time is right, you'll understand control. Raefield will be so pleased," Nicholas said.

Why would he say Raefield would be pleased? Don't listen to him, Lauren. It's just another scare tactic.

"What makes you think I'll fall to Raefield?"

Quinn quickly shot me a warning. I couldn't stand here and let this snarling man dictate my life and control the actions of the people I cared about.

Nicholas looked amused. The deep lines in his face moved with his twisted mouth. "They always do. Nobody can resist Raefield. Let yourself be free. He'll guide you." He laughed artfully. "My master will be pleased indeed. Quinn, Lauren has grown to be quite willful. She'll be an asset."

"No she won't, Nicholas. She won't surrender to your cause. And I won't let you near her without a fight." Quinn's strength surfaced from that quiet control he had carefully hidden. I felt his energy pushing at the edge of his skin.

"Are you threatening me?" Nicholas snarled.

"Only protecting what's mine," Quinn said, gritting his teeth.

"Should we test this out?"

Nicholas had already calculated Quinn's move and released a painful energy surge towards us before I could push it away. The stinging pulsation felt unbearable, and strong enough to push us against a wall. I could feel the current still moving along my spine. Then, Quinn's arm became free. The energy force leaped out from Quinn, taking a strangle hold onto Nicholas's neck. The man began to choke on his words as he reached for his overstretched neck, trying to release that invisible strangle on his throat.

"Let go of me or you'll pay for this," Nicholas gasped.

"Not until I'm sure you'll leave us alone," Quinn shouted back in a deep voice.

The wing had cleared of any bystanders afraid of the white lights and angry voices of the willful men.

"I . . . promise . . . I'll . . . keep . . . my . . . distance."

The release on Nicholas's throat was slowly removed but not by Quinn's mercy. I watched in horror as pain shot down Quinn's back, running directly into his legs. He dropped to the ground.

Mercedes.

"I leave you alone to wander the city and you get into a confrontation with them? *Fool!* We have work to do. Raefield is expected."

Raefield . . . no. He's dead. He can't be coming. I began to sob deep inside. I knew he wasn't dead. He was living in another time. If he could find a way into the portal, if the mist was coming, than he would cross over. He would be in present day Chicago. My anger seeped out.

Steady, steady. Wait, stay strong.

Quinn climbed to his feet. His breathing slowed. He began to prepare again.

"Don't even think of trying anything else. My next move won't be so kind," Mercedes barked.

Quinn retreated. "What do you mean Raefield is coming?"

"Exactly as I said. A storm is coming, a storm that you and I have passed through to get to where we are today. It's finally coming." Mercedes laughed.

"Yes, the storm is coming," Nicholas chanted. "My master will be here, and he's bringing his people."

No, he can't. He can't come here. I won't allow it. I must do something.

It came out of me. But it wasn't the rage that let it go. It wasn't even the gem reshaping itself. I had let it go. It was now surfacing, fighting to be set free. *I* became its keeper.

"How? I haven't sensed anything," Quinn demanded.

"Let's just say we've been able to track it. If everything goes according to plan, than we can expect Raefield at the first sign of autumn. *The harvest moon is at hand!*" she declared. "We'll be one big happy family. You'll see, Lauren. You'll find your place in this world. You'll be at Raefield's side as it was intended."

"I won't do it. I won't go down that murderous path. *I won't be one of them!*" Quinn held me tightly as I trembled in his arms. My control was slipping.

"But you will. You'll have no choice, and you'll see once order has been restored, as it should be. We've been persecuted for so long. *But no more!* This world will be redefined and the new order will rise." Mercedes then spoke in an ancient, long dead language.

"Go. Have your childish life and dreamy days. Enjoy this weak existence. When the time comes, you will follow. We'll be able to keep the portal open." Mercedes glared at Quinn. "Dr. Sendal was able to call the portal open with that rock inside her head. It was unexpected. We waited for you to pass through. It was wise of you to try to close the way once you entered. Clever."

"If your family causes any trouble, we'll make things harder for them," Nicholas stated in a stern voice.

"They were too nosey, especially Helen. She's like her twin in that way," Mercedes sneered.

"Leave my family alone! If you ever come near them, I'll destroy you."

Mercedes and Nicholas laughed. "Child, you wouldn't know how to unleash that strength on your own," Mercedes taunted.

But I knew better. I had opened the gates. I would take the strength given to me and unleash its power.

The walls within the temple shook at my command. Mercedes and Nicholas looked horrified. I held the glass to the aquarium secure so that it wouldn't break onto the ground. The water stirred within. Mercedes, still fixed on my unearthly abilities, extended her arms to strike me down. I quickly seized her will and subdued it. She cursed at me through her screeching voice. My attention remained focused.

The floor began to shake as a quake set off inside the earth. They gripped the marble walls for balance, knowing that my wrath had been awakened. Quinn remained steady at my side, unsure if he needed to intervene or cover for his own life. Nicholas's dark, scorned eyes looked at me first with vexation then complete satisfaction.

I wanted to slap the delight from his eyes. Instead, I released the pain and set free its needlelike precision onto the pair that forced my hand.

"Stop it! Stop doing that! **It's killing me!***"* Mercedes screamed. She held onto her head, writhing in pain.

"Argh, argh, ha, ha, ha," Nicholas vented. *"Ha, ha, ha! Yesss,* let the hate flow. Show us your strength. *Argh, argh."*

"Lauren, show mercy!" Mercedes begged.

I held firm, not pushing the limit any further yet unwilling to pull back.

"Lauren, that's enough. Let go. You're killing them," Quinn urged.

I was startled. I looked at a wide-eyed Quinn. *What am I doing?* I started to release the hold. I was shaking inside. The energy slowly flowed back to me, recoiling inside my body to the core of its domain.

Mercedes tried to catch her breath. The heaviness slowed down. Her once doubtful eyes now reflected fear and trepidation. "Nicholas! Let's get out of here."

My heart raced. It wasn't from my strength, but from the realization of what I had done. I was the monster they wanted to see. I was the evil waiting to be unleashed.

I looked at Quinn for solace. My hands shook. "Quinn, am I a terrible person? Tell me. Was it wrong?"

"No, you had no control. You were pushed."

I knew better. I did have control. I wanted revenge.

"Lauren, they were threatening you. You knew when to stop. That's what's important."

I nodded. I'd promised to learn restraint, to use and to protect, but not to destroy. Could I? Would I need to destroy or be destroyed? My hands were steady, but something felt different. A surge lingered. It felt good and right. My eyes danced with joy and my lips curved upward at the thought.

"Let's get out of here," Quinn suggested.

I glanced at the glassed-in ocean as she resumed her peaceful flow, filled with the sea life safely swimming behind the unbreakable glass.

CHAPTER 17

A Pagan Life

I SPENT MANY nights worrying about Raefield's arrival. Quinn displayed no concern. He repeatedly told me it was impossible to predict a storm's arrival and that Raefield could easily fall into another era.

"But wouldn't it alter the present day if he arrived five years ago or ten years ago?"

"You'd think it could, but today is already set. It can't be changed. That's why you can't go back to save your parents. You can live in that time, relive a moment, but the course has already been set—the end result is the same. It's the future we don't know about." Quinn gave me a reassuring smile.

"So, when I came to Portland, it was the present day, but I had regressed. I was four years old again."

"Exactly. Your life in New Haven ended when you were twenty-two, in 1900. I was twenty-six. That past was the current time, but we travel through the mist for a long time even though it doesn't seem that way. You fell into an opening and your age was reset, a rebirth so to speak. It's just fortunate that the Reeds were able to find you."

Something else troubled my newfound belief in time travel. "What if we go back in time? What if Raefield is able to come here and take me back to the New Haven we knew?"

"He could try to do that. I wouldn't let him," Quinn reassured me. "You need to remember that your time ended there in 1900. After that, you fall into a different situation, you live a different life or you're just a bystander. And there's a chance you'd just fade away. If you hadn't gone through the portal, your life would have ended at the beginning of the century. Remember, you were hurt. We had to get you out for you to survive."

"I know that now. There wasn't an option. And if by chance I lived through my injuries, I probably would've fallen under Raefield's control."

"Fallen," Quinn repeated.

"And if Raefield is able to find a rift in time, then what?"

"Lauren, I can't say for certain he wouldn't try to find that hole. I'm just not aware that it can be done. I'll be concerned if he actually makes it here and finds a way to control your powers for his own use. That's why we need to make sure we can close the portal."

"Dr. Sendal."

We both stood, moving quickly to his place. In record time, we were driving down his street.

"Quinn, I felt your presence as far away as a few blocks. It's amazing what good sleep and a healthy diet can do. Come, I've prepared us a light snack," Dr. Sendal said to us, as we stepped into his home.

I scanned his immaculate condo. This time, I knew what to expect.

"Lauren, how have you been? Are you able to find more control?"

"Yes. I'm getting a better handle on things. And the headaches aren't as bad. I'm able to call it out, more than it's able to take control of me. I feel stronger."

"Excellent. It's working with you. It's recognizing you as the controller." He placed the food samples and fresh cut fruit on our plates. Then he poured us some water from a plastic bottle he'd opened. "Just water."

I watched Quinn drink from his glass. I couldn't help but think back to the coffee shop when I'd first told him about my adoption. I wondered if he should have left me alone so that his life could at least be less complicated and unburdened by my past.

"Lauren, I don't mean to bring up anything that would upset you, but have the voices come back?"

"You mean my parents? No. I haven't heard from them since that time in the hospital. I've tried to contact them, but nothing has happened. It's good to know they're remembered."

He looked at me with understanding in his eyes. "They're not the kind of people you can forget so easily—the best of people. I wanted to know how much they tried to guide you."

"I'm on my own, Dr. Sendal."

"It's what I expected. It's what your parents would have wanted."

"Should I expect more?"

Dr. Sendal paused for a moment. "It's hard to say. I don't fully understand the relationship between the rock and your parents' spirit. Essentially, it's the essence of your parents. In time, I believe it'll lessen until they no longer communicate with you. When that occurs, the gem may be ready to be removed."

I wasn't ready to lose the only direct link I had left to my parents. I'd just found them. I wanted to hold on to them as long as possible, even if they weren't physically real. The thought gnawed at me as it mixed alongside the nerve impulses going to my head.

"They're always going to be a part of you. Their love will carry on in you," Quinn said to me.

"You're right. They would want me to have the most out of life. I can't wallow in what could have been. And I can't bring them back," I said firmly. "This life needs to be lived."

"Your happiness is their greatest gift," Dr. Sendal stated.

"Dr. Sendal, when the stone is removed, will I remember everything?"

"All of it. Your life, as you once lived it, and everything that has happened thus far in this life. It will all come back."

I beamed at Quinn. "Our life then and our life today."

Dr. Sendal's face turned more serious. "Now, let's get to the heart of the reason for your visit. Quinn briefed me on the recent events at the aquarium. What else can you tell me?"

"They were sure they could predict when the mist would come. I don't see how that's possible," Quinn mentioned.

"The only way I know how is through a rock. I'm sure she could draw up a storm with Nicholas's help, but to bring forth a portal, I can't believe it."

"Do you suspect she has a gem?" Quinn inquired.

"No. I doubt it. There aren't many in existence."

"What do you mean *in existence*? How hard is it to find?" I asked Dr. Sendal.

"It's quite difficult."

"What, is it some kind of sacred mine?" I was getting annoyed.

"Lauren, you must understand that your parents were special people. They were gifted, each having a tremendous amount of power."

"But they couldn't even save themselves."

"No, they were tricked by Raefield. He found a weakness. You see, he was very close to your father. Your father trusted him. But when he suspected Raefield was plotting a cataclysmic event, he threatened to expose Raefield to our people and strip away his powers. Your father could do that. He had the ability to take a person's talents and render him mortal. Your *mother* could do it, too. Together, they were invincible. And they never abused their power," Dr. Sendal said, looking moved.

"Then how . . . how could they have fallen into Raefield's hands?"

Dr. Sendal looked at Quinn cautiously. "Because they thought he was remorseful. He begged for their forgiveness. He pleaded with them that he could change. And he did, or so it seemed. He followed their ways and obeyed them like an obedient son. He was very convincing. Your parents loved him . . . like family. They had good hearts. They believed Raefield had mended his ways.

"And when they appeared most vulnerable, he turned on your parents. I was told that in their sleep, he sent a powerful fume—the most deadly kind—paralyzing them in their bed. Then Raefield's men bled them, to weaken them further. They removed your parents from their room and held them prisoner in Raefield's mansion."

I tried to contain my anger and grief. It swelled at every facet in my body. My parents had suffered at the hands of someone they'd trusted! I felt enraged.

Do not let it go. Find that control. You can win.

"Lauren, it's only natural that your inner emotions set off what is innately at the core of your strength. It's what triggers your powers. You have to feel those emotions to let go of the energy and turn on its force. Your control is the key in shaping your power."

I took in small deep breaths. I held the energy within. "What happened next?" I asked, gritting my teeth.

"He only wanted to weaken them. He wanted them to bend their views and not push him to extremes," Dr. Sendal continued.

"But they didn't."

"No, your parents fought. And in their struggle—"

"Stop. I don't want to hear anymore." I felt cold. It was the kind of chill one felt when you're isolated and left to fend for yourself.

"Lauren, we can go if you'd like," Quinn said.

I shook my head. "No. We came here for a reason." I turned to Dr. Sendal. "What about the stone? What else do you know about the portal?"

"The stone . . . the stone is essentially the spirit of your parents. They're the same. Only very gifted people possess a stone. And when they die, the stone is formed. Your parents have been captured within you. It's how we saved you. It gives life. It's what gives you tremendous powers that we're just finding out."

I took a step back. The spirit of my parents and their powers was literally inside my head.

"Dr. Sendal, could it be possible for Lauren to have her own gem?" Quinn asked.

"In her case, it's very likely. That could be why Raefield wants her so much. The gem will only go with the person it sees as a worthy fit, naturally, in this case Lauren because she's their child. He may have known that her parents would possess a stone and deduct that she could as well, making her quite valuable. In death, she's no use to him."

I was a tool to Raefield, a way to manipulate the greatest strength and turn that into the deadliest weapon. Nobody would be safe if I fell into his hands, and if he could control my actions, then all could be lost. My stomach soured.

"Lauren, are you ill? Your color is fading," Quinn asked.

I gathered myself quickly. "No . . . not at all. I'm just taking this all in, the time component and my parents' abilities. Really, I'm fine."

Quinn's eyes narrowed, but he turned back to Dr. Sendal. "Tell us what you know about the portal. You've traveled through it more than once. What can you tell us about its limits?"

Dr. Sendal leaned forward. "I was fortunate enough to cross through time on several occasions. One might say that it was rather risky of me to venture beyond the safety of familiar grounds. But what is security if danger was lurking nearby? Defend yourself—yes—but know that each time you turned around, a death warrant waited for you."

I found myself agreeing with everything Dr. Sendal said. I understood the need to run, to escape at all cost. I couldn't let them see my fear.

"I was the second child born to a family who lived in the territory we call Utah today. It was 1610, ten years before the pilgrims founded Plymouth colony. By this time, it was over a hundred years since

Columbus landed in the Caribbean, making way for the Conquistadores to venture to the new land. The Vikings had already come to North America, followed by Cabot and his men. I'm not sure how we got there, perhaps when a storm passed through some of our people traveled to that land. My grandmother was Shoshone—Comanche—as they are known today. She was a healer, a revered woman. You could say I was destined to follow in her footsteps.

"The Shoshone moved to Wyoming and Colorado; my family went with them. We worked side by side, hunting for game and building a stable life. When I turned fifteen, I was a grown man. I ventured off to study the plant life. I stumbled into a mist; this vapor with its blue hues surrounded me. When I tried to escape, it engulfed me. I was locked inside with nowhere to run. That's when I remembered the stories from my parents about this powerful mist that took us to places we never imagined." Dr. Sendal caught his breath.

"When did you realize you had special powers?" I asked.

"Since I was a little boy. My parents warned me not to use them. They were afraid that the Shoshone would fear us, believing us to be the evil spirits from the dead returning to end their lives with our dark magic. I was unsure of my powers. It scared me when I tried to use my talents, so I kept them hidden just as my parents requested. They told me we were different . . . different from the native people who roamed the land, different than the men who explored the land.

"When I stopped traveling, I found myself in 1690 Boston. It was there that I learned to use magic. I was in my late twenties. I knew I was older. Every memory of my life with the tribe and my family was imbedded in my head. The portal had transformed me. I remembered my parents saying that much."

"That was a dangerous time to practice magic," Quinn stated.

"Yes, it was two years later that the Salem witch trials began. Even though I was living in Boston, we felt the cruelty and injustice."

"We?" Quinn and I both asked.

"I became a court member to Sabina, the princess of the night. I served her for two years when the trials began. She was a wily one. She was very cunning and beautiful. She had men at her feet and powers like no one else—similar to Raefield. Her innocent violet eyes and full red lips could lure anyone from the dead. And she killed people who stood in her way. People listened to her. They were afraid of her. I was . . . caught up in her allure . . . bewitched by her influence to see what she really was.

"I was the healer, the doctor of the court. It was her court, a coven of witches, made up of people like us. We lived amongst mortals, but separate from the colonist who could never understand our ways, could never know our secret. I learned how to use my magic. I belonged to that secret world."

I understood the need to journey in order to find that place to be complete.

"She was furious with those foolish children and the superstitious people who engaged in those trials. Accusations flew. In those days, mental illness and accidental drug use were unheard of. Sabina never feared the colonists; they were fodder to her games. Her rage was set off when they captured a wizard, her lover. They suspected him of practicing witchcraft because he was so boastful. One night, a group of angry people surprised him in his state of inebriation, tying his arms and stabbing him with a temporary paralytic. They took him to a cell. They questioned him relentlessly. When they were through with him, they stabbed him in the heart with a poison that could kill a witch. Somehow, they knew what to use. I suspect a jealous lover of Sabina told them what to do.

"She was enraged. When she found her lover's body burned at the stake in an open field, it set her off. Sabina went on a killing spree. Her delirium took over, and she became sloppy. We were exposed. It wasn't safe for any of us. There was nowhere to run, no place to hide. In fear and from a lack of leadership, some of the members began to target one another. That's when I learned that killing your own made you stronger, but it also set off a chain reaction.

"Even though I became stronger and more powerful, I still ran from the chaos and the mob. I could defend myself, but I wouldn't kill for revenge. I promised to heal, to protect those who needed my assistance. But in the end, I had to kill some of my own in order to survive." Dr. Sendal fell silent.

"How were you able to leave?" I finally asked.

"I hid in the countryside. For days, I roamed the territory, trying to find a safe place to survive, hoping that a great mist would carry me away. When it didn't, I moved on. Finally, I ran into some compassionate people. They'd heard of the massacre in Boston. They knew of Sabina's spree. They told me that she went into one of the mob leader's home, a minister, while he slept safely in his bed. She pressed her body against his and took him under her control. Sabina sliced her wrist so that the minister could taste from her blood. This wasn't the blood of the afterlife. Her blood was acid. One drink and death would ensue for the unfortunate soul.

"Hiding within the dark corner of the room was the scorned lover. She was caught by surprise but ran to him like a lost child. In her moment of weakness, he struck her down, taking the life of the woman he loved. He quickly got out of the minister's house, and there in the dark, open field, he set her body on fire."

I was in Quinn's arms. I felt a strange sense of loss and despair. "What happened to that man?"

"He drank the poison that can kill a witch. In death, I assumed, he could be with her forever."

A love tragedy turned worse. I was glad my life wasn't so complicated. Still, the mayhem that spread across the land in those fanatical times stayed in my mind as a warning of magic's destruction. "Dr. Sendal, how did you get out?"

"Kayden, one of the gentle people that I met, had a stone imbedded in his head. He was able to call the great mist. He told me of the powers of the stone as Sabina had done, but I actually never met someone who had one."

"And that's when you came to New Haven in 1885," Quinn recalled.

"Sort of. My first time was actually in 1890. I was only going through the motions of 1890 because it wasn't set. That's when I knew I had stumbled into the future."

"Amazing . . . the unknown future," Quinn spoke in awe. "What did New Haven look like? Was the hotel as you remembered?"

"Nothing was clear. There were fragmented images of the hotel. And the people . . . one minute they were present and in the next moment, they were gone. I was lucky that the portal stayed opened in the unfinished future."

"If Raefield wasn't in New Haven when Quinn arrived in the present day, then where is he?"

"That's a very good question. All of us had gone into another time at that point. I suspect that he stayed in New Haven for some time before entering the portal, or I should say before another mist came through. The question is . . . where did he go?" Dr. Sendal said.

If Raefield left New Haven, could he be in the present as a younger person with a different identity? Would I be so lucky and maybe he'd already passed away? No, Mercedes and Nicholas expected him.

"Lauren, I have a feeling that Raefield is still alive. I can't say if Mercedes and Nicholas were just trying to scare us, but unless they have a stone, I can't imagine they're able to predict when the mist will pass through. And there's no way to know if Raefield will be here when fall arrives. You can't control where the mist will take you and when." Quinn shook his head. "I don't know what they're up to. I do know you surprised them. I bet they never expected you to be so advanced."

Advanced. I wasn't trying to be advanced. I was trying to protect Quinn and myself from their undermining ways. But it did feel exciting and natural to release that kind of mental prowess. I felt rejuvenated.

Somewhere, that eagerness reared its resourceful head again.

"It's late. I think you two have had your fill of ghoulish stories for today. Lauren, I think you should talk this over with your parents. Prepare them for what might occur. In the meantime, I'll do some digging around, see what I can find out. I think it's best that we start to hone in on your skills—just in case. It's time you cultivate what's yours." Dr. Sendal sounded fatherly. "And please, go on with your life as you normally would. Don't allow the thought of Raefield to consume your happiness." Dr. Sendal turned to Quinn. "I'll be in touch."

The silence during the car drive home grated on my nerves. "Quinn, how can you be so relaxed about all of this? Aren't you a little concerned?"

"Curious, yes. Worried . . . no. Once I know what they're up to, then I'll decide if we should worry. I know this sounds crazy, but I think this might be a ploy."

I was glad that one of us felt confident.

"Lauren, it's only natural to worry. I don't want to minimize the possibility that Raefield could come here. In fact, he may even be here, but I think we would know that by now. My instinct tells me those two are up to something else. Why give us warning of his arrival? Why not surprise us with his presence? It would be to their advantage."

Quinn had a point. Why tell us in advance unless they wanted to brag. They've been known to be overly confident, as Quinn had said. And I highly doubt they were being generous.

"You're right. It seems too convenient for them to lay their plan out for us, especially the arrival of someone like Raefield. We'd only react to what they tell us. We could run."

"I'm not running."

"Why? Why wouldn't you run?"

"I've turned the other way before. I want to be here if Raefield shows his face. I'm not saying I want a fight, but I'm not going to hide every time someone makes a threat. Sure, your safety and welfare *is* my concern, but your home is here. *My* home is here with you. If Raefield has to be destroyed, so be it." Quinn was very focused on the road ahead. His stern face never wavered.

"This isn't the time to be a hero."

Quinn remained silent, his head never turned in my direction. I didn't want him to think that I didn't appreciate his efforts. He didn't need to prove his manhood; I already knew he was strong. His devotion said it all. I just didn't want him killed.

I felt sick again. I needed a plan.

"Tell your family to meet us tomorrow evening. We should keep them informed of any new changes. They may even have some news of their own," Quinn ordered. "Lauren, your parents have been tracking the whereabouts of Mercedes and Nicholas for some time."

"And?"

"So, it's safe to say they're probably watching out for Raefield, too."

We crept into his silent house. You could hear Garrett snoring upstairs. I suspect Raegan was still up, watching TV or talking on the phone. I texted her to say I would be staying with Quinn tonight.

"I'll call Alex and the gang tomorrow."

"Let me talk to Alex," Quinn said.

"Are you sure? You don't have to do it."

"I think its better that I talk to him directly. He'll have questions, and maybe some accusations. I'll take the hit if he starts up. He'll want to know everything."

"Right."

I was accustomed to carrying an extra bag of my personal belongings since we switched off where the other person would stay. I quickly got ready for bed, and then climbed into his waiting arms on my side of the bed. It felt nice to be close to him.

Fatigue came over me despite the nagging in my mind. "Quinn?"

"What is it?"

"There's something I forgot to mention to you." I turned to him in the dark. "When my friends were over, I overheard them talking about odd changes and visitors. Do you suppose they actually felt intruders coming?"

"Between all of them, it's possible. But I doubt they can tell this far in advance if Raefield or his men would happen to cross the portal. We're talking about time periods, not time zones."

"Then what do you suppose they meant?"

"You'll have to ask them," Quinn said, his voice fading into sleep.

I searched again. How could my supernatural friends feel something approaching, something eventful that could take place? I decided that the random anomalies stirring, which I have felt over and over again, were not the same thing they felt. My signs seem to be unknown forces, spirit-like in nature and at times an unexplained sense of threat looming nearby. Whether it was a shadow hovering over me or around a hidden corner, or the drastic change in weather, and even the presence of my parents, they seemed to cross at irregular intervals. Neither Quinn nor Dr. Sendal felt the same perplexing forces as I've felt. Could what I have felt be parallel to what my friends were experiencing?

My mind jolted. "Quinn!" I hissed in the darkness. "What about the group from West Virginia? Could they be coming this way?" I jerked the sheets off of him.

"What is it?"

"Remember when Garrett told you about Alex's fire marks? He must have told you how he got them."

"Yeah," Quinn grumbled.

"What if Mercedes and Nicholas were somehow involved with that coven? Could they be using them to call open a portal?"

Quinn's eyes opened wide. His body stiffened. "Even if they knew about this band of outcasts, I can't see them bringing any of those members out in the open. Didn't your friends say they feared being away from the safety of their home, that living in the outside world was too much?"

"Yes, but what if Mercedes and Nicholas were able to convince just a few of them to follow . . . to believe in their cause, like they were on the same team?"

"It still wouldn't matter. Their powers combined wouldn't have the ability to create a mist. That nest sounded deranged. I can't imagine they have the mental capacity. The only way they could have that much power is if one member had . . . "

"A stone," we said in unison.

"It's impossible," Quinn said. "A person needs to have a strong mind in order to hold onto the stone and wield its power. If a person isn't of sound mind, the gem could easily take over that person and ultimately destroy him."

"But what if one of them was strong enough to withstand the powers of a gem? Then he could open the doors of chaos. Quinn, what if it's true?"

"Then we have a lot to be concerned about," he replied.

Quinn didn't say anything else. My mind, however, continued to race. I knew it was premature to assume this could happen, but still, the idea that one or some of them could come here and force their control over us alarmed me. Did one of the West Virginia witches possess a stone?

"It's late. Let's save our energy for tomorrow. We'll talk to your family and your friends to find out what they know. Together, we can come up with a definitive plan."

Sleep. My mind wasn't on sleep. Mercedes and Nicholas intended to bring Raefield to the present day with the possible help of a crazed witch. How could I sleep? Yet, as my thoughts traveled from my immediate family to Quinn and to the friends and family he'd left in New Haven, sleep manifested in the deepest corners of my mind. I trailed somewhere between here and that other world of unconsciousness.

⊷▭ ▭⊶

It seemed like a long night to me, a night that would never end, but somehow the sunlight permeated Quinn's room, waking me from a hazy state of mind. I looked over to his side of the bed.

"Quinn . . . Quinn?"

The room was light and airy; the window was open to let in the morning breeze. I felt warm, moist air fill his room. His organized sanctuary remained untouched.

"Quinn?"

He still didn't answer. I finally climbed out of bed, stumbling to the bathroom. I almost didn't notice a white piece of paper dangling from his tack board.

Lauren, I didn't want to wake you. You stirred most of the night. I thought you could use the sleep. Went to work. Contacted Uri. I'll see you later.

Always,

Q

What time was it? I looked at the clock: noon. I smiled to myself, thinking of his thoughtfulness. I was so lucky to have him in my life, a miracle that he'd come along and found me again. I quickly grabbed my belongings and dashed across the front porch to my place. Raegan had left the fans on. The summer heat spread everywhere. I quickly got myself ready. Hunger still hadn't found me. Had Dr. Sendal sprinkled some of his fairy dust onto the food? By this time, I would have consumed two meals.

I quickly ate a light snack in case the need to replenish came on strong. I pressed the speed button to call Mom.

"Mom, it's Lauren . . . No, I'm fine. Listen, Quinn and I need to talk to you and Dad this evening. It's important . . . No, I can't go into detail . . . Yes, it's about them."

I knew what was coming next.

"Lauren, you know when it comes to them, you need to let us know right away."

"I'm telling you now." The line went silent. I waited for her to respond.

"Okay, I didn't give you the chance. Go ahead."

"First of all, we're fine. We just want to pull everything together, see what you know and tell you what we know."

"And?" Mom asked.

"And . . . we ran into them again. But everything is under control. I handled it."

"What do you mean 'handled it'? You can't just say you ran into them and everything is fine. It's never fine with those two."

"Mom, just trust me, okay? I'll tell you tonight when we're all together. I don't want to get into details over the phone. I'm also calling Isaak and Chelsea." I could feel her tension on the other line, but I wasn't about to cave in. This was more my problem, and I needed to handle things my way.

Mom let out a heavy sigh. "Alright, Lauren. I'll expect a full report. I keep forgetting you're an adult, too. But we're your—"

"Yes, family is the most important thing. Love you, Mom." I ended the call, feeling a stronger bond with my family.

My whole life had been protected by the careful ways of my parents. I posed a risk to them, yet they'd taken on that task wholeheartedly and raised me as their own. They kept vigilant all these years so that one day, when I was ready, I would know the real story. Or the stone would force my hand.

I reached for my phone again to text Isaak and Chelsea. I was sure my parents kept them fully informed of any situation. Isaak returned my text immediately.

THIS SHOULD BE GOOD. HAVE BEEN WONDERING WHAT YOU'RE UP TO.

I haven't spoken to Isaak directly about any of this—meetings with Dr. Sendal, running into Mercedes and Nicholas, and the West Virginia theory. There'd been no time and too much to explain. I knew my parents told him everything. He'd known about my past before I did. And how much did Quinn share with Isaak? The last time we dined with my parents, I remembered a unified kinship forming between my brother and Quinn.

Someone was calling me. "Alex?"

"What the hell is going on, Lauren?"

I rolled my eyes.

"Got a call from your *boy*friend."

"I know. He thought it best to talk to you directly."

"What did he do now?"

"Nothing. He's not doing anything wrong. It's me. I'm the one who's putting everyone at risk."

I stopped to let him fire the questions. Better to let him make his point then to sugar coat the situation.

"Quinn isn't stirring up trouble?"

"No, quite the opposite."

Alex became silent, then said in a less accusing tone, "So, there might be some connection between the West Virginia clan and the other two clowns?"

"Possibly. We're not sure if the West Virginia clan came into contact with Mercedes and Nicholas, but they're threatening us. They're saying Raefield is coming through a portal."

"What? Can he do that?"

"It's just a theory we have. I don't want to alarm everyone. We're meeting my family tonight."

"He talked to Cameron, too, and now the others know."

"Good. We'll want to compare everything, even any strange feelings you've experienced."

"Alright. Just wanna make sure."

"We can talk more when we're all together again."

"Hey, Lauren?" Alex began. "Don't take it personally about Quinn. I'm not trying to give him a hard time. We just . . . can't be too trusting."

"I know. Try. That's all I ask." I ended the call with Alex. I didn't want to lose any friends over this unresolved controversy before we could pull everything together.

Tonight would be interesting. I wanted to know what my parents really knew. They'd had such a major role in handling powerful people and orchestrating this present life. I found it rather amusing that Mom was so passionate about American history and culture. We lived it. We were that past. We had flourished alongside common man. Had any of our true nature made its way into the mainstream in an ugly turn of events and exposed us to the paranoid masses, there may have been greater chaos and rebellion. Even the authors of the *Malleus Maleficarum* would have turned over in their graves. Little did the Inquisitors know they'd persecuted the wrong people throughout Europe and young America. I wondered how many true witches they'd in their possession. I felt certain a few powerful souls had guided the hunters into the afterlife.

My phone buzzed on the kitchen counter. I raced from the living room, knowing who would be on the other line.

"Quinn, where are you?" I was almost breathless.

"Getting some work done."

"Alex told me you called. It wasn't as bad as I thought. Everyone will be at my parents' place. I haven't heard from Chelsea, but I'm sure she'll come."

"Think your family will handle the news okay? About Raefield possibly coming?"

"I feel good about things, like one big family coming together in a show of support. It's going to work out. I can feel it."

"I hope so. Regardless, they'll support you. Love you."

"Love you, too."

The rest of the afternoon sped by in a whirlwind. I managed to get in a power run and took a solid nap just in case the gathering lasted into the late hours. I didn't have to be at work until one the next afternoon.

→─▶◉ ◉◀─←

Quinn's dark car pulled into the shared driveway. I watched as he got out of his car wearing light business attire. He looked fresh and energetic, like he hadn't worked all day—a man in line with his destiny. He reached into the passenger seat for his canvas messenger bag and then turned to retrieve some grocery bags from the backseat of the car. He grinned. I quickly pulled away from the window. I moved further into the house to find something to keep me busy. The door to his house opened and closed, followed by silence.

Oscar started to bark. "Shh, Oscar. Keep it down."

I quickly scurried around the kitchen, trying to find something to clean even though the house didn't need cleaning. A book managed to find its way into my ready hands, and I miraculously transported myself onto the sofa when, after a minute, a light rap sounded on the door.

"This is between us." I slowly walked to the door, knowing who would be on the other side.

"Hi. I thought you were home. I picked up Italian so you wouldn't have to cook." Quinn lifted up the plastic bags and came through the door. He'd already changed into his khaki shorts and a striped shirt that I've never seen.

"Oh, I'm glad you thought of it. That'll save me some time so we don't have to rush to get to my parents' place." I opened up the Styrofoam containers.

I set up the small feast, adding seasonal fruit and fresh greens for our sides. It felt like a happy little home. He entertained me, and he dined me. He left all notions of fear aside, leaving an atmosphere of hope and safety.

"We should head out."

We climbed into Quinn's car and drove to my parents' home. We were silent the whole way, but the quietness between us was understood.

I recognized Chelsea's silver Audi coupe and Isaak's practical Lexus SUV. I didn't recognize the oversized black Escalade and a non-descript Civic parked in front of the house.

"There are others," Quinn commented.

I fished for the keys to let us in. The house was temperate and inviting like I remembered. We paused under the chandelier in the high-ceilinged foyer and I heard voices coming from the family room down the hallway to the right. My mother soon appeared to greet us.

"Lauren, Quinn, we're all here. Have you eaten?"

"We've already eaten." I looked at Mom curiously. "You asked the Brandts and the Fozis to join us? Have they been involved this whole time?"

"They've been informed of certain matters since we've moved here. They're like us in many ways except for the long journey."

I'd always wondered about the Brandts and the Fozis. Now, their sudden and hurried friendship with my parents on the recommendation of Dr. Sendal made sense. One moment we lived in small town Idaho, and the next minute we moved to upscale Chicago.

"I didn't see Dr. Sendal's car. Is he running late?"

"No, the Brandts drove him."

"That would explain the government style Escalade," I said to Mom. My mother nodded.

The three of us walked into the living room where everyone sat comfortably, talking amongst themselves about everyday things. All eyes turned to Quinn and me, particularly me. I felt self-conscious, something I usually don't experience. Their eyes bore through me like the brightest of spotlights, blinding me so that I couldn't see and somehow causing my voice to disappear. And the floor felt closer in proximity. Quinn squeezed my hand.

"Lauren, I'm so glad to see you again. We haven't seen you in some time. You should stop by. Our youngest has her license now and she's excited to show anyone her driving skills," Nadja Fozi said, twirling her fawn-colored hair.

"Is that her Honda outside?"

"No, we borrowed our son's car."

"She's been a little concerned since the time we rushed off to Connecticut with your parents. It's made her . . . uneasy. She feels better switching cars," Julian informed us.

"Driving different cars isn't going to make you safer, Nadja," Leslie Brandt remarked. "No one will get to us." Leslie looked at me for confirmation.

"Is that why you're driving that monster of a car?" Nadja responded.

"We've been looking for something bigger for family trips and taking my daughter's friends around."

Aaron Brandt looked impatient. "Ladies, this isn't the time to exchange car preferences or who may have the best decoy. It really doesn't make a difference." He turned his deep amber eyes on me. "Lauren, is there something you'd like to share with us?"

All eyes were on me again. Even my normally outspoken brother decided to keep quiet.

Mom? Dad? Where's my support?

"Just take your time, Lauren," Chelsea spoke up.

The weight of the world somehow managed to drop from the sky and onto my shoulders. I considered my options. What would be best for the people I knew and for me. One wrong decision could mean the abrupt change in people's lives. I wasn't ready to be the kind of leader they could turn to. What possible direction could I give them when I didn't know myself? Run and hide?

I opted for something closer to home. "For starters, I'd like everyone to meet Quinn. He's been an important part of my life."

"Of course, of course. Where are our manners? This must be the Quinn your parents have mentioned," Leslie said, glancing at my mother. "I'm Leslie Brandt, and this is my husband, Aaron. We've been friends with Lauren's parents since they moved to Chicago. And this is Nadja and Julian Fozi," Leslie said. "You already know Dr. Sendal. Let's just say we've been a tight knit community since, and we'd like to keep it that way."

"I understand completely," Quinn responded. "I can assure you that preserving this life is what I want. I'm sure we're all here for the same reasons, seeking the same answers. Raefield has made quite an impression on everyone, despite never meeting some of you in person. His legend seems to carry throughout time."

"Oh, we've met him a few times. We know what he's capable of doing," Nadja responded. "We prefer to stay as far away from him as possible." Her hand twitched.

"What my wife is trying to convey is that we've witnessed him in action, and we've seen his methods of persuasion and how he deals with those who interfere," Julian added quietly. "We've passed through that time, long enough to be acquainted with Dr. Sendal, Helen and Oren, and to briefly meet your parents."

A warm feeling passed through me. This important gathering involved everyone, not me wallowing in self-pity. Their lives could be compromised, too. The gifted minds now formed a close-knit circle around the rectangular coffee table where my mother laid out the spread of food, now half eaten, for the purposeful long evening. Our welfare and future appeared unclear.

I took a deep breath. "What we know is the existence of Raefield and some of his followers. Obviously, Mercedes and Nicholas found a way to be here in present day. They've managed to keep a low profile until this summer." Everyone nodded or mumbled in agreement. "They haven't made any direct threats, only stressing the importance that, some day, I would be at Raefield's side. He wants to use me for my powers."

"Which I will never let happen," Quinn asserted.

"Neither would we," Isaak finally spoke up.

"However, Mercedes has revealed to us for some unknown reason, perhaps to scare us, that the portal can be opened." I looked at my mother.

"What do you mean, Lauren?" My mother turned to my father and her natural born children.

I decided to omit the aquarium confrontation. "They said a storm was coming, that the portal can be opened, and Raefield and his people would be coming."

"*What?* That's impossible! Raefield is in reach?" Nadja exclaimed. "You can't mean that they know when a storm is coming. No one predicts a great mist. They could only call a storm if they had a stone." Nadja looked terrified. "*No* . . . no! They can't have one. How? *Who* is in their possession?"

Everyone except Quinn and Dr. Sendal buzzed with concern.

"My worst fears are coming true. Raefield intends to destroy our lives and take Lauren away. I won't have this!" Mom insisted.

My father attempted to console my mother. Chelsea and Isaak just looked at each other.

Nadja shook her head. "We have to run. We have to get as far away as possible."

Julian turned to me, and I saw panic in his cocoa eyes. "Lauren, how did they say Raefield would arrive?"

"I guess through the portal. She said they were able to track a storm. She didn't say how." My next statement would be another blow. My voice held steady. "Raefield will be here by the start of fall."

"By the September equinox?" my father asked. "Uri, can this be true?"

My parents turned to Dr. Sendal for answers. "I can't foresee that they would know where Raefield was located, unless he's able to pass back and forth through time and communicate with them periodically. It's unpredictable. We would have sensed it if Raefield had come within range of us."

"She spoke about the first sign of autumn and the harvest moon, which falls in October this year," I told them, remembering what Mercedes had said.

"What's this nonsense about a stone in their possession? I thought it was a rarity," Aaron questioned.

"It is. We don't know if they're bluffing just to throw us off or to scare us. They don't have one in their possession here in Chicago. We've located their place of residence," Dr. Sendal explained.

"So, this leads us to an idea that came to Lauren last night. It may be farfetched, but I think we should examine it carefully. I don't want to miss anything," Quinn said.

"Lauren, what else do you know?" Mom asked, her insistent hazel eyes probed into me.

"It's something Alex mentioned. When he was in West Virginia, he ran into a reclusive but powerful group of witches and wizards. They weren't elegant or refined, nor were they mainstreamed into society. And from what my friends said, they didn't resemble a cooperative lifestyle like even the nomadic tribes in the west. Alex, Elsie, and Justin described them as 'disturbed'."

"These are your camp friends, the ones your parents entrusted to keep watch over you?" Leslie inquired.

"Yes, the group I met in high school. We've formed a strong bond. And just so you know, we've compared abilities."

"I would assume so. Your parents said they were like us, but can they all be trusted?" Leslie asked.

"Absolutely. I've always had a good feeling about my friends."

"You never know," Leslie remarked, still unconvinced that anyone could be trusted. She focused on Quinn, her eyes narrowed.

"Leslie, Oren and I made sure they were sound. I wouldn't jeopardize Lauren's safety. They've proved to be loyal and trustworthy friends."

"We'll get through this, my dear," Aaron gently said to his wife. "It's a challenge we knew we would some day face."

I suddenly felt guilty. If it weren't for this stupid rock or me, my family and their friends wouldn't be in danger. My friends wouldn't be pawns in Raefield's ultimate plan. We wouldn't be here comparing ideas and devising ways to stay alive.

I wanted to run.

"Let's get back to the matter at hand. Lauren, finish telling us your theory," Dad urged.

"What if Mercedes and Nicholas have been in contact with the clan?"

"We've heard of this group out east. They may have been in contact with this rogue group," my father mentioned.

"Since there seems to be a mystery around this coven, could it be possible that one member has a stone?"

The voices started again, exchanging thoughts and concerns.

"Frankly, we don't know. None of us has come close enough to them. If they do, I'm not sure they understand the power of the stone," Dad said.

"Exactly. Only Alex has been in their lair. And he wasn't fully coherent and strong enough to find out."

Isaak sat up this time. "What you're saying is that one of the West Virginia people could have a stone and that Mercedes has somehow managed to gain their trust, enough to use them to call open a portal?"

"Yes."

"Dad, is this true?"

My father looked flushed and angered. He turned to Dr. Sendal and said, "Uri, I've never heard of someone from the past entering the present at precisely a set time. It's inconceivable! That person may not come out the same. Take Lauren, for instance."

Everyone tried not to look directly at me. Quinn held me close to him.

"You're right. It's too hard to predict, but we have to take their threats seriously. Even if a portal was open, there's still a slight chance that Raefield could cross over. In the meantime, we have to be very aware of our surroundings. Any signs and any information *must* be shared. I suggest we resume our lives. We don't want to give them reasons to make us weaker. We can't let them take over our lives," Dr. Sendal suggested.

My observant sister, who'd remained quiet the entire evening, finally spoke. "I think that's the best we can do. From what I've heard, I don't believe Raefield is much for diplomacy, but it seems to me he doesn't want to harm Lauren. Perhaps in his arrogance, he'll reveal to us his long awaited plan. If we could convince him that the stone is ready to be removed from Lauren, then she can't be of value to him."

"That would be ideal, but I doubt he'll be so gullible," Leslie remarked. "Is it that close to coming out, Uri?"

"I have my doubts. I thought she was in the beginning stages of extraction when she was hospitalized, but it seems to have molded into her more deeply."

"What about an exchange? If the West Virginia people have a stone, then maybe Raefield would take that person over Lauren," Isaak suggested.

"I wish that were the case, but we know that Lauren is his conquest. Her rock is superior," Quinn stated, his tone grim.

I would never be free of this burden. *Oh, Mother and Father, why was I given this obligation? Please forgive me for what I plan to do. I need to protect these people.*

Mom started to get up. "I think we have a lot to think about. It's not our wish to place any of you in danger, but if you feel staying together could only improve the outcome, then we'd gladly accept your support. If you feel you must leave, then we wouldn't hold it against you. We're all friends," she said with quiet dignity. "We will find ways to bring Raefield and his followers down if it comes to a confrontation. Some of Lauren's friends will be moving here soon. They feel their lives may be at risk, so staying together could be beneficial."

"It may not be an easy task. We'll do everything we can to avoid casualties," my father said. "Just as Uri said, we can't let them weaken us. If they infiltrate our group, then we'll all perish."

A strong mind, I thought to myself. I hated this gift.

"No, Oren, we can't let them destroy us. It would be the end of our people, the good people who have lived for centuries in building this life," Aaron concurred. "We would always stand together."

The room quieted again, but I could hear the silent nods and the voices of reason bowing to what needed to be done, and what lay ahead in order to secure our fate.

"It's been a long evening. Thank you all for coming. We'll be in contact," Mom said, and everyone prepared to leave.

I felt worn out. I thought I could eat some of the delicious food in front of me despite the meal I'd consumed earlier. My appetite disappeared during my need to escape.

Mom stopped me before I reached the door. "Lauren, after we spoke this morning, I got a call from your friend, Elsie. I didn't want to speak prematurely on behalf of your friends, but she said they were planning to move here, anyway. She was certain that staying close during this time was the best thing to do." She gave me a thoughtful look. "And please don't think you're a burden to them. They're your friends, and they care a great deal about you. Their lives are on the line, too."

Great. More people became involved because of me. I couldn't prevent my friends who didn't even live here from becoming more entangled in this web. Little insects we were, waiting to be taken, cocooned, and stored as food.

The Fozis left first, followed by the Brandts. Chelsea stood in the foyer with my parents. Dr. Sendal, Isaak, and Quinn huddled near the stone fireplace. I heard their whispers from across the room.

"Let's take a look from all sides. I think we have a greater advantage than we believe," Dr. Sendal mumbled.

"I agree. I have a feeling we'll be running into Mercedes and Nicholas in the near future. Let's see if we can't get something out of them. Lauren caught them off guard. I have a feeling they won't take it lightly. They'll want to show us up," Quinn whispered.

"That's really keeping your enemies close. What about the West Virginia clan? Should we seek them out, maybe send an envoy to see what we can find out?" Isaak asked.

"It might be too risky, although I'm just as curious as you are. It would be advantageous to see who and what we're dealing with," Quinn murmured.

The front door closed and my parents returned to the living room. I heard Chelsea's car engine came to life before she quickly sped out of the driveway.

"Helen, we were just saying goodnight," Dr. Sendal said.

"Hmm. You all look too conspiratorial. In any case, we're grateful for everyone here tonight," Mom said, kissing me goodnight before she headed for the stairway.

My father waited at the doorway until Quinn, Dr. Sendal, and I were seated in the car. I watched him from the back seat, waving to us as we began to leave. The bountiful moon looked brilliant in the sky—full and glowing with an abundant illumination. Patient. It was the harvest moon I feared. It wouldn't be long before the final sign of peace faded and the crossover would take place. For now, the sky appeared still except for the breeze moving through the air. It caused the trees to sway. The maple leaves now ushered toward the house, protecting my family vicariously in its cloak-like branches. I watched until I could no longer see the two-story home as we moved farther and farther away.

CHAPTER 18

Call Me

I VOWED THAT I wouldn't let the intruders—our inherited enemies—disrupt my life. I didn't want enemies. They'd chosen to be antagonists. They bullied us like common peasants with their malicious threats and their abuse of power. Magical Powers. Who do they think they are? Don't they realize we have just as much power, if not more?

I'll show them.

Take it easy, Lauren. You have to do better.

Life would continue regardless of this obstacle. Everyone took the new information in stride, except for Mrs. Fozi on occasion. She would have to find her way. I wasn't going to hide under my bed and wait for them to arrive, if Raefield truly was coming. *Deal with him when he comes* was my newly acquired motto. I had other exciting and fun-filled days ahead. The Fourth of July festivities was this weekend, our house party the next weekend. I didn't have time to worry nor did I care. I even welcomed the humdrum complaints that came with work and the normalness of everyday life. At night, I found solace knowing that Raegan was safe while I stayed with Quinn.

Yes, I even stayed vigilant for any character changes in my friends.

Keeping that in mind, I continued to practice my skills with Quinn at every possible moment while receiving healthy doses of education from Dr. Sendal. He understood the importance of working on the craft—how the forces came together and breathed life into what we could do. I felt stronger and agile with my skills. The connection between the mysterious rock and myself fused more and more into one. My thoughts and my actions became synonymous as the energy flowed through me like blood and water. We couldn't function without each other. We couldn't survive if one failed.

I think the two of them actually enjoyed stretching the limits of their power. Their teaching helped me to discover my potential.

"Are you going to play with that remote all evening, or can I have it to watch my show?" Raegan asked, staring at me wide-eyed.

"Huh? Oh sure, take it. I'm not watching anything special."

"Obviously. Lauren, you're a million miles away. What's going on with you?"

"I just have a lot on my plate. It's nothing to be concerned about," I said, giving her my best front.

Raegan's bright green eyes narrowed. I saw a lecture forming from her lips. "You know what your problem is? And because I'm your best friend, and I love you like family, I'm going to be straight with you because that's what we're supposed to do. You, Lauren Reed, always need to be in control."

My mouth opened to form the words I wanted to say. She halted my reply with a raised hand.

"You have some kind of strange notion that you need to be perfect all the time, that everyone expects that of you. That everyone depends on you for all the answers," Raegan gently lectured. "It's not natural. It's impossible to shoulder the world on your own, so please stop trying."

"I'm not trying to carry everyone's load, just the ones that depend on me to do the right thing," I replied.

She wasn't convinced. "Well, you've been handed a lot, more than your share. No, let me rephrase that, *beyond everyone's share.*"

"I know. I just don't want to be a burden to everyone. I feel . . . responsible."

"Lauren! Have you heard anything I've said? You're not a burden. And it's not *your* responsibility to save the world." She looked exasperated and flushed. "You've got some crazy witch and a few cracked up magicians on your case. Hell, *I* would be a little disturbed!"

I recapped everything in my head, all of the pros and the cons neatly lined up in their respective columns. All the players were positioned around this dimensional board, connected somehow, and waiting to make their stealthy moves. I had no intention of being a pawn.

"I guess you're right. It hasn't been easy learning about my birth parents, my *special abilities*, and, of course, those freaks on my trail." *And Quinn.*

"Ah, duh. And look at the fate you were given. A stupid rock imbedded in your head, tying you to great powers that people are after . . . would *kill* for," Raegan reminded me in a whisper. "Don't get me wrong, having magical powers is way cool, minus the other stuff."

I sighed. Instead of feeling all emotional inside that I could talk to Raegan about my troubles, I felt hollow. Numbness crept along the edges of my true feelings. I was grateful that I could confide in her, yet still leaving out a few minor details—the time exchange, actually being from the past. Knowing Raegan, she would be fascinated having a friend who was born before 1900, was well preserved, and frozen in time. Raegan needed to know from me who I was and not second hand from Alex.

"Lauren, you don't need to live this perfect person image. It's okay to be unsure. It's normal to rely on other people. Until Quinn, I wasn't sure if you ever needed anyone or anything."

Oh, how she knew me too well. It's true. He's the one that I've waited for. He'd seen me break down into little pieces and helped me glue myself back together again.

"I mean, nothing seems to faze you. You don't let anything bother you. I'm just afraid that, one day, you're going to crack from being so strong all the time."

I chuckled to myself. "Believe me, I've had my moments. I haven't stayed completely calm through all of this. It's been a lot to take in, but knowing I have such great friends and a wonderful family has really helped."

This time, Raegan looked convinced of my sincerity.

"We're not close to being through with all of this. There's still so much we don't know. I'm just saving my energy for bigger things to come."

Raegan didn't press any further. I was glad for some peace of mind, but it proved short-lived. Moments after Raegan left for the evening to meet friends, something aroused in me. It wasn't a gentle tug or a sudden ache. It felt more like a muscle spasm. Then, it escalated in severity. It began to pull at my insides slice-by-slice, until it became irrepressible. I was losing myself to this newfound pain. This powerful force, this overwhelming compulsion dragged my body upstairs. It called to me as if it cried and spoke only to me in some language meant for my sensitive ears.

I'm coming. I hear you.

What would be waiting for me upstairs? Something terrible? Something wonderful? Was it a monster under my bed? Whatever wanton force it might be, I needed to know. I belonged to it, and it belonged to me.

Quinn. He wouldn't be here for another hour.

No, I shouldn't go.

What if it's dangerous? I would recognize a trap. Wouldn't I? Surely I possessed that power. But it still urged me to move towards it.

My hands longed to reach out, and my body moved closer to the unknown. It took every ounce of strength in me to stop moving.

Caution. Be cautious.

I slowly glazed over my pendant with my index finger with just enough icing to delicately cover the prized jewel, transforming it into a work for display. I'm not sure what I hoped to find by touching the bracelet, but something in me believed an answer would surface.

I'm here now. I'm with you.

My bedroom door stood ajar. It waited for me, patiently waited to draw me in.

See me, it echoed sweetly.

I surrendered. I was like a madwoman with one goal in mind: The absolute need to re examine the infamous box. It called to me again, and I answered its appeal. I don't know why, I just had to look at it. It was the box that housed my special charm, placed there for safekeeping. It spoke to me from the hidden corners of my room.

I stood here before in the same live dream, summoned by the pull of the magic box. Whatever control I believed I possessed was taken over by a greater force. Pointless to resist. Everything connected.

In seconds, I hovered over the desk where my precious gift slept. The drawer opened on its own, as if waiting for me was no longer an option. I reached to the back of the drawer where I'd placed the ethereal box. The grooves were all too familiar. Like a dutiful servant, I removed the little treasure from its hidden cove.

I turned my box left and right like a ballerina on display so that I could admire its charm from different angles. The fine grooves of an intricate design caught my attention with its array of curves, leading to the eyelet. Subtle. Bejeweled on both ends with semi-precious gems of deep amethyst and murky citrine. The heaviness and color of this box went beyond gold, a mixture of a transitional metal such as platinum or iridium. My treasure looked like an antique, yet not dull or tarnished.

The sides formed architectural frames without the busyness seen in elaborate designs with window-like structures overlapping each other. My fingers traced the etched formation assembled to beautify my box. I didn't understand the meaning behind the artistic masterpiece.

The lid appeared flat in structure without shingles or tiles. It did have the similar mastery reflected on the sides of the box.

The most puzzling feature was the neglected back. Mine was no inferior. I touched the carvings along the back wall. Why this formation? I traced each edge, and each turn seemed to lead to a dead end and back to the beginning until I finally made my way to the center of the maze.

Shaking my head, I decided to move on from the puzzle. Any other person would have searched for a key. My nimble fingers knew better.

Flesh overlaid the eyelet, bringing the box to life. Just as before, the magic box opened at my command. Empty. Everything appeared the same. The ruby velvet covering remained in place. Again, I turned the box upside down and side to side. Nothing. I closed the lid and pushed it away.

Why was I drawn to that ridiculous maze? It made no sense. My fingers ran over the interweaving lines again. *Talk to me. Tell me what I need to know.* Over and over, I traced the lines until my fingers began to feel the wear from my repetitive action.

What do you want from me?

As if hearing my voiceless pleas, the lid opened. It was the same emptiness from moments ago. I then touched every corner, every wall that formed the box feeling each separation that formed the velvety fabric. Still nothing.

I finally noticed a slight variation at the upper right corner of the base. I gently lifted the fabric. *Careful . . . easy.* It wasn't bound by resin or paste.

Like out of some lost fairy tale, a note found its way underneath the fabric. I rechecked the base of the box. No trap door. I seized the parchment paper, which felt similar to my mother's only written communication to me, between my clenched fingers. Gently, I opened the note to find these words:

Save Me

Save me. Save whom? Who was this *me*? I shook my head, feeling confused. My family? Quinn? My friends? Me?

I didn't know whom to save. *What* would I save them from? My mind moved in circles. It reached and pulled and reviewed everyone I knew. If the activity in my head were recorded at this moment, it would be off the charts. The sketch wires would be out of control: Broken machine, no longer in service.

Who needed my help? This went nowhere. It wreaked havoc on my every thought, but I couldn't ignore the message staring right at me. It was a blatant request. Someone was in trouble. Someone needed help.

Mother, is this from you? Were you trying to tell me that you and my father were in trouble?

No, it couldn't have been.

It was too late. The message arrived too late. I had been a player in a fatal scheme, an unwilling and unknowing pawn in a larger plan that caused the downfall of my family. In another time and another place had I just been stronger. . . .

My thoughts shifted to Quinn. He was there, too. He struggled to save me, and then became a victim before he could escape.

Quinn . . . run! They're coming.

No . . . no!

Quinn . . . hurry. Get up!

I began to pace. I wasn't sure what was real anymore. Everything seemed to collide and overlap. And I wasn't always there. I scrambled everywhere. I needed to crack this message before time ran out.

Someone needed help. Someone in trouble. I needed a sign. I needed more answers.

It felt useless. I wasn't getting anywhere.

Then, suddenly, a melodic rap grew louder as it took me elsewhere.

CHAPTER 19

Sign In

"DID YOU HEAR me? I've been standing at the door thinking of ways to pry it open without breaking it down," Quinn asked me with a slight alarm hanging from his voice.

"I . . . yes. I heard you. I was on my way." My hand played nervously with my bracelet. "I lost track of time with the music on. You know how it is when something catches you and you're in your own world." I released the bracelet.

Quinn stared at me. "Uh huh. What gives?" He ran his hand through his low-maintenance hair.

"I'm not sure what you mean. I was going over some old things. I guess I got distracted." I followed him into the living room where he made himself at home.

Quinn frowned. "Lauren, you're pretty transparent. I know you can multitask well, and there wasn't any music on. Tell me what's really going on."

I wanted to tell him everything that had just happened like I normally can share my thoughts with him. I wanted to free myself of the secret message that my magic box had produced, how it called to me.

My concerns became his concerns. I could go to him and feel he could placate my worries into a working theme, a *talk this through agenda*, so that we could work to resolve whatever issue or concern came our way. In return, he gave me the same. But today, I felt a need to withhold just this once. I couldn't add another burden.

"I'm waiting," he said gently, a hint of sadness in his gray eyes.

"I was thinking back to the first time we met—officially in the present day—at the clothing store when you caught me off guard." To this day, I can still feel the warmth I had when we met.

His eyes and lips softened. "I remember it well. You were . . . flustered, arguing about some piece of clothing."

"What? I was distracted, as you should remember. I was placing you somewhere. I felt that I knew you but didn't know why. And I was drawn to that place, not knowing everything was blocked." I reached to him, to keep him here with me.

"You did look somewhat confused. I could see the brainstorming going on."

"It was a tug, an invisible force telling me you were somehow familiar." I released his arms, despite my desire to keep him with me at all times.

"You looked as beautiful to me as I remembered." He reached out to touch my warm face. "Just as you are now."

Beautiful. I never thought that word described me. Beautiful was reserved for models or actresses or the most sought after girl in school. It was used to describe a dress, a picture, a home, and pieces of jewelry. As for me, I never thought twice. Beautiful. How could I be beautiful?

Quinn reached for my hand. "Yes, beautiful. You. Everything I remembered turned real in front of me."

I became that person, beyond simple, and not just pretty or nice-looking or even attractive as I thought that was the best I could be. Beautiful—that was me in his eyes.

I basked in the moment, yet beyond his enduring words was actual concern for another person's well-being. Selflessness in contrast to selfishness. And while the world teetered around us, we lived in our own little happy globe.

What else could be stronger than love?

Quinn brought me down to reality. "Lauren, what did you find upstairs?"

"Find upstairs?"

"I think you know what I'm talking about."

"Oh. Find upstairs."

Quinn's face reddened. I could hear the heavy sigh coming from him. He took hold of my arms, trying not to squeeze them tightly. He narrowed his eyes with the seriousness that only a stormy gray cloud could produce. Fear and anxiety and a touch of rage fused behind his glass windows.

"Lauren, I will *not* lose you again."

My heart quivered. "Why would you lose me?"

"I'm serious."

"I am, too. I'm not going anywhere. Remember, I don't go anywhere you don't go."

His grip didn't ease. "Why do you need to be this way?"

"And what way is that?" I freed myself from his hold.

"Trying so hard to do the right thing to make everybody happy. To take care of everything when you're the one that needs to be looked after."

"What, are you and Raegan in on something? I can take care of myself."

"I didn't say you couldn't take care of yourself. You, of all people, are very capable of handling a tough situation."

"Then what do you mean?"

"Just hear me out."

Take it easy, Lauren. He's just concerned.

"Where should I start?" Quinn sighed. "My Lauren, how easy it is for me to love you." His fingers traced the sides of my face.

Whatever irritation I had moments ago disappeared. Even the energy surge subsided.

"I can't explain the reasons for your powers or why you've found yourself in this situation. I don't know if it was the cosmos that's brought us together or God or some other deity beyond this world." Quinn looked at me until I felt the seriousness and the depth of what he was trying to say. He dug into the very foundation of my existence.

Quinn sank back into the couch, assuming a contemplative manner for a few seconds before straightening up again. "I don't have the answers. I just know that, despite all of the challenges for you, for me, and your family, it's been the most wonderful life."

I understood him clearly now.

Quinn glanced upstairs. "So when I tell you that I cannot lose you to something I could have prevented, I mean, I won't allow us to be separated like before. *Ever.* I cannot allow you to go through the risks you've gone through again."

I reached out to console him. "I won't go anywhere."

Quinn looked at me. "Tell me, Lauren. What happened upstairs?" he whispered.

Defeat found its place in me. I couldn't ignore the soft pleas of the man who carried my heart.

"I don't understand it completely. I just found it today."

"Keep going."

"I didn't want everybody worrying, especially you. I know you'd want to know, and I wasn't trying to keep it from you. I was hoping to figure it out before I told you."

"Just tell me what it is," Quinn pressed.

"It was in my box that held my bracelet. It . . . called to me. I was downstairs, and Raegan had just left. It was so strong, a force that pulled me and connected with me and seemed to tell me in its silent voice that I needed to go to it."

Quinn shook his head.

"You have to understand that I'm supposed to see this. I believe it was meant for me to see."

"What was in the box?"

"It was a note, just like the one my mother left. On the same type of paper, but the handwriting was different," I told him. "Actually, it wasn't inside the box but underneath the velvet lining. I didn't think twice at first until I saw a tattered corner."

"What was written on the note?"

I paused and deliberated. "Save Me." I mouthed the words out loud so that they could circulate and be free to roam on the outskirts of my mind.

"It's a message handler."

"A what? What's a message handler?"

"It's a transfer of signs or messages given solely to random people, *special* people, such as yourself. It's the Pony Express without the horse or the carrier," he explained.

"I'm getting secret notes passed to me by some invisible force? Can't they just call?"

Quinn chuckled. "It's not that easy. There's a clue or code, which gets sent to its owner by some invisible force or thing. Magic, I guess would be the culprit. The person usually senses a delivery. Case in point, you made the connection."

"But it's so abstract. I was worried and upset because it didn't have a solid meaning. Quinn, can you see how troubling the words *Save Me* have been? That's why I couldn't tell you. I didn't want either of us jumping to conclusions. I don't know whom the note refers to," I pleaded with him.

"Hmmm, you have a point. The problem with a message handler is just that. It has no concrete meaning. It's not designed to give direct purpose to its owner, only an effective tip. It can help or harm if taken the wrong way."

Riddles and riddles and more riddles.

"I don't believe it's a physical or spiritual person. It's connected to the powers of a person who possesses great strength. And it's not like you can command it to appear. It can't be controlled," Quinn explained.

"What if it can be altered or pushed on request? Maybe I could probe into it so it would produce a clearer message."

"Doubt it."

"How do you know? Have you seen it tested?" I implored. I wasn't going to settle for the status quo. I needed to take it to the next level, whatever that may be, and in return wield it in my favor. I believed I could do it. I knew I had a chance. It was in my blood and in my powers to go beyond the norm and extract what couldn't be done by any other witch.

Quinn studied me. "I can't read what you're thinking, love, but because I do know you well enough, please tell me you're not conjuring up ways to control the messages."

"Why would I do that? You said it couldn't be altered. I'd be wasting a lot of extra energy that I needed."

Quinn grinned. "Because that beautiful head of yours is always on the move."

Beautiful was back! *Just give me this moment.*

"I didn't want you to get in over your head, thinking you can set the handler in motion and hope it can bring you what you want." Quinn moved several strands of my hair away from my face. "I've never known it to be done. Of course, it would be advantageous if it could tell us more."

Quinn and I inadvertently turned our heads to the looming staircase. I knew what he was thinking.

"Let's go," we said in unison.

He followed closely behind me, his hands on my waist as we ascended the curved staircase. I felt cautious and hesitant. Funny how a small box could do that to me. We inched closer to my room; the heaviness in my legs grew. Quinn nudged me along until we reached the half opened door.

"Everything looks the same."

"Did you expect it would look different?" Quinn asked.

"Not different, just rearranged in a way that would surprise me. Get my attention."

The box rested in the exact place I'd left it. I grabbed it. It was cool already, as if nobody had touched the ornament in a long time. With a quick scan of my room, I assured myself that nothing had been adjusted.

"I don't see anything unusual," Quinn said, looking around my bedroom with hawk-like eyes.

We sat on my bed, hovering around the weighted chest. The lines were the same, the edges unscathed, the box closed to the outside world. No attic door or underground hatch suddenly appeared.

"Everything is as it was," I told him.

And like any magical being, I traced the eyelet for the second time today, opening the adorned box to my command.

Empty. Unchanged. Quiet.

"I lifted this corner. See?" I showed Quinn exactly what I did, carefully removing the velvet off the floor. The note folded up was easily removed from its hiding spot.

"You're right, it's the same type." He studied every detail—the writing, the paper, the feel of the edges, and the ink. He held the note up to light. "Nothing unusual."

"So, where do we go from here?"

"We don't." Quinn put the paper back underneath the cloth. He closed the lid then examined the outside of the box, tracing the lines, the corners, and studying the bottom of the case as I had done.

"We can't sit here and do nothing. It's a clue. It has to be solved!"

"Lauren, you know we can't act on this. We don't know who the note is talking about and what it actually means."

"But someone's in trouble. We can't sit here and do nothing! Someone needs our help. *My help.*" I was fuming. I don't know what took over my serenity, but I couldn't sit around and wait for some tragic event to show its face, harming anyone close to me.

I couldn't let it happen again!

I grabbed the gold-plated box. The energy began to swirl within me, charging me with exceptional strength, and flowing through me from the command center to my core and down into my limbs. The force and the electricity exhilarated. I wanted this. I belonged to this. My true self awoke.

"Lauren, don't do this," Quinn warned. He attempted to pull my arms away from the box. All his strength couldn't budge my grip.

I ignored him. My mind was convinced.

"*Lauren,* we can try something else. Stop this!"

The excitement of energy materialized through me. It was every-where! It felt good to release it.

"*Lauren, don't do this! Let it go!"* Quinn shouted. He shifted away from me. He repeatedly massaged his palms and fingers to relieve the painful sensation from his grip on me.

My desk began to rattle. The lamp on my bedside table flickered on and off. Papers began to float, as did the once neatly lined books within the bookcase. The room even started to tremble. Quinn looked afraid, but I stayed focused.

Talk to me. Tell me what you know. I'm here, feel me calling.

The closet door shook, too. The papers and the books and any trin-ket that belonged in my room circulated in the air and began to pick up speed. I kept the objects from harming Quinn.

Why can't you hear me? I'm ordering you.

I was still concentrating. I looked over to see Quinn firmly against the wall. His face went blank.

I had no worries. I was the controller.

What's this—heat? Warmth in my hands, courtesy of the box. The electricity started to prickle. I think a message was forming. I reached out for the calling.

Nothing happened.

The box became hot and my hands began to burn. I looked around the room to see objects moving in disarray. I let a few items land on the floor. I felt tired, like I was laboring too hard. *Why isn't this working?*

My body started to ache. My head pounded. The electricity sent out jolts. I looked at a still Quinn. The shock was apparent on his face. I felt hurt. I couldn't control the energy any longer.

The heat . . . it's getting too hot.

"*Quinn!* It's burning. My hands are burning!" I tried to pull away but failed. Papers flew into my face. A book slammed into the side of my head. "My head is really hurting!"

I could feel myself losing balance from the throbbing pain. The rock was very much alive, giving me the repercussions I deserved. Quinn finally came to his feet. Standing behind me, he contained my arms and helped me to take control.

"It's so hot. My hands are so hot!"

"Focus, let it go. Tell yourself to *let go*," he ordered.

Ignoring the excruciating pain, I summoned whatever power I had left to release me from this wretched box.

Do as I command.

My silent calling surfaced. Another surge came through me. The flying objects slowed, eventually all falling to the ground or on top of nearby furniture. The room finally stopped shaking. Calmness found its way back in. However, the pain in my head and hands lingered.

"Steady . . . keep focusing . . . okay!" Quinn pulled me away from the box with both of us landing safely on the bed.

I looked at my red hands. They weren't as scorched as I'd expected they would be. My pride, however, was another story. My fingers moved steadily, yet not completely agile as before.

"I'm such an idiot!"

"Don't be so hard on yourself. You thought you could control it."

"I could have hurt someone! I didn't know what I was doing. I thought I was so smart." The child in me had emerged, not the adult ready to make crucial decisions and control other people's fate. I couldn't control my own powers.

I turned to Quinn. "Are you hurt?" I surveyed his arms, head, and chest.

Quinn laughed. "I'm fine. My ego is a bit dented. I couldn't pull you away."

"*Your ego?* More like mine. I was the know-it-all who didn't know anything," I babbled, falling back across the bed. A heavy sigh escaped from my lips.

Quinn turned to me. "You didn't know. Every powerful person has the desire to see what she or he can do. It's in us. We use what we have."

His reasoning was solid and natural. I should have listened when he said that the handler couldn't be altered. *Need to work on the craft.*

"You're right. I got in over my head."

"Don't be so hard on yourself. I couldn't even pry you away from the box. I would never let anything happen to you. Not like before," he vowed. Quinn planted a few lingering kisses on my moist lips.

"I held you back," I whispered.

"I would have fought to get to you." He cradled my face in his hands and then shifted them to the small of my back. "Because you're my . . . "

"Your?"

"My life. Mine."

"I'm glad I belong to you," I confessed, my voice drowned out by my pounding heart.

Our lips met again, this time with more fervor and resilience. We searched, and we hungered, and we found all of the places we knew so well. I couldn't get enough. I wanted more; I called out for more.

My calls were met. Our hunger would be satiated.

That wonderful ache below my waist called out again.

⋅→▣◎ ◎▣←⋅

Lauren, come help me.

"What? Is someone there?" I whispered. I was shaking. Cold slithered through my body from the damp night air. I saw the feather light curtains billowing at the open window.

Lauren . . . Lauren, I'm here.

"Who you are?" I glanced over at a sleeping Quinn. The clock beamed 1:00 am. I quietly got out of bed, grabbing my robe for comfort.

I heard only the silence of the night. This wasn't a dream. This voice I didn't recognize. It wasn't my mother's voice on the first night I heard her reach out to me, and it wasn't from my parents when I'd been hospitalized. Definitely a female voice. And I don't believe this nameless being meant to harm me.

Something compelled me to make my way downstairs. A nightlight had been left on, giving life to the shadows that lingered in the living room. *I shall not fear. I shall not fear.* I roamed the night. I belonged to this night.

Oscar was scurrying around in Raegan's room. His high-pitched whimper cried out to the mysterious voice calling in the night.

My walk through the house ended with another pull in the direction of the kitchen. *Go to the door,* it seemed to command me to do. I did so with purpose. The door whisked open and I faced the night. Outside,

I needed to go outside. I looked across the yard. Who waited for me behind the mighty elm trees in the darkened corner along the russet-colored fence?

I didn't know. I knew something waited for me.

My neck tensed as my feet moved me forward into the night. My breathing became shallow and quick, the air thick and heavy. I began to pant. My footsteps slowed, wetness covering my bare feet, but I kept moving despite the chill to my skin. The sweet air blended with the fragrant flowers that surrounded the house and the sap of the maple tree in the right corner of my enchanting yard.

I felt adrift. I inhaled nature's fragrances. Particularly the lilacs, which circled and thickened the air.

A light sweetness from the roses joined the sensory chorus. Powdery perfume and delicious fruity scents began to compete with the aromatic lilacs. They couldn't overpower the heady cologne of the bushes.

Even the tulips were no match. They were the spring champions, the brightest and the showiest flowers growing around the yard. Their blooms faltered in the deepening summer.

My pace slowed until I came to a complete standstill. The perfumed air surrounded me until it became difficult to breath. Noxious. I shivered in the moist air.

I trudged forward, seeking the place I needed to go. A brittle spice seeped into the air. It came from the far left corner where the fireflies lighted the darkened path. Were the elm trees attempting to break the heavy cologne of the lilacs? Propelling winds came in from the north.

Lauren.

The waving branches summoned me. My steps moved quickly towards the voice in the darkness coming from the left corner where the trees and the bushes hovered in clusters. My heart remained steady.

It was so dark. The fireflies had left the scene. The towering elm trees blocked the light. I stood in the corner near the place where my mother had stood when she'd watched the shadow trespass across the shrubs.

I wasn't afraid.

Nature's whisper awakened me to the stillness of the night.

What's happening? I looked around as I stood in the corner of the yard, still wearing my nightclothes. Why had I come here? I glanced back at the house and caught the yellow flicker that glowed from the room in which I slept.

"Quinn!"

I took off. In seconds, I flew up the stairs to the closed door of my room. A dim light flickered from beneath the doorway. I opened the door. It was dark again, but my keen senses visualized the night. Maneuvering quietly, I looked over to Quinn. He slept peacefully. My gaze shifted to the metal box sitting on my desk. It called to me again. For the third time since this new revelation, I swiftly opened the box and lifted the fabric to find the words waiting for me.

CHAPTER 20

In Good Company

"So GLAD WE moved the party to after the Fourth. It'll be great to see everyone we haven't seen this summer!" Raegan rejoiced as she unpacked disposable dishes and party favors. We'd bought the usual cookout food—chips, dips, side dishes, and drinks. Raegan and I had made a few dishes and some desserts the previous night. Isaak would bring the burgers and do the grilling. Quinn, Alex, and Justin volunteered to help him.

Having the party after the Fourth allowed other friends to join us. Since our Minnesota friends had moved down the street from us less than two weeks ago, the timing was perfect. Raegan benefitted the most from their move.

We couldn't persuade Gavin and Cameron to move down here sooner. They wanted to visit a powerful witch in Clam Lake before moving to Chicago. They agreed staying together would be beneficial, but they didn't want to draw attention to us by having so many witches and wizards suddenly show up. Our combined energy could easily make us a moving target.

"I can't believe how much food we made, and all the other stuff we bought," Raegan commented. "I mean I know *some* of you can handle a lot." She turned to give me a mischievous grin.

"I'll try to hold back."

Raegan tossed a few colorful sprinkles on top of the cake. She hesitated before starting her next art project. "Do you think about your previous life? This is probably really different from what you'd be doing on a Saturday morning."

"Sometimes."

I finally told her about the time traveling. I retold the story of my life in Connecticut and how I'd met Quinn at his family's hotel, The Maxwell Inn. She knew I was born before the 1900s, she knew about the loss of my birth parents, and that Raefield was after my stone. She also knew that I had been *reborn* as a small child after I crossed over to the present day. And, yes, she knew that my parents, the Reeds, were actually my aunt and uncle. I still didn't know who'd brought me to the hospital or who delivered me to the orphanage and devised my new identity.

I recently told the others about my past. It could help them understand our history and give them the tools they needed for what they might be facing. And we agreed, as our coven grew, that discretion would safeguard all our lives.

"It's amazing that the Reeds found you in Oregon at the orphanage, moved you from city to city, and here you end up in Chicago with me as your best friend," she said as she put away the desserts and helped me with the potato salad.

"Yeah, it's ironic how it all happened, and how we're all going to be in the same place."

"So, let me get this straight, Isaak and Chelsea were not from that time?"

"Correct. They were born to the Reeds in the present day," I explained. "Even though I left when I was twenty-two, technically, I'm older than Isaak and Chelsea if you count years since birth. But the time travel shaved off a section of time, and I restarted at a different age making me the youngest in the family. Kind of like cryogenics meets reincarnation."

"That makes sense . . . sort of." Raegan transferred the eggs, the onions, and the potatoes that I'd cut up into a large bowl. "I guess you couldn't live that long since penicillin wasn't discovered until after the

1900s, and vaccinations weren't common. And who lives to be over a hundred anyways?" The future vet spooned a large amount of leftover chocolate fudge frosting into her mouth.

"You're right. Most people don't live to be a hundred or more. As long as I'm healthy, my immune system thrives. I'm not sure how long I can live." *Or when my life might be taken.*

I added the mayonnaise mixture to the potatoes. "Remember, people during that era grew up faster and were considered adults at an earlier age. Being twenty-two then was like being thirty-five now. And people probably only lived to be in their fifties or sixties."

Raegan laughed. "You were already a mature woman."

"Not as old as I am now."

"You're not old, just recycled," she chuckled. "And I suppose if you were able to travel again, you would keep living at a different age. You might even live forever."

"Forever is a long time to live by yourself," I responded, shaking off that melancholic thought. "Sure, I could end up much older or very young. Even though Quinn estimates he's in his late twenties, he thinks and feels more like someone who is in his thirties or early forties because he remembers everything."

"At least the two of you seem to be closer in age by the way you act. And you definitely are more mature than most people in their twenties. I always knew you were advanced."

I smiled. "I'll take that as a complement."

A few of our Northwestern friends began to arrive at four-thirty. We'd told everyone the party would start at five. Other college friends would join us later. The rest were former high school classmates, friends of friends, and work and activity related friends.

Quinn and Garrett arrived at four to help out, along with two women friends of Garrett's. They reminded me of the Medusa sisters, without the hovering display over Quinn. When they offered to help, I knew otherwise. Alex, Cameron, and Gavin showed up after Quinn and Garrett.

Raegan and I set out the food. We left extra food at Elsie's place. A large fold up table and two gas grills were set up on the deck. More people began to arrive.

The day moved perfectly. The weather cooperated and the food disappeared quickly. Everybody seemed to be in a festive mood.

"You guys have a great place, and look at your backyard. How lucky of you to find something with this much space. We couldn't find anything decent except for a small house with an even smaller yard," admired Stephanie, a Northwestern friend.

"I know. I love this place and its location. My Minnesota friends just moved down the street," I said. "I'm glad my parents knew who to contact."

"Everything looks great." She put some food on her plate as I added more selections on the table.

I felt Quinn's eyes on me, and smiled. I looked up at the spacious yard filled with guests and the scenery in the background. The image of the wily yard had vanished from my stroll through the yard.

"Tell me what you're thinking," Quinn said as he joined me.

"Just setting everything out."

"You were deep in thought. What's going on up there?"

"Was I being obvious about something?"

I looked up at the front door to see Raegan greeting old friends from high school, followed by a couple that lived down the street.

I greeted the newcomers with Quinn at my side, dodging any further questions as I directed everyone through the kitchen. I no longer recognized all of our guests. Voices grew louder outside against the music that was playing.

Quinn mingled and stopped questioning me. I would tell him soon about my late-night walk.

The landline rang. I grabbed the phone. "Hello?"

"Lauren, is that you?"

"Who is this?" I saw Quinn pause from his conversation in the corner.

"Lauren, I need to talk to you."

The voiced sounded familiar. "I'm sorry, who are you?"

A long pause on the other line. The man breathed heavily. "Hello? I'm hanging up now."

"Lauren, I need to tell you. It's getting dangerous."

"Who *are* you and *how* did you get this number?" I turned away from the crowd, irritated by the caller. I didn't want to see Quinn's face.

"I've always been a friend. It's important that you use your gifts wisely."

"Then tell me. What danger is coming, and what gifts are you talking about?"

"They want to use you. They want to destroy. Don't let them! Look within. Use what you have."

"How would I know what to do?"

Silence.

"*Please*, tell me what you know."

The line went dead.

"Lauren, who were you talking to?" Quinn slipped his arm around my waist, taking the phone from me.

I didn't respond right away. I wanted to know more. I wouldn't get the chance unless he approached me again. Would it be too late? I looked up at Quinn with resignation. "It was the man from the store. I recognized his voice."

"He *called* you? How did he know how to find you?"

"I don't know, just like I didn't know before. But I think he was trying to help me," I said. I needed to get back to our guests.

"What did he say? And don't leave out any details," Quinn said.

I told Quinn what the stranger had said to me. "I don't think he wants to harm me. He's middle-aged with completely white hair. He wasn't worn down by life. His face looked younger than his age. It was the hair. Average build and average height, someone who wouldn't stand out in the crowd. He reminds me of a teacher or a trusted relative."

Quinn looked distant, as if scanning every face he might have encountered in this life or the previous one. I was sure he reviewed everyone I might have crossed paths with in my former life.

Click, click. Snap, snap. Image after image.

"No, I can't say I know him," he finally said.

"I didn't think so."

I suddenly noticed the crowd growing larger inside my house with more people still arriving. It hadn't reached mob capacity, although space became limited. Raegan waved to me from the deck to come outside.

"Look, why don't we focus on the party? Have a good time. This mystery man will have to wait," Quinn said.

"You're right. This gathering means a lot to Raegan and me. I don't want it ruined on account of something that may or may not happen, especially by a man who can't give me a straight answer."

Quinn gave me a reassuring hug. I felt more relaxed, having shared the burden of my uncertainty with Quinn. "I think you have some special visitors." Quinn pointed at the people who stood on the deck near the serving table.

"They said they would make an appearance. 'Be like shadows' and 'See how things are going.'"

"So they have, like camouflage. I didn't feel them coming," Quinn remarked. "It must be some control mechanism they're using. They're good. They know how to cultivate a strong block. I'm not sure I could wield such a disguise. I can usually tell when someone is trying to hide."

I scanned the kitchen and dining table to see if anything needed to be replenished before heading outside to meet the newcomers who managed to strike up a conversation with some of my college friends. They appeared comfortable and satisfied with the outcome of the barbecue.

A man reached for my arm. "Looks like everyone is having fun. Are you expecting more people?"

"Hi, Mom. Hi, Dad. I'm glad you came over." I hugged them both. "So far, it's going well. We have enough to eat and drink, and everyone seems to be having fun."

"Lauren, do you know all these people?" Mom inquired.

"No. Some are friends of friends."

"Is that wise?"

"We're keeping our eyes open, Helen," Quinn interrupted. Dad patted Quinn on the back. He looked confident.

"Mom, it's okay. It's no different than being at school or any large public gathering. Besides, I think an outsider would be detected with all the gifted people here."

"I guess you're right," Mom conceded. "We haven't noticed anything suspicious. And there doesn't seem to be any exterior forces planning to take over."

"Helen, let's hope no invasions are imminent," Dad said. "The kids need to have a normal life, enjoy what they have and what's around them. They need to move forward. We all do."

My mother nodded. "Lauren, I brought more food."

I looked under the covers of each plate but left the protective wrap on over the salads to keep away the bugs. We'd surrounded the deck with citronella lanterns and torches and had insect repellent and lotions readily available. The mosquitoes didn't seem interested in my blood. Perhaps I naturally repelled that type of invaders.

"Let's make a few rounds. I want to see who else is here."

I said my hellos to the people we passed and to see if everybody had enough to eat. Some of the guests planted themselves in the folding and lounge chairs while a few of the guys were throwing a football along the back fence of the yard. Even Oscar enjoyed all the excitement, running around the yard from group to group.

I passed another group from school—Michelle, Gabrielle, Linda, Tina, and Matt surrounded by faces I didn't recognize. We also stumbled upon a few people making out along the side of the house.

"Lauren, you've got a great place. Glad we're able to make it to your party," said a blond I recognized from school.

It was already after eight. The party seemed to grow to more than fifty people. Even the fire pit had a tight-knit circle formed around it. My parents had left an hour ago after making a final inspection.

"Hey, Lauren, come over here." Elsie motioned to me from the living room while the poker game intensified. A pile of money sat at the center of the table with more being tossed into the mix. I left Quinn and Garrett with some of the other guys. They headed outside.

"What is it?" I asked Elsie.

"It's strange. I've been back and forth at this spot several times today. Twice now, I've noticed this dark yellow, sporty car drive by. It wasn't until the second time that the car slowed down before speeding up."

I looked outside. I only saw the cars parked along the street and some of the partygoers hanging out on the porch. I turned back to Elsie. "Was it small with two doors and a curved roof—a Crossfire?"

"I'm not good with cars, so I don't know the brand, but it was a small, yellowish, two-door car."

I thought back. I remembered the hum of the engine. "I think I've seen that car before. It's not very common. I'm not even sure they make them anymore. And I don't think it's someone looking to go to a barbecue."

"Really?" Elsie asked apprehensively. "Do you know who it is?"

"I couldn't see the person. But I remember a glimpse of wavy hair—dark blonde. The face was shadowed, and the person wore sunglasses. Did you see the face?"

"No, only the back of the car. From inside the house, it's hard to tell. Definitely not magic."

"That doesn't give us much to go on, just the possible car. We could be overreacting."

"I think we should tell the others," she insisted.

"I think so, too, but don't get them worked up. Keep it quiet. We don't know if it's anything."

"Better to be one step ahead," Elsie cautioned. "Alex and Justin are downstairs. And I can feel Cameron and Gavin heading this way."

She was right. They walked towards us. I needed to learn how to go around my protective aura in order to sense someone approaching. What a disadvantage!

"Great party, Lauren. You should see some of them making complete fools of themselves. You go to school with these people?" Cameron asked. "I wish I had a camcorder to record every person that— "

"Yeah."

"What are you girls talking about by the window?" asked Gavin.

"Probably their boyfriends; and how special they make them feel. And what irritates them about their men," taunted Cameron.

"Shut up, dummy. Seriously, what's going on?" Gavin asked again.

"I'm going outside. Just let them know. It's nothing to get excited about," I said, leaving my three friends behind.

"What's she talking about?" asked a now serious Cameron.

I found Quinn with my family. He was talking to them and some friends from high school.

"I won't have to take that many credits this year in order to grad—"

"Can I borrow you?"

"Sure." I led him away from the group, not missing Chelsea's wary look.

I shared Elsie's comments and reminded him of my encounter with a similar vehicle and perhaps the same driver.

"I don't want anybody to jump to conclusions. It's just a coincidence, but it can't be ignored," I said to him.

"And we don't know if that person, that woman, is a friend or not."

"Right, and not a witch. She didn't feel anything," I responded.

I looked over to catch Chelsea's watchful eyes. Her expression went blank, and she frowned. She leaned over to Isaak as he chatted with some former classmates. She whispered in his ear. Isaak stopped abruptly and looked up at us. I looked back at them with pleading eyes to be patient.

"Let's just file this for now. We don't have anything else except for on two occasions, a golden Crossfire with a possible female driver passed by. We don't know what it means," I reminded him.

"Okay, but let's stay alert just in case. I don't want any surprises," he ordered gently. "How are you holding up?"

"I feel good. I'm not tired at all. I made sure to replenish here and there, keep it steady."

"Good. Let's keep things in perspective. So far, nothing has happened. We'll figure this out."

I nodded, but I couldn't help the guilt surfacing around me. My fault, again. I was the problem. I caused the inconvenience and forced everyone to be elusive. But why should we change our lives and run like little children? We were the ones who had power in greater numbers. I couldn't let someone ruin *my* day. It was perfect!

I left Quinn to go back inside. He went to tell my siblings and Finn about the drive by. I still needed to tell everyone about the phone call. Only Quinn knew about the first encounter at the grocery store. Now that he's made contact twice, I'd have to let everyone know.

"Lauren, what's this about someone doing a drive by of your place?" asked Alex. Raegan, Cameron, Gavin, Elsie, and Noelle were on his heels.

"I'm not really sure. It's just a strange coincidence that I'm trying to put together. We know nothing. We haven't even seen this person's face to make any conclusions. I don't think there's anything to get excited about," I explained hastily. "She could be a friend."

"Well, I don't like it. It's always something minor that turns into something major, and I don't like not knowing what it could be," Alex insisted.

"Relax, man. We can't react to what we don't know. I think it's best to just keep this piece of info to ourselves until we find out more. It's no use getting worked up," Gavin reasoned, adjusting his glasses.

"Alex, he's right. Let's just keep our eyes open. Nothing's happened tonight. It's been a fun party with no mishaps," Justin said. He looked at me for confirmation. "Lauren, is there anything else?"

I was the animal in the cage, caught in the corner. And it was too late; I was surrounded. I knew what I had to do. With a speech ready in my mind, I told them about the white-haired man at the grocery store and the phone call I received today, which I believed to be the same person.

"Geez, Lauren. Why didn't you say something?" Alex demanded, sounding more irritated. "And this occurred around the time you met that crazy old woman at the soup kitchen?"

"Alex, she's not crazy. She was helping Lauren," Raegan said, justifying my silence. "I'm sorry, Lauren. I shouldn't have told him."

"No, it's fine. I assumed you told him, and that he told everyone." I looked at all my friends for the answers. Their faces said it all.

"Not me, but I'm sure *someone* will fill me in," Noelle muttered. She was the last to know about the powers, the way of life, and the time traveling.

"So you see, both people have been trying to help me in their own way. It's a disadvantage that I don't know who they are. Hopefully, this third person is an ally, too."

"We don't know that for sure. She could be on the other side," Alex remarked.

Raegan glared at him without him reacting. She then turned to me. "Lauren, didn't you say the elderly woman knew your mother?"

I nodded. "She said she knew my mother. She even knew me when I was younger, assuming it's from that time, which means she passed through a portal. I don't think she's a witch. She seemed to lack the strength."

"A normal human has come through. Interesting," Cameron commented. "I wonder if that gentleman is part of the past, as well."

"That, I don't know," I replied. Everyone looked satisfied with my explanation and my suspicion that the driver of the Crossfire could be a friend.

"Okay, let's just keep all the players recorded. You guys know this is all tied together, don't you?" Alex added. Everyone nodded. "Let's get back to this party."

We dispersed in different directions. Noelle and Elsie stayed with me to straighten up the kitchen. The players at the poker table remained too engrossed in the game to know what we were discussing.

"Everything looks in order. Let's go find my family."

It was after nine, and I started to feel a twinge of fatigue from the long day. The constant food gave me some needed energy since this cookout could last pass midnight. More people came as some left through the back yard.

I found Quinn and Garrett with my family. They stood near the maple trees by the back fence. The full green leaves fanned the background in their airy motion. They all stared at me except for Finn, who looked somewhat puzzled that the circle had suddenly become quiet.

"Lauren, you must be in trouble again," Finn commented. Chelsea gave him a heated glare. He shrugged.

"Just ignore him, Lauren," Chelsea said. Her look wasn't insistent and vigilant like before, but it contained the undertone of *we need to talk*.

I told them about the man at the grocery store and the phone call; both times he tried to warn me. I also mentioned the older woman at the soup kitchen who knew my birth mother.

"I think they're from the past. Somehow, they crossed over. I know what you're probably thinking. Why didn't I say something sooner? Well, for starters, it wouldn't have been complete," I said, looking mainly at Chelsea and Isaak. "It wasn't until the phone call today and then the drive by that I felt it might be something significant."

"Lauren, you need to let us know what's going on. You can't keep these things to yourself," Chelsea stated in a motherly tone. "This isn't only about you."

"I'm telling you now, am I not?"

"That's beside the point. We didn't know about the other incidents until today. What if something had happened to you?" Chelsea responded.

"Nothing happened. And I can handle it. Everything's under control."

"Chelsea's right. You need to inform us of anything that ties you to your past, or anything that might seem bizarre," Isaak added.

"Isaak, why are you against me?"

"Nobody is ganging up on you, especially not me. But it's a little irresponsible of you to think that any of these so-called interactions are nothing. It affects all of us," Isaak replied.

"Don't you trust that I can pick through the contacts and figure out what it means?"

"Lauren, of course they do. They just want to be involved," Quinn added.

"Stay out of this, Quinn!" Raegan, Elsie, Noelle, and Finn all took a step back. I suddenly felt regretful, and looked over to see if I had wounded Quinn. He displayed neither hurt nor anger by my words. I pleaded silently for understanding, but I was met with a neutral expression.

It was now Chelsea who changed her tune. Her face softened into the wise and beautiful sister I knew. "Lauren, you're my sister. I don't want anything to happen to you," she said. "You can't do this alone. It's too much. We have to work together. We can't risk any harm to anyone."

I heaved a sigh.

"So, instead of waiting, I called Mom and Dad to let them know. They're coming back over."

"Oh, Chelsea! Why did you do that?"

"Because they need to know," she said matter-of-factly. "They want to be here."

"Oh, boy," Finn commented.

"Shh," Chelsea hissed.

I wasn't going to lose it. I would stand my ground. "Mom is going to worry for no good reason. Then I'm going to be on double patrol. She'll get Dad to find some way to *always* be in contact, like when I was in high school. I can take care of myself. I'm a grown woman."

"Hardly," Finn added with certainty.

"Shut up, Finn," Chelsea and I said in unison.

This wasn't going to end on a sour note. I planned to handle my parents and make sure they understood I was still in control—set the boundaries. I love my parents and everything they've done for me, but I just can't let this get out of hand. It's *my* night, *my* party. *My* problem.

Boundaries.

"Just forget it, Chelsea. It doesn't matter. I'll talk to them," I said to her calmly. I looked over at Quinn. I extended my hand to him, feeling remorseful. He reciprocated by reaching out to me.

"Okay, let's put all seriousness aside. There's a party going on and there are people wondering where the lovely hostesses disappeared to." Isaak motioned for us to scatter like the wind.

"*Yeah!*" quipped Raegan. "There's a party going on, and *I* need to be there."

"Why was everyone so serious?" whispered Noelle as the two walked away.

"I'll tell you later."

Quinn, Elsie, and I were the last ones standing in a loosely huddled circle. I still gripped his hand. Then Elsie said, "Don't worry too much, Lauren. I'm sure your parents just want to be close by. They'll give you space."

"Sure."

"Guess I'll go find Justin. I hope he didn't gamble away a fortune, like his car. Justin's good, but Alex has more tricks to pull. You know how he always has to win."

"Right," I responded, less interested in what my friends were doing with their money. She sped off into the crowd, weaving through the clusters of people laughing and talking and dancing the night away.

I turned to give Quinn a gripping hug. "I'm sorry for snapping at you. I didn't mean it."

"Hey, why so tight? I'm not dying."

"*Don't* say that."

"Sorry, poor choice of words." His face softened. "I'm not mad. I know you didn't mean it."

"Are you sure?"

"C'mon, it was nothing. You were just caught up in the moment. It happens," he muttered. "Besides, I wouldn't be a real man if I ran every time you have a less-than-perfect moment."

"But I was so . . . mean."

"It was an accident. You can't scare me that easily."

My guilt dissipated. "I don't know why I said that. I would never want you to stay out."

"I know."

"Promise me you won't stay away."

"Shh. It's forgotten." He planted his gentle lips on mine, the softness that would make me forget why there was ever any guilt.

I found my place next to Quinn again. I was in the happy zone, and surrounding us was the invisible bubble that kept the not-so-perfect world out for the few moments.

Good boundaries.

"Lauren, they're here."

"Uh . . . what?"

"Your parents are coming."

Broken boundaries. *Get around the block* needed to be mastered, and soon.

"Hello, Quinn."

"Helen . . . Oren, it's good to see you again."

They casually strolled up to us. I could feel myself getting warmer. My mother wouldn't look at me. I tried to read her face, but she hid her concerns. My dad said something to Quinn, but I blocked out his voice. My mother just stood there, as patient as a ticking clock. I knew what she was thinking.

"Lauren, we wouldn't have come back," Mom finally said.

"I know."

"Honey, you and Raegan did a wonderful job with setting up this party. It looks like a success," Dad commented almost too enthusiastically.

"Uh-huh. It turned out well. I think everyone is having fun."

"It seems that way." She still wouldn't look at me. She seemed to be distracted by something nonspecific. I looked around to see what might have caught her attention, but I saw nothing. Mom finally looked in my direction but not directly at me.

"Everything seems to be in place. It's been a good night for you. There's still a lot of energy."

I grinned at Quinn. "And it's still early."

His deep slate eyes shifted to the space around us, avoiding any eye contact while keeping his smooth lips stationary.

"Well, I think we'll go find Chelsea and Finn. We can talk about this later," Mom said in a soft voice.

"Mom, thanks for coming. I . . . can't do this alone."

She nodded her head. Her eyes no longer radiated tension. She became a friend who would listen and who would stand with you when trouble reared its head. I watched them walk through the crowd, avoiding any unruly and slightly exuberant guests in their path. They seemed to ignore any potential mishaps while blending unnoticed in the youthful crowd.

"You should go mingle with your guests. It's not everyday you have this many people you know in one place."

"But . . . "

"Raegan may need your help. The night *is* still early."

I smiled, my insides turning as Quinn stared at me.

"Bright."

"What are?"

"Go find your friends, and we'll meet up later," he said, his voice a little ragged.

I walked away, my steps light and airy, crossing between naive girl and resolute woman. I let him watch. An innocent giggle sprang from my lips as I walked from group to group. I listened in on the conversations, and I talked to the people I knew and didn't know. He was right. I should see the people I haven't seen. It might be a long time before I would see them again. My head cleared and my thoughts didn't drift into an anticipated doom.

It was already after ten. The stars and the moon appeared to be shining brighter on this special summer night. Even they could tell nothing would go wrong. I could almost hear the stars giggling and the moon chuckling at us with approval.

I crossed Quinn's path a few times. Our eyes connected for a few quiet moments. I even saw my parents relax and engage in light conversations with the college students around them. Who would believe my parents could blend in with the masses?

"We did the right thing by moving down here," Elsie said. "I wasn't sure at first, but Alex pushed the idea and Justin went along with it, as he usually does, unless he has a strong feeling against something."

I wrapped her in a warm embrace. "I'm happy that you did. Raegan and I couldn't wait, and I'm sure Noelle wanted the same thing."

"No more long commute to see you. No more waiting for the right weekend so that we can meet as a group. Now we can see what Chicago really has to—"

Raegan came running after Oscar. "Oscar, what's wrong? Lauren, I don't know why he's acting this way," she abruptly said, coming from the direction of the house.

Oscar was whimpering. I watched him paw at his delicate furry ears in irritation. The normally sweet dog wailed and scowled incessantly. I stopped what I was doing. An uncomfortable pitch moved closer to the house. It grew louder, then softer, then lower. I turned back to Elsie and watched her rub her forehead in annoyance. To the right of me, I saw Alex massage his neck to ease some unknown discomfort. And Gavin and Cameron appeared disoriented, standing by themselves in the distance.

"Lauren, are you listening to me? *Do* something. He's hurting," Raegan demanded.

I meant to go to the ailing dog when I heard his cries. I just couldn't. I stood there frozen in place like a dramatic actress, waiting for the cue to signal it was my turn to perform. But my slow and deliberate response shifted focus to the silent stare of Quinn and the wide-eyed expression of my mother.

"*What* is going on?" Alex grumbled, scanning the yard.

My mother's alarmed stare shot at me. She opened her mouth to say something gravely important. The yard seemed to be spinning, and I barely held onto the brakes to stop this merry-go-round from soaring out of control.

I reached inside, and I fought the wave of imbalance.

Quinn ran towards me, only not as fast as he could move. I knew what was happening.

"*Nooo!*"

The rippling effect shook the disabling guise from my normally gifted family and friends back to clarity. I watched, furious as uninvited guests approached the back yard.

Chapter 21

Witch Tales and Tribunals

"Nice digs, man. Is there a show going on?"

"Foxy lady, where are you going tonight? The party's here."

"Shut up, Ron. You're such a pig."

The crowd stood back, gawking at Mercedes and Nicholas coming down the parted path. The snickering and whispering quieted. They ignored the bystanders.

As they came closer, the tulips along the house curled downward and began to lose their color. The majestic branches and the fully mature leaves of the maple tree bowed back. A sudden stream of cold air weaved throughout my backyard, lingering along the borders of this protective domain. Even the once-twinkling sky became shadowed in a dull haze. Oscar continued to bark incessantly.

I heard the cries of a woman. I quickly turned to where my mother stood with terror on her face. She wasn't weeping. There was no time for tears. The echoes of sobbing called out again. It didn't come from anyone here. Was I the only one who heard the cries?

Quinn gripped my hand. Any tighter, and I might lose sensation. His brows furrowed and his eyes narrowed at the approaching intruders. He cursed under his breath.

"How did this happen!" Alex barked. Gavin, Cameron, Elsie, and Justin stood in a tight line, waiting for any reaction.

Garrett moved next to Quinn with the same conviction as the others. My father put his arms around my mother to console her. Her eyes remained wide, her fear turned into anger.

"Lauren, is this who I think it is?" Raegan whispered in a trembling voice.

"Just stay back, both of you," I ordered Raegan and Noelle. They scurried around me, standing a few steps away with arms linked. Oscar ran to Raegan, wrapping himself around her leg.

To my left, Isaak, Chelsea, and Finn stood motionless in their small circle, watching the strangers approach.

"I don't think they were on the list," Finn remarked.

"No way," Isaak adamantly replied.

The uninvited guests laughed. The path opened wider, allowing the dreaded pair to approach us. None of the other guests seemed to care who came to the party even if the new arrivals were overly dressed. The party resumed to its previous state.

"Lauren, it's so good of you to invite us to your little gathering. The masses are all here!" Mercedes shrieked. She scanned the yard and the house.

"You *weren't* invited."

"Tsk, tsk. Is that how you treat your guests?" Mercedes remarked. She turned to the scarred-faced man who for the first time looked as if he were enjoying a night out. "Nicholas, I think Lauren has developed quite the attitude."

"She seems to be that way."

"Such a strong and capable girl—*woman*, I mean. Isn't she?"

"I completely agree with you," Nicholas responded in a stately manner. "She's coming into her own. She's growing into what we expect her to be. More driven, more purpose. I can see it in those eyes."

"See? *We* can get along. I think it would be prudent if you follow our example," she continued.

"Cut the crap, Mercedes. What do you want now?" Quinn snapped.

Mercedes's face turned less cheerful. A small pout formed on her scarlet lips. "Quinn, is that necessary? I realized we haven't been so kind to one another, but that was the past. We must forget about what once was and focus on a new bond. Let's say a new beginning for people like us," Mercedes said, her expression turning soft and sincere. To my ears, every word made tiny cuts into my skin. I felt sickened by her overkill of sweetness.

"I highly doubt you want to make amends. If I remember correctly, the last encounter was provoked by you," Quinn pointed out to Nicholas.

"Clearly a misunderstanding. I only meant to provide Lauren the assistance she needed to ignite what is rightfully hers," Nicholas defended. "She took it to the next level as a threat, unleashing her will. Premature—yes—she's advancing nicely. I knew she was strong."

Quinn glowered.

"Let's get this over with. I'm sick of listening to these jokers," Alex snapped back. He charged the pair. They'd already clasped their hands together in anticipation of a threat.

"Stop it, everyone!" Mom ordered. She stepped out of the shadows. She moved closer to Mercedes and Nicholas, Dad following behind. She stood at a vulnerable place along the same line as I did.

"Oren and Helen Reed, my favorite guardians. I knew I could count on you to provide reason," Mercedes cooed. "It's been so long—*too* long. I've missed our little *tête-à-tête*." She threw back her wavy mane, reshaping the large curls as if making herself more presentable. The low cut, black shimmering dress managed to stay in place even if the slit of the dress was overly revealing. "Oh, how I've missed those days of social decency. What *has* happened to this world?" Mercedes let out a chilling laugh.

"No respect for authority," Nicholas added.

My mother held her composure even as the tension in her eyes grew weary. Her pursed lips and sharp eyes remained steadfast. "Respect cannot be forced."

"I am in total agreement with you, Helen. Those who have the will should command it. And the people who lack respect for authority should be dealt with judiciously," Mercedes said, looking justified.

"That's not what she meant," my dad intervened.

"Ah yes, the law abiding attorney. I'm glad you've decided to join us in this delightful conversation, Oren. You've been missed in court."

"That was a long time ago."

"A lifetime ago. Although it was brief, you were a valuable asset," she recalled.

"Mercedes, you didn't come here to make a trip down memory lane. What do you want with my family?" Mom questioned, taking a solid step forward.

A former classmate strolled into our lair near the back fence of the yard. "Whoa, Lauren, sorry to interrupt, but do you have anymore ice? You're all out."

"The freezer downstairs," I replied, not wanting him to become the clueless bug caught in the black widow's web.

"Cool." Peter noticed their blank expressions. "Like the outfit, Mister. Very retro."

"How nice of you," Nicholas responded flatly.

Peter walked away without looking back.

"Can we not have anymore mindless interruptions?" Mercedes scoffed. With that, she and Nicholas lifted their hands towards the sky, turned their attention upward, and focused on the circulating clouds above.

Another burst of cold air descended upon us, bringing rain and thunder. It caught our guests by surprise. They never anticipated a home-brewed storm.

The wind picked up speed and the crash of thunder pulsated across the bleak sky. Darkness reached out—black as soot—bringing with it bright lights in a disproportionate light show. Next, the whistling wind resurfaced strong and heavy, stealing center stage. I heard my guests calling out to take cover. We weren't affected by this change in nature. With the wave of her hand, she made the people come to a standstill like she had at the concert, only this time the rain and the flicker of lightning continued.

"Much better. Less nuisance," she stated.

"My friends will get sick." My fist was arched above my head, ready to strike.

"Now, now. Let's not get carried away. You may be powerful, but you're inexperienced," Mercedes reminded me. She positioned her right palm in front of her face, ready to block what I might hurl at her. "It's only temporary. Besides, you'd want a quick shower to cleanse all that happiness away."

"Happiness?"

"The mood dust," Mom spoke up.

"*Very* good, Helen. You've kept up with your studies."

It all made sense. Everything felt too good—too perfect—even when I tried to find something that could go wrong. How could I have been so distracted?

Have to do better, Lauren.

Mercedes lifted her hand to the sky again and the moisture dissipated along with the lightning. Then she sent the heated air to dry up the perimeter.

"There, just like new." Mercedes revealed a full set of dazzling white teeth. "Yes, Lauren. Even you were fooled. I wasn't sure if you would have picked up on the alteration in behavior. I'm sure you were surprised to see *all* of your cohorts in such a party mood," she gloated.

"*What* exactly did you do to us?" Alex demanded. Quinn quickly put his arm in front of Alex.

"That's right, Quinn. Teach your hot-headed friend from making a mistake he'll regret dearly," Mercedes lectured. Alex pulled back. "Stay put if you know what's good for you."

Nicholas smirked at Mercedes's remark.

She turned to Quinn. "Quinn understands these delicate matters. He *knows* the consequences of being hasty and negligent." Mercedes gave him a superior grin. I didn't look his way.

"Did you come here to give us empty threats and show us how to alter the weather? Rather mediocre, don't you think?" Alex challenged.

Mercedes began to laugh, a loud and boisterous laugh, shifting from high pitch to spasmodic. Only Nicholas joined in on her humor although his laugh was more subdued. She suddenly stopped her caroling. She walked directly to Alex. Her face was now inches from his. "I've killed many in my day. Adding another subject—a wizard such as yourself—would only set me higher."

Alex didn't flinch. He kept his focus on Mercedes.

"But I didn't come here to start a fight. There will be time for that in the future."

"What are you talking about, Mercedes?" Mom demanded.

"Helen, you know what's always been the plan," she replied.

"The plan?" I asked.

"Oh, that's right. You've lost your memory. Yes, the plan. I'm sure your parents can fill you in," Mercedes began. "Or should I say your aunt and uncle?"

It was deeper than an accidental cut. The blade wiggled in the same spot, rubbing against flesh. *Fight it. They're just words. Don't give in.* Quinn slid his arm around my waist, bringing us closer. I wasn't alone.

"That's insane. It'll never work. You're reaching again, Mercedes," Dad remarked.

"Are you sure about that, Oren? It's really simplistic, almost inevitable. Nature tells us so. When the worlds come together, and we are one—strong and more powerful—let's see who comes out ahead. Let's see how the weaker gene survives."

"But they're our friends. This is their world, too," Elsie said, almost in tears.

I turned to look at Raegan and Noelle frozen in time. They were no less important than anyone standing in this yard. They were the innocents. They were merely protected from the brief storm by standing next to us, but they were the most vulnerable at the same time. I wouldn't let them fall.

Alex gritted his teeth.

"Don't be naive. The superior class always beats out the inferior species. There isn't room for both," she told Elsie.

"We can teach you much. You're already gifted, a natural-born witch. All you need is to be trained," Nicholas added persuasively.

She moved closer to Justin, Gavin, and Cameron. "I won't follow you."

"How do you know?" Nicholas asked.

"Because she's not like you. These are people. They're human beings, not your disposable toys. We're the same as they are. Only we have special abilities," Justin attempted to reason.

"Exactly my point. The selected ones are and will be stronger, thus more able to survive. No room for the weak," Mercedes justified.

"You're crazy," Justin remarked.

"Crazy, or right?"

Justin turned away.

"We'll see when the time comes who follows."

"Mercedes, this is an outrageous plan. *We* did not agree to this coup nor will we be a part of it. Only you and your minions wish to overtake the world by eliminating anyone that doesn't agree with your beliefs," Mom said, her voice stern.

"Not fiction, Helen. It will happen. Our time is near. And if you wish to be a part of the higher order, then I suggest you take advantage of what was given to you, and use it accordingly," she replied. She continued to look directly at my mother. "But in the meantime, we shall reacquaint ourselves with Lauren and get to know her friends and your extended family." Mercedes made eye contact with Chelsea and Isaak.

Mom let out a quiet gasp.

"I don't think so, Mercedes," Quinn said as he raised up a hand.

"Relax, brave one. I'm not going to harm her. She's too important for me to destroy. I'd like to *get to know her again*. Is that too much to ask?" Mercedes asked.

"Yes, *way* too much." Quinn moved us back a step.

"Quinn, my word is gold. If we wanted to harm her, we wouldn't be able to get close enough. Look around. You, as a group, could easily take us."

I needed to speak freely. "Then why the mood dust? Why threaten us?"

"To make sure it would be a reassuring environment to enter knowing an entire coven was present," Nicholas replied. "You can never be too certain how a group will react."

I had been overconfident. "The female in the Crossfire . . . she's one of you."

"Careless on my part to involve a simpleton. She's not one of us, but yes, she wanted to provide her assistance." Nicholas strolled like nobility in front of us along the invisible line that separated us from them. He hardly glanced at us. "Perhaps she believed some miraculous transference of power would occur if she associated with the right people. Foolish girl. One cannot be given such gifts! And I dare not think she could believe a bite on the neck would do her justice. Such tall tales!" Nicholas asserted.

My friends and family looked at each other. I knew they would be more vigilant from now on.

"The girl in the library. It was her," I said to Quinn.

Quinn didn't look surprised. He had been here before. "To avoid detection," he quietly said.

"Exactly. We needed her to survey the place when Lauren moved in and when this fete started to take shape," Nicholas admitted. "She insisted on driving one of my pet cars one too many times, unfortunately."

My mother let out another small gasp.

"Did you believe we would never find her? It was a miracle to end up in the present day that allowed us this privilege. Otherwise, we would have been caught in another time—any *random* time—and forced to wait for another great mist," Mercedes recalled.

My parents fumed.

"Knowing how resourceful the two of you are, I'm sure you've kept a close watch over us. But nevertheless, we weren't in hiding," Mercedes added. She looked at my parents who refused to look directly at her. "But we were surprised to find Quinn had crossed over, too."

"And you're surprised I wouldn't try?" he replied sternly.

"Of course we knew you would, only amazed that you ended up in the present day and managed to relocate next door. Very clever . . . and convenient," she confessed. "At first, we didn't realize you had moved in. Through our source, she mentioned a dark-haired man moving in. Well, we decided to look for ourselves, but were wholly surprised that another warlock was living next door. I wasn't sure if he picked up on our presence. We didn't stay long enough to find out." She turned to face a somber Garrett who, if I had to guess, hadn't picked up on their eavesdropping.

"Well, Mercedes, it's quite noble of you to inform us of your transgressions. I can see that we have nothing to worry about now that you've decided to be so open and honest with us," my father said.

"But, of course. I want nothing more than open dialogue and trust between the parties. I want us to have a fresh start. We are like blood."

"Just because we possess similar powers and have the will to survive—stay alive—doesn't quite make us kin," Alex remarked squarely.

She ignored his comments as she strolled before us. Mercedes's careful movements were lithe and precise, always keeping a watchful eye on us. Her confidence reigned. She knew she had moved to a higher standing. She knew we would have to listen.

Then, I made the move. I became like dust, leaving no fragments behind. The air flowed clearly as my empty cavity dispersed. Mind took over matter. My steps moved above ground.

"Where is she?" Mercedes called out.

My friends and family looked everywhere. Mom only turned at angles.

Nicholas scanned the yard. His arm reached out to feel for my presence. Nothing. He also searched the ground.

I didn't plan to be inattentive to details this time. I would make things right.

Mercedes's anger burst into life. Her face burned with redness and her eyes sought vengeance.

"Better not try anything funny, sister. You wouldn't want us to retaliate," Alex remarked.

Mercedes hissed at him. She rescinded the rage she displayed moments ago. Her eyes moved from one side to the other. She couldn't find me.

I moved around Chelsea, taking care not to give myself away. My beautiful and poised sister instinctively remained still.

Nicholas halted. His eyes shifted to the frozen statues in my yard. He then turned away from the crowd and back to us. He grinned malevolently.

I stopped moving. Not an inch, not even a heavy sigh would escape from me. But I was ready. I watched the notorious pair come closer together. Nicholas continued to smile in a perverse way. Mercedes was no longer infuriated. Her deep brows formed an arch so angular and her lips moved with a satisfactory smirk that resembled a clown.

"Lauren, dear. Come out so that we can see you. There's no reason to hide," she cooed.

"Like you said, she's coming into her own. She's making her own decisions," Quinn responded.

"Exactly how we'd like her to be, her own person. However, this charade of abracadabra is sheer nonsense. There's no reason to hide. We're on the same team. It's imperative that we work together," Mercedes said, raising her voice.

Mom chuckled. "Mercedes, you can be amusing when you put your mind to it. Do you honestly believe we would go along with any of this? Really, it's useless trying to point out the fundamental differences we have here."

"Helen, I'm aware of your hesitation, and I *completely* understand your reservations. It's not like before. There were obstacles we didn't foresee. All of this will make sense when everything is complete, when we reign once more."

Mom looked at her with the coldest of cold eyes. I've never seen my mother penetrate deep into the bone. She stood in a treacherous place, only inches away from Nicholas.

"*Reservations? Obstacles?* You mean the betrayal and death of my family—Lauren's parents? *Am I supposed to think it's nothing at all?*" Mom lashed out.

Don't cry. Don't cry.

Dad grabbed Mom's hand, holding her back. I wished he hadn't responded so quickly because I *really* wanted to do the same thing.

During this heated conversation, Isaak left the spot where he and Chelsea stood to be closer to their parents. Chelsea stayed back to keep watch over a frozen Finn. She outlined his completely still face. My friends were learning more about me than I expected. The complex past and the elusive present came together in front of them to shape a future no one really knew.

Mercedes looked up in the air. "Lauren, I know you can hear us. It's not what you think. We weren't the enemies of your parents." She turned away with a humbling look. "I can say for myself and Nicholas, and go one step further and speak on behalf of Raefield, that it was of great loss that Phillip and Faye had passed on from a tragic accident."

"*Liar!*" Mom took Mercedes by surprise, leaping for the unprepared witch.

Dad and Isaak grabbed Mom before contact could be made, avoiding a war of the witches.

Crashes of thunder began to deafen the night sky.

"*Let go of me, you two! I'm fine,*" Mom seethed.

Mercedes actually looked frightened as she faced Mom. She became more withdrawn. Nicholas appeared solemn after Mercedes mentioned the death of my parents. Did he feel any guilt? I tried to hold back. *I'm sorry, Mom and Dad.*

"At least we know there doesn't seem to be a standard on who gets killed. Let's start by eliminating them so that we can even the score," Alex suggested enthusiastically.

"No, Alex. We don't kill for pleasure. Don't cross over to their side," Dad warned.

"But, Mr. Reed, we'll become stronger."

"We can't be like them."

"They crossed the line first. This is how we should deal with the problem. Situation solved," Alex pointed out.

Mom looked grimly at Alex. She paused, taking in a deep breath. "They didn't kill her parents . . . directly." She turned to Mercedes. "They knew about the disagreement between Raefield and her parents. They knew he wanted no interferences from anyone that would undermine his plans. They were told he would deal with the De Boers family directly. So, no, Mercedes and Nicholas did not *directly* have blood on their hands."

"But they knew," Alex finished what my mother meant to say.

Nicholas cleared his throat. "Raefield is very powerful. What Raefield wants, Raefield—"

"*Stop . . . her. I. Can't. Breathe,*" moaned Mercedes.

This night became too long. It was out of my control. Alex was right, end this now.

"No, Lauren! Don't do it! You're better than this!" Quinn shouted.

My stealthy hand locked around Mercedes's neck in a tight grip so that she couldn't escape. One wrong move, and snap! My left arm pinned her curled arms behind her back. She struggled like a wild animal. All I had to do was channel my thoughts directly to her and force the energy violently into her.

Alex and Justin charged toward Nicholas before he could attack them. They each held Nicholas's arm in a tight grip.

Quinn jumped from his spot, attempting to pull my invisible self off from a trapped Mercedes.

"Stay back, Quinn. This is my battle, not yours," I commanded him. I sent an electric current at him; he jumped back.

"Ouch!"

I'm sorry, Quinn. I know your hands will only burn for a moment.

I started the release.

"What are you doing to me?" Mercedes called out. *"I'm burning up!"*

"Lauren . . . *please!* Your parents wouldn't want you to do this. Think of them—and yourself. Don't let them die in vain," Mom pleaded.

"It's the only way to stop this. They had to suffer trying to save others. Mercedes and Nicholas knew that Raefield wanted to kill them, and they did nothing," I responded vehemently. "The cycle ends tonight." I wasn't hiding any longer. My family and friends would witness what I was capable of doing. I would take full responsibility. I had to ensure that the world might have a chance at being safer.

Kill, or be killed.

I was sure they saw the vengeance in my eyes. It was all I had at the moment.

"Their death is not a guarantee that Raefield won't come. With or without them, he's still a threat," Dad reasoned.

"That's why we need to lessen the threats. They're not of this world. They don't belong here. They won't be missed."

"We're not of this world, either."

"Let go of me, demon child!" Mercedes shouted in between gasps.

Quinn approached us as close as he could get without making contact with the invisible electric fence I set up. Garrett stood behind Quinn, hands ready. "Lauren, let go. The hate won't bring your parents back. Their love is with you. Everything's for you."

The tears already fell. "Quinn, I can't stop. It's beyond me."

"Yes, you can. *Try.* Your mind is strong. You control the power. It doesn't control you."

"It's too much."

"You're stronger. Focus. Use your mind. Control what ignites within."

"I . . . I feel so much anger. It takes over."

"I know. Turn that into your vise. Hold onto it. Draw it back in."

I did what he told me to do. With complete focus and sheer will, I felt a shift in command. Something moved in another direction. I pulled it in; I controlled the flow. The current moved out of Mercedes and back into me. My grip slowly let her go.

"It's working. I can feel it go into me," I told him.

"Take it all back in slowly."

Mercedes was completely loose. She scrambled out of my hold, turning to face me with her rage. *"Lauren, you could have killed me!"* she screamed.

I tried to focus on what she was saying, but all I could see were her lips moving. *"Ohhh!"* The ache in my head exploded. I began to fall toward the ground.

"Lauren!" Mom screamed.

I hadn't pulled everything back in yet. The previous energy storm had not been capped. It released again after the pain erupted in my mind. Like a renegade cable that snapped from the electric pole and floated in the wind, the eruption and the uncapped energy moved wildly. The ricocheted energy floated around us, bouncing onto the ground and causing it to shake, resembling an earthquake. From the fall, I managed to land safely on the ground. But my head still spun. I couldn't focus entirely on the scene; the vibrating ground took precedence. I attempted to get up, but lost my balance again.

Pull yourself together.

I curled into a ball, trying to find ways to bring the uncontrolled energy back in. I was too weak.

"What the hell?" Alex called out. He inadvertently released Nicholas.

Nicholas freed himself from Alex and Justin, then struck each of them in the face. Both men fell onto the rumbling ground.

Nicholas quickly took off before they could go after him. He became a shadow in the night, slipping from reality to the obscure.

"He's getting away," Alex moaned, pulling himself up from the ground. He touched his sore face where Nicholas struck him hard.

"Let him go. He's too far ahead. We've got to get this energy under control," Quinn ordered. He helped Alex to his feet then reached for Justin.

I moved up slowly. Although my head still hurt, it didn't last as long as the previous major episode. I was more alert this time and recovered quicker. The ground still shook in waves of moderate to heavy shaking.

Now, standing firm, I pulled the loose energy back in. The chaotic force moved in an orderly fashion. I absorbed the rich energy. It felt good. But to my surprise, I was met with a painful, sharp slice across my stomach.

"Huh!"

I looked up to see the blood stained eyes of Mercedes staring back at me.

"Lauren!" I heard Chelsea scream.

What I remembered next was slowly falling backwards. The sensation along my stomach burned fiercely as I gasped in pain. I tried to speak again, but I lost the words in my throat. I reached to comfort my newfound wound only to feel wetness seeping through my clothes. That's when I felt the wind of Mercedes leaving the scene.

Sizzle, sizzle, it was the first thought to describe what was happening across my stomach. Then, I felt the numbness settle over the wound. It didn't hurt that much anymore. I suddenly felt light and airy, floating in a bed of clouds. My thoughts faded into hazy, swirling images and colors that ranged from gray and white to smoky black. Light and dark flickered in and out of my mind.

"Someone catch her!" Mom ordered. She sounded so faint as if she were walking away.

"Mom." I reached out to her.

The ground stopped moving. I fell into someone's arms. Was there an earthquake in Chicago? My eyes moved up into my head. I couldn't think anymore.

Am I falling asleep?

That was the last thing I remembered before everything disappeared.

Epilogue
In Life and Death

I KNEW OF a place where people go to when they no longer belonged to this world. Everyone avoided this excursion until the end. Saving money for this big day wasn't required.

I wanted to be surrounded by nice people, who felt lost and whose cares disappeared.

To be free and to let go. . . .

No urgency. No routine. Goals and monetary gain inconsequential. All grief and sorrow set aside. All past doings recorded and shelved. Everyone moved forward.

Perfumed orchards and cognac-laced flowers floated in the air. And the fresh cut grass! I remembered the fragrance of green lawns after a heavy rain.

So dark in here. I waited for the fluffy white clouds and the tree of life to appear.

I must be in transition. Soon, a door would open to the beautiful open plain. Reborn. Perhaps we reverted into molecules to float in space and observe from the heavens.

Something smells good. Fresh baked muffins like Mom's. Famished. Shouldn't hunger go away?

Mom. *Please don't be sad. I'm moving to a good place. It'll get easier.*

Quinn. *Don't forget me. You'll always be with me.*

My excitement climbed another notch. No book could explain this event. Not much longer. I felt something else.

Fear.

Tires skidding? So loud and obnoxious. This is too real. And the smell; I remembered it. Exhaust fumes and wheels rubbing on a surface—friction—like a match. Something could catch fire.

Fire?

Burning. . . .

Mercedes!

"*Huh!*" I flailed atop my bed to free myself from the memory of Mercedes's assault. My eyes shot wide open.

"*Lauren . . . Lauren*, you're going to be okay. Take it easy. We're all here," Chelsea said. "Dr. Sendal, she's breathing too fast."

I heard him shuffle closer. "Listen to me, Lauren. You need to slow things down. There's no reason to get excited. No one will hurt you. Breathe deep and slow. That's it, Lauren. Don't gulp for air. Let it fill your lungs," Dr. Sendal instructed. "Focus. Bring yourself to the present day. You're in your room. It's daylight. Last night is over."

Clarity returned. Mercedes and Nicholas had disappeared last night. And I wasn't caught in transition to give my spirit a new home. I remained in my room, along with my belongings.

I opened my eyes to see familiar faces hovering over me. They waited for me to speak.

"Hey, Lauren. Some party we threw last night," Raegan teased. Her wavy red hair appeared brighter.

"I'll say. You were something else. *Wick-ed,*" remarked Cameron.

"Okay, give her some space. Everyone, move back," Mom ordered. Everyone took steps back. "Lauren, the mark is gone. You don't have to hold onto your stomach. The damage has cleared."

I lifted up my hand, expecting to see a sharp object penetrating my belly. The blade left a vivid memory—piercing, deep, and intentional.

But the stinging pain disappeared and the emotions leading up to last night's event passed.

"How did I survive?" I sat up in bed to look at everyone.

"She had a sharp blade. I think it was only meant to maim you. It was laced with a fatal poison," Mom explained, choking on her own words.

"She knew you'd survive. Any regular human would be dead, but she knew it would temporarily put you out of commission. Her great escape," Dr. Sendal added.

"I . . . I didn't see it coming. I was too caught up in the moment." I lowered my head.

"We wanted to give you time to heal. The energy, which lives inside and gives you strength, worked its way toward the wound to heal you from the inside out. The poison was encapsulated and pushed outward. I covered your wound with a special ointment to assist in cell regeneration," Dr. Sendal explained.

A plastic needle protruded from my right arm, hooked up to a yellow bag suspended from a pole.

"Let me close that off." Dr. Sendal reached for the intravenous line and removed it without putting pressure on my arm. My blood clotted and the puncture sight sealed up.

"All good, back to normal," he said.

Alex stepped forward, a smirk on his face. "You look like—,"

"Alex, you don't need to tell her that," Dad interrupted.

"I was going to say she looked like nothing happened." He turned back to me. "Lauren, I'm glad you're still alive. We're all glad it didn't turn out worse. Isn't that right, Quinn?" Alex rubbed his face where Nicholas had made a lasting impression.

Quinn didn't say anything. He looked at me with deep, pewter-colored eyes. I saw reluctance and conflict. I searched for the fearless survivor who supported me. He never appeared. His eyes told me everything.

He'd lost trust in me. He didn't recognize the person I'd become. But, as a respectful and polite person, Quinn approached me, sat on my bed, and touched my quivering hands.

"We didn't know what kind of damage Mercedes did to you until Dr. Sendal examined you. You were going in and out of consciousness. Poison sounded like the most logical answer. Good thing Dr. Sendal came right away," Quinn said.

"I gave you something you had taken before to help curb your need for nutrition and to keep you vital so your body could heal," Dr. Sendal explained. "I was confident you'd reject the poison and return to your old self."

"I'm glad you have faith in my abilities to heal, Dr. Sendal." I turned to the others. With a sobering and heartfelt approach, I reached for the people around me. "I won't let that happen again. My lack of judgment put everyone at risk. I . . . wanted them to feel the pain that I felt. I'm sorry. It was wrong of me to act out. I would never hurt anyone intentionally."

Mom reached out first. "Of course, you didn't mean to let it go that far. Your powers are strong, something you need to learn to curb and control. In time, it'll get easier. For now, side with caution until you fully understand what you're able to accomplish." She hugged me. Mothers seem to forgive you at all cost.

I returned her embrace, glancing over at Quinn. He appeared solemn. I knew his thoughts. He didn't love me anymore. I'd become a disappointment and a menace to everyone around me.

"Don't think about it twice, Lauren. If it were me, I would have done the same thing, only I would have eliminated them earlier," Alex said.

"Kind of like how Nicholas knocked you out," Gavin retorted.

"Shut up, Gavin. That was unexpected. A quake took us by surprise. I had him. If the ground hadn't thrown us off, I would have taken him out," Alex boasted.

"My doing," I pointed out.

"Lauren, it's not your fault. Your powers seem unpredictable. You did your best under the circumstances," Elsie chimed in.

"She knows that. She's working on it, aren't you, Lauren?" Raegan asked.

"Yeah, work in progress."

"All right. I think that's enough excitement for one weekend. I don't believe Mercedes and Nicholas will be back anytime soon. They might want to reconsider their undisputed plan after this weekend's events went awry. Mercedes succeeded in hurting Lauren. Thank goodness nothing more," Mom said to everyone. "Lauren needs her rest, and I'm sure we all have things to accomplish today."

"I've got some journals to read. Mom's right. Getting more shut eye might do you good," Isaak said.

"Call us if you need us," Chelsea said.

Dr. Sendal chuckled. "I wouldn't worry too much about it, Lauren. It was bound to happen sooner or later. Now, you know. Move beyond this weekend's transgressions. Don't dwell on what you might have done differently." He turned to Dad. "Quite some party, Oren. I'm glad I didn't stop over for that visit. It's been some time since I've exchanged words with them."

"Hmmm, I agree with you on that one, Uri. I'm not certain what the dynamic duo would have done in your presence," Dad replied. "We'd have to listen to them manipulate us further."

"Let's get something to eat. Gavin's buying," Cameron suggested.

"Since when?" he replied.

One by one, my family and friends left the room. It had been a long night for them. From Dr. Sendal's description, I'd barely avoided a perilous condition.

"Call me if anything changes," Dr. Sendal said.

Quinn straightened up from the corner of my bed.

"Please stay," I said quietly.

"If you want me to."

I felt defeated.

Mom flashed a look of disappointment at Quinn, then appeared thoughtful. "It would be nice if you could stay. I'm sure Lauren could use the support."

Quinn nodded.

Raegan and Alex left last. Quinn moved near the corner of my room. The distance between us intensified.

"Why are you so far away? Am I so horrible that you can't stand the sight of me?"

He looked at me, eyes blank.

"Can you forgive me? I didn't mean to do those things. The anger was too much. The energy consumed me beyond my control."

He walked closer to me. "It's not that."

"Then, what? Tell me what I need to do to make it right so that you won't look at me this way. In disgust." My throat felt dry.

The suggestions circled my mind. I had received hints and signs from Quinn, but chose to ignore them.

"You don't love me anymore. I saw the hate in your eyes."

Quinn looked confused. I knew I was right. I'd lost his love last night when I went into my rage and put everyone in danger. I had become unstable.

Quinn shook his head. He sighed, then began to chuckle. The amusement soon turned into laughter.

"Did I miss something?"

"I can't believe you," he finally said.

"What's so funny? Tell me what you really think and spare me any false hope," I snapped.

Quinn looked serious this time, his eyes sympathetic. "You have this way of conjuring up a different image from what I'm portraying. For someone who's supposed to be insightful, you're completely off. Your radar needs fine tuning."

"Huh?"

"I *don't* hate you. And I'm still completely in love with you."

"Oh."

Quinn chuckled again. "I think you're going to have to learn how to separate emotion from intuition before it gets you into trouble."

I sighed. "Then why so distant?"

Quinn paused. "Last night . . . what I saw in your eyes . . . was sheer rage. I've never seen anyone as caring as you turn that into hatred. I was caught off guard."

"I know. And I'm sorry. It won't happen again."

"It's not that. I know you didn't mean it, and I know you weren't that enraged. I think the rock is too strong."

"I can control it. I'm getting stronger, and when I understand it more, I'll be able to call the shots. Everyone says so. Dr. Sendal believes in me. Even Mom agrees."

Quinn appeared skeptical. "I can't watch the stone consume you."

"What are you saying?"

"I feel like I'm losing you again. I just got you back after two years of searching. You almost died before you entered the portal. Even though the rock saved you, it's hurting you. The episodes are unpredictable. I thought it would lessen."

A part of me wanted to scream. The only remnant I had left of my parents was slowly killing me.

"What should we do?"

"Initially, I wanted the stone removed, but it's too intertwined into your psyche. Removing it too soon could harm you."

"I can't run from it."

He thought for a moment. "No, but you could leave where it might be safer. I can take you somewhere else."

The idea of leaving sounded promising. A temporary solution would give us time. Quinn would be with me.

"I guess you're right. We might not have any other choice," I said, feeling isolation drift through me. "We'd always have to be on the move."

Quinn nodded. "Ready to leave at any given moment," he muttered. "I don't like it anymore than you do, but I don't see how staying much longer can benefit anyone. They'd keep coming back, and who knows, the threats might actually come true. The reinforcements could be real."

A growing enemy list. Mercedes and Nicholas already here, Raefield and company could come, and a few deranged witches from the deep forests of West Virginia all wanted to control me. They would have to catch me first. I would die before allowing them to use me.

"If only my powers were constant, I wouldn't have to run." I thought back to the aquarium incident and the backyard when I nearly drained Mercedes's power. I felt different; something had changed.

"If only," Quinn repeated.

Determination ruled me. I knew I could be that person. For now, the calmness of summer and the safety of home ruled all disparity. The shadows of autumn and a harvest moon awaited me. They would have to wait.

Leaving. My family would understand. I'd be doing them a favor. Sometimes sacrifices needed to be made in order to protect people. My friends wouldn't feel burdened any longer. They would have a chance at a normal life.

Quinn, on the other hand, felt we belonged together, for better or for worse. He didn't owe me anything by staying with me. I didn't care. It must have been the bond we'd formed in that life long ago. I welcomed it with all selfishness.

.